THE KILLDEER

Northcott Mayes

T0204785

NEW YORK
VIRGINIA

The Killdeer
by Northcott Mayes

ISBN 9781938467172

Editing by Joe Coccaro
Cover Design by John Köehler
Text Design by Marshall McClure

Published by

 köehlerbooks™
an imprint of Morgan James Publishing

5 Penn Plaza, 23rd floor
c/o Morgan James Publishing
New York, NY 10001
212-574-7939
www.koehlerbooks.com

 Habitat for Humanity® Peninsula and Greater Williamsburg Building Partner

In an effort to support local communities, raise awareness and funds, Morgan James Publishing donates a percentage of all book sales for the life of each book to Habitat for Humanity Peninsula and Greater Williamsburg.

Get involved today, visit www.MorganJamesBuilds.com

ACKNOWLEDGEMENTS

To Stella and Spencer who inspire with their passion every day.

To Joe for unending and unconditional support.

My eternal gratitude goes to Joe, Marti, Geri, Marc,
and Wilma for wading through the rough drafts.

Thank you Köehler Books Publishing for having
the courage to think outside the box.

Special thanks to John Köehler for his beautiful artwork.

A heartfelt thank you to Joe Coccaro for
the care he took with my story.

Thank you to Cheryl for her diligence in rooting out the errors.

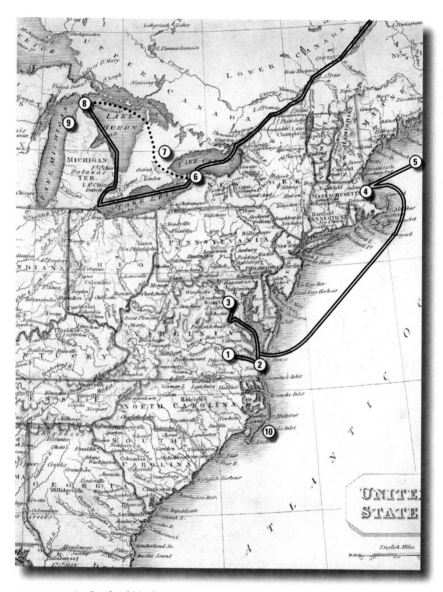

1 - Scotland Neck
2 - Norfolk
3- Washington, DC
4 - Boston
5 - towards Halifax
6 - Wellend Rapids

7 - Richard Jordan on foot
8 - Mackinac Island
9 - Beaver Island
10 - Wreck of the Vindicta

INTRODUCTION

All seven men piled into the whorehouse with little regard for gentlemanly behavior. They hooted and laughed and pushed each other chest-to-back into the ornate house in a fashionable neighborhood above the harbor. It wasn't actually a whorehouse, but rather a rented house that this night was to function in that capacity. The men were young naval officers, veterans of a recent, daring success over the Barbary Pirates, and soon to be the darlings of the American public at home and abroad. What they were getting tonight was just a taste of how grateful their nation would be and what heroes they would become once the news spread further than the north of Africa. They were about to begin a long series of public celebrations, but tonight's affair was private. It was the gift of a wealthy shipping merchant whose fleet was now safe to sail the North African coast, no longer forced to pay tribute for safe passage. The business of this same merchant had been strangled by insurance fees when insurance was even available, so any men who could give a good slap to these "damned pirates" deserved a night to remember. The merchant's gold and the right connections had bought just such an evening for these young officers. They were being provided a huge and luxurious house, well-stocked with liquor, food, and numerous ladies of the evening.

Most of the officers had paid to consort with whatever tradeswomen were available in North Africa, Syracuse, or even Gibraltar, but tonight's ladies were of a vastly different set than what they had sampled in the Mediterranean. These women were not common whores raked in for hasty work, but elegant creatures approaching the caliber of courtesans, well-read, beautiful, and very, very skilled. The officers ranged in age from seventeen to twenty-seven, and they were all raucous and randy, but after one look at their hostesses, they settled down. The dozen or so ladies seated around the room tonight resembled sleek and elegant cats, and just like housecats, they came in a variety of colors and coats. They were all beautiful, and each had a pinch of danger for flavoring.

One of the men was Lieutenant Richard Holmwood, a tall blonde with amazing blue-green eyes. His face was burnished by the sun and his hair bleached almost white. Richard was one of those men with light-brown hair which turns blond when touched by the sun. Darker hair in his brows and lashes set off his eyes. Richard looked around the room at the women and suddenly felt nervous. He sensed as they entered the room that it was the men being measured up tonight rather than the other way around. An older woman stepped forward and introduced herself as the "sponsor" of the ladies, then urged them all in to dinner. Two of the women appeared on either side of Richard, and he found himself escorting them into the dining room. The women looked hungry for more than just food, and Richard eyed them fearing it was quite possible he would embarrass himself before morning. The two women who had taken his arm could sense his anxiety, and they found it absolutely charming. They winked a silent pact with each other to share this youngster and guide him faithfully.

The sun was nearly up the next morning when the seven men tumbled into two waiting carriages to return to their inn. They had been in bed most of the night although none of them had slept a wink. Richard found himself in a carriage with the three youngest officers, and they lolled on each other barely able to sit upright. The carriage had not gone two hundred yards before all four were slumped over each other asleep like a litter of exhausted and sated puppies.

CHAPTER 1

SISTERS have an easy time of finding their place in a family, but for brothers it is vastly different. Richard was next to the youngest of the four sons of Gabriel Holmwood, a merchant captain, and they lived near Hampton, Virginia. A gap in age between the elder two and the younger two sons left Richard somewhat of an outcast. Micah and Thomas were the older brothers, and as such, the young gods of the household. Richard was too young to be included in the older boys' exploits and too old to have fun with his younger brother, David. The baby of the family was Susanna, and her brothers alternated between tolerating, tormenting, and adoring her. For Richard, finding his place was a daily struggle.

Gabriel Holmwood's fleet was comprised of two good-sized barques and six smaller vessels. He traded strictly in the Chesapeake Bay. He had ventured far up and down the coast during the War of Independence and he preferred now to sail within the comfortable sight of the Bay shoreline. There were other seamen who claimed the blue waters of the deep ocean, but Gabriel would stick with the green and brown of the Chesapeake. He had prospered staying close to home and saw no need to leave his family any longer than necessary. His clients were happy with his services and he had made a tidy sum. His sons inherited his love of sailing and were like a swarm of water bugs up and down the river in any number of the family's small sailing vessels. A neighbor was once heard to say, "You mean to tell me there are only four of those boys. I swear there must be eight or ten. For God's sake you see 'em wherever you go on the water!"

Micah and Thomas would always take the best of the vessels moored at their father's pier. They would go off on their adventures which amounted to little more than catching fish and racing with other boys, leaving Richard with whatever vessel was left. He usually had to make some repair or adjustment to the boat before he could use it, but Richard loved to tinker and tend the boats as much as he loved to sail them. He would get a vessel in such good shape that it was one his brothers would take next time. It wasn't just that he repaired and cleaned, but he adjusted the rigging as well until it was as efficient as possible for catching the wind. Over the summer, the Holmwood boats would become faster and more seaworthy as Richard continually refined them, until they could not be touched by any other little fleet. Richard took Micah and Thomas' abuse in stride, and by constantly repairing the boats, he became a master of squeezing every ounce of power from the wind. At age eleven he was a much better sailor than either of his brothers and many fully-grown men.

Occasionally, Richard would give in and take seven-year-old David with him. They would haunt the creek banks looking for crabs or snakes or try their luck for fish on a crude line they had set out. More than once Richard and David successfully caught fish and had been roasting them over a fire when the older Holmwood boys swarmed in and took the feast by the simple right of more muscle and height. At these times David would cry, but Richard saw it simply as the way of power in the world. After one particularly nasty incident of piracy though, Richard set about to get even with Thomas and Micah.

The next time he and David were out fishing, Richard made a big display to his elder brothers of the fish they had caught by holding them up on their stringer, letting the sun glint off their wriggling bodies. Richard and David then sailed away to cook their fish on the bank of a small island near the western shore of Point Comfort.

The older boys waited until they thought the fish was just about ready to eat and then commenced their raid. Micah and Thomas stalked the cooking spot, but found it deserted; however, on a crude spit over the fire were two fish about eight inches long, perfectly cooked. The fish had been raised up off the fire to let them cool, and to their delight Micah and Thomas found Richard had been kind enough this time to add pepper and salt. The fish were the perfect size and small enough that their bones became soft in cooking so that they could be held in one hand and eaten whole like a banana. The younger boys had been obliging enough to take the heads off the fish, and now Micah and Thomas stood with their conquest in their hands, ready to take the first bite. "I bet I can eat mine faster than you," Micah dared Thomas.

"You shouldn't eat those," Richard said as he stepped forward from the trees, sounding braver than he felt.

"Yeah? Who is gonna stop us? Certainly not you, Toad," Thomas sneered at Richard. Richard looked at his brother's leering face and noticed Thomas was getting a beard. It was not as thick as Micah's, who had just turned fifteen, but it was beginning. Thomas was only three years older than Richard, but the gap in boys at that age might as well be a century. As Thomas held his stolen fish, he felt the power of every one of those years he had over his little brother and said, "Just try to take it from me."

Richard stood mute while Thomas and Micah eyed each other holding their fish. Micah counted, and on three they both took a huge bite. On the same count of three, Richard bolted back toward the shore where David stood holding the boat with its sail already up and luffing in the breeze. As Richard crossed the low dunes near the shore, he heard howls of disgust and rage behind him. He waited grinning while David, his eyes huge with terror, begged him to get back into the boat. Richard shook his head with a wicked smile and said, "Just wait."

Richard and David had cleaned the fish as they always did, but this time they had placed fresh, well-formed dog turds in the body cavity of each just as it finished cooking. The heat from the fire warmed the feces and turned it to a noxious paste just waiting to be gobbled by the greedy older brothers. The dog custard had only been the first act, and Richard waited now for the encore.

That morning both he and David had forced themselves to drink as much as they could from the spring before they left the house, and their bladders had been nearly bursting as they showed off their catch to Micah and Thomas. When they reached the island to do their cooking, and before they even built their fire, they peed into two large beer mugs, smiling and sighing as they relieved themselves. They then placed the mugs in plain sight of the fire as they did their cooking.

Micah and Thomas had instinctively reached for the beer mugs to wash the dog mess from their mouths only to find it wasn't beer at all. They came crashing and smashing for the beach just as Richard and David shoved off and the wind filled their little sail. Richard looked back over his shoulder and saw the older boys lying face down on the sand, sucking up the brackish water they would normally never drink as they alternated between cursing Richard and spitting jets of water. Richard turned his back grinning, but headed straight for home. It would probably be best to be in the house and under the aegis of his mother or their nurse, Wrennet, before the older boys caught up with them. David looked back at the shore, and though he was still scared, he flashed a small conspiratorial grin at Richard, who winked back at him from his perch by the tiller.

The older Holmwood boys were never inventive enough for real vengeance, so they simply pushed and shoved Richard when they could get away with it, but this had little lasting effect on his sturdy frame. Richard knew they wouldn't dare hurt him seriously for fear of what their father or mother would do to them, and he tried to convince David of this, but David lived in constant terror of his eldest brothers. The older boys tried to get Richard in trouble with their father, but Gabriel Holmwood was easygoing, if not indulgent, so it usually came to nothing. The older Holmwood boys continued their ineffective bullying of Richard, but it only served to make him tougher. This war between brothers might have continued for years had it not been for an event that altered their lives forever.

THE SILENCE of the sleeping house was shattered by screams and the pounding of running bare feet. Richard met Micah and Thomas in the upstairs hallway, their faces white with shock. "What's wrong?" Richard asked as Micah held up his hand for him to be quiet. They listened and then there were more moans and a scream. "It sounds like Zanna," Richard said, referring to his sister by her nickname, but then another scream ripped through the house and this time there was no mistaking it as David's. "Something is happening to both of them," Richard said as all three moved down the hall toward their parents' room. They crowded through the door to find David, Susannah, and their mother writhing in agony on the bed. Wrennet and their father, still in their nightclothes, were bent over the three.

"I'll go check on the other boys," Wrennet said, turning to leave when she caught sight of them staring wide-eyed in the doorway. She asked, "Are any of you ill?" They all shook their heads, staring in mute horror at the others on the bed. "Come with me," Wrennet said, pulling them from the room and closing the door. "Micah and Thomas, you must go and get Doctor Wailey. Go together, and go quickly. Your mother, Susannah, and David are very sick. I think it's something they ate." Micah and Thomas nodded and ran to get dressed. Within minutes they were riding barebacked-double on their father's horse. Thomas held a lantern in one hand as he clung to Micah's waist, and Wrennet urged them, "Be careful, but go fast, and then you come right back here!"

Wrennet had given all three of the sick ones tartar emetic, causing them to vomit explosively. She feared too much time had elapsed and the unknown poison had invaded their blood. She had thought to give them another dose of the emetic but concluded it would not do any good. Little Susannah had nearly choked to death with the first dose. She had been vomiting when a painful spasm struck her abdomen. She inhaled to scream, sucking the vomit into her lungs. Wrennet had turned her upside down to help clear her lungs, but the damage was done.

The whole family, including Wrennet, had eaten the same thing, so why would only the three of them be ill? Wrennet stood by the side of the bed while Gabriel waited by the front door, barefooted with his nightshirt hastily tucked into his trousers.

Dr. Wailey, Micah, and Thomas arrived within twenty minutes, and the doctor examined the three patients. He ordered more tartar emetic and bled them, but he only added to their agony. The screams went on for several more hours and Richard overheard Dr. Wailey say to his father in the hallway that he did not believe they would survive the night. It appeared to be poisoning, probably from mushrooms. "But we all ate the mushrooms," Gabriel said. "Why only these three?"

"That is the way with mushrooms. You can eat them twenty times, and the twenty-first time you eat them, they kill you. I know people who have picked them successfully for forty years, and then one day they pick the wrong one," Dr. Wailey said as he dabbed with a cloth at some vomit on his waistcoat. He added sadly, "I also think the mushrooms build up in the blood, and one final dose is too much. It is strange that three people would be affected at the same time, but it is not unheard of. Mrs. Holmwood was ill with a fever a month back, and the little ones would not be able to fight the poison as well, so the three of them were weaker. I am sorry, Gabriel, but there is nothing I can do. You can already see the cyanosis in the little ones. Their lips and fingernails are beginning to turn blue." Richard had listened to what was supposed to be a private conversation, and then he tore silently down the stairs and into his father's study where he stood leaning against the closed door. Panic more than sadness overwhelmed him. His mother had been the rock of his life, and with her gone, and David and Zanna too, he would be left as the sole target for Micah and Thomas. Catherine Holmwood had a way of making everything better for her children and Richard couldn't imagine life without her.

After an hour in the study, Richard crept out from his hiding place and hid under the stairs, wanting to be closer to people but still shielded from the agony upstairs. He sat digging his nails into his palms until he could not stand it any longer, and then he put his hands over his ears. He felt like a coward, but he had to block the noise. He began to pray that they would stop screaming, and around three in the morning he began to pray they would die. If they couldn't survive, why did they have to suffer? His prayer was answered after another hour as the screams turned to moans, the moans to sobs, and then the sobs to silence.

Gabriel came for Richard and took him upstairs. "You must hurry if you want to see Mama while she is still alive." He stepped now into his parents' room and saw his mother propped up against the lace-trimmed pillows. Had she not been in her own room and wearing her own nightdress, he never would have recognized her. He quickly averted his eyes only to see David and Susannah's small bodies wrapped in sheets on the floor near the window. Richard had no idea David and Susannah had already expired. Catherine had insisted, while she still had strength, that she and her babies would stay together until the end and leave the house together.

Richard walked slowly to the bedside, wanting to look at his mother, but not wanting to see her either. He reached out and touched her face, and her eyelids fluttered. For just a second he had a glimpse of her indigo eyes. Catherine tried to reach for him, but she was too weak. Richard caught her hand and held it as he sat on the edge of the bed with the smell of vomit threatening to gag him. Once more he saw her blue eyes, and then she was still. Richard felt a hand on his shoulder and looked up to see Micah. This was not the goading, threatening Micah, but one stricken and softened by grief. He gently pulled Richard away to stand next to him so their father could sit on the bed next to Catherine. Thomas stood on his other side, and the three brothers witnessed their mother die. Richard felt Thomas slip his arm around his waist and then Micah put his arm across his shoulders, holding him. The three watched their father hold their mother's hand until her last breath, and then they slowly left the room. She would now become no more than a shape wrapped in a sheet beside her youngest children, and they had no need to see it.

The cemetery service was a blur, and several times over the next week Richard was awakened from his sleep by David or Susannah calling to him. Twice he had gotten out of bed and dressed, determined to go to the cemetery and dig them up, but as he stepped outside in the cold, the reality of the chilly air would chase the tendrils of the dream away, and he would assure himself they were indeed dead. He shouldn't have been fooled by the dreams because he had touched them both in their coffins, and they felt cold like a stone floor underfoot, and they would never rise again.

TIME IS THE GREATEST of healers, and as the Holmwoods went through the motions of living, their world slowly returned to some sense of normalcy though they knew it had altered forever. Micah and Thomas called a truce in their warfare against Richard, but they replaced it with something even more painful. They completely ignored him. They still took the best boat at the pier, and they still bossed him out of the way, but they really didn't put their hearts into their abuse unless they had some friends to witness it.

This ignoring of Richard made the humiliation of the brothers all the more acute, when in front of everyone they knew, Richard took first place in the small river regatta Hampton hosted on Independence Day that summer. Had Micah and Thomas been completely honest with themselves they had known for a while that Richard was a breed apart when it came to sailing. Unfortunately, for them, all of Hampton Roads now knew they had been bested by their little brother. Richard took first place over two dozen boys, most of whom were older.

Richard possessed that sixth sense shared only by the very finest seamen. It was an awareness of the wind and the sea that cannot be taught, learned, or bought, but like any other gift from God, exists freely. This gift did not just exist in Richard Holmwood, it thrived.

CHAPTER 2

JOSHUA HUMPHREYS had recently been hired to build six frigates for the American Navy. Unable to justify the cost, Congress had dismantled the Navy after the War of Independence. America was to find that without the protection of Great Britain, many parts of the world began to bully the vessels of the infant nation. There was after all a very great need for a navy, and Congress set about to rebuild one. The United States could not build a navy as great as Britain, but Congress even then showed the trait that would make Americans famous; it decided to build bigger and faster ships than its rivals.

Humphreys was spending some time in Gosport Navy Yard in Portsmouth just across the harbor from Hampton. He was looking at the French ship *Sempian* there for repairs. He wanted to see exactly how her bracing was constructed under the waterline. His designs were nearly complete, but there was one more feature he wanted to confirm before beginning construction on what he believed would be the six most efficient ships of war in the world. As he had stated to as many would listen, his ships would be the size of a ship of the line but possess the speed of a frigate.

Humphreys was also visiting his sister in Hampton, and due to the observance of Independence Day, the shipyard was closed. He now halfheartedly watched the youngsters race in the regatta. He was lounging in his chair, not caring who won, until a sturdy blonde boy pulled ahead of the pack and never gave up the lead. Suddenly, Joshua sat up with interest and retrieved his spyglass to watch the young man sail.

The race required the contestants to sail a long oval course, negotiate around a buoy, and then head back toward the starting line. The return leg brought the young sailors against the wind and forced them to tack. The blonde boy took the lead within two hundred yards and was well around the buoy tacking like the devil before the rest even reached it. Humphreys stood now and watched the race. He called over to his sister and asked the boy's name. She looked through the glass, and then said, "One of the Holmwood boys. They have run wild since their poor mother, God rest her soul, passed away a few years back. The Holmwoods lost two other children at the same time, a boy and a girl. I heard it was bad mushrooms that killed them." Helen would have gladly provided him more grisly details of the deaths if Joshua hadn't risen and taken the glass back from her to watch the young sailor approach the finish line stretched between two boats. He watched Richard as he clung to the tiller. He was bracing himself with a tanned bare foot against the gunwale, his hair bleached almost white, and though he had yet to pack on muscle, the frame that would eventually carry it was already in place. Humphreys cheered silently for him and then sat down and made a note to find out more about this Holmwood victor. The ships he was building were special, requiring a new breed of seamen. Unless he was very wrong, the young man whom he watched win the regatta would mature into just such a man. Humphreys was determined to make sure the lad's invaluable talent was not wasted in some other trade.

Richard was preparing a rod to go fishing after dinner when a carriage arrived in front of the house. He set the rod aside and walked down to unlatch the gate in the little picketed yard which was bordered by flower beds his mother had kept so meticulously, but which had now been invaded by sugar pine saplings and weeds through which only a few remaining perennials struggled for life. He watched as a stoutly built man climbed down from the carriage and adjusted his wig. Richard smiled to himself. He had not seen a wig in years, and even his father, who clung stubbornly to the past like glue, had abandoned his several years ago when all three boys had threatened to throw it in the fire. The man stretched, heaved his waistcoat around from where it had bunched at his side, and then extended his hand, "Joshua Humphreys, and I am looking for the Holmwood family."

Richard smiled at Humphreys' florid face and reached out his hand, grateful his father had shown him how to greet someone properly. He still remembered being lined up with his brothers while his father moved down the line shaking their hands, forcing them to look him right in the eye as they pretended he was various townspeople they were greeting. He now said politely, "You have come to the right house, sir."

"If I am not mistaken, standing before me is the recent victor of the regatta, correct?" Humphreys asked, grinning.

"Correct again, sir," Richard said, this time grinning, and Humphreys nodded to himself, impressed with the lad's manners and poise. Richard stood back and waited for Humphreys to enter and then latched the gate behind him. His mother had admonished them all for years to close the gate so the little ones did not wander off, and even now, years after there had been no children younger than Richard, the whole family still carefully closed the gate every time they went through. Richard turned to face Humphreys now and said, "May I help you, sir?"

"I come begging to speak with your father. Is he about?" Humphreys said, looking about the yard and porch.

Richard nodded, "Yes, sir. He is in his study. Please come, and I'll show you." Richard led Humphreys into the house and past Wrennet, who was doing her best to clean up after the evening meal, and he introduced Joshua Humphreys to his father and then left. As he was crossing the yard he heard his name mentioned. He had never been much of an eavesdropper, but something told him to be one now, so he slipped up under the open window in his father's study and listened.

Both men were settled with a glass of port after their introductions and Humphreys' lavish praise of Richard, but Humphreys now got down to the business that brought him, and he said, "I would like to take your boy, the one who showed me in here."

Gabriel started and raised an eyebrow. "Take him? Make yourself clear, sir."

"I have been staying with my sister, and I have kept my eye on him since I saw him win the regatta last week. He is a singular sailor, and I think it would be a waste to allow him into any other occupation except the sea."

"He will sail. All my boys will come right into my business. They can take over from me in a few years, and then I can rest at home," Gabriel said, smiling.

Joshua Humphreys leaned closer and said, "Sir, with due respect, I don't mean for him to be tripping along in sight of the coast. I mean deep blue water for him, weeks from port, navigating by the sun and the stars on a spanking new frigate of the Navy of the United States. Your boy has the makings of a fine naval officer, and I wish to put him on that track."

Gabriel stared at Humphreys, speechless. "Richard is the baby of the family. Why him?"

Humphreys looked at Gabriel and smiled as he said, "Sir, you have seen the boy on the water. No other explanation is necessary." Gabriel stood. He no longer had any taste for his port, and he walked toward the window to toss it out. Richard heard him coming and scooted away, his heart pounding at what he had heard. He wanted desperately to hear the rest of their conversation, but he had pushed his luck too far already. He tore off for the river and spent the time until dusk poking around the bank, never really using his fishing rod.

Much later that night, after he had been deep asleep, Richard awoke to find his father standing over him with a lamp, staring down. Richard pretended to be asleep, and after a few minutes Gabriel left his room. Richard stared into the dark wondering what was going on, and he was still thinking about it as he drifted back off to sleep.

The following morning Richard wanted desperately to ask his father about the conversation with Joshua Humphreys, but he had no way to bring it up without revealing he had been listening. Unbelievably, it was Thomas who opened the conversation. "Papa, who was that man who came here yesterday?"

Gabriel looked at Thomas and then at Richard and he finally said, "He is Mr. Humphreys, and he designs ships. He was interested in visiting a ship at Gosport Yard." Now this explanation would never have been good enough for Richard, but Thomas was not as sharp, and he swallowed it with a nod, taking biscuits off the platter being set down by Wrennet.

Richard saw his chance and asked, "Papa, what advice did he need from you?"

Gabriel looked trapped for a moment and then mumbled some nonsense about draft, and then he quickly rose from the table and went to his study and closed the door. Richard stared after his father wanting to press him more, but could not. When he looked back to his plate, he found Thomas had stolen his bacon, but it didn't matter because Richard was too jittery to eat this morning. Wrennet saw him playing with his food, and she came and felt his forehead. He struggled against her halfheartedly and she released him announcing he had no fever. When she suggested whipping up a tonic for him, he bolted from the table and disappeared out the door.

Two days later, after watching his father leave the house, Richard quietly crept into the study and looked over the things on his father's desk. There he found a letter to Joshua Humphreys allowing Richard to accompany him back to Boston. It was understood that Richard would become part of a crew on a cutter in the Revenue Marine until the frigates were built. He would then be signed on as a midshipman to train as a naval officer. There were some stipulations as to Richard continuing his education while at sea. There were also admonitions to Humphreys for the care and welfare of his youngest son, but Richard skimmed over them until he saw his father's signature at the bottom. Richard picked up the letter and read it again. It was his ticket out of Hampton and away from his father, who was clinging to him more and more each day. Last night he had awakened again to find Gabriel with his lamp staring at him while he slept. This time Richard had asked, "Papa, what's wrong?"

Gabriel had answered, "Nothing, I was just checking on my baby." Richard hated being called the baby. He was the youngest by default. Richard had rolled his eyes and flopped over facedown until Gabriel left the room. He then kicked off the covers, flipped over, and stared into the darkness at the pattern the moonlight made on his sheets.

Richard went the following morning to Gabriel's study and found it empty. There was a letter on the desk, again addressed to Joshua Humphreys, however this letter thanked him for the kind offer, but stated that he could not reconcile sending his youngest son so far away just now. Richard stared at the letter and then replaced it on the desk. Next to it was the earlier letter giving Humphreys permission to take Richard with him. He stared at both letters and made up his mind, tearing the declining letter to shreds, tossing it in the fireplace, and raking it under the ashes. He grabbed the affirmative letter and stole upstairs. Richard packed a small sack with the clothing he thought he would need, took all the money he had in the world, a single gold eagle his father had given him for transporting empty barrels to the dock upstream at Jamestown, and finally the paper and pen from his small desk. He crept down the stairs certain he would be stopped at any moment, and raced out the front door not even bothering to shut the gate. He ran all the way to the address on the letter where Mr. Humphreys was staying and arrived there about forty-five minutes later.

Richard knocked on the door trying to calm his breathing. Helen Humphreys answered the door and looked Richard over from head to toe. She told him to stand there and she would fetch her brother. In less than a minute, Joshua Humphreys was at the door, and Richard handed him the letter with a grin. Humphreys read it through quickly and looked up at Richard and smiled. "Well, son, it looks like you will go to sea after all."

"When do we leave?" Richard asked, wanting to be away before he was discovered missing.

Joshua looked him over. "Whoa, there, we won't leave until tomorrow morning, but you are welcome to stay with my sister and me until it is time for us to go," Joshua said, holding the door for him. "Come right in, and make yourself at home." Helen Humphreys gave Richard a critical inspection and stalked off muttering about hair combing and face washing. Richard realized he had not even washed his face or combed his hair that morning, and after running all the way there from home, he probably did look and smell like he deserved her scorn. "We were about to take our noon meal. Why don't you join us," Joshua said, "and you can get cleaned up through here." He motioned and Richard followed to a small guest room. Joshua brought him hot water and a towel, and Richard attempted to remove as much of the accumulated dust as possible.

Wrennet had tried to keep the boys neat, but that was a job beyond her capacity. She would often lay down the law and they would scrub up, but even then, it was hit or miss. Gabriel would occasionally raise his head and look around the table and determine that tonight was the night for a bath. He would then send them into the kitchen telling them not to come back out until they were clean. He would yell after them, "Just look at the three of you. If your poor mother wasn't already dead she would die of shame to see the state of you. There isn't a clean neck among the three of you, and Richard's face is so dirty he looks like he needs a shave!" This would always bring a hoot from Micah and Thomas as they made fun of Richard's smooth face. At thirteen, he still had a face as hairless as a girl's.

Richard now washed carefully, trying not to slosh too much water around, smoothed his hair, and put on a clean shirt. He did his best to shine each of his boots on the back of the opposite leg and then determined he was done. When he walked back out, Helen Humphreys smiled at him like her face would crack from the strain. She had obviously been cajoled by her brother into being kind.

They sat down to a dinner of roasted chicken and potatoes with cucumbers and radishes. Richard ate everything put before him, but he remembered not to take seconds even when they were offered. His mother's training did not go so far as refusing dessert, though, and his face broke into a grin when Helen set before him a large slice of plum cake with lemon sauce and patted his shoulder. She had softened to him. Any boy that would eat her poor attempts at cooking with such gusto certainly was not all bad.

Richard again earned a smile when he complimented her food, and after dinner the three settled easily into the evening hours and would have been quite comfortable if Gabriel Holmwood had not arrived.

It was a horrible scene for all concerned. Holmwood Senior accused Humphreys of luring his boy away and went so far as to suggest he wanted Richard for some dark and unnatural purpose, which caused Helen Humphreys to run shrieking from the house for the constable. Humphreys tried to explain, tried to show the letter Gabriel had written, but Gabriel was so worked up he wouldn't listen to reason. For him it was as if he were back on that horrible night when he had lost his wife and youngest children. He had been helpless then, but he was not helpless now, and by God, he was not losing another son. Gabriel grabbed Richard and held him tightly, while Humphreys and Richard pleaded with him to calm down. Finally Richard screamed, "Papa, stop! You are not losing me, I am going to sea. It's what you do, and it's what I want to do." Gabriel stopped ranting and looked at Richard who added, "Papa, I don't want to hate you, but I will if you don't let me do this. I am good at this, Papa, and I want to get better."

Humphreys looked from father to son and stood silently watching, then finally said gently, "Captain Holmwood, this lad has a mighty gift, and he will seek to use it. You can't keep that kind of potential at home forever. Trips on the Bay will never be enough for him, and one of these times you will turn your back and he will be gone. At least this way, you will know where he has gone." Gabriel locked his eyes on his youngest, released his grip as his shoulders fell, and sank heavily into the chair, shaking his head.

Just then Helen Humphreys and the fat constable, who still had his dinner napkin stuffed in his necktie, piled into the room, and Helen yelped, pointing, "There. That man is attacking my brother and this poor, dear boy."

The matter was soon cleared up, and Richard stood next to his father's carriage outside Helen Humphreys' gate. Gabriel held back the tears he knew would embarrass Richard, but which he would shed once he was out of sight. He tried to lock every image of Richard's face into his mind to hold onto until he could set eyes on him again. "Oh, Papa, I'll write to you, I promise," Richard said with the impatience of youth, "and I'll see you again, so don't worry." Gabriel nodded and stroked Richard's cheek, gripping his chin in his hand, and, for once, Richard had the good grace to hold still and not pull away. Gabriel had already admonished Humphreys to take care of Richard, and there was nothing left to say, so he got into his carriage and left, not waving or looking back as is the way of sailors.

THERE WERE SEVERAL obstacles, but Joshua Humphreys was able to get Richard accepted as a midshipman. The first of his frigates, simply referred to as Frigate A, was due out later in the year, but until then the boys who would be her midshipmen were scattered out to be trained on board the cutters of the Revenue Marine, recently created by the Department of the Treasury to deal with tariff violators. Richard was sent on to Boston to meet his ship, and he was joined by three other midshipmen.

The captain of the *Washington*, a seven-gun cutter about eighty feet long, was a man named Lee, and he greeted the four boys who would be in his care as they came aboard. The boys had not even stowed their things when the *Washington* got underway and set off on patrol.

The boys ran about the deck looking with delight at everything as they sailed out of Boston Harbor into the open sea. Within an hour of being on the open sea, the four boys were sick. Richard vomited up everything he had eaten that day and then everything he believed he had ever eaten in his life. After another hour of heaving, one of the old sailors pulled him and the other youngsters aside and forced them to eat some cold salt pork and half a biscuit, promising them it was just the thing for their stomachs. He also told them kindly, though using the foulest language any of them had ever heard, that the worst thing they could do for seasickness was to sit around. They needed to be up walking, going about their duty, or going to the bow and keeping their eyes on the horizon, "And don't be lettin' yer head loll back and forth stirring yer stomach like a spoon." He assured them that the more they moved, the better they would feel. Richard gagged the food down and then went to the fore of the ship and before long was amazed at how much better the salty food and fresh air did make him feel. Being new, he and the others had yet to be given a watch, so they were free to explore the ship, and they scrambled in and out of every section like ants in a pantry. When they got to the large swivel gun mounted in the middle of the forward main deck, they stopped and stared, fascinated. Richard walked to the open end of the gun's barrel and hoped to look down into its maw, but there was a protective wooden cover plugging it. Captain Lee saw them gawking at the gun and smiled. They might as well be interested, before long they would be aboard a frigate whose guns would dwarf the one that now had them captivated.

Much to their delight, the boys discovered six more guns hidden under their canvas covers. They peeked under the canvas and emerged having gotten their first whiff of gunpowder.

The boys were lined up the following morning and broken into two watches. They were also told that from now on they would be referred to as Mister, followed by their surname. They were to call each other by that title while on duty or when referring to each other when speaking to an officer or any other crew member. Richard stood the first watch with a boy named Leonard Travis. Travis was also from a seafaring family, but instead of begging to become a midshipman like Richard, he had been forced to do so. Young Mr. Travis wanted nothing more than to be back at home, but he had been bustled off, "for his own good," as his father had put it. Richard eyed Travis carefully, but Travis had not met Richard's gaze all morning. He had heard Travis crying himself to sleep last night, and at one point had almost thrown a shoe to get him to shut up. Finally, in frustration he had yelled at him. Travis had continued to sob, but had done so into his pillow. He was still sobbing when Richard fell asleep.

Over the next few days, the boys were shown their duty and drilled on maritime vocabulary, history, and seamanship. They were dizzied by the myriad knots they would have to learn, some of which Richard already knew, and the cat's cradle of rigging. Much to Richard's delight, it all came very easily. The running rigging for any ship was the same as that for the tiny vessels he had sailed, it was just multiplied several times over. If he followed each line up and through its blocks, it all made sense.

The Revenue cutters were all gaff-rigged, not quite schooner-rigged, and certainly not square-rigged, and Richard had never been on a vessel like them. He saw how this set of sails gave the ship great maneuvering ease, but also how it could be manned by a fairly small crew. Richard had no way to know, but the entire crew of twenty-five was equal to the amount of men it would take to just haul up the mainsail on the new frigate he would eventually join. The cutter's foremast flew a square sail above the large quadrilateral mainsail and Richard noted the deep belly on the mainsail, and he mentioned it to the crew member next to him, who simply shrugged. Captain Lee overheard him though, and moved closer saying, "Good question, Mr. Holmwood. The belly is to hold the wind longer. It isn't pretty, but when we're turning, and we always seem to be turning when patrolling the coast, it certainly helps." Richard nodded, looking up at the square sail. What Lee said made perfect sense.

The following week the boys were schooled in what Captain Lee referred to as "authoritative deportment." He walked back and forth in front of the line of four boys while he spoke. "I know that you will not be with us as a career. You have been promised to the Navy, but until its frigates are ready, you have been entrusted to my care. Until that time you will be members of the Revenue Marine. Do any of you know what it is that we do?" All four boys shook their heads no. Lee looked them over and asked, "Do any of you know what revenue is?" Richard stepped forward, and Lee addressed him: "Mr. Holmwood?"

"Sir, revenue is money earned," Richard said, speaking it as a question.

"Exactly correct, Mr. Holmwood. Please step back in line," Lee smiled, waited for Richard to find his place back in line, and then continued, "Only we are talking about the earnings of our nation rather than the earnings of an individual. When goods come into or leave this country, there is a fee imposed by our government. That fee is called a tariff. It is our duty to see that ships coming in, going out, or even in port, have paid their tariff. If we find they have not, we may seize the cargo, the ship, or the crew, depending on the circumstances. Many of the ships we deal with will be owned by American merchantmen. We must then at all times show them respect. We should be firm and resolute, but we must always remember we are dealing with American citizens. They may turn out to be criminals, even smugglers, but they are American citizens first. Do you understand me?" He looked down the line of nodding boys, letting his gaze linger on them until they began to feel uncomfortable and looked down or away. Only young Holmwood held the captain's gaze, refusing to lower his eyes, and Lee finally relented and smiled at him.

At the end of the first week, both watches were lined up for gunnery practice, and the boys were quivering with excitement. Part of each boy's duty was to clean and check the guns, but they had yet to witness them being fired. Now that the time had come, they could hardly wait. They watched in fascination as the crew went through its loading ritual. First, a tightly packed bag containing the six-pound gunpowder charge was placed far down in the gun, and a felt wad was rammed down snugly against it with a long-handled ramrod. Next came the actual twelve-pound cannonball followed by more wadding, and then the whole load was jammed tight. It was explained to them that if the seas were rolling, another wad would be rammed down tight on top of the whole thing to keep the ball from rolling back up toward the muzzle as the waves tipped the ship's side downward. The boys had involuntarily moved closer with each step in the loading process, and they were now only a few feet away.

They watched in fascination as the gun captain ran a small corkscrew-like pin down into the touchhole, that tiny hole in the upper part of the rear of the cannon no larger than a nail, and punctured the gunpowder charge bag. He then poured a small amount of the highest quality gunpowder, "First rate powder," he explained, into the opening and closed the levers which sealed the touchhole tightly. When a cord was pulled, a spark would ignite the powder to blast the shot out of the muzzle of the gun. The gun captain now looked over his shoulder and bellowed at the boys to get back. They held their ears as well as their breath as the gun captain pulled the firing cord.

The explosion was like nothing Richard had imagined. First there was an initial "whomp," as the charge exploded, and a split second later the gun recoiled backward straining at its rope tackle while unleashing the most tremendous blast. All four boys stood with their eyes huge and mouths gaping, and then Richard and two of the others let loose with a whoop of elation. Travis remained silent. He had been terrified by the noise, wetting his pants before the firing cord was even pulled.

Richard stood with his eyes glowing and Captain Lee smiled. Lee remembered well his first thrill at firing a gun, and for the next few days this gunnery practice would have the feel of adventure, but within a month these four boys would be molded into gun captains commanding a six-man crew with members older than the boys' fathers. As young officers, their authority would be absolute.

It was fortunate the midshipmen were schooled in gunnery, for not long after, Captain Lee received word that the United States was at war with France. All ships bearing that flag, naval or merchant, were fair game. Richard stood in the middle of a group of men reading aloud to them from a newspaper brought aboard the ship with the mail. Most of the ordinary sailors could not read or write and they crowded around to hear. While Richard was reading the paper on deck, Captain Lee was reading his orders below. The first of the Navy's frigates, U.S.S. *United States*, was now ready, and there had been a general call for officers and crew to report. Richard and the others except Travis were beside themselves with anticipation. Travis had retreated to his bunk when he heard the news.

Although the *United States* was ready in May, the boys assigned to Captain Lee were not destined for her but for the second frigate, *Constellation*, and they had to wait until September when she was rigged and ready. When the word finally came, Captain Lee lined the boys up and wished them well using their Christian names for the only time ever. He gave them his blessing and was startled when Travis, in a violent breach of etiquette, hugged him around the waist. Captain Lee choked a bit, but sternly and with a wooden face loaded them into the ship's boat and watched as they were rowed to the waiting and magnificent *Constellation*.

CHAPTER 3

RICHARD and the other midshipmen gawked at the *Constellation* as they approached her through the choppy seas off the coast of Massachusetts. She was fretting at her anchor like a great black dragon struggling to slip a chain, and she was the most beautiful thing Richard had ever seen. Compared to the feisty little *Washington*, the *Constellation* was massive. She looked sleek and sinister with her seemingly endless gun ports, and he could hardly wait to be aboard her. Funding for the frigates had been on-again-off-again. What was originally to have been only a few months aboard the Revenue Marine cutters had stretched into two years for the midshipmen. As Richard climbed the side of the heaving frigate, he was three days shy of his fifteenth birthday. He resembled a man more than a boy, and shaving was now a daily ritual.

Once on board, Richard found himself one of thirty midshipmen, ranging in age from fourteen to eighteen. Some, like him, were beside themselves with excitement, while others, like Travis, seemed pensive. The boys were quickly presented to the officers on watch and then shown their mess and berthing areas where all the boys would sleep tightly packed as they swung in their hammocks like hams in a smokehouse. They stowed their few things and were then divided into watches. Richard hadn't been on board a full two hours when his first watch began. It became readily apparent to the deck officers that the sailing experience of the midshipmen ranged from absolutely none to a gratifyingly decent amount. Richard was definitely in the latter category, and during gunnery drill that very afternoon he demonstrated his prowess by leading the fastest team to load, fire, and reload. As a result he was assigned a gun crew. This made him the youngest officer on the ship to have his own crew.

Constellation was under the command of Captain Thomas Truxton, and most of his officers were excellent and treated the midshipmen sternly though well, but there was an exception, Second Lieutenant Theodore Yancy.

Yancy, twenty-two, and a veteran of the merchant trade, was not on duty when the new midshipmen arrived, but later as officer of the watch, he looked over their names and swore silently under his breath. Two years earlier, Yancy had pooled his money with his brother and another man and purchased a half-interest in a ship which had an existing and rather lucrative tobacco run that included Richmond. Within two years of purchasing the ship and its contracts, however, they lost the Richmond contract to Gabriel Holmwood. Curing tobacco is an exact art, and the plantation owners wanted to be sure it was moving to market at its peak, not sitting on a wharf in the hot sun waiting for the uncertain arrival of a ship. Gabriel provided that service and kept to a strict schedule of transport stops that became a very profitable circuit. Yancy's ship was tardy and losing the Richmond stop forced him to sell his portion of the ship and eventually join the Navy for employment. He hated everything about it which showed in the way he dealt with subordinates.

Yancy located Richard off duty in the midshipmen's mess and began to drill him to see if he had any connection to the despised Holmwoods of Hampton Roads. When he found Richard was not only related to, but the son of the man he believed had ruined him, he said archly, "Oh my, the son of a thief has washed up here. Why don't you go back and spend your time on your father's ships and leave the real sailing to those fit for it?" Richard had no idea what Yancy was referring to, but he steered clear of him mostly by keeping to himself and studying.

The Navy wanted to make certain its midshipmen would be not only skilled seamen, but also gentlemen. Each ship provided a schoolmaster who had oversight of at least ten midshipmen. On smaller ships with less than ten midshipmen, their education would fall solely on the captain and his officers.

The *Constellation* had a schoolmaster to instruct the boys in Latin and Greek, history, mathematics, natural history, literature, and composition. Other officers, especially the captain, would also teach the midshipmen navigation and seamanship, both of which relied heavily on mathematics. The midshipmen's education would not be the soundest, but it could be supplemented by constant reading. A schoolmaster always came aboard with far more books than he could ever hope to get through, and he was willing to lend what he did not use in class to anyone who wanted them.

The schoolmaster was often a theology student taking a break to earn money to continue his studies. The day the schoolmaster reported for duty was usually the first time he had stepped onto a ship, and it seemed that schoolmasters, as a breed, suffered from seasickness. Although not physical, the job was still not an easy one. Rambunctious midshipmen, anxious to leave the classroom and get back on deck, tormented the schoolmaster with pranks, like cutting the ropes on his hammock or salting his tea. The boys suffered often from coughing fits which struck several of them simultaneously, or if not coughing, then bouts of flatulence for which they heartily apologized. Occasionally, it was even a lethal combination of flatulence brought on by the coughing. Although he was armed with a stout bamboo cane and given the authority to use it at his discretion, the schoolmaster found that the boys, who were quite a bright lot, eventually gave in to their natural desire to learn and they settled down. A schoolmaster who tried to beat knowledge into his pupils soon found that the tone of their pranks quickly turned from mischievous to vicious.

A temporary classroom was created by stretching canvas around some tables and benches just feet from the midshipmen's mess, but at any time a drummer might be ordered to beat to quarters, and the canvas was ripped down. The classroom would be dismantled and returned to what it really was, a gun deck. The schoolmaster's books, slates, paper, and the like would be trampled underfoot as the crew, including the boys, scrambled to their positions and rolled out the guns. Several schoolmasters had been nearly crushed while scrambling on their hands and knees, gathering materials when the heavy guns were rolled backward to be loaded.

Richard found himself encumbered on the *Constellation* with a schoolmaster named Waite. He was about twenty-two, thin and small, and very soft-spoken. Most of the midshipmen were tall enough to look him right in the eye, and four of them outweighed him by more than twenty pounds. He may have been slight, but he was quick-witted and above all, tolerant. Despite his looks, he laughed at their pranks and eventually won the boys over, and they succumbed to his instruction if only to please him.

Richard was bright, and Waite recognized it right away. He asked if Richard might like to supplement his study of ancient Rome. When Richard shook his head eagerly, Waite placed in his hands a small ornately bound book, *Julius Caesar*. Thumbing through the pages, Richard found it was not a history but instead a play written by William Shakespeare. He was doubtful, but took it with him to his hammock. Within pages he was interested and by the end of Act I he was enthralled. Whenever he had time over the next week, he read more, and when he was finished, he read it again. The flowing speeches, combined with the treachery and the valor were the substance of legend, and he was hooked. One phrase that kept running through his head was, *Cry havoc, and let slip the dogs of war.* It conjured up in Richard's mind great, beastly dogs, half-starved, fierce, and kept on stout chains just waiting, with no other purpose but to be freed to run among the enemy destroying and conquering. He saw the frigate in the same way, a creature existing for a single purpose, war, and he loved the thought of it. He had yet to be tried in a battle, but the drills and gunnery practice were enough to make him glad he was nowhere else. If the drills were this thrilling, what must a real battle be like?

Waite inspired Richard to read literature, and Truxton inspired in him a love of navigation. It was the captain's duty to see that the midshipmen were instructed well in that field, and they were secretly delighted when Truxton himself, and not one of the other officers, instructed them. The boys spent almost as much time looking at his scars as they did looking through their sextants. They were too afraid to ask how he had gotten them, so they made up fantastic stories in their mess explaining each scar they could see. It would have thrilled them to know that quite a few of their outlandish stories were spot-on. What they knew for a fact was that Truxton had been a successful privateer in the War of Independence, and he never once had to strike his own colors. He had done everything a seaman could do, and had been everywhere, even to China, on trading voyages. The boys worshipped him. The midshipmen dreaded instruction under Lieutenant Yancy, and no one dreaded it more than Richard.

Lieutenant Yancy would always give Richard some nautical calculation that even Yancy could not have solved in the time allotted. When Richard fumbled or needed more time, Yancy would humiliate him as incompetent. On the occasions when to Yancy's disgust Richard would arrive at the correct answer, the disbelieving Yancy would still find fault. Richard would not have specified the miles as nautical, or have indicated a specific measurement, and he would then berate him or strike him with a slender bamboo cane in front of the other midshipmen. Richard knew better than to react, it would cost him his career, but he yearned to get even with Yancy.

Truxton's instruction was a bright spot for the midshipmen in the otherwise mind-numbing duty of merchant convoy escort. French privateers were now hunting the trade routes for prizes, and the American merchant ships had begun travelling under the protection of a frigate at all times. The frigate's crew hated the duty. It was slow, they felt the skills of the merchant crews were inferior, and they basically sailed in huge circles. It was in this way that Richard spent his first year on the beautiful *Constellation*, the monotony broken only by gunnery practice and Yancy's ridicule.

The *Constellation* finally received orders to leave convoy duty the following December to battle the French in the West Indies. As they sailed south, Richard spent his third Christmas away from home. He had not been back for so much as a visit, and his father and brothers would barely have recognized the tall and muscular young man he had become in those years.

They had hardly arrived in the Indies and settled in their patrol when they spotted the forty gun French *L'Insurgente*. The crew had drilled until gunnery was second nature, but now they faced the real thing. Richard and the other midshipmen were barely able to contain their excitement. This was not target practice where he might win a small cash prize, or, better yet, praise from Truxton. This was for real. On the little *Washington* they had used twelve-pound guns, but *Constellation* fired a ball twice that weight and Richard had yet to see the real damage a shot like that could inflict.

The marine drummer beat to quarters, and they flew in all directions to take up their battle stations as the *Constellation* prepared to intercept the French ship. Richard stood behind his gun in the tropical heat, absolutely roasting in his regulation wool uniform waiting with his gun crew for the order to fire. He grinned over his shoulder at the lieutenant behind him, but the lieutenant, a veteran of other battles, did not return the smile.

The French had the wind in their favor, but *Constellation*'s greater maneuverability would make up for the disparity. The gun crews waited tense and silent as the *L'Insurgente* came astern firing her bow chasers to test the range. From the stern windows, Richard could see the smoke long before he heard the report of the gun, and he watched as the shot fell harmlessly into the sea fifty yards shy. Richard's gun was located on the starboard quarter, and he could easily see the oncoming French ship through the windows of the captain's cabin which was part of the gun deck. The bulkheads which had given Truxton privacy, his furniture, and even the checkered floor tarpaulin, had been removed and stowed. Some of it was in the hold, and some in the ship's boats which were being towed along behind like a flotilla of ducks. The furniture was removed to prevent it from becoming deadly splinters by heavy shot.

Truxton used the test shots of the French to gauge his own range. A few moments later Richard felt the ship turn sharply, and as she settled sideways to the waves, she rocked considerably. The order came down the line to fire only on the up-roll to gain altitude for the shots. "You will fire amidships when she bears," came the additional order from the lieutenant nearest him. Richard waited to see the ship through the space around the barrel of the gun as it protruded from its port. Suddenly the guns nearest the bow began to fire and the firing proceeded down the line toward him. After six guns had fired, there was a dreadful explosion as a French shot roared though the *Constellation*'s side knocking men and a gun with its carriage flying. The air filled with deadly splinters, some nearly two feet long from the *Constellation*'s oak hull. They became deadly spears exploding in all directions while wounded men's screams were drowned as *Constellation* continued to fire her guns.

Richard now saw the French ship come into view through his gun port, and he was waiting for her midships to come square into his sights when the gun next to him was hit. The shot roared through the side of the ship tipping the two-and-a-half-ton gun off its carriage and onto its crew.

Richard saw for a second the severed arms and head of a man he knew from his watch and then turned his attention back to his own gun. The *L'Insurgente* was now centered in his sights, and he waited for the up-roll to fire. With a roar the gun rolled backwards as it hurled its double shot. As the recoiling gun gathered speed, Richard watched the wheels rolled effortlessly over body parts which had fallen in the way. With a soundless pop a head flattened and its contents sprayed over Richard and the others in his crew.

Richard's gun was arrested by its heavy tackle and stopped rolling backwards, and his crew began to reload and haul it back into place to fire again. *Constellation* was now turning and though Richard could not hear them yelling, he knew the opposite crews were preparing a broadside. Richard tried to take stock of the wounded around him. He saw the Surgeon's crew arrive to collect the wounded, and they began to haul some of them away, but, to Richard's horror, the pieces and parts, including the headless body, were tossed overboard through the open gun port to get them out of the way. Richard's eyes burned from the gunpowder, and he wiped them with his hand, but as he pulled his hand back from his face, he saw it was covered with blood and bits of brain from the dead and injured men around him. He gulped down his gorge and made ready to fire again.

Richard could hear, or rather feel, the firing of the guns on the port side as he waited for the ship to turn again and expose his quarter. "We are laying it to them," the lieutenant next to him shouted cheerfully right in his ear. Knowing what they were going through in the *Constellation*, he could not imagine how bad it must be on the *L'Insurgente* if the French were getting the worst of the punishment. Two guns down he could see Leonard Travis, his face set grimly as he watched his gun crew reload, run out, and tie down. Travis stared straight ahead, waiting for the order to fire again.

The starboard battery once again opened up, and the deck was filled with smoke and noise. Richard saw out of the corner of his left eye the bulkhead explode as another French shot roared through. He felt something strike the brim of his hat, and he glanced sideways to see a ten-inch splinter sticking out of the oak beam just behind his head. He could see down the gun deck, and there was nothing but smoke and rubble where Travis had been standing seconds before. He forced himself to breathe and fired his gun again, knowing at any moment the world around him would explode, and he would be blown to smithereens. He had to fight the urge to duck and pull his head down into his shoulders, but he had been admonished repeatedly to stand straight and do his duty. One old sailor had tried to comfort him saying, "Don't worry 'bout them shots around you. It's just like lightnin', you'll never even see the one 'at gets you. If it hits 'round you, and you're still standing, you're fine." All the weeks and months Richard had been firing for practice, he now realized it was the splinters that killed men and rarely the actual cannonball. He was barely breathing as he ordered his gun to be reloaded, certain the area around him would erupt into splinters at any second. His crew was able to fire again before the ship turned to unleash the port battery. The *Constellation* was doing well and didn't seem to be taking any hits except in the area of the starboard quarter, exactly where Richard's crew was located.

They fired over and over again, moving the dead and wounded as necessary. The gun to his right took a direct hit that killed its midshipmen and four of its crew members along with two from his own crew. Richard ordered the unwounded men from the next gun to take the place of the dead men in his crew, and they continued to reload and fire repeatedly for what seemed an eternity. His existence consisted only of loading and firing. He could barely hear anything above the ringing in his ears, but he had the presence of mind to remember to reduce the amount of powder used. As the gun heated up, less powder was needed, and to put in a full load now would damage the gun. All around him the stern bulkhead was eroding as it took hit after hit from the French. One of his men, impaled in the thigh with a splinter that was at least a foot long and nearly two inches across, crumpled to the deck. As he was hauled away to sickbay he was still insisting he could work. Richard could no longer hear his firing orders, so he turned to the lieutenant behind him hoping to read his lips. He understood he was being ordered to increase his gun's elevation to attempt to bring down the *L'Insurgente*'s mast and rigging. Richard was looking right at the lieutenant affirming he understood his order when a spider shot, two deadly metal rods hooked to a short chain, blasted through a hole in the *Constellation* and took the lieutenant's head off just below his jaw. To Richard's horror, the lieutenant stood there headless for a second then sank slowly like he was kneeling at a church altar before he toppled backwards. Richard tore his eyes away from the corpse, but not before he saw the lieutenant's severed head tucked up neatly under his dead arm.

The incoming shots were steady now as the *L'Insurgente* fired over and over like a trapped wasp's stings, and Richard felt the hits all around him. He lost two more of his gun crew, and looked down the line where three men were standing by a gun so damaged it would not fire. The remainder of their crew had been killed, and Richard motioned for them to come and fill the vacancies. Two of them made it to him, but the third disappeared in a blast of smoke and splinters.

The firing went on for another ten minutes, as the French unerringly hit the starboard quarter over and over. Richard was no longer aware of the smell of gunpowder; he was just trying to stay alive and keep firing at the enemy rigging.

A cheer erupted as the *L'Insurgente* lost her foremast, but Richard was practically deaf and oblivious to it. He did hear a shot strike ten yards away hitting directly on the side of a disabled gun and making a tremendous clang before it deflected onto the deck to spin there like a deadly top.

With the foremast gone from the *L'Insurgente*, the *Constellation* now had a true advantage in maneuverability. Each of the *Constellation's* guns could fire straight into the unprotected stern of the French ship. The impact would shred her innards, and it would be her doom. The entire port battery let fly as they came upon the enemy. Richard's crew was now the only one in the starboard section still intact, and they prepared to fire again. As soon as the captain of the *L'Insurgente* saw his stern would be crossed again, he ordered his ship to strike her colors and surrendered.

A cheer rang out all along the gun deck of the *Constellation*, and someone motioned to Richard it was over. He just stared around, stunned. Everywhere he looked, hands, arms, legs, and other unidentifiable gore littered the deck. There was movement around him, and he could feel the thumping of feet on the deck through the soles of his boots, but he could not hear a thing except the ringing in his ears. He did not hear the boatswain's whistle ordering the retrieval of the ship's boats, nor did he hear Captain Truxton speaking to him. Truxton waded through the debris of bodies and damaged guns. He stood next to Richard and tried to talk, and Richard could only read his lips as he said, "You got the worst of it right here, Mr. Holmwood." Truxton eyed Richard carefully trying not to show his disgust at a large piece of scalp, with the black hair still attached, clinging to the collar of Richard's waistcoat. Richard stared back. This was war, and it was not the game he had been playing at gunnery practice. He had been wrong to think it could be fun. Let slip the dogs of war? There were no great beasts of war. They were men, men who were forced to do their duty and become dogs until it was over. He had done his duty, and no one could fault him for it, but now that it was over he began to shake and Truxton led him away. As they passed Travis's gun, Richard saw him being hauled away by the surgeon's men. Richard realized, revoltingly, that he could recognize individual sailors' body parts even when they were detached from the body. He recognized the hand of a sailor named White from the snake tattoo that wove around an index finger, and a large chunk of shoulder that was marked with a distinct sword scar belonging to the carpenter's mate.

Truxton now had Richard by the arm and led him toward his cabin which was quickly being put back to rights. Richard could hear a bit now, and as Truxton reached his cabin he turned to Richard in the doorway and said with a voice that sounded to Richard as though it was coming from the end of a tunnel, "You took a terrible beating today and took it like a man. It's all right to feel it when it's over, but never let it show. You have five minutes to compose yourself in my cabin. Cry if you can, and then you come out and complete your watch." Richard nodded numbly, and Truxton added more softly, "I couldn't be more proud of you if you were my own son." He urged Richard gently by the shoulder into his cabin and said, "Now go, and, Mr. Holmwood, five minutes only."

Richard arrived on deck in less than five minutes. The Boatswain looked at him, knuckled his forehead in obedience and then calmly flicked off the chunk of flesh still clinging to Richard's collar. Richard looked down at the section of scalp on the deck and swallowed hard.

The report of the dead and wounded was relayed through him to the officer of the deck. There were nineteen dead and thirty-seven wounded, but it was one of those unpredictable whims of war that the midshipmen bore the brunt of the fatalities in this encounter. Of the thirty boys on board, ten were now dead and six wounded, two of them seriously. It was any captain's nightmare to report the death of a boy put into his care, and poor Truxton had the duty of writing nearly a dozen such letters. He would be nauseous by the time he finished.

Richard watched as the dead were sewn in their hammocks by seamen of their rank. Richard was touched by the items their friends placed in the hammocks with them, ranging from Bibles to sewing palms to mugs for drinking rum. Each hammock was then sewn up with a double shot. A quick prayer was said over the bodies, their names and rank called, and they were sent over the side. The weight of the cannonballs pulled them into the cobalt depths leaving only bubbles rising to the surface. Life was then expected to return to normal. There were still watches to be manned, duties to be completed, a ship to run, and a prize to sail home. It seemed odd to Richard how quickly life just picked up again. When his mother, brother, and sister had died, everyone walked around in a fog. There was no regular schedule for days, and friends and neighbors had turned out to help with food and chores. On the *Constellation*, the decks would soon be washed of the blood and gore, the damage repaired and painted, bodies given over to the sea, and the ordered and regular life would return. Richard realized it was that very routine that allowed them to cope today and find strength to fight again tomorrow.

Richard thought again of the line from Shakespeare: *"Cry havoc, and let slip the dogs of war."* The first time he read it, the words sounded like magic, but now that he had seen war, he knew the beasts in chains were not dogs at all—they were everyday men who wore the invisible chains of civilization. Once those chains were slipped, they would kill and they even found honor, valor, and glory in the killing. Men in war did what they could not imagine in peace, and he was glad to feel the heavy links of civilization returning.

Richard went down to the sickbay to check on Travis. He climbed down the steep stairs and entered the dim and stale surgeon's realm which still smelled of gore. Even though the deck had been rinsed and scrubbed, his boots still crackled on bits of sand that had earlier been spread to absorb blood and keep the surgeon from slipping as he worked. Richard found Travis in a hammock, amazingly conscious. Travis smiled crookedly when he saw Richard approaching. Richard knew Travis' wounds were severe but was not prepared for what he saw. Travis was missing his left eye, his left arm below the elbow, and most of his left leg. Richard touched his shoulder and offered his sympathy, but Travis stopped him and said with a smile, "No, it's all right. Don't you see? I get to go home now. Isn't it wonderful!" Richard stared at him stunned. How could Travis hate the Navy so much he considered it a worthwhile trade to lose his arm and leg and half his sight to be free? Richard smiled trying not to let his horror show. He stayed only a few minutes then wished Travis well, promising he would visit soon, but knowing for certain when he left he would never come back. It was all he could do not to run from the crowded and dank sickbay, and he gulped in the fresh air as he came on deck.

He learned a few hours later that Travis had died shortly after he left him, so Richard and two other midshipmen prepared him in his hammock for burial. Just as they tightened the last few stitches, Richard slipped inside it a stack of letters Travis had received from home. He felt Travis would rather have them with him than anything nautical.

The *L'Insurgente* required fewer repairs than was first believed, and when they were complete, she was a pretty sight. She had been scrubbed up, her sails and rigging repaired, and now wore a shiny black and yellow coat of paint like *Constellation*. She was fit, and all she needed was a prize crew to sail her. The *Constellation's* first lieutenant was wounded, and fit only for light duty, so he stayed where he was, and Second Lieutenant Yancy was given command of the *L'Insurgente*. The watches were adjusted to make up for missing men and, much to his regret, Richard found himself in Yancy's watch. Yancy gave him a wicked sneer as he climbed over the railing and onto the *L'Insurgente*. Richard's first duty was to assist in getting the French sailors who could not be trusted to help sail the *L'Insurgente* down into the brig, and Yancy berated him the whole time.

Earlier, they had been becalmed after the battle was over, and had simply lashed the two ships together for ease of proceeding with repairs and tending to the wounded. All the while the repairs were being made, the sea was as smooth as glass, but now an obliging breeze had sprung up, and it was necessary to board quickly to separate the ships which were beginning to toss and rub against each other impatiently. Richard looked back at *Constellation,* hoping it would not be too long before he was back aboard her.

They sailed in convoy with the Stars and Stripes flying high above the French flag announcing to all who might come upon them that *L'Insurgente* was a captured prize. Richard did his best to steer clear of Yancy and only spoke to him when he was required to do so. There were no dinners at the captain's mess on this ship. Any meals out of the ordinary fare were at the captain's expense. Yancy had no money for such luxuries, so he ate his salt pork and peas alone in his cabin.

About three weeks later *Constellation* and her prize gave chase to two ships they believed to be French. Much of the *L'Insurgente*'s new rigging had stretched under the strain of sailing, and the crew had been constantly tightening it down and taking in the slack. Richard reported to Yancy that a good deal of the standing rigging on the topmost mizzen was loose and should be tightened. It could be done in an hour. The mast could still fly straight canvas, but the strain of tight maneuvering in a battle could cause the top section of the mast to carry away. Yancy snorted at the suggestion, but he followed Richard to the stern where he stared at the mizzenmast for nearly five minutes without speaking. He then said, "I will note your worrisome comment in the log, but I see no reason to do anything of the sort. Leave it as it is, Mr. Holmwood." Richard touched the brim of his hat in salute, and Yancy elbowed past him. Yancy then turned and added, "Mr. Holmwood, we have a sailing master on board to tell me these things, and I am sure if there were any problems with the mast, he would have reported them to me. You have your own duties to keep you occupied, so keep to them. If they are not enough, I can double them for you." Richard saluted again, gritting his teeth. He would do his best to bring it to the attention of the sailing master, but he didn't hold out much hope. Richard believed the sailing master was nearly incompetent, and he was also thick as thieves with Yancy, so there wasn't much hope for the mast getting repaired.

The fleeing French ships were now aware that the frigate was gaining on them, and they piled on more sail, but the sleek *Constellation* and its refitted prize were very fast and continued to close the gap. The drummer signaled for the crew and the small contingent of marines on the *L'Insurgente* to beat to quarters, and everyone scrambled to their battle stations. Richard took a deep breath and took his place. He no longer had the giddy anticipation he had before the fight with the *L'Insurgente* but had a grim determination to do his duty and get through it alive. Let slip the dogs.

The French ships were within range now, and *L'Insurgente* turned sharply to port to train her guns on the closest ship, leaving *Constellation* to deal with the other vessel. Richard's crew fired and was reloading when the *L'Insurgente* turned sharply. There was a sudden cracking and tearing of canvas as the top half of the mizzenmast snapped and fell forward onto the mainmast, cracking the top off it as well. The debris then fell onto the deck.

The ship wallowed as the crew looked to Yancy for orders. Word passed quickly that he had been crushed under the falling mainsail yards and had sustained several injuries to his ribs. There was no doubt that his collarbone was broken as the shattered end pushed up the skin. The first lieutenant had been standing next to Yancy when the mast fell, and he was also injured badly. Richard was the senior midshipman on board, and the crew now looked to him for orders.

L'Insurgente sat helpless in the water, and the French turned to finish them off. Richard stared over the rail at the oncoming ship and quickly ordered the men to begin clearing the fallen mast which was acting like a sea anchor and creating tremendous drag. They needed to gain some control of the ship. The French broadsided Richard's ship, tearing through the debris and converting it to lethal flying shards. The French attacker now performed a shallow turn and lined up on the stern of the *L'Insurgente*. Richard could see it coming, but there was nothing he could do. The *L'Insurgente* was not fitted with stern chasers to fire behind them and was defenseless. The crew huddled waiting for the attack, and it came with all the violence they anticipated. At least three shots tore right through the belly of the ship and one destroyed the rudder. They were dead in the water and could not steer the ship. Richard was about to tell them to strike the colors when he noticed that the flag had come down with the mizzenmast. He saw a crew member at the first platform on the foremast nailing the colors back up with a belaying pin.

Richard ran to the rail waiting for the French ship to deal the fatal blow, but to his surprise it was sailing away. The French captain knew they were helpless, and he had gone to help bring down the *Constellation*.

Richard ordered the crew to clear the debris on deck and give him a damage report. The good news was that the shots through her stern had not hit any vital supports though it put six of the guns out of commission. There were no holes through the hull that were leaking, but the rudder was paralyzed. As they chopped away more of the debris, the ship turned parallel to the wind and rocked sickeningly.

Richard ordered the foremast rigged to carry as much sail as possible while he turned to the problem of steering. He wondered if they could create a drag like a sea anchor that would provide some rudimentary control. He looked around on deck and saw a pile of short staves and metal hoops, the remains of several smashed fire buckets. This gave Richard an idea and he ordered two crew members to bring up ten barrel hoops from the hold. As each barrel was emptied during a voyage, it was broken down into staves and hoops which were stored flat to save space. The men quickly found the hoops and returned to the deck. Richard placed one hoop flat on the deck and then another four around it so that it resembled a child's drawing of a fat flower. He then instructed his crew to use stout lines to attach two sails which overlapped each other to the hoops forming two giant pouches. One of the sails could be given more or less slack which increased or decreased the drag allowing them theoretically to steer the ship. The whole apparatus was then fastened to the ship with heavy leads and some floats to reduce the strain on the lines.

The crew lowered the contraption over the side but only allowed it to fill a bit and then released the lines to allow the water to flow through again. When the lines were taut, the ship had veered a bit to that side which gave them some hope it would work. They hauled it back on board to reinforce the lines holding it, and while it hung there with its double sack dripping on the deck, a sailor immediately christened it "The Scrotum."

The other drag was completed using more barrel hoops, and both were put into place one on each side of the stern. The crew loaded the foremast with as much canvas as they dared, and then created a rough-looking sail made from a chunk of canvas suspended from the snapped mast by temporary yards. It was an ugly arrangement, but they were finally able to move in a straight line, closing the distance to the *Constellation*.

They could see the *Constellation* fighting it out with the two French sea wolves who circled for the kill. *Constellation* belched out so much flame and smoke as she fired from both sides that Richard twice thought she had exploded. She was a magnificent sight as she kept up a near continuous barrage of twenty-four pound shot. Richard calculated that if only three-quarters of her forty-four guns were firing, she would have at any one time seven or eight hundred pounds of shot hurling toward the enemy. The sound of the gunfire was deafening, but Richard could still hear the screams of injured men and the whirring of the ropes as they hauled the guns back out to fire again.

A full broadside from the *Constellation* connected with the French ship which had been its antagonist from the beginning of the action. When the smoke cleared, an eight-foot section of the French captain's cabin was visible through the hull. His quarter gallery with its relatively luxurious commode was gone, and if he somehow managed to keep his ship he would find himself using a bucket like the rest of his crew.

Richard made for the ship that had attacked him earlier, and her captain was so intent on damaging the *Constellation* he didn't see them until *L'Insurgente* was within range. Richard would have loved to see the look on the captain's face when he realized he was being attacked by what he dismissed as a dead ship. The French ship now tried to turn and fire, and in doing so exposed her stern. The bizarrely-rigged *L'Insurgente* unloaded her shot, which slammed into the Frenchmen's stern. "Right up the ass, sir!" a crew member next to him shouted. The French ship now tried to turn again, but *L'Insurgente* unleashed a second volley, which tore off her mainmast. Richard urged the *L'Insurgente* forward, and to his surprise he saw the enemy strike her colors. What the hell was he supposed to do now? He sailed closer trying to keep his eye on the other French ship which was busy fending off *Constellation*. It seemed too good to be true, and Richard wondered if it was some kind of trick. The French captain, with the flag in his hand, and about thirty of his crew were standing on the deck looking grim as *L'Insurgente* approached.

Richard had his French prize lashed to the wallowing *L'Insurgente*. He and six of his crew stepped across the rail and took control of the ship while the others held muskets aimed at the French crew. Richard picked up a sword from the deck as he walked toward the French captain. The French crew grumbled when they saw the victorious youth. Even the captain smirked and said something in French, which Richard did not understand. The captain made a mocking lunge at him, but Richard did not see it as a stunt by the captain to take the sting out of being bested by a child. Richard leaped forward, executing a textbook perfect lunge. It looked exactly like the diagrams that hung in the midshipmen's mess, a perfect diagonal line from the tip of his sword to his planted back foot. He stopped with his sword tip right under the captain's jaw. All he had to do now to kill him was raise up on the ball of his foot. The French captain lost his smirk instantly, and through clenched teeth Richard said, "I'll have your sword, sir."

The captain didn't dare move his head, but he craned his eyes to see Richard's hand and said in clear English steeped with a heavy accent, "You have it in your hand," and after a pause added, "sir." Richard lowered his sword, pointed to the *L'Insurgente* and said, "You and your officers will be escorted to that ship." The captain nodded and climbed slowly across the railing where he was held at gunpoint near the stumpy mainmast. Richard said to the French crew remaining on the surrendered ship, "Please see if your surgeon needs assistance."

The sailors looked at him blankly, and then the French captain asked from the deck where he was being held, "May I tell them, sir?" Richard nodded and the captain called across, "*S'il vous plaît voir si votre chirurgien a besoin de l'assistance.*" One of the French disappeared below deck. Richard had no idea what the French captain said, but the last word did sound like assistance, so he waited. The crew member returned and said something in French, and the captain translated. "Our surgeon has been killed, and we would be grateful for any medical assistance you can give us." Richard sent men to check on his own wounded and to see if there was a medical officer to spare.

As he was about to turn away, two sailors from the French ship stepped forward. One with a nasty wound to his shoulder said, "Sir, we are Americans. We were pressed by the British and then traded through smugglers. They traded us, sir, to the French for sugar."

Richard looked at them and said, "From where do you hail?"

The other man now spoke. "We are both from Baltimore, sir. We sailed from there on the merchant ship *Elsbeth*, but she was stopped by the British and they claimed we were British citizens and took us. There weren't nothing the *Elsbeth* captain could do. He wasn't armed, and there were only about twenty-five men in our whole crew."

Richard looked back at the French captain and he confirmed it sourly. Richard called to two crew members on the *L'Insurgente*, "Help these men to sickbay, and treat them well. They are Americans." The two men seemed to sag with relief as they were helped down to sickbay. Richard turned again to the French captain and asked, "Do you have more Americans aboard this ship?" The French captain shook his head and then was taken below under guard.

The *Constellation* had captured and secured her prize. A boat came alongside and the first officer of the *Constellation* climbed up the side of *L'Insurgente* and stood looking at the makeshift mainsail and the damage to the ship. He asked, "Where is your commander? Where is Lieutenant Yancy?"

"Lieutenant Yancy was injured, sir, in the initial attack from the French ship, as was Lieutenant Brims," Richard explained.

"You did this?" The officer looked around again at the repairs and then walked to the stern where both scrotum-like sea anchors sagged on the deck. He looked at them and then at Richard and arched his eyebrows.

"I didn't know what else to do, sir. Those things have been the rudder since ours was shot away," Richard explained.

The officer stood dumbfounded, and again said, "You did this?"

"Yes, sir, we had to give what assistance we could to the *Constellation*," Richard replied, pointing over to her. He remembered he had the French captain's sword in his hand, and he added, "And I have the French captain's sword for Captain Truxton."

"Truxton? Hell, you'll be keeping that sword. Do you realize you have captured a prize? You'll get paid at a captain's rate for this ship if she is sold." He looked around again and then stared at Richard. "Exactly how old are you, Mr. Holmwood?"

"I'm sixteen, sir, and a month," Richard said softly, not wanting the rest of the crew to hear.

"Sixteen!" the officer smiled. "Well, nevertheless, damned good job! Have you seen to your wounded and secured the enemy officers?"

Richard nodded, and then added, "I have also sent a surgeon's assistant to care for the French wounded, sir, as their surgeon was killed." The officer just shook his head amazed, and then Richard added, "Sir, we took two men off this ship who claim to be Americans from Baltimore. Their wounds are being seen to, but I believe they may have some information that will be of interest to us."

The officer again shook his head and smiled, "Jesus, what a job you have done here, Mr. Holmwood. Prepare your dead for burial and assist the French in doing the same. As soon as I have orders for you, I will send them over." Richard saluted, gripping the brim of his hat.

Richard didn't have to wait long. Repairs commenced within the hour to the four ships, and the small squadron set sail for Kingston to refit in port. They caught up with some mail from a southbound convoy and there were three letters for Richard from his father. It had been close to a year since Richard had written to him. When he tried to write a letter to his father, it seemed hollow and boastful to say what he had done and claim any glory when men under his command had died. In the end, he described the port, the ships they captured, and a full page of mundane things about life at sea. He signed it and put it with the other letters that were being bundled and sent on a northbound ship.

Richard may not have been boastful about his accomplishments, but Truxton certainly was. In his letters to Gabriel Holmwood, as well as to the Navy Commission, he left out no detail of the courage, ingenuity, and seamanship Richard had shown during his brief command of the *L'Insurgente.*

After six weeks of refitting, the four ships were ready to depart and begin their patrol again. Most of the crew had spent their time off duty drinking copious amounts of rum, sampling the local whores, and dancing. The midshipmen were allowed the drinking and dancing, but were kept chastely away from any of the tradeswomen.

Richard had acquired a crate of books, and he now settled in the midshipmen's mess with his treasure. The varied collection contained histories, Shakespeare's *Hamlet*, a half-dozen sappy novels, some botanicals with fantastic etchings, a book on raising chickens, about a half-dozen more without covers he had yet to identify, and a book written in French.

Inside the French book was a reference to someone named Sun Tzu, the sixth century before Christ, and also a Frenchman named Jean Joseph Marie Amiot. The book had been through several pairs of hands that could read both French and English and its pages were littered with scribbled translations. One that caught his eye was *Know Your Enemy*. He flipped back to the inside cover and the same hand had written in large letters *The Art of War.*

He took it to Waite, the schoolmaster, who smiled as he held the book in his hands. Waite had an English translation of the book and traded it with Richard. It was dense material that would take him a long time to read, but to a midshipman more than likely returning to convoy duty, time was something he had in abundance.

Richard secretly hoped that when they left port he would be put in command of the prize captured by *L'Insurgente*, but Truxton put all notions of that to bed when he lined up the officers and midshipmen from the various ships and made his reassignments. Richard found himself back on board the *Constellation* and to further disappoint him, he learned he was to be in Yancy's watch.

Yancy's injuries were painful and took some time to heal. During his convalescence, he heard nothing but the exploits of Midshipman Richard Holmwood. The story had been embellished a bit, as men will when bragging about someone in whom they take pride, but the essential truth was still there and it rankled Yancy. He could not refute any of it and endured the praise heaped on Richard day after day. Yancy seethed inside that the son of a thief would get such treatment when all he had gotten was pain and shame. He would meet with young Holmwood when there was no one else around, and this new little star would find out just what it was like to get some of his shine wiped away.

Richard was oblivious to just how much Yancy hated him. In the following four months the convoy had destroyed two small French ships that had been stalking merchants. The ships had been so damaged in the battle there was nothing left to do but burn them. Richard watched the flames creep up the remaining rigging of one of the French ships and wondered if it would have been better to just sit by and wait for their surrender. With the much larger crew of the *Constellation* they could have boarded and taken the Frenchmen without destroying them in the gun battle. He had no sooner had the thought than he remembered how he had viewed a gun battle before he was actually in one. Boarding a ship was not as glorious as it sounded, either.

The next morning they encountered the *Constitution* and her escort, *Nautilus*. *Constitution* was a sister ship, one of the same litter of six frigates the Navy had first produced. She had mail and orders, and something else that set Richard's heart pounding. The *Constitution* had twelve carronades lashed to her spar deck. Each carronade was capable of projecting a thirty-two pound ball about a hundred yards. Their range was much shorter than the three or four hundred feet of *Constellation's* guns, but a carronade shot could be devastating. Six of the monsters *Constitution* carried were destined for the *Constellation*.

The carronades were much shorter than the nine-foot guns Richard was used to, and they weighed about a ton, only half the weight of the long guns. Still, a ton was not easily moved from one deck to the other, so they made for the nearest port where the carronades were unloaded and placed on their carriages. Richard and the others who had not seen a carronade before stood watching. Each sat on a sliding carriage rather than on wheels, and instead of having two iron projections or trunnions out each side to mount it to the carriage, there was a simple large lug on the underbelly. Its elevation was controlled with a screw like that of cannons used on land.

During his watch Richard received a message that he was to report to Captain Truxton's day cabin as soon as he came off duty. Richard wondered what he had done wrong to warrant a private scolding, as midshipmen were not ordinarily called to the captain's cabin. He pondered it for the remaining hour and a half of his watch, and then brushed up his uniform jacket and reported. Truxton's steward announced him and held the door open for him to enter. Truxton looked up from his correspondence as Richard walked in and stood before him. "Have the carronades been lashed down properly?" Truxton asked without looking up from his correspondence. Richard affirmed they had, as well as the shot to be used in them. Truxton did not motion for him to sit, and Richard stood at attention staring at a point above the captain's head. Truxton put a flourish on what he was writing and then stood and turned to Richard. "Relax, I have some news for you about the *Danse Sur La Mer*," he said, referring to the ship Richard had captured. "I have been informed she is not to be sold as a prize, but to be renamed and used by the Navy as an escort." He looked at Richard and said, "I am sorry, Mr. Holmwood, but there will be no prize money for you. I have, however, been instructed to give you a concession fee for your good work." Truxton handed him a draft for fifty dollars. Richard was disappointed, but took the draft politely. A midshipman was paid nineteen dollars a month, and this fifty dollars represented three months' work without the sweat and danger, so it was certainly better than nothing.

"Thank you, sir," Richard said, and then added, sounding very much a boy, "Am I still allowed to keep the sword?"

Truxton laughed. "Absolutely. You earned it, so you keep it." Truxton then cleared his throat and said seriously, "I wrote to the Navy Commission about your capture of the *Danse Sur La Mer*, and I have to say I did not stint on the details, nor did I embellish them. I made an accurate report of the incident. I did make a request in my correspondence, but being so used to having my requests denied, I thought no further on it until I received this information today from the Navy Commission." He waved a paper and said, "I could not be happier to impart it to you." He looked at Richard and rose smiling. "Pack your trunk. You will be moving again." Richard's heart sank at the news, and when Truxton saw it he grinned and said, "You will move your things from the midshipmen's berthing area to the first cabin on the starboard gun deck."

Richard stood confused, then uttered, "Sir, I don't understand. That is an. . ."

Truxton interrupted him, "An officer's cabin you were going to say? Well, you would be correct." Truxton smiled and held out his hand. "And it's yours, Lieutenant Holmwood."

Richard stared at him stunned and Truxton added, "Here is your commission signed and sealed. Congratulations." Richard shook Truxton's hand and took the commission with trembling fingers. Truxton tapped his shoulder and said, "You will need to get yourself a long coat here soon." He gestured at Richard's short midshipman coat, "And you will have to get used to a collar, but I think if you see Lieutenant Brims, he will loan you his old uniform until you can get your own." Richard smiled, still shocked, and looked around wondering what he should do. "Time to pack, Lieutenant," Truxton said, nodding toward the door. As Richard was walking through he added, "I am dining with my officers tonight, and I expect to see you there." Richard saluted and walked away clutching his commission, still stunned. Truxton smiled after he left and shook his head approvingly. To his knowledge, Richard was one of the youngest lieutenants in the Navy.

Word spread through the ship like tar on fire and soon the crew knew Richard had been promoted. Everyone he met congratulated him, everyone except Theodore Yancy. When Yancy heard, he snorted and then walked away. In the wardroom, Yancy would pretend like Richard wasn't there and at times interrupted him, but Richard let it pass.

Richard was fencing with another young lieutenant one day when Yancy appeared and called a challenge to the winner of the round. Richard won and prepared to face Yancy, but Yancy was not fencing to touch. Richard followed the wardroom rules and tapped him twice on the chest in what would have been fatal injuries if they were fighting for real, but Yancy in turn sliced a shallow cut in Richard's forearm before one of the other officers intervened, saying, "Come on, Yancy, he's got two good taps on you already." Yancy grinned and then backed off, but his eyes were not smiling as he made a vague apology and left.

The other lieutenants on the ship were kind and accepting, but Richard found himself again in that no-man's land where he was too young to really be one of the officers and yet no longer one of the midshipmen. He passed the following year in this lonely manner and Theodore Yancy dogged him every minute of it.

CHAPTER 4

WITH THE WAR with France finally over, the *Constellation* was ordered to the North African coast in the Mediterranean. The Algerians were collecting tribute to allow ships to pass without attack. Prior to the War of Independence, American ships had been under the protection of the British Navy and tribute paid by the British for safe passage extended to American colonial ships as well. Now American ships were vulnerable to capture and the ransom of passengers by Algerian pirates. If no one was willing or able to pay the ransom for the captured Americans they would be sold as white slaves. America had neither the money nor the mindset for this treatment, so several of the frigates were sent to deal with the situation, including the *Constellation*.

Before the *Constellation* left to cross the Atlantic she put in again at Gosport Shipyard in Portsmouth for refitting, allowing Richard to visit his family just a few miles across the James River in Hampton. When Micah and Thomas received the news Richard would be home, they planned to pin him to the ground as punishment for not writing. One look at their little brother though made them reconsider. Richard was as tall as they and possibly broader. He looked magnificent in his uniform, which set off his blond hair and startling blue eyes. It was more than just his size that gave them pause. Both brothers could see that Richard moved with the ease and grace of a predator, a large cat perhaps, and they could tell without testing him that his responses would be like lightning. Gabriel stood with tears streaming as he pulled Richard's cheek down so he could kiss it. He patted Richard's arm, as he repeated, "My baby boy is home again!" Wrennet ran down the walk when she heard his carriage arrive and threw herself into his arms. To her surprise, Richard wrapped his arms around her and lifted her right off the ground. It was amazing what four years had done to the boy Wrennet had last seen at thirteen.

Richard visited his family for a week and then reported back to *Constellation* at Gosport. Though he would visit home again for dinner, such occasions were usually marred by Yancy who would ride him about his family each time he returned.

Richard had finally purchased a new uniform of his own, and he was modeling it for Brim when Yancy came into the wardroom. Yancy looked at both of them and said, "I never trust a man who worries about his clothes. The Navy don't need that fuss, and I don't much like pretty boys."

Richard and Brim could not resist and said to each other as they left the wardroom, "What kind of boys do you like?" They could hear a few chuckles which were drowned out by Yancy's bellowing.

"Come back here!" Yancy screamed, and Richard and Brim both looked at each other puzzled and returned to the wardroom. Yancy pointed to Richard and said to the other officers assembled, "This man has insulted me and made a claim of unnatural and immoral actions on my part." Yancy was shaking with rage, and the officers in the wardroom who had been laughing at the rude comment now stood and looked uncertainly at each other. Yancy said through clenched teeth, "I call you out Lieutenant Holmwood. Give me the satisfaction." The wardroom went silent and everyone looked at Yancy. They were startled by Yancy's challenge to a duel over something obviously said in jest. Insubordinate it might possibly have been, but no one had taken it seriously. They were shocked at Yancy's call and even more so with an opponent so much younger than himself.

"Name your time and place, sir," Richard said flatly. This situation had gone on long enough and needed to be put to rest by defeating Yancy.

Richard knew absolutely nothing about dueling, so he asked Lieutenant Brim. Brim's experience consisted of participating in one halfhearted duel and witnessing two others, but he accepted Richard's request to be his second. Brim was only twenty, but by tradition he would negotiate the terms of the duel and the weapons of choice. Brim questioned Richard who admitted he was not that comfortable using a pistol and asked instead if he could use his dirk, that short blade many times made from a broken sword that midshipmen are required to wear at all times on duty.

Brim spoke to Yancy's second, who showed some reluctance to use dirks, but Brim silenced him by saying, "Your man has years more experience than my man, and surely he can handle a dirk. If he is that much of a coward, he should not have challenged Lieutenant Holmwood."

Yancy's second tried again, "With pistols, it is a fair match."

Brim snorted, "Since when has it ever been fair. Mr. Holmwood is barely seventeen years old. Don't talk to me about fair! We have requested the use of dirks." Yancy's second blanched and they bantered back and forth for another three-quarters of an hour, but in the end, it was left with dirks at the extremely close distance of three paces. The time was set for eight the following morning on the north side of Craney Island across the Bay. It was late when Brim returned from his negotiations and found

Richard, who was on duty, to give him information.

Leave was freely given to most off-duty officers. Richard and Brim had no trouble getting off the ship and over to Craney Island the following morning. They found they had arrived at the dueling spot before Yancy and his second, so Brim used this time to instruct Richard in the details of a duel and its finer etiquette. He explained there would be a reiteration of the cause of the duel, the chance to withdraw without losing honor, the actual count and pacing, and then he explained one rather delicate point, "Just before we start, the two of you will turn away from us and relieve yourselves." He saw Richard's expression and explained, "It serves a couple of purposes. First, if you are injured in the abdomen, it is better if your bladder is empty, and secondly, if you get scared, it won't be quite so obvious to everyone else here."

Richard looked at him incredulously. "Yancy and I are supposed to piss together? Is this a prank?" Brim shook his head no. Richard realized he was not kidding and smiled weakly as he said, "I doubt I can squeeze out a drop, but I'll do my best."

Yancy arrived with his second and their small entourage and were gathered about twenty yards away. Yancy was strutting about smugly while watching Richard closely.

Richard walked toward him and said more bravely than he felt, "Are you certain this is what you want, Lieutenant Yancy? There is no guarantee of the outcome."

"You upstart! You think because you have been in a couple of battles and tagged along at the tail end of a boarding party you qualify as any type of a threat to me. You little prick, you have been nothing but trouble to me since I set eyes on you, so, yes, this is what I want, unless you want to beg. You and your family have damned my honor," Yancy said, shaking with rage.

"You have certainly damned mine, so let's to it, sir," Richard said through his teeth, then swallowed hard.

Yancy closed the gap between them and they turned their backs to the others and quickly relieved themselves. Richard thought ironically that he and Yancy were no better than two backyard dogs marking their territory before a fight. They were then each presented with identical dirks that had never been used by either combatant.

Richard held the dirk in his hand shifting it to feel for its balance. He had chosen this weapon mostly because he knew he would have stood no chance with a pistol, and he knew Yancy was damned good with a sword. Richard did have some talent with a knife and the dirk was as close as he could come.

As a youngster neglected by his older brothers, Richard was forced to entertain himself. One of the ways he had passed the time was to throw a knife at a tree, counting how often he could hit in a small chalk circle he had drawn. He had become quite good at it, and his life now depended on that accuracy. Yancy outweighed him by at least forty pounds and was three inches taller. Richard knew that he would be killed if Yancy got hold of him. If Richard threw his dirk and missed, he would be without a weapon and at Yancy's mercy. He could probably outrun the larger man, but Richard promised himself he would die before doing so.

Richard and Yancy lined up back to back. The rules were again recited and both men nodded. It seemed to take forever for the count to reach three, but finally it arrived and Richard and Yancy turned at the same time. Yancy sneered and stepped toward Richard with his arms stretched out to the side like he was going to crush him. Richard planted his right foot, turned slightly at an angle, and threw the dirk. Before Yancy could throw or even react, the dirk was embedded in his chest to the right of his heart. Yancy staggered and fell clutching the knife with both hands trying to pull it loose while Richard stood staring at him.

"You've killed me, you little shit!" Yancy bellowed.

"No, sir, I have not," Richard said flatly and then added, "You have been hit in muscle only. That dirk is not long enough to puncture your lung, so you'll patch up well enough." He walked to where Yancy was rolling on his back and hissed, "Is your honor now satisfied, or shall we line up again?"

"Just go!" Yancy bellowed. "Get out of my sight!"

"You still have your turn to throw, Mr. Yancy," Richard said flatly.

"Go away," Yancy whined and curled on his side, cradling the hilt of the blade.

Richard turned and picked up his jacket and hat and put them on. He turned to Brim and said quietly, "Is there anything I am supposed to do now, or is it over?"

"It's over, Richard," Brim said. They walked toward their boat and once they were off the island, Brim asked, "Was it a lucky throw, or did you aim?"

"I aimed for his chest, but not his heart. He has a chest like a barrel, and I figured the muscle could absorb the dirk without too much injury," Richard said.

"Then you could have killed him?" Brim asked as they rowed across the Bay.

"Certainly, but what good would that do?" Richard asked.

The news of Yancy's defeat spread through the ship. If Yancy had thought his defeat of Richard Holmwood could ever have restored his honor, he was sadly mistaken. Most of the officers thought Yancy was callow for the challenge and thought even less of him now that he had been defeated by someone so young.

The other officers only forgot Richard's youth when it came to seamanship, and there he was unequalled. He secretly swelled with pride when he overheard the sailing master, who was recovering from pneumonia, say to Truxton that all would have been well even if he didn't recover, for, "Young Mr. Holmwood there could easily take my place. I never saw such an eye for sails and rigging, even in the dark, and he is what eighteen, nineteen?"

The sailing master was corrected by Truxton's reply, "Lieutenant Holmwood is but seventeen."

Six weeks later they set sail from Portsmouth across the Atlantic to the North African coast where, to Richard's chagrin, they were once again on convoy duty, this time protecting American merchant ships from the Barbary Pirates rather than the French. Same duty, different enemy, but just as boring.

The first three convoys they escorted went without incident; however, in the fourth convoy was a ship manned by the worst crew Richard had ever seen. *Cumberland* wallowed along with her sails luffing and flapping slowing down the entire convoy. The small sloops of war favored by the Barbary Pirates swarmed just out of range like jackals waiting for the frigate to break formation to guard the slower ship and leave the others stretched over several miles unprotected. The pirates even held hope that the *Cumberland* would be abandoned for the greater good. The slower the *Cumberland* sailed, the longer the convoy stretched and the closer the pirate sloops approached.

The *Constellation* slipped back to hail the *Cumberland*, now christened "Cumbersome" by the frigate's crew, to find out what was wrong. They learned that nearly a third of the crew was very ill and could not even muster for duty.

Truxton hatched a plan that might work, but it was risky. He turned and looked hard at Richard and said, "I am sending you over to take command. You understand, Lieutenant Holmwood, that should you be unable to get the ship moving faster you will be defenseless, since we will be forced to leave you behind?"

"Yes, sir, I understand, but I think something can be done to allow her to gain speed, and I would like to at least try," Richard said.

Truxton shook his head and nodded, "Best get to it then. You may take two midshipmen with you." Richard mumbled a quick "aye, aye" and began to retreat from the captain's cabin when Truxton stopped him and added, "Richard, do you know what cargo the *Cumberland* is carrying and why we have not abandoned her sooner?" Richard shook his head no, and Truxton smiled saying, "Good. It's best not to know." He stopped smiling then and was serious as he added, "Good luck, and Godspeed."

AT FIRST RICHARD THOUGHT they would send him over in one of the ship's boats, but they could not slow down enough for that, so it was determined they would leap from the larger *Constellation* to the smaller ship. Richard grasped the ratlines and stood watching as the *Cumberland* came within range. He thought initially it would be simpler to leap into her rigging or try for her ratlines but realized that if he missed his footing or his hand slipped he would fall into the sea. Good swimmer or not, they would more than likely not be able to pull him from the sea before he drowned. Jumping on the deck involved possible broken bones, but at least if he slipped there he would fall to the deck, not into the water.

The matronly old *Cumberland* was now less than fifty yards away and Richard tensed to make his jump. Beside him were the two midshipmen who were to accompany him, Williamson and Shaw, and they made ready to leap as well. He had warned them not to jump into each other for fear they would all fall into the sea. When the range was right he shouted to Williamson and Shaw, "Jump just as we start our down roll. We'll be closest then." Both young men nodded, not taking their eyes off the ship they were overtaking. They edged out as far as they could, holding with one arm, and on Richard's yell, they leaped to *Cumberland*'s deck. Richard landed and rolled back up to his feet, unable to believe he was not hurt. Williamson rolled too, but he did not get up as quickly, and Shaw jumped so high and late he was tangled in some of the mainmast running rigging, and it was a few seconds before he untangled himself to stand embarrassed on the deck. Shaw had a nasty bruise on his cheekbone, but assured Richard he was fine.

The captain of the *Cumberland* stood staring at the three men. When he found his voice he said, "Lieutenant, thank you for coming to help us. We're a bit shorthanded at the moment." Richard looked around and saw only seven men. They looked like they were just recovering from some illness. As if reading his thoughts the captain explained, "A little over two dozen of my men went on leave in Marrakech, but they got tainted rum there and six of them died. Another dozen are still sick, and you're looking at the ones fit for duty."

Richard smiled sympathetically at the sick sailors. Already walking the deck looking up into the rigging, he said, "I'm sorry to hear that sir, but we must get to work if we are going to pick up some speed." He saw several places where he could improve the sail surface for catching wind, but the ship was rolling heavily, recovering slowly from the waves, and Richard knew before he checked that they were carrying a great deal of water.

"We need to check the hold, sir," Richard said, and the captain led him down the companionway steps and onto the second deck. It was there that he saw the cargo the *Cumberland* was hauling: Girls, at least twenty, ranging in age from twelve to about seventeen or eighteen. They stared at him startled, and recovering themselves edged forward. Suddenly, erupting from the middle of the girls was a monstrous rutabaga of a woman obviously in charge.

She rushed forward bristling with fury and said in a thick accent which Richard could not readily identify, "Sir, I am Mrs. Adeline Fisk, and this deck is for my girls! These are young ladies, not accustomed to this kind of treatment with men barging into their quarters without even identifying themselves or knocking." She took in a great shuddering breath and continued, "I was assured by the captain my girls would not be gawked at, or in any way molested." She tugged her dress down over her prow of a chest and ordered, "You will identify yourself, so I may report you to the captain, and then you will leave."

Richard looked at the hissing woman and quietly identified himself, Williamson, and Shaw, and then said, "Ma'am, I assure you I am just passing through, but I need to check the hold to see if we are taking on water." Then he added with a glare, "and it would be best if I did that before we sink to the bottom." Without waiting for an answer, Richard moved through the mob gently parting the girls who were pressing forward for a better look.

Richard and Williamson reached the entrance to the hold and removed the grating, but Shaw had been cut off and surrounded like a weak animal picked from the herd. He was unsure of what to do and kept backing up until he stood flat against the companionway steps where he just stared at the hungry girls.

Williamson lowered himself down into the hold and then reported to Richard that there was at least two feet of water sloshing in the hold. This meant that the bilge water was now up into the hold area and would have contaminated everything there. It was not a recent leak, and Richard realized some of the trunks and cases were actually growing mold. He turned to Shaw and said, "Start throwing these crates overboard to help lighten the load."

Mrs. Fisk heard him and pounded on his back with her fan, screeching, "I heard that, young man. You cannot throw away our gowns. We will be unfit to be presented anywhere."

Richard stared at her and then repeated his order to Williamson. He turned now to the woman and said, "Ma'am, if we don't lighten this ship, the only place you will be presented is at the bottom of the sea." A gasp went up from the girls and some started to howl. Richard cursed himself for saying it out loud, and then turned to them and tried to say soothingly, "Ladies, I think we will be fine, but we have got to get rid of some of this weight. I am sorry, but the trunks must go."

From the back of the crowd a girl's voice called out in less than ladylike volume, "Good! I wasn't looking forward to wearing those rags anyway!"

Another voice called in answer, "Only because your ass is now as wide as an axe handle, and none of them fit you!" Richard and Shaw exchanged a glance as a storm of words ensued. The mob separated to reveal two girls on the deck fighting and cursing. They didn't fight like girls who usually just tear at each other's hair and clothes, but each was standing in a good, solid, knees-bent stance with their fists clenched ready for action. One girl spit into her hand and motioned for the other to come again. Shaw saw his chance to escape the companionway and ran to Richard's side where the three of them stood staring dumbfounded at the girls. Mrs. Fisk rushed in with a blanket and threw it over one girl's head and the other girl was surrounded and restrained by her peers.

"Ladies! Where are your manners?" Fisk bellowed. She took a deep breath to compose herself and then turned to Richard and with a voice dripping honey said, "I must apologize for these girls. It's this confinement that is working on them. They are not used to such rough use and have been so carefully raised they sometimes forget themselves." Richard looked at the two combatants. The blanket had been removed from the one and they stood glaring daggers at each other. He doubted strongly it was the confinement of the ship that had caused them to forget their manners. He didn't believe they ever had any.

Within a few hours, the hold was empty of everything that could be jettisoned. Having tossed her foul innards, *Cumberland* moved along a bit lighter, but she was still wallowing. Richard made adjustments to the sails that gained a few knots of speed, but the ship was still heavy with water and lagging behind the rest of the convoy. There wasn't enough crew left to sail the ship and work the pumps at the same time. He had no choice, he needed more hands, and as he looked around at the milling girls he made his decision. He sought out the dreaded Mrs. Fisk and suggested that her girls might be able to take short shifts on the pumps.

If he had suggested they open a bordello, it probably would have gone over better with Mrs. Fisk. She reared back to give him a horrifying view down both barrels of her nostrils and then raked him, "Lieutenant Holmwood, I can't have these girls working like laborers. They come from some of the finest families in America and Europe. They don't work! They don't even know how, and I am not going to be the one to teach them!" With her multiple chins flapping and her prow thrust forward, she resembled a large, rousted hen. Richard looked over at the girls. Two of them bore the bruises of an earlier fight and stood with their hands on their cocked hips looking anything but fine bred and frail. As he gazed at them, two of the girls actually wet their lips in a hungry and sultry gesture as they examined him from head to toe, lingering long and hard in the middle.

"Come with me, madam," Richard said, taking hold of Mrs. Fisk's arm. He pulled her to the taffrail and then pointed. She followed the line of his hand as he explained, "Do you see those ships?" She nodded, seeing the pirate sloops for the first time. "They are not friendly, and they are hunting us. We have dropped far behind the convoy, and those hostile ships are gaining on us. They will catch us by nightfall, and although they won't bother us at night, they will certainly attack us at dawn. Unless we can get the water out of this ship and get it moving faster, we will be at their mercy." He looked at Mrs. Fisk, and she stared back into his blue-green eyes. He added with a steady voice, "When they board us, those of your girls they cannot sell for slaves, they will rape to death. Those they find useless for either purpose, they will feed to their dogs." He let this sink in and then added, "Now, if by some chance you should survive, I think you will have a difficult time explaining to these high-placed parents you mentioned that, but for the risk of some blisters and hard work, their daughters might still be alive." Richard leveled his gaze, "I am not asking them to do anything immoral; I am asking them to stay alive. They don't look frail to me, and I need their help."

Mrs. Fisk looked as if she would vomit as she stared at the enemy ships on the horizon, but she slowly nodded her head. "Tell us what to do, sir," she finally offered. Richard smiled weakly, for even with their help on the pumps, the ship would most likely be overrun by the pirates at dawn.

Richard lined the girls up on each side of the eight-foot iron bar that was the handle of the pump, and as he started to explain, two of them began slapping each other. He separated the antagonists and tried again. Normally, four men stand on one side to push and pull. Richard had manned pumps before, and it was murderous work, so he put six girls on each side, so they could help push and pull each way. He had instructed them to wrap their hands in sailcloth to prevent blisters, but even with the cloth, their palms would be shredded after about twenty minutes. He had spoken with Shaw and Williamson, and they would each take a group of the girls and help them pump, altering their crews every twenty minutes.

The pump handles barely budged at first, but after four or five revolutions they moved easier, and after another half-dozen turns, the water began to flow down the pump dales and out of the ship. The girls found it to be somewhat of an adventure at first, giggling and gaping at Williamson and Shaw, but after an hour of taking their twenty-minute shifts, they looked a little worn, and Richard felt for them. Everyone on the ship, including the captain and Richard, took their turn at the pump, and by the end of the second hour, there was a discernable drop in the water. Richard and Shaw went back down and found many leaks just below the waterline.

They used every strand of oakum on board, and even a few shredded evening gowns that had been set aside as contraband when the others were thrown overboard, to plug the holes. The girls proved more hardy than Richard would have believed and stuck to the pumps long after they were exhausted, mainly because the ringleaders had made a competition of it, and they struggled on if only to show each other up.

Richard's doubts about the fine breeding of the girls were confirmed as he watched two of them compete in a spitting contest. Richard shuddered as he watched them hawk back and then laugh as the sea gulls dove to catch the globs they launched. He was absolutely certain he could not spit as far as either of the contestants. In truth, their families had more money than manners and had come into the former recently in industrial or mercantile endeavors. Mrs. Fisk adopted the philosophy that if she treated them like they were well-bred, they would adopt that behavior. She certainly had her work cut out for her when it came to her charges. They all cursed like sailors, and their predatory looks practically terrified Williamson and Shaw.

Mrs. Fisk's job was to domesticate these creatures, no doubt with the purpose of eventually passing them off as well-bred girls to wealthy husbands, and Richard felt for her in her task. She had a rough road ahead if she hoped to keep them chaste long enough to teach them manners.

On the third day after he boarded, they caught up to the convoy, and Richard saluted Captain Truxton with a flourish and a huge grin as he sailed past them into the *Cumberland*'s original place near the front. Truxton murmured to his first officer as Richard passed them, "You know if he wasn't quite so damned good, he would be offensive." They both smiled and waved back to Richard who was standing on the gunwale holding tightly to the ratlines, his blond hair blown forward over his face by the following wind. He was wearing his uniform jacket, but stood hatless with his hungry female crew arrayed behind him. The girls had given up on formality days before, finding that their gowns only hampered their turn at the pumps, so they stood now loose-hipped in not much more than their chemises. Captain Truxton added with a grim smile, "Mr. Holmwood won't be quite so full of glee when he learns what must await him when we reach Syracuse." After Richard assessed the situation on the *Cumberland*, he had reported back to Truxton by flag signals that there were six dead and twelve dangerously ill. This would have to be reported to the harbormaster when they arrived in Syracuse. Truxton smiled sadly knowing what would result from that report.

They were due to raise Syracuse the following day, and the unruly girls saw this as their last chance at Richard or his midshipmen. When they came off watch, Williamson and Shaw arrived in Richard's cabin seeking refuge from the female onslaught. Richard went on deck for duty, telling the midshipmen to lock themselves in if need be but to stay away from the girls. He told them, "Just gut it out one more day, and we'll be shed of these hyenas forever." Twice he had awakened to find girls in his cabin, and he had almost rudely shoved them out.

Richard was as randy as the next man, but somehow a gentleman's appetite for food is lessened if he is thrown into a vat of it. It was the same with these wanton girls. He was smart enough to know that to cull one of them out of the herd would incite a riot in the others. It would be like tossing a grape into the monkey house at a zoo. Cry havoc, indeed.

The *Cumberland* waited to be assigned a berth in Syracuse. Richard should have been alarmed when they were sent to an anchorage on the edge of the harbor rather than a pier, but he was just so relieved to be getting off the ship.

A few moments after they dropped their anchors, a boat came out from the pier and another from the *Constellation*. Richard, Williamson, and Shaw had gathered their meager belongings and were standing near the rail waiting evacuation. Being manned by stout naval jacks, the *Constellation*'s boat took the lead. Richard elbowed Williamson and Shaw and whispered, "Let's get the hell off this barge." The *Constellation*'s boat came within hailing distance, but would come no closer, and Richard felt the first pang of worry.

Captain Truxton himself was in the boat, and he congratulated the three on their rescue of the *Cumberland*, her crew, and passengers. Truxton congratulated them again, and then added in a serious tone, "You have all done your duty admirably, but you know the rules of contagion. A ship reporting more than two deaths by anything other than bodily harm must be quarantined."

"But, sir," Richard replied, "those men died from drinking rum that was toxic. There is no contagion here."

"Yes, Mr. Holmwood, I know, but rules are rules, and we must all obey them if we choose to call again in this port," Truxton said sympathetically. "I have here orders for the three of you to report to the first American naval ship that calls here after your quarantine is over. We cannot stay, as we also had orders waiting for us that call us away as soon as we take on provisions." He said softer, "I am sorry, gentlemen." Richard's heart sank lower when he recognized his locker in the boat along with those belonging to Williamson and Shaw.

Richard stood watching as the *Cumberland*'s boat was lowered. Their lockers were transferred from the *Constellation*'s boat to it, and then Truxton returned to his ship. Richard, Williamson, and Shaw watched with pale faces until Truxton was back on the *Constellation*. They turned and looked back over their shoulders at the girls who had heard every word Truxton had said. Seemingly at a signal, the girls stepped forward, closing ranks like wolves on their prey. Richard knew then what it felt to be hunted. More of the *Cumberland*'s crew recovered each day, until Richard, Williamson, and Shaw had very little to do. He instructed the midshipmen in navigation and general seamanship, but since there were no books on board to teach any other subject, Richard was limited to his memory for material.

Richard had a tiny cabin, really no more than a locker, just forward of the stern officer cabins, and Shaw and Williamson had staked out a berthing area just outside his cabin where they hung their hammocks. Now that there was no escape for the three men, the girls began to forage out like cockroaches during the night. Richard finally let the boys seek refuge in his cabin. Mrs. Fisk's girls were not only randy, they were relentless, and Richard repeatedly warned the midshipmen to stay away from them. "If you touch one of them it will cause a stampede in the others, and by the time we hauled them off, there would be nothing left of you but some grease on the deck."

Richard thought he had succeeded in keeping his two charges safe, until the night before their quarantine ended when Shaw stumbled into his cabin nearly naked, completely disheveled, and trembling. Richard stared at him and then said, "Mr. Shaw, where is your uniform?"

"They kept it, sir. Fought over it like dogs with scraps, they did, taking buttons and tearing strips of cloth," he said and pushed his mangled hair out of his eyes. "All I did was go with two of them to help with a jammed door, but they blocked me in, and then swarmed out! I was like a beetle that had stumbled onto an anthill. They were everywhere, and I tried my best, but then they started fighting over me, and I had to do what they wanted."

"Are you all right?" Richard asked, more amused than alarmed.

Shaw looked wildly around the room and then blurted out, "Sir, is it possible for a man to be raped . . . more than once?"

CHAPTER 5

THE MOMENT the quarantine was over, Richard and the two midshipmen moved from the *Cumberland* to an inn where they gorged on Italian food. They had to wait there three weeks, but one morning they awoke to the news of a large American frigate in the harbor. They shaved and dressed double quick and with their orders in hand, stood waiting on the pier. They watched as the *United States* dropped her anchors and was met by the harbor pilot. As they were rowed out, Richard noted that she was a beautiful ship, perhaps not as lovely as the *Constellation*, nor as menacing as the *Constitution*, but she was still wonderful.

Richard found that command of the *United States* was being transferred in Syracuse to Edward Preble. He was to arrive with a convoy in three weeks. The previous captain, being very unwell, left on a ship bound for Philadelphia. During those three weeks, the ship would be under the command of its first lieutenant. Richard reported to him and then stowed his things in his cabin. He was the youngest officer on the ship, and as such got the smallest cabin, not much larger than that on the *Cumberland*, and thirty midshipmen hung their hammocks just outside his door. His cabin on old *Cumberland* had been made of wood with a door, but this was no more than some canvas partitions on wooden braces. The majority of his cabin was taken up by the nine-foot gun over which swung his hammock. He had room for his locker which also served as a chair, and he had the luxury of a chamber pot plus a steward to empty it, but it was austere living to be sure.

The *United States* led a squadron of six smaller vessels. When Commodore Preble finally arrived, all the officers from those ships crowded onto the deck to greet him. He took one look over the mass of young officers assembled and mumbled, "This is nothing but a pack of boys. Am I to go to war with school boys?"

Regardless, he started work right away to fulfill his orders. The Navy was, at last, going to deal with the problem of the Barbary Pirates. He had been given permission to do what other commanders had only dreamed of, taking the war right to the pirates' principal city. Preble's orders were to bring the pirates down in any way he could, including direct bombardment of Tripoli.

Upon hearing this, every young officer fantasized about hurling shot right into the palace in Tripoli, but it would be months, nearly a year, before they got their chance. In the meantime, while drilling and drilling, the fleet was also on convoy duty. Sometimes their convoy group swelled to fifty or sixty merchant ships as those of neutral countries joined them, relying on the well-known adage of safety in numbers.

Preble had indeed inherited young officers, and with their age came cockiness and a brash assurance that they were indeed the ones to put an end to the Barbary nuisance. They lacked discipline to the standard Preble demanded, and it was going to be a tough tour for them all. Among the young lieutenants in this squadron was Stephen Decatur from Philadelphia. Stephen, Richard, and another lieutenant, Richard Somers, all drawn together by the adversity they shared, became fast friends.

Commodore Preble was absolutely strict about etiquette and protocol and drew up over one hundred new regulations for the North African fleet. Any officer who fell afoul of these regulations was required to submit to Preble in writing the reason for his failure, the consequences that resulted, and how the same could be avoided in the future. For officers with an excellent command of written English like Richard, composition was no problem. For others, Stephen Decatur among them, writing was hell. He had not been the best of students unless the topic interested him, and while mathematics came easily, he avoided reading. On several occasions Richard dictated while Stephen wrote discipline reports that needed to be submitted to Preble within the allotted twelve hours.

Preble drilled them constantly and it began to pay off. His goal, he told them plainly, was to have each of them able to react in a battle and know what to do as the situation changed. They would drill all possibilities, and eventually each officer could anticipate what was needed next. Preble reasoned that it was dangerous for them to always have to look to him for signals during a battle, "I might not be able to signal you, or I might be killed. You need to know what to do without me telling you." This was a novel idea in a time when the battle plan could be altered only from the commander's ship, but Preble made a good point. It was very possible in the middle of a battle that signals could fail or be misread.

It wasn't only the lieutenants who suffered under Preble, but the captains as well. Among them was William Bainbridge of the *Philadelphia*, who was in his late twenties. Bainbridge had a reputation as having bad luck, though mostly with cards and women. What made the greatest impression on Richard was Bainbridge's rather free use of the lash. Richard transferred to the *Philadelphia* to act as Bainbridge's first lieutenant, while that officer commanded one of the smaller escorts for practice. Richard had heard and now confirmed that Bainbridge ordered more men flogged on his ship than all the other captains combined. He seemed to think it a necessary component of the workings of the ship, and he practically boasted about it. Richard secretly thought Bainbridge did it to take out his frustration on his crew, caused by the pressure he was receiving from Preble.

Bainbridge was also a showoff, which rankled Richard to no end. Bainbridge was versed in literature and history and knew several languages. He also liked to share little anecdotes guaranteed to monopolize the conversation. Richard was just as well-read, but saw no need to prove it.

Under Preble, captains like Bainbridge, accustomed to absolute obedience on their ships, had to fall in line as well, even to the point of writing discipline reports just like the younger officers. On one occasion during drills, Bainbridge had failed to move into a position to cover an imaginary enemy squadron that had split into three sections, and he was forced to write a report explaining his failure. He completed his report and then stormed about his ship. It was difficult to get out of this huge man's way, and after he ran into them, he had three sailors flogged on a charge of disobedience, telling them they were lucky it wasn't for striking an officer.

Richard sailed with Bainbridge for nearly six months and it was all he could do to stand silently and watch the punishment meted out to the crew. He knew the pain a lash could cause, and saw its indifferent use as almost obscene. Once in a fit of boyhood misjudgment, Richard and two other midshipmen had hit each other with a rope lash like that used for flogging. They each took a turn hitting the other and Richard's turn came last. He had underestimated the damage done to the backs of the others. When the rope slapped across his back, he gasped with surprise. The pain was unbelievable. There was the initial sting from the impact of the frayed rope followed by a searing burn like someone had placed a red-hot poker on his back, and then even that melded into a murderous throbbing that lasted for several hours. It hurt much more than any of them anticipated, and they had only received one lash. It may have been a foolish boyhood prank, but in each of them it left the determination that they would have a man flogged only as a last resort.

The *Philadelphia* was due to go on reconnaissance, and its regular first officer returned from his short escort command. Richard was allowed to return to the *United States*, and though he was right under the close scrutiny of Preble, he was at least far from Bainbridge. It turned out that he wasn't there long, as Preble gave him command of a sloop captured earlier from the French called *Le Scoot*. The sloop wasn't much to look at, but after a week under Richard's command, she at least handled better than when he got her and quite likely better than she ever had in her life. He sailed her into Syracuse's harbor where the entire fleet was to gather for orders. They would be there a while waiting for Bainbridge's *Philadelphia* and her three escorts to arrive. Decatur was commanding another of Preble's escorts as was Richard Somers. The three friends met at a tavern in Syracuse frequented by American officers when they were in port. When Richard arrived, Stephen and Richard Somers were already sitting with six other officers, and they made room for him at the table. Stephen looked up as Richard settled in and said, "Have you heard? They are putting off the attack on Tripoli until better weather in the spring. We are all headed to Boston. Apparently, the *Constellation* and the *United States* are to be refitted with more guns before we come back here to deal with the Barbary Pirates, so we will get a nice long leave, they say, perhaps all winter. If that's so, then I am headed to Philadelphia where the merriest pair of blue eyes await me. What about you?"

Richard shook his head, and said, "Alas, no blue eyes await me, but I have three maiden aunts right in Boston who will spoil me rotten, so I think I'll just drop anchor there, and let them have a go at me."

RICHARD STEPPED OFF the ship in Boston and headed for the home of his aunts, actually his great aunts, as they were his father's aunts. Their home reminded him of a child's playhouse. The three Holmwood sisters were spinsters, tiny and old, all well under five feet tall, very delicately built, but each with a will of iron and absolutely no hesitation to speak her mind. Richard had referred to them for years behind their backs as the Puppets. He gave them the name after visiting with them as a boy. During this visit, all three, Grace, Dorothy, and Ruth, were on the settee listening as conversations switched from one end of the room to the other, their heads swiveling in synchronized movement left and right. Richard thought they looked amazingly like puppets in a show.

The three small women had suffered the problems and indignities of living in a house created for normal-sized people, so they built a house that was, as they said, "our size." The ceilings and doorways were low, as were the counters and the cupboards. Richard had the uncomfortable feeling when he visited them that he had crawled inside a dollhouse. They had one normal-sized bed for guests, but other than that, everything was child-sized, or more correctly, Puppet-sized.

On his second day in Boston, he offered to run errands for them, and they promptly gave him an extensive list with accompanying notations about where to get each item and stores to be avoided. Richard had tried to eat breakfast at their terribly small table with his knees pressed against the bottom, but it was so uncomfortable he had to leave before he was full. He stopped then at the first tea shop he came across to get something to eat to fortify himself for his errands. As he entered the shop, everyone looked up at him. He looked around and found the place packed. Just as he turned to leave, a striking woman by the door motioned for him to sit next to her.

Richard sat down and stared at the woman as she motioned for a waitress. They ordered more tea and cakes and then settled back to wait. Richard leaned closer, mesmerized by her sparkling eyes, and he thanked her, "Lieutenant Richard Holmwood, ma'am, and thank you again."

She looked at him in his smart uniform and smiled, "Lorraine Portman, and it is my pleasure. Please understand, I don't. . . I mean I never have offered my table to a strange man." Richard smiled and studied her more closely. Even though she was sitting down, Richard could tell she was tall. Her hair was blond-white and her eyes brilliant blue. She was absolutely and without question the most beautiful woman he had ever seen. She looked perhaps twenty-one or so which made her all the more attractive. As Lorraine stared at him, Richard had the sensation of being devoured. Her look was unnerving, but he wouldn't have left that table then for anything in the world.

They chatted long after their tea was gone and only made a move to leave when the proprietor, needing their table, basically stood over them. "I really must run some errands for my aunts," Richard said, dreading to break the spell.

"Where do you have to go?" Lorraine asked almost desperately. Richard explained and Lorraine rose and suggested, "Then perhaps we can run our errands together. What do you say?" Richard nodded and quickly paid for the tea. With Lorraine on his arm, they walked toward the Quincy quarter where Richard filled Aunt Dorothy's exacting list scribed in her nearly microscopic handwriting. They laughed and commented on the things they saw, ate a late lunch and finally parted, as there was no way to prolong the day. As they passed the little tea shop where they had started, Lorraine said, "I can't believe I am doing this, but visit me if you wish. I am staying at a cottage north of town, and I will begin my stay there in three days. It is called Rosalind Cottage. I don't care why you come, but please visit me there." Lorraine looked desperate and somewhat afraid. Richard reached out and touched her hand, nodded, and then watched her turn into an inn across the road. Richard slowly walked back to the tiny Puppet house with his mind in a fog. Every cell of his brain was screaming for him to forget this possibly troubled and possibly unsavory woman, but her appeal overwhelmed him.

On the third day, cramped in his bed in its tiny bedroom at his aunts' house, Richard answered the call of common sense, resisting the urge to visit Lorraine. He held fast on the fourth day as well, but on the fifth night, he could stand it no longer. It was nearly midnight, but he packed a few clothes, wrote a note to his aunts explaining that he had to return to the ship, and quietly stepped out into the night. There was only one road leading north from Boston, which he followed on foot. He was doubtful he could find a carriage or rent a horse at this hour, and besides he wanted to walk to give himself every opportunity to change his mind. He was still conflicted two hours later when it began to rain. It was bitterly cold, and he was wearing only a light-wool overcoat, and he wished desperately for a great coat like the one he had left at his aunts' house.

Lorraine had said the cottage was a mile past the Tern Creek Bridge, but he had yet to pass Tern Creek. He finally came to the bridge and saw a man hunkering under a canvas shelter on a little barge tucked out of the rain under the low bridge. Richard yelled down to the man, "Sir, do you know where I can find Rosalind Cottage?"

The man looked startled and then said, "I ain't from here, but before it started to rain, I could see the light from a cottage just there." He pointed north, "I don't know what it's called, but it's the only cottage I've seen." Richard thanked him and continued up the road which became narrower and rougher. The cold rain hissed off the lantern he was carrying, and he was shivering miserably, still not exactly sure why he was doing this, only knowing that he had to see her again.

After what seemed like several miles, Richard came upon a small path that led off to the right toward the oceanfront. After about three hundred yards he saw the lighted window of a small cottage ahead. If it wasn't the right cottage, perhaps they could give him shelter, and he could search for it again in the morning. He knocked softly at the door, and after a short time Lorraine answered. She didn't open it warily like most women would in the middle of the night. Richard stood dripping and shivering on the doorstep. Lorraine smiled, "I should have given up hope, but something told me you would come tonight, and that is why I was awake." She pulled Richard into the room and over to the fire. "My God, you are soaked and freezing. Come by the fire and get warm." She helped him out of his coat and pulled a chair close to the fire. There was also a little stove burning, radiating warmth. Richard sat shivering and Lorraine finally said, "You have got to get out of these wet clothes. Go upstairs to the loft and change. Do you have dry clothes with you?" Richard nodded yes. His waxed canvas case from the ship was practically impervious to water, and he quickly climbed the stairs and changed. The warm clothes felt like heaven against his cold arms and thighs. Richard came back down carrying his wet clothes and Lorraine handed him a blanket and a glass of brandy as she took his shirt, pants, and socks to dry by the stove. He wrapped himself in the blanket and relaxed as sips of brandy warmed his chest. There was a chair directly across from him, and she sat in it dressed in a plain-white nightgown. Richard should have felt awkward here with a strange woman dressed in her bedclothes, but didn't. Actually, he felt very much at home. When Lorraine got up to get a shawl, she tucked the blanket closer across his shoulders, which seemed like the most natural thing in the world for her to do.

They sat quietly by the fire and chatted until Richard felt his eyelids droop. His neck snapped up and Lorraine smiled. "Off to bed with you, now, no arguing." Richard climbed the steep stairs to the loft above and collapsed into the deep featherbed, immediately falling asleep. He was dead to the world until he heard Lorraine moving downstairs in the morning sunlight.

Richard found a basin of water at a stand nearby and, stooping against the steep roof, he washed, shaved, and then dressed and climbed down the steps that were more of a ladder than stairs. "Good morning!" Lorraine greeted him with a mug of coffee, "There isn't much to eat here this morning, but Mrs. Goodword, the lady who comes, will bring us enough food for the next few days. Please tell me you can stay awhile."

"I don't have to be anywhere for awhile, so if you want me to stay I can," Richard said, not taking his eyes off her. If possible, she was even more beautiful than at the tea shop and much taller than he remembered. Richard stood about six feet, yet she could look him in the eyes. He restoked the fire and they ate bread and cheese and then dressed warmly before a walk down a small path to the beach. The waves were still pounding from last night's storm, but the sky was clear. The sunlight dazzled on the water as they explored for items washed up during the storm. They found a boat oar and several empty crates. They took the crates back to burn in the fire and staked the oar in the top of a dune like a flagpole to which Lorraine tied her scarf which fluttered in the wind.

Back at the house, they found Mrs. Goodword was busy inside cleaning. Lorraine looked from Richard to Mrs. Goodword, and then pleading with her eyes for Richard to play along, said, "Mrs. Goodword, may I introduce my brother, Richard, just on leave from the Navy." Richard bowed politely, and the older woman nodded back, continuing with her duties.

"I have left you beef stew, some biscuits, a cooked ham, more cheese and jam, and some beans that I put there in the fire." Mrs. Goodword pointed to a small pot in the ashes to the side of the fire. "Now, you leave them there on the edge until dinner time, and they'll be ready. Will you be needing anything before I come again on Friday?" Lorraine and Richard both shook their heads. As she was about to walk out the door she said to Lorraine, "Ma'am, I am glad your brother's here. I was worried about you being all on your own." With that, she nodded to them and left the cottage.

Lorraine turned to Richard and said, "Thank you for going along with my story."

"No problem. If you want me to be your brother, I can do that," Richard said, smiling.

"I don't know what you are, but I am so glad you came. I feel like I have known you all my life, but really I only met you last week. Strange isn't it?" Lorraine took off her bonnet and hung it by the door. She wrapped her shawl around her shoulders and then poured two glasses of wine. "I know it's early, but would you mind having a glass with me?" Richard drank wine on the ship at almost every meal, including breakfast, so he took the glass without hesitation and clinked hers.

In the afternoon they walked on the beach again, exploring the dunes west of the cottage where great storms of the past had piled the sand thirty feet. They climbed up the front and ran down the back of one dune only to trip and fall in a heap all tangled together. They stayed in the sand laughing until Richard stood and pulled Lorraine onto her feet. She giggled and said, "God, it feels so good to laugh. I haven't laughed in years and years, not like this at least." Richard smiled and offered her his arm, which she took. They returned to the cottage and ate lunch. Lorraine wasn't a very good cook, but it didn't really matter, because Richard could eat nearly anything. Having been at sea eating the worst food imaginable, he had learned not to be fussy. Walking in the wind and the fresh air had left them both tired, so they lounged about the rest of the afternoon talking and reading to each other.

After a dinner of ham and beans they sat talking by the fire and became quieter as the night wore on. They retreated into private thoughts before Lorraine said it was time they retired. She squeezed Richard's hand, then walked to her bedroom and closed the door. Richard sat staring at the fire, listening for any sounds from Lorraine's bedroom. Hearing none, he quietly climbed the ladder to his loft, took off his shirt and boots and then walked to the tiny window beside his bed and looked out at the ocean. The moon was swimming on the surface like mercury, a sight he never tired of seeing. He then heard a board creak behind him and turned. Lorraine was standing at the top of the ladder staring at him. "What's wrong?" he asked. She didn't answer but stepped up into the room. She came slowly toward him and put her hand on his chest. His muscles tensed like horseflesh at her touch, and he stood staring at her, not daring to breathe.

"Please, I am not a loose woman, you must remember that," Lorraine whispered, "but I want to know what it is like to be with a man, a real man." She faltered for a moment and then made up her mind to continue, "My husband was not really a man, and now that he is gone, I want to know." Richard stood staring at her, unsure what to do. She looked at his chest where her hand rested and said, "Look at you. You are magnificent. I have never been with anyone except my husband who was old when we married. I have tried not to imagine what it would be like, but when I saw you, I don't know what happened." She smiled and then touched his face, and he looked at her. "Please, Richard, please show me." She stepped closer and put her cheek on his neck, and Richard inhaled her scent of lemons and violets. She said with her face against him, "Please." Richard pulled her face up to his and kissed her. She wrapped her arms around him and then begged him again. He pulled back looking in her eyes to make sure, and then he pushed up her nightgown. Lorraine raised her arms, and he pulled the gown over her head and dropped it on the floor. He picked her up and put her on the bed, then kissed her again, marveling at how thin and delicate she was; her breasts, no more than a handful, were beautiful. She was breathing so hard he thought she might choke, and he stood and fumbled wildly with his trouser buttons until they finally yielded, and he stepped out of them. Lorraine reached for him, "Please don't be gentle with me. I want to know what a real man feels like."

"Lorraine, I don't want to hurt you," Richard started to say, but she cut him off.

"I don't care if you hurt me, just get inside me!" she begged. He forced his way into her like a bull, and she screamed, begging him not to stop, not to ever stop. Mercifully, there was no one within earshot of the cottage.

RICHARD LAY on his back with Lorraine curled against his chest. As he stroked her hair he said with a soft chuckle, "I hope you are not like this with all your brothers." Lorraine laughed and moved closer until he kissed the top of her head, and, then unable to resist, he asked her, "Well?"

Lorraine sighed and said, "Ten thousand times better than I thought."

They talked and after a bit Lorraine pulled Richard over onto her again, but this time they were gentle and let themselves enjoy each other until they finally passed out. There was no awkwardness or regret between them as they awakened tangled together; they simply got up and got dressed, ate breakfast, and explored the area around the cottage.

Richard learned that Lorraine was older than he assumed. In fact she had recently turned twenty-eight. It was a bit of a jolt when Lorraine learned he was a decade younger, but it really no longer mattered. On rainy days they stayed indoors and lounged about, and on some days they didn't get out of bed until noon. One morning they woke to find it snowing, and they ran around barefooted outside like children. They stoked the fireplace and the stove as hot as possible and then hauled in water to heat and poured it into a huge tub where they took turns soaping and rinsing each other. They saw no one but Mrs. Goodword several times a week, and other than her, they were completely in each other's company day and night. In this way Richard spent the next several weeks in absolute bliss.

Richard and Lorraine had moved downstairs to her room, and he woke one morning just before noon to find himself alone there. He felt groggy and the cottage had a forgotten feel. He got out of bed and found all Lorraine's things were gone and his case packed and sitting in the middle of the floor by the fireplace. He quickly dressed and stepped out the door, shielding his eyes from the bright sunlight, startling an old man lounging on the front seat of a carriage. The man stood up and waved at Richard on the doorstep. Richard ran to him and asked if he knew where he could find Lorraine. The old man rubbed his chin and said, "I took Mrs. Portman back to town early this morning. She said she had to meet her husband, due in Boston Harbor in the next few days. She said I was to come back here and take her little brother back to town when he woke up. That must be you, sir. If you are ready, I'll take you now." Richard walked numbly back and got his case. His head was swimming and he suspected he had been drugged. He was normally the lightest of sleepers, yet Lorraine had managed to pack and leave without him waking.

He took one look around the tiny cottage, slammed the door and left. He rode in silence nearly all the way to Boston and then asked the driver again who Lorraine was meeting. The driver looked at him strangely and said, "Her husband."

"What husband?" Richard asked, still trying to understand.

The driver looked suspiciously at him and said, "Being her brother, I would think you would know her husband, wouldn't you?"

Richard glowered but recovered himself. "She's been married to so many of them, and I wondered which husband she was referring to this time."

The old driver chuckled and said, "She is meeting her current husband, Commodore Portman. I'll bet you know him, he is quite high up in the Navy these days."

Richard felt like someone had kicked him in the head, and he asked, "Commodore Anthony Portman?" Richard had never met him, though he had certainly heard the name.

"Yup, that's the one," the old driver beamed. Richard sat stunned and only spoke to give directions to his aunt's house. The driver dropped him off, and Richard paid him, not waiting for change. The old man took it to be a generous tip.

Richard quickly freshened up and prepared to return to the ship. His aunts begged him to stay for dinner, but he told them he had to report for duty without delay. Grace pleaded, "But, dear, we have barely visited with you since you've been here." Richard shrugged and kissed them each on the cheek and apologized as he raced out of the house. The Puppets stood on the doorstep like little birds on a fence rail as they saw him off.

He boarded just as they were slipping their lines. "Mr. Holmwood, glad you got the message," Preble said. "I know you have a few more days on leave, but we need to get back to Washington for the change of command. I thought you might have to come in a later vessel, but glad to see you made it." Richard had received no message but kept that to himself as he walked to the wardroom, by far the best place to gather information on the ship. He got some coffee and then sat at a table. Soon a new lieutenant who had reported to the ship while Richard was at Rosalind Cottage introduced himself.

Richard was able to learn from him the news. Apparently there was to be a change in the overall naval command. The lieutenant explained, "Well, Commodore Boswell suffered a stroke and cannot continue, so the new Navy commandant will be Commodore Anthony Portman." Richard's heart seized, and the lieutenant continued, unaware that Richard was barely breathing. "I haven't heard much about this Portman except that when he is around, the rum certainly flows." As an afterthought he said, "I also hear he has a beautiful wife who is young enough to be his granddaughter. I wonder how he caught her?" The lieutenant laughed and took his coffee up on deck. Richard sat stunned. Not only had he repeatedly bedded a married woman, but one married to a commanding officer, no, the commanding officer!

When they reached Washington, Richard asked permission of the captain to go on ahead to schedule the refitting of the ship's rigging at Gosport Navy Shipyard in Portsmouth. "If I get there ahead of you, I can reserve a slip."

"Only if you agree to visit your father while you're there. I wouldn't mind a long visit with my family when I get there, either," Preble smiled. His family originally hailed from Hampton and his wife was still there.

Richard caught a merchant ship that afternoon bound for Hampton, grateful to miss the change of command ceremony for Commodore Portman.

For the next several days, every time a carriage slowed in front of the house, he expected to see marines climbing out to arrest him. More than his guilt and fear, or even knowledge, that he had been used, Richard agonized with a sense of overwhelming loss. He thought about Lorraine endlessly.

The *United States* arrived in Portsmouth just over three weeks later. Richard was ready to board when he learned there were whole new orders for everyone. Preble was assigned the *Constitution*, which had just finished an extensive refitting and was ready to sail from Gosport. So the crews traded places, and they left within a week to rendezvous with the *Enterprise*, already in African waters. Richard was relieved they were leaving and still naïve enough to think it was possible to put miles between himself and his guilt. He didn't care where they went, as long as they kept him too busy to obsess over Lorraine Portman.

CHAPTER 6

RICHARD, Stephen Decatur, and Isaac Hull, all three of whom had felt the business end of Preble's whip hand, were now fine officers. They had rotated the command and first and second officer positions on the *Constitution* all the way across the Atlantic. Richard, now acting as second lieutenant, came on duty in Syracuse and was looking over the Italian harbor just as the *Constitution* was being hailed by a small sloop. When the sloop captain was brought on board, he had dire news for them.

The plan had been for the *Philadelphia* to rendezvous with the *Constitution* and the *Enterprise* to assist in blockading Tripoli and then aid in an all-out bombardment of the city to destroy the Barbary Pirates. Unfortunately, the sloop captain told them the *Philadelphia* had been run aground by Captain Bainbridge in Tripoli Harbor. The ship was now in Tripolitan hands and Captain Bainbridge and his crew of three hundred were held captive. No doubt the pirates would seek an outrageous ransom for their release. Preble sat stunned by the news. The loss of the ship reduced his battle strength by a third, and though the *Philadelphia* had a huge gash in her side and there was damage to her foremast from slamming to a sudden stop on a hidden reef, she could be repaired, and if she was repaired by the Tripolitans, she would be a force equal to either the *Enterprise* or the *Constitution*. *Philadelphia* would be the most wondrous pirate ship in the world.

Preble dispatched the *Nautilus* with requests to Washington for more ships and men. It would be months before there was an answer, so he immediately set a course for Tripoli. When the *Enterprise* and her escorts arrived later in the month, they watched and waited. They could not risk grounding another ship in the harbor in the foul weather of the North African winter. The *Philadelphia* wasn't going anywhere either, and there would be few repairs made on her until the weather improved in the spring. They waited, watched, and hatched a plan.

The *Philadelphia* had to be recovered or destroyed, a terrible option for such a magnificent ship. As time went on, the pirates made repairs faster than had been anticipated. The plan to destroy her became the only option discussed.

Earlier in the winter, the squadron had captured a small Turkish-built ketch which they renamed *Intrepid*. The *Intrepid*, commanded by Stephen Decatur, and the *Siren*, commanded by another of Preble's young officers, Charles Stewart, would sail into Tripoli Harbor and burn the *Philadelphia* to the waterline right where she was moored. The *Intrepid* would actually destroy the *Philadelphia* while the *Siren* would guard the mouth of the harbor and cover the retreat of the *Intrepid*.

The plan was the brainchild of Stephen Decatur, Richard Holmwood, Charles Stewart, Isaac Hull, and Richard Somers, and it was just the sort of daring, dangerous plot these young, cocky men would concoct. No one could think of a better plan. At dusk on the second day of February, they sailed in their two little ships away from the *Enterprise* and *Constitution* which had ceased their blockade and lulled the Tripolitans to lower their guard.

For days before they set sail, Decatur had insisted the men eat local food and find native clothing to disguise their American uniforms. "We have to blend in as best we can," he told them as they downed the highly spiced local fare of highly gaseous chickpeas or garbanzo beans. They found clothing in the refuse they had taken off the *Intrepid* when she was captured. The coarse tunic Richard belted at his waist smelled like a goat with an undertone of something faintly resembling rotten cheese. Some of the men went so far as to smear their teeth with tar to resemble the tobacco stains common in North Africa.

Richard would command the *Intrepid* and had studied intensely the available charts of the harbor. He knew all the marked reefs, but having been in the harbor only twice, still remembered the strange air currents moving there caused by the long natural breakwater and the wind off the hills behind the city. His main concern was how to maneuver when in the lee of the *Philadelphia*. There, they could be cut off from the wind needed to escape the burning ship. If they could not get away, they would have no time to lower men over the side in boats to pull the ship away before either the Tripolitan shore batteries blew them to pieces or they were incinerated by the fire engulfing the *Philadelphia*.

Stephen came to him three nights before they were set to leave and said, "Richard, we need to look like a native ship, so none of your fancy sailing on the way in. It's great on the way out, but into the harbor we need to look lubberly and like we need a good pump-out."

When the plan had first been set down on paper and taken to Preble, he had put Decatur in charge. Preble had discussed with Decatur who should go along and what role each would play, and they agreed Richard Holmwood would actually command the *Intrepid*. Stephen would lead the boarding party, but Richard would sail them in and out of the hostile harbor. "I can think of no one better," Preble had said, "and whether or not you succeed in destroying the *Philadelphia*, your success in getting back out alive will rest in his hands. Your lives could not be in better hands; he is a singular seaman."

They left at dusk the next day and Preble stood staring at them long after they were swallowed by the horizon. He would not know for days if they had been successful, and every one of those days would seem like a week. These were not just officers under his command being sent on a dangerous mission. He had raised most of them from their teens, and they were like sons to him. His prayers were now filled with entreaties for their safe return.

On board the *Intrepid* was a man who spoke the local language to help communicate should the need arise. The British flag was run up so that they appeared as a Maltese trading vessel. Richard had a drag rigged which made the ship wallow a bit and appear overloaded with cargo. They had no actual cargo except seventy-five horribly crowded men smelling of unwashed garments, spicy food and its aftereffects, and massive amounts of incendiary material and weapons. The crew had been admonished not to use muskets or pistols in the attack, as it would raise the alarm to the shore batteries right away. They would accomplish all the work with swords only.

The majority of men stayed below and only a handful were ever visible on deck at any time. Nonetheless, their spirits were high when they arrived at the mouth of the harbor and tacked back and forth waiting for the *Siren* which they had lost about five miles back. The wind was shifting and Stephen didn't want to wait any longer and possibly lose it, so he motioned for Richard to tack toward the city. If this wind would just hold, their retreat would be much easier.

It took almost two hours to get to the moored *Philadelphia*. They had to communicate with each other in whispers, for sound travels easily on water, and one word of English on what was supposedly a Maltese trader would bring the shore batteries on them instantly. When close enough to hail the small crew on the *Philadelphia*, they asked in the native language for permission to tie up to the huge frigate as they had lost their anchor in a gale. The bait was taken and a line tossed over to the *Intrepid*'s deck. They secured the bowline and began tying up to the stern when one of the marines in the group belched thunderously as his stomach reacted to the foreign food. Another tried to shush him, and this gave them away: "Americanos!" the alarm went up. Stephen, cursing, gave the order to board.

Decatur's boarding party swarmed up the side of *Philadelphia* in a single mass, and in less than five minutes they had secured it. They had been ready for a brutal boarding rush, but there were only about ten men onboard, and those that were not killed immediately jumped overboard rather than face Decatur and his crew.

The boarding crew immediately began placing the explosives and combustible material they brought with them around the ship. Any tar found on board was poured all over the deck, and they threw pitch as high as they could on the masts and rigging. Some of the flammable material was staged to burn down into the powder magazine. Stephen noted that the magazine was only about half emptied in Bainbridge's failed attempt to scuttle the ship. Bainbridge had thrown the guns overboard, but left most of the powder for the enemy. Stephen gave the signal to light the fire, and then he waited to see his men safely off the ship. The fire roared to life, and Decatur barely got off in time and even then was forced to leap into the rigging of the moving *Intrepid*. As the *Intrepid* sailed along the *Philadelphia*'s side, Richard and Stephen watched the fire leap up her rigging and begin to glow in the gun ports. It was moving faster than they believed possible, and the air seemed filled with heat and noise. Just when it seemed it couldn't get any hotter, the wind suddenly died.

The men looked at Richard, horrified. Setting a ship on fire is not an exact science, and there was no telling how long it would be before the powder magazine exploded, but they knew they didn't want to be anywhere near the *Philadelphia* when it happened. Richard had thought of the possibility of a lee behind the ship, and now with the last of the *Intrepid*'s forward momentum, he turned the ship tightly to starboard so she was headed right back toward the *Philadelphia*. "Jesus, Richard, she is set to blow! What are you doing?" screamed Decatur.

"Getting us the hell out of here, just watch," Richard yelled, staring up at the rigging. The growing fire created its own draft, and it was enough to push the *Intrepid* forward out of the lee where she could catch the wind. The crew stared horrified at the burning ship, and *Intrepid* seemed barely to move at all, but suddenly the sails snapped and Richard yelled orders to haul on the sails to catch the wind.

The shore batteries had heard the screams as the boarding party raided the *Philadelphia*, and they now opened fire on the tiny *Intrepid*. The raging fire lighted up the harbor. The shots from the batteries fell all about them, but the men cheered at each one trusting in that old advice that you can't see the one that gets you. They were so flushed with their success that they yelled ribald suggestions to the gunners on shore and clapped when a shot fell near. Some shot fell close enough that the splash fell on the deck, and the crew watched the fire reflected through the plumes of water like fireworks. The men in the *Intrepid* hooted and hollered and pounded each other on the back. Not a single one of them had been lost, and with the exception of a few burns and Stephen's sprained ankle from his leap to the rigging, they were unhurt.

They carried on celebrating as they watched the flames on the *Philadelphia* now completely engulf her. The wind, which had been so kind to them, began to fail. Still in high spirits they lowered the boats to begin rowing for the mouth of the harbor where they could at last see the *Siren* waiting desperately for them.

In the harbor the *Philadelphia* burned through her anchor cables and began to drift in lazy circles. The Tripolitans had used her guns for practice and left them loaded, and as the flames began now to heat them up, they fired indiscriminately in all directions. *Philadelphia's* guns posed more danger to the retreating *Intrepid* than the shore batteries, and it would have been sorry luck indeed to be destroyed by friendly fire after such a daring maneuver.

As they gained the open ocean, the sky was alight over the city and could be seen for miles. The two small ships rendezvoused and sailed in company for the *Constitution* and *Enterprise*. The last they saw of the *Philadelphia* she had run aground in the middle of the Tripoli waterfront, and somewhat later they heard the tremendous explosion that shook and shattered the shoreline.

The little flotilla had been gone for seventeen days. When Preble finally saw them on the horizon, he signaled impatiently for the outcome. When the *Siren* signaled it was successful, the entire squadron erupted in celebration.

The squadron returned to Syracuse where a grateful American merchant feted them with a feast. His national pride made him magnanimous, so the night following the feast he threw a private party for the seven officers of the *Siren* and the *Intrepid*.

The seven men tried to walk calmly into the huge house where they were met by enchanting women. They piled through the door at roughly the same time. "Gentlemen," said a large woman who was obviously in charge, "there will be plenty to go around, I assure you, so why don't we have a drink and you can tell us your tales over dinner. As for dessert, well, we'll save the best for last." She winked knowingly. The women came forward and Richard found two of them on each side, holding his arm. The woman on Richard's right had white-blond hair and deep-blue eyes. Richard had been haunted by dreams of Lorraine Portman since she abandoned him at Rosalind Cottage, but as the other woman, a fetching brunette, engaged his free arm, he thought that with enough wine and the right encouragement he might be convinced, for at least tonight, that he could slay the ghost of Lorraine Portman. He smiled a bit nervously at the women, and they licked their lips. The blonde admonished him, "Food slows a man down; do eat lightly."

It took nearly a day to recover from the celebration, but as soon as he was sober, Richard realized Lorraine still haunted him. He had done his best to drive her out of his life that night, but she remained there like a bloodstain.

CHAPTER 7

THE *CONSTITUTION* arrived in Charleston having spent many months along the northern coast of Africa after burning the *Philadelphia*. They had hailed outbound ships coming across the Atlantic and received news as they continued their crossing. While taking on fresh water and food in Charleston, they also received mail. Richard had no letters, but there were two newspapers from Washington, which he devoured, reading each article, then the advertisements, the notices, and even animal husbandry tips. He knew he was looking for, yet dreading he would find, some news of Lorraine Portman. The information he was seeking did not come by way of the newspaper, but in old-fashioned gossip.

Preble and his officers hosted dinner with the captain of a ship just out from Baltimore. They learned that they had missed a marathon of drinking earlier in the year hosted by Commodore Portman as he celebrated the birth of his first child, a son, after nearly a decade of marriage. The real gossip was that Portman got roaring drunk and fell off a stage where he had been accepting congratulations. He broke two ribs and lost a tooth, but still held onto the bottle of rum.

Richard listened to all of this with his heart in his throat and a frozen smile as he calculated time and possibilities. *Did I leave more than my heart behind in Rosalind Cottage?*

After two months in the South Atlantic, the *Constitution* arrived in Washington just in time to celebrate Independence Day. Decatur sent word to Richard and the others that he was hosting a reunion of sorts of "Preble's Boys." It was nothing more than an excuse for a party.

Richard was having a good time reuniting with old friends at the party when someone grabbed his arm. He looked straight into the Arctic blue eyes of Lorraine Portman who grinned back at him. For a moment he couldn't breathe, but when he could, he turned on his heel and walked away. The smile fell from her face like she had been slapped.

"Richard, wait!" Lorraine pleaded as she caught up with him and pulled him by the sleeve of his coat to a stop. "Please listen to me, please."

Richard turned to her, stone-faced. Lorraine pulled him closer by the arm, reaching for his face with trembling fingers. Richard yanked away from her, but she hung on his arm desperately. He snapped under his breath, "Stop it! People will see you hanging on me. Go back to your husband!" He had been downing Norfolk Punch most of the night, and she could smell the heavy rum on his breath. "You told me your husband was dead."

"I did not," Lorraine whispered, "I said he was gone."

Richard leaned toward her, and hissed through clenched teeth, "Leave me alone." Lorraine looked like she was about to cry as Richard wrenched his arm loose and walked out the door, leaving the party without even making his farewell to his host or any of his friends. He stormed back to the ship and flung himself on his bunk, staring at the ceiling for what seemed hours.

Lorraine had looked even more beautiful than he remembered and seemed so happy to see him. He tried now to call up her face from the party and take back what he had said. For him, staring at her eyes was like rushing toward a great blue iceberg which threatened to crush him with both its danger and its beauty. He wanted to rush back to Stephen's and call her out as a whore and a liar, but he also wanted more than anything to be alone with her again like they had been at Rosalind Cottage. He felt inadequate and used, yet wavered between despair and lust for hours until the rum took over and knocked him out.

He awoke the next morning to a splitting headache and swore he would never speak to Lorraine Portman again. Even more he would never again think about her, the corrupt, deceitful, lying . . . soft, beautiful, elegant, funny creature that haunted his dreams and every waking moment.

A MONTH LATER, Richard and most of the other officers involved in burning the *Philadelphia*, and a good many who now claimed to have been there, were attending a party in Washington in honor of the second anniversary of the destruction of the ship. Richard was just nursing a drink until he could politely leave. It was a command performance for all the officers, and he was doing his bit. The party was held at the home of Captain Benright, a legendary smuggler during the Revolution, who was now ancient, but who still hosted a fantastic party, and the turnout was huge.

To kill time, Richard wandered over to study some wall paintings of ships struggling in heavy weather. He found more paintings in a small alcove farther down the hall. As he studied them a shadow fell across his arm. His heart skipped a beat as he recognized Lorraine. He groaned, "Oh, God."

Lorraine touched his lips with her fingers to quiet him, and then said softly, "Hear me out, Richard, please? Meet me outside by the springhouse in half an hour. Please, you must, half an hour." Before he could answer, two women came giggling conspiratorially into the alcove. The women stared awkwardly at Richard and Lorraine until he bowed and slipped away.

He strolled around the perimeter of the rooms making small talk and putting on a jovial face. Twice he caught himself looking for Lorraine in the crowd, but each time he cursed himself and stopped. Finally, he had been there long enough that he could politely leave, saying goodbye to Benright and his wife.

Richard entered the little building by the river and stood in the doorway, waiting. Lorraine, standing in the shadows, finally risked calling his name, and he snapped, "What if it hadn't been me, Lorraine, what would you have said then? It was stupid to call me by name. You should have learned by now to play the deceiver's game better than that."

"I knew you would come," Lorraine rushed forward and wrapped her arms around him. He resisted the urge to hold her, but the tantalizing smell of lemon and violets wafted from her tresses. The smell hauled him back to those astonishing weeks in the cottage, which brought stinging tears. He roughly shoved her away, and asked again what she wanted. "I have to talk to you, Richard. I want you to understand what I did."

"I know what you did, Lorraine. I was there the whole time," Richard said with a snarl.

"But you don't know why. Do you?" Lorraine touched his face, and this time he let her. "I was a good wife for years. I never looked at another man. Anthony was fifty-seven when I married him. I was eighteen, Richard, eighteen years old. I traded the possibility of a young husband for the security of a wealthy old man, and I was willing to live with that trade," she faltered, "until I met you." Lorraine touched his face and ran her fingers over his lips. "Richard, I had to have you once I met you. I had to know."

"Had to know what, Lorraine?" Richard moved back a step from her and shut the springhouse door behind him, plunging them into absolute blackness.

"I had to know what it would be like if I hadn't sold my youth to an old man. I had to know what it was like to have a real man, not an old man, in bed with me, inside me," she stepped toward him, and he retreated until his shoulders were against the closed door. There was not a speck of light and both their eyes ached as they tried to see each other.

"So you used me to satisfy your curiosity? Did you think I was just some boy you could play with and then dismiss?" Richard growled.

"I never once thought of you as a boy, Richard, not once." Lorraine felt for his face and took it in both her hands and whispered close to his ear, "You are far from a boy, but I know you felt something too, something that was undeniable, something that had to be sated, and it wasn't just lust. You tell me you didn't, and I will walk out of here and never speak to you again." Richard didn't respond, and she continued. "Yes, Richard, I wanted you to bed me. You can call me whatever you want, but you wanted me too. Finding women would be no problem for you, so why did you come to me? You walked eight miles, some of it in the freezing rain to see me, so don't tell me it was just that you were hoping for a willing woman. You could have stayed warm and dry and gotten that in Boston." Richard was silent in the dark, and Lorraine continued, "Yes, I used you. I used you to satisfy my desire, so it came as a horrible inconvenience to me when I realized I had fallen in love with you." Richard started, and she continued, "By the time I realized it, it was too late. Richard, I have thought about nothing but you since then. I've had to pretend and smile when I wanted to scream. I dream every day you will come and take us away." Lorraine sobbed against his chest, and he patted her back.

Her words sunk in, and he asked, already knowing the answer, "The child is mine, isn't it?"

"Yes," she said softly, "and he is beautiful. I named him Richard Owen, after you."

"What the hell are you doing Lorraine, trying to see me hang, just to see what that would be like, too?" Richard said, but there was no edge to his voice this time.

"Anthony's father was named Richard, so it was easy to give the baby that name, and then I added your middle name, Owen, which is what I call him," Lorraine explained. She wrapped her arms around Richard's waist and said, "I just want us to be together, the three of us. I just want to run away and never look back."

"Life isn't that easy, Lorraine, though I wish it were," Richard held her tight and closed his eyes against the pain of his constricting throat.

Lorraine said desperately, "I tried to forget you, honestly, I did, but it's no use. If I didn't think it would ruin his life and yours, I would have you walk into that party right now and claim him as your son to everyone there, and then we could leave, but you're right, life is not that simple." Lorraine lowered her head to his chest, and he held her close for several minutes and then gently pushed Lorraine back at arm's length and said, "God, I wish I could see your face now, but I see it enough in my dreams." He gripped her hands and said, "This has to be the last time we meet alone. Nothing good will come from us sneaking around. What is done is done, but so long as you are married to someone else, I will never be alone with you again."

"Tell me you love me, Richard, tell me just once, because it has to last me a lifetime," Lorraine sobbed clinging to him.

Richard hesitated and then whispered, "I love you, Lorraine. God help me, but I love you."

"Kiss me," Lorraine begged, and when Richard told her no she said, "Please, Richard, what harm can one kiss do?" Lorraine stepped forward, and her lemon scent washed over him. Richard inhaled it and abandoned any hope of escape. He kissed her softly and then more urgently. The attraction between them was still unbidden and undeniable. Within minutes they were pawing at each other's clothes. "Please, Richard," she tugged at the buttons on his trousers, "please."

"My God, you will be the death of me, Lorraine," Richard said as he tore off his blue uniform jacket and put it on the stone floor of the springhouse, "but what a death!" Lorraine hiked up her dress as she sprawled on his jacket. She fumbled with the ties on her drawers, and when she couldn't release the ribbons, Richard simply tore them loose at her waist and ripped them off her in the dark. There was no technique or manners in what they did. Richard plowed into her, and Lorraine wrapped her legs around his waist as she raked deep furrows in his lower back with her fingernails.

Afterward, they lay panting on the floor, and finally Lorraine spoke, "Does it feel different since I had Owen?"

"No, you feel wonderful," Richard said and kissed her lips.

"Richard, what are we going to do? We can't live like this." Lorraine touched his face with her fingers, "We can't be together, and I can't live without you. I'm doomed, because you will haunt me the rest of my life."

"We'll think of something. Portman can't live forever the way he drinks. We'll work this out, but we can't meet like this again. If we get caught, it will ruin everything for us, and for Owen." Richard pulled her to her feet saying gently, "Come on." Lorraine tried to smooth her dress in the darkness and felt her hair which seemed, surprisingly, not too out of place.

"My drawers. I can't leave them here for someone to find," Lorraine felt around for them, and Richard did as well. He finally felt soft fabric under his boot and picked them up. He handed them to her, and she said giggling, "I can't wear them; you tore them right off me." She touched his face again and said, "Are you coming back inside to the party?"

"No, I said goodbye when I came out here, but you have to go back in now." Richard kissed her and added, "Hurry, you can't be caught here."

Lorraine pulled him close and said, "Right now, I don't care."

"You will care if you lose our son. Listen, go back to the side door and lie down on the ground and start calling for help. Call like you have been yelling forever. Someone will hear you, and you can say you went out for fresh air and fell off the steps and twisted your ankle. Blame it on the step, or blame it on the wine, but it will at least explain the state of your dress which I can't see, but which has to be a mess."

"All right, Richard. What do I do with these?" she touched his hand with her wadded drawers.

"Give them to me, and I'll get rid of them," Richard said, putting them in his pocket. He kissed her one last time and whispered, "Be careful, Lorraine, and remember, I love you. We will work this out, but just be patient." Richard opened the door to the springhouse and the moonlight flooded the tiny room. He turned to Lorraine and smiled. She saw the flash of his teeth for a second before he gently nudged her forward. Richard waited as she sprinted across the lawn, and then he saw her lie down by the side door. As she started a very convincing series of calls for help, Richard walked in the opposite direction along the river then curved around the front of the house. He passed the cressets marking the end of the drive and added more wood to each one. As the flames rose higher, he dropped in Lorraine's drawers. He listened and could hear murmurs coming back from the house where Lorraine had been discovered. The spirits had been flowing heavily all night at the party, so her little mishap would hardly raise an eyebrow.

Richard saw Lorraine twice more in that year, both times at a party. They had resisted the urge to sneak away, but each time they had found a quiet edge to the crowd and in a hasty clench of hands, almost like a handshake, affirmed that nothing had changed. They had agreed they would not correspond by letter, though both desperately wanted to do so, and they took no one into their confidence, so they would remain alone in their desperation.

RICHARD VISITED his family in Hampton for a few weeks while his ship underwent storm repairs at Gosport Navy Yard in Portsmouth. He paced around the house irritably and on a very short fuse as he thought of a way to see Lorraine. Micah said teasingly, "I bet he's not used to going this long without a variety of girls or even the buxom wife of some absent officer!" Micah had barely gotten the words out before Richard was on him, grabbing him by the lapels of his jacket and shoving him across the room. Gabriel grabbed them both and hauled them apart. Micah stood rubbing his chest while Richard stood panting, his nostrils flared and his fists clenched.

"What in God's name is wrong with you, boy?" Gabriel demanded.

Richard turned on him and screamed almost like a petulant child, "I am not a boy! Do you understand me, Father, I am a long ways from a goddamned boy!"

Old Holmwood looked stricken and reached for Richard gingerly like he would reach for a panicked horse about to rear and strike out. "Richard, I never meant it that way, but you are my boy. You will always be my baby boy," his voice cracked, and he sat on the fireplace fender trying to catch his breath. Richard stared at him, his jaw still clenched.

Micah, still looking confused, offered, "Rich, I didn't mean anything by it. God knows, we think the world of you and everything you've done. If I said something that touched a sore spot, I take it back right now."

Richard flopped down in a chair across from his father and said, while staring at the ceiling, "I'm sorry. I'm just on edge."

"No kidding!" Micah tried to laugh. Richard had always been full of fight, but he was full of mischief then too, but these days all that remained in him was the fight. Micah secretly wondered if some of the things his brother had been forced to do at such a young age had left him violent. The closest Micah or even Thomas ever came to a battle was breaking up a brawl at the local tavern. Micah had no real comprehension of the rage of war, and the thought of it secretly frightened him, but he kept his fear well-closeted, humiliated that he owned it at all.

Although they would never admit it, Richard's brothers and father had lived vicariously through Richard's numerous exploits. The glowing dispatches and letters home by Richard's commanders had amazed them. They shared the tales of his glory as if they had done the deeds themselves.

Richard shifted now and tried to clear the air, "I am sorry. I just don't like being called the baby."

Old Holmwood stood now and walked to where Richard sat. He put his hand on Richard's shoulder and said in a weary voice, "I can't help it, Richard. When your mother died along with the two little ones, you became the baby of the family, my little baby boy. I didn't want to let you go, and when I saw you growing up, it only made it harder to take that I was getting old. I don't think of you as a lad or anything like that. We know the reports we get back here of your deeds are only half of the brave things you have done, but you don't need to lash out at us son. We are your biggest supporters."

Richard smiled and nodded silently. He took a deep breath and said, "I'm just at loose ends, Papa. Please don't think on it anymore." Old Holmwood nodded and said he was going to check on when they might hope to get dinner. Micah smiled at Richard and left the room then too. After both men had left, Wrennet came quietly into the room. She found Richard sitting near the fire and pulled his chin up, so he was forced to look at her. She had heard the whole thing. Richard looked at her steadily, taking in all the old familiar features. She was beginning to gray, but was still a handsome woman. With a slow and steady voice Wrennet asked, "Who is she?" Richard looked at her, trying to act puzzled, and she added, "Don't sit there and try to deny it. A man only acts like you are acting when there is a woman involved. Who is she, and what is the problem?"

It was no use. He had never been able to keep anything from Wrennet, and in truth over the years she had been a confidante of sorts. Even so, he could not tell her the details of this volatile secret, so he simply gave her what he could and said, "She is another man's wife."

Wrennet took no moral high ground and made no judgment. She simply said rather sadly, "Ah, those are usually the hardest to get over. I will keep you in my prayers." She smiled and patted his hand and added, "Even more than you are already." She rose to see about dinner but turned at the door and said, "I am good at keeping secrets; you know that. If you need someone to help you carry this load, I am always here, Richard."

He looked up at her and smiled, and his eyes softened and creased as he said, "I know, Wrennet, I know." Richard got up and joined the family in the dining room a few moments later. Dinner was peaceful, as were the three days that followed before his departure. Richard left for Portsmouth and sailed for North Africa in command of the escort ship, *Gallant*.

THEY HAD BEEN away for seven months and once again sailed into the harbor at Syracuse. Richard waited impatiently on the *Gallant* until she was laboriously maneuvered next to her pier. He then mustered his crew for the dispersal of the mail which had just come aboard. He waited, trying to appear casual as the purser called out names for mail. He did not really expect anything from Lorraine, but couldn't completely quash his hope.

There were great plans among the crew for a bout of heavy drinking and carousing, and as soon as the last bit of mail was passed out, he dismissed the off watch to begin their debauchery ashore. He made his way to the *Constitution* to see what orders they had received, but when he boarded there was a tight knot of officers from several of the escort ships clustered near the taffrail. Richard reached the group just in time to hear the captain announce, "I have just learned that Commodore Portman has died." He looked at the date on the correspondence and then clarified, "Just over two months ago. Commodore Portman spent over forty years in service to his country. He did his part in the War of Independence, and has served us well as our Commandant. I would like to observe a minute of silence in respect of his passing."

Richard stood with his head bowed, but his heart was beating so quickly he could hardly take a breath. The moment of silence seemed to stretch into hours, and his mind raced with possibilities, but finally the captain put his hat back on. There were no immediate orders, so they would take on food and water and continue to provide convoy escort for merchantmen and reconnaissance when they were able. Just as Richard was about to return to his ship, he was handed a letter which had been addressed to him in care of the *Constitution*. His heart raced with possibility as he recognized Lorraine's handwriting, and he walked as calmly as he could back to the *Gallant* and once in his cabin, he broke the seal with his thumb and read the letter. Lorraine had not risked signing it, but to his amazement it was written the day Portman had died. To an outsider reading the letter, they would not have known what she was talking about, but Richard knew very well what was contained in the short and cryptic note:

> Dearest Richard,
> I find myself alone. We had prayed for help, and it came
> from an unexpected but not surprising quarter – a bottle.
> I am leaving to mourn with Rosalind. Please join
> us when you can. I know it may be a while before you can be
> with us, but I am patient, and nothing has changed.
> Your loving sister,
> L

Richard read the letter three times, and then he leaned back against the bulkhead of his cabin and sighed with relief. Lorraine was at Rosalind Cottage waiting for him, and she would be there until he arrived. He looked at the date of the letter again, and knew that Lorraine had probably not left for the cottage for a month or six weeks after the funeral, but she would certainly be there by now. All he needed was a way to get back to Boston, but they were scheduled to return to Tripoli, and they would be there for months perhaps even a year. He briefly thought about jumping ship, but he quickly dismissed it as ridiculous. He would have no way to support Lorraine and Owen if he were court-martialed, so he quickly penned an equally cryptic letter letting her know he had received her letter and would be there when he could. There was a packet of outgoing mail leaving the *Constitution*, and he slipped his letter inside the canvas packet just as they were about to seal it. He waited while the red wax for the seal was applied over the curled ribbon and the large eagle seal applied, walking away only after he saw it being bound with marlin line and the lead seal clamped over the knot. The packet would be passed over to a ship heading westward, and Richard wondered how long it would be before Lorraine received the letter.

CHAPTER 8

PREBLE and his officers hatched another plan to destroy the corsair fleet in Tripoli. This one was just as simple as the others and involved loading explosives on the valiant little ketch *Intrepid*, which Richard had commanded when the *Philadelphia* was put to the torch. She would be crammed with as many kegs of powder and incendiaries as she would hold and then sail right amongst the corsairs on the Tripoli waterfront. A small crew would ignite the flammable material and then row away in the *Intrepid's* cutter hoping to get out of the harbor unnoticed by the shore batteries in the ensuing panic that would follow the detonation of the ketch.

Richard Somers had been involved in the planning of the *Philadelphia* raid, but when they set off on the mission, he had been very ill with a fever, and could not go, but he would get his chance now as the leader of this equally dangerous plot. The *Gallant* was to wait outside the harbor at Tripoli to provide whatever defense she could for Somers and his crew to escape and pick up the cutter when she cleared the harbor. The raid would take place in September when the weather was mild and the wind favorable but very slight. There would be a land breeze later as the warmer water pulled the air off the coastline, but even then it would probably come down to rowing like hell to get back out of the harbor alive.

All was now in motion, and the *Gallant* waited about a mile outside the harbor and tacked back and forth in lazy circles. The corsair captains kept a close eye on *Gallant,* so they were less attentive to a ragged looking ketch overloaded with what appeared to be cowhides as she slipped into the harbor and made for the corsair fleet moored less than fifty feet from the outer city walls. Somers had made the comment that the walls would provide a good deal of flying material when they exploded inward on the city from the force of the *Intrepid* blast.

As true darkness fell, the *Gallant* turned until she was only about a hundred yards outside the long spit of rock that guarded the harbor and there she drifted silently. The *Intrepid* could be easily seen edging her way across the harbor. Everything was going according to the original plan, but the temperature dropped, forming an odd fog over the harbor. It was a narrow band about twenty feet thick that started about ten feet above the water. It looked exactly like a thick blanket stretched across the harbor. The *Intrepid* now disappeared into this dense cover and continued to make her way toward the moored corsair fleet. From the *Gallant*, Richard could see the topsail and a dark shadow where *Intrepid's* hull glided through the water, but he could not see anything on her decks. Another forty minutes passed without incident. Then, just as a slight breeze sprang up that swirled the bottom of the fog layer, there was a tremendous explosion where the *Intrepid* had been. The entire fog layer seemed to light up in a horizontal blaze across the harbor, and both of *Intrepid's* masts shot straight up, flaming like rockets before turning in midair and spiraling back down to the water. Fiery pieces of the *Intrepid* and her crew rained down in flames. No one on the *Gallant* spoke for nearly five minutes. They watched in horror as each piece fell from the sky to blink out in the water, and they could almost hear it hiss as it touched the sea. Finally, Decatur, standing next to Richard, said, "Oh, Jesus, this cannot be."

The *Gallant* waited for hours hoping against hope to see the cutter making for the mouth of the harbor, but it was in vain. Richard knew Somers had not ignited the explosives according to the plan because he was still a half-mile from the corsair fleet. There were two possibilities that would explain what happened. First, the explosion could have been an accident. A tiny spark was all that was needed to set off all that gunpowder. The other possibility was that the *Intrepid* was halted or in some way found out, and Somers had decided to destroy the ship rather than let it and its huge load of explosives fall into enemy hands. The truth was hidden in that fog bank and any chance of finding it vanished as the fog disbursed the following morning.

Captain William Bainbridge and his officers, still prisoners in Tripoli, were led down to the beach where some of the bodies washed up. He was able to identify Richard Somers and two others, but of the crew of thirteen, only those three bodies were ever recovered. It was assumed the others, who had been in the hold when the ship exploded, were simply vaporized. Bainbridge wrote a note to this effect and was able to have it smuggled out of the prison where it was brought to the *Gallant*, still waiting three days later outside the harbor. There was nothing left to do but return to the *Constitution* and deliver the dreadful message to Edward Preble.

Preble had requested to be relieved in North Africa months ago as he was suffering from stomach problems which he rightly believed to be cancer. He now waited in desperate pain for the answer to his request.

When the *Gallant* appeared on the horizon, *Constitution* promptly signaled with her flags asking for success or failure. The sad answer was sent back and met with absolute silence on the decks of the frigate and her escorts. Immediately upon arrival, Richard made his report to Preble, who collapsed into his chair and sat with his head in his hands. His request for relief came a week later. When Preble asked for one of the escort officers to accompany him back to Washington, Richard eagerly volunteered.

After delivering Preble in Washington in very poor health for a much needed rest, Richard took leave. He did not travel south to Hampton to see his father, but north as fast as he could to Boston. Richard now remembered the last thing Wrennet had said to him when he saw her last. She had said, "Oh, Richard, be careful. Not just of your neck, but of your heart." She touched his cheek. "You run a terrible risk, you know, and I wish you the best of luck." Richard had smiled and kissed her on the cheek, but now Wrennet didn't have to worry. Soon everything would be fine, and he could be with Lorraine publicly, legally, and morally, if he could but just get there.

RICHARD ARRIVED in Boston near dusk, but it was closer to midnight when he finally knocked on the door of Rosalind Cottage. Lorraine opened it smiling. Richard stepped into the cottage and wrapped her in his arms. He held her for a long time and then pulled her back to look at her again. "God, I have missed you," he said and kissed her. She helped him peel off his greatcoat and jacket and then held him close, burying her face in his neck. He held her for several minutes, and then held her at arm's length and said, "My God, you get more beautiful every time I see you!" Lorraine pulled him close to the fire and the lamp and the light fell on him.

"Look at you! You look more handsome than even in my dreams," Lorraine said, touching his face. He kissed her again and then she picked up a lamp from the nearby table and said, "You must see him right away." Richard nodded and followed her into the small bedroom where she and Owen were sleeping. Richard took the lamp from Lorraine and held it over the sleeping boy. Owen was curled up with his head on the pillow, and Richard bent down to look at him closely. Owen's head was covered with blond curls, and he slept with his mouth slightly ajar. Tiny white teeth were visible through his parted lips and he had a few scattered freckles. He was a beautiful child and even asleep he resembled Richard a great deal. Richard stood staring and then sheepishly realized he was no better than his own father, staring at his son by lamplight in the middle of the night.

"He's beautiful, Lorraine, absolutely beautiful," Richard said, looking at her in awe. "I can't believe he's mine."

"Oh he is yours, Richard. He looks just like you, and more so each year," Lorraine smiled and then pulled Richard out of the room and softly closed the door. "Do you want something to eat, or can I get you a drink?"

Lorraine asked, suddenly shy, though she didn't know why. She looked at Richard again and realized he had grown even taller and had filled out considerably from when they were first in Rosalind Cottage. The change from a man of nineteen to that of twenty-three is remarkable, just as a two-year-old thoroughbred is considered mature, but is not the fleshed-out animal that it will be in another year with an arch to its neck and massive shoulders. As it was with the colt, so it was with Richard, and Lorraine raked him over with her eyes noting the girth of his neck and the thickness of his arms and shoulders.

Richard shook his head no. "I don't want anything but to hold you," he said, pulling her close. They lasted perhaps five minutes longer before they went, clawing at each other as they climbed, to the loft and the bed where they had first been together.

Richard awoke to find Lorraine already downstairs. He could hear her talking to Owen. Richard didn't know what to do, how to make his entrance, so he washed and shaved and then simply climbed downstairs. Owen stared at Richard as he crossed to where the child was seated in his chair. He glanced from his mother to Richard, but didn't look frightened. "Owen, this is a friend of mine. His name is Richard," Lorraine said.

Richard smiled and squatted next to Owen, who broke into a grin and offered Richard a sliver of toast on which he had been nibbling. Richard opened his mouth and received Owen's slobbery and cold offering. Owen was delighted and offered him more, but Lorraine saved Richard by pointing to a chair across the small table where he and Owen could size each other up as they ate.

After breakfast they prepared to go for a walk. As Lorraine was adding several more layers of clothing to Owen than were necessary, he broke loose and ran to Richard and hid behind his legs. Richard turned and scooped him up, smiling at Lorraine and said, "Enough, or he won't be able to walk." He then turned holding Owen and looked into the mirror that hung over the fireplace.

Owen looked at their reflection and said, "You look like me!"

"No," Richard chuckled, "You look like me. I had this face first!" Owen found that tremendously funny and squirmed, laughing in Richard's arms. Lorraine reached to take him from Richard, but Owen shook his head and wrapped his arms around Richard's neck. "You stay right here with me," Richard said, rubbing his back.

They walked out into the cold morning to find strong winds. They decided to go inland where the dunes would give them some protection. Owen was content to ride on Richard's shoulder until they got beyond the dune, and then he wanted down. He scrambled ahead as Richard and Lorraine walked close together behind him. They walked for nearly an hour, just ambling slowly on the lee side of the dune. Finally, they came to a place where the wax myrtle trees formed a solid wall and made it impossible to go any further, so they turned back. Owen was dragging now, so Richard scooped him up and cradled him as they walked back toward the cottage. In these simple ways, Richard and Owen began to know each other as Richard and Lorraine got reacquainted.

After Owen had been put to bed, Richard stoked the fire and they sprawled before it on thick quilts. They talked for hours, finding again that same comfort in each other's company. The fire had burned down but still had flames enough to illuminate Richard and Lorraine as they stretched out naked together. Richard rolled over so he could look down on Lorraine's face. She did not look a day over twenty-five though she was now well over thirty. He kissed her and ran his hands over her body. She laughed deep in her throat and pulled him closer. They spent hours talking and loving and, at times, even dozed.

Something awakened Owen in the dark and he reached for his mother, but she was not there. There was a thin line of light under the door coming from the main room of the cottage, and he quietly opened it and peeked out. He heard a moan like his mother was in pain and saw her on the floor and Richard bending over her. Owen watched, both engrossed and horrified, as Richard ran his tongue down his mother's neck. She moaned again and then smiled. She pulled him closer and laughed throatily. His mother did not laugh often, and Owen was enchanted at how this big, blonde man could make her laugh just by kissing her. Owen was mesmerized as he watched the two of them. At times Owen thought his mother was being injured, but she seemed to cling to the man and call him by name, and Owen knew she wouldn't do that if he was hurting her. Owen watched until they rolled apart, and then he scurried back to bed and dove under the covers pulling the pillow over his head and holding it tight for a long time, until his heart stopped pounding and he fell asleep.

The next morning Owen watched Richard walk across the floor and sit down at the table. He was much taller than Owen's papa, Commodore Portman, and much younger too. Owen was still confused about where his papa had gone, and though Lorraine told him he was in heaven, she didn't say when he would be back. He now crawled into his mother's lap and she held him close. He turned and kneeled in her lap and she laughed and held his hands. He kissed her on the lips and she kissed him back, telling him how beautiful he was. Emboldened, he stuck out his tongue and ran it down her throat as Richard had done. She yanked him back, so she could look in his face and told him to never do that again. "Owen, why did you do that to me? That is vulgar. Don't you ever do it again!" she scolded him. Owen, stunned, sat pouting and confused, suddenly not liking this interloper who sat across from them at the table.

Owen was determined to succeed, and so he tried again the next day. He crawled over to Lorraine while she was napping with him and kissed her the way he had seen Richard kiss her. Lorraine's eyes flew open, and she pushed him away. "You will have to sleep alone if you do that again." Owen stared at her, pouted, and began to howl. They weren't real sobs and there were no tears, but he knew how to get his mother's attention. Lorraine gasped, pulled him onto her lap, and rocked him, saying, "Owen, you are my beautiful boy, my best boy, my only boy. I could never have another little boy as wonderful as you. Please don't cry." She hushed Owen and rocked him. Richard came through the door, looking concerned. Lorraine looked up at him and said, "I think he just had a bad dream. Why don't you just leave us alone for a while, and he'll be fine. Richard nodded and quietly closed the door. Owen smiled triumphantly and curled closer to his mother as she rocked him on her lap.

Richard's leave was quickly being used up, and he had only one night left at Rosalind Cottage. Lorraine tried not to think about him leaving again. There was no telling how long it would be before they would be alone again. Owen had been a baby the last time she had seen Richard and how he was nearly four. Time was flying by, and she was getting no younger. That night Richard leaned up on his elbow in their loft bed and ran his finger along her jaw. "I can't believe I have to leave you and Owen tomorrow. It seems like I just got here." They made love desperately and rather than a sound of pleasure, what escaped Lorraine's throat was more a bittersweet sob.

EVERYTHING ANTHONY PORTMAN owned was held in trust for Lorraine and Owen. In an acknowledgment of the age gap between him and his wife, Portman specified that should Lorraine remarry, half the property and funds in his estate would transfer to the new husband. Lorraine could not legally own property, so it was a way for her to benefit from his largesse. If she remained single, the trust would keep her well for the duration of her life. It was final evidence of how good Anthony could have been to her had he ever been able to conquer his worst enemy—alcohol.

Lorraine waited in the huge Portman house for her time of mourning to end, and when it was up she waited for Richard's return to Boston. They corresponded by letter, but even those were few and far between, and they still had to be very careful. Richard thought they would marry when the year was up, but Lorraine insisted they make it appear as if she came out of mourning, and then Richard began courting her. They married in a quiet ceremony about four months after that torturous year-long wait. Richard asked for two weeks of leave, "because I am getting married." The rumors had already started.

Gabriel Holmwood sat stunned, reading the short note from Richard announcing his marriage. Richard had never mentioned any girl in particular, and now, suddenly, he was married. The note had stated they would come to visit when they could, but it might be a while before that was possible.

It was nearly a year later that Gabriel received word that Richard and his bride would soon be in Hampton Roads. They took rooms at the inn up the road and arrived one afternoon just around tea time. As the horse's hooves clumped to a stop outside the gate, Gabriel could not restrain himself any longer, and he was peeking out the window at Richard and his wife as they came up the brick walkway. Wrennet flung open the door and stood with her arms out. Richard loped the last few steps and gave her a hug. She was laughing and crying at the same time and holding the door for Richard as he turned back and helped Lorraine and Owen into the house. They walked into the sitting room and Gabriel rose to meet them. Whatever he had expected from Richard's bride, Lorraine was not it. Gabriel had pictured some little blushing creature, but instead Lorraine was stunningly beautiful, tall, and poised, and older than Richard, though Gabriel would never have guessed a decade older. There had been no mention of a child, but now as Gabriel looked at the little boy introduced to him as Owen, things, whispered things, and long forgotten incidents, fell into place, and he knew his own blood coursed through the veins of the child. Gabriel looked from Lorraine to Richard and nodded slightly letting them know he knew. Lorraine stood looking warily at Gabriel, and he came forward and kissed her cheek. She relaxed and smiled and looked even more beautiful if that was possible. Gabriel patted his knee, "Come here, Owen, can you give your Grandpapa a hug?" Owen looked back up at Lorraine to see if it was all right, and she smiled and shook her head. Owen barreled across the room and jumped onto Gabriel's lap and let the jolly old man hug him and muss his curls. Owen knew men Gabriel's age had magnificent pockets that contained watches, and penknives, and sweets, and he began to explore them with relish.

There was a general rumbling and bumping at the front door and Micah strode into the room talking as he came, "Papa said you were coming, and we saw your carriage pass so we came along too." He stopped in front of Richard and for the first time in his life, looked up at his little brother. He had not seen Richard in nearly four years and in that time Richard had filled out splendidly. "Look at you!" Micah said smiling, and Richard held out his hand to greet him. Micah scoffed, pushed his hand away, and pulled Richard into a crushing hug. While Richard had grown upward and broadened out, Micah had merely broadened. Richard looked over Micah's shoulder and saw the cause of his brother's amplification. Micah introduced Richard and Lorraine to Margery, who looked like one of those large, bossy, but good-natured women who live only to cook for men and run their lives. It was true, for within a month of their marriage, Margery had relieved Micah of the

onerous burden of ever again having to make a decision. Margery had
in her arms a little blonde boy of crawling age, and there was another
about age three clinging to her skirts. She put the child down and he
started across the floor to Gabriel. The little one clinging to her skirts
followed and they too climbed onto their grandfather's lap. Owen smiled
at them, but kept a firm grip on the gold watch he had just extricated
from its little waistcoat pocket. Gabriel beamed at his lap full of blonde
boys and motioned for everyone to sit down. Margery and Lorraine sized
up each other. Lorraine thought Margery could loosen her hair and look
a little less severe, while Margery devised an eating regimen that would
put some meat on Lorraine's bones, though she had to admit Lorraine
was remarkably beautiful.

As they were finishing tea, Thomas arrived with his bride, Lydia.
She was a simple looking, rather pale and nondescript girl of about
nineteen. She adored Thomas and worshiped him. No one was a better
husband, sailor, provider, or anything else that could be suggested. She
extended her admiration to Micah as the older brother, and now she was
about to bestow her awe on Richard and Lorraine. Thomas introduced
her, and Richard and Lorraine each bowed to meet her. She giggled and
blushed, then sat staring unabashedly at them with jaw dropped. Lydia
had never seen such beautiful people. Richard, with his blond hair and
magnificent eyes, not to mention his dazzling uniform, and Lorraine,
with her mass of curls that glistened in the light like a pile of gold coins,
seemed to shimmer and glow. She thought they looked like two gods
descended from Olympus to cast favor upon the family, and she thought
it the most wonderful luck in the world that she could claim them as
family. She smiled at Gabriel with his lap of boys and patted her belly. It
was only a few months now until she would have her own to hold and
she couldn't wait.

They settled into a rather raucous dinner as they tried to catch up
with each other down the length of the table. After the meal, the men
stayed at the table to conspire while the women and Wrennet and the
children retreated to the sitting room where Margery took command of
the port and began passing it around freely. Lorraine sat back and listened
while Margery discussed the value of port, and then the questions began
as Lorraine knew they would. Where was Lorraine from? How had she
met Richard? Had Owen been a healthy baby? The questions continued
until Lorraine was desperate for Richard to return. Her new sisters-in-
law meant well, but Lorraine had been secluded and private so long, it
was difficult to remember she was now legally married to Richard and
no longer had anything to hide. Female small talk did not come easily to
her, never had, though neither Margery nor Lydia saw through her polite
comments.

Richard and Lorraine toured Hampton Roads the next day, and

Lorraine was enchanted. There was nearly as much harbor traffic as in Boston, but somehow it didn't seem as seedy and overrun with the detritus of maintaining ships and sailors. She mentioned this to Richard, and he said, laughing, "There are sections of Norfolk that come close!" It occurred to both Richard and Lorraine that they could escape the wagging tongues and innuendo if they were to relocate to Hampton Roads. Richard was there as often as he was in Boston, and Lorraine, though she had little in common with Margery and Lydia, would at least have the Holmwood family for support. They made their decision over breakfast and that day set out to look for a house. They came upon a very large brick house that was nearly finished, but all work had stopped and the construction site was overgrown with weeds and grass. Richard inquired and found the owner was very ill and had no desire to complete the house. His wife had no desire to live in the house without him, so it sat waiting to be auctioned, which, by luck would be the following day. Richard obtained the information about the sale and then asked if it was possible to tour the house. He contacted a land agent who still had a key and arranged to look over the house that afternoon.

Richard had already swallowed his pride with regard to Lorraine's money. By the terms of Anthony's will, half the money was now Richard's, though Richard felt it would always be Lorraine's. It was not lost on him that with his salary of barely a hundred dollars a month, they could never afford such a place. Lorraine insisted that the only really kind thing Anthony had ever done for her was to make such a will. "I was never anything but something for him to show off. Well, now I am going to show off a bit on my own. I earned this money Richard, every cent of it in all the years I put up with his drunkenness. Now let's look at this house and forget the past."

They found the house to be even nicer inside than they imagined. No expense had been spared in importing marble for the foyer, nor had there been a lack of skilled craftsmen working on the moldings and trim. There were six bedrooms, far more than they needed, but Richard said, smiling, "We could find a way to fill them up!" Lorraine was enchanted and decided right then that no one would have that house but her.

At nine o'clock the next morning, Richard bid at auction and got it for less than it was actually worth. It was the first of several shrewd bargains he would make. The house builders were put back on their task and said it could be ready in three or four months.

As Richard signed the papers transferring ownership, he was stunned to see the name Preble. Richard couldn't believe what had just happened. He had purchased the house Edward Preble had started to build when he retired from the Navy. Preble's family hailed from Hampton Roads, and he had decided to settle back there to recover. As he realized the truth, Richard smiled to himself and whispered, "One of your boys will take good care of this for you, Commodore."

Richard and Lorraine returned to Boston as Richard was due to leave the following week. He would be gone six or eight months at least, but Lorraine assured him she could see to the transport of anything she wanted from the Boston house on her own. "The next time I see you, it will be in Hampton in our own house," Lorraine said as she kissed him goodbye.

THE NEXT TIME Lorraine saw Richard, he had earned his captaincy, and she smiled as she saw his uniform with the two gold epaulets rather than just one. He was only able to be in Hampton a month as he had orders to travel to Boston and take command of the *Reliant*, a large barque built in Boston about ten years before. He was to bring her to Gosport for refitting before sailing to support the *Constellation* in North Africa.

Richard was taking over command from Captain Charles Lort, who was being relieved after he had rammed a ship not only leaving harbor but upon reentering it as well. It was the final straw in a career already marred by alcohol. He had only been able to stay in the Navy because he was a distant cousin of Commodore Portman, but with the death of Portman, Lort should have known his days in command were numbered.

Word had reached the *Reliant* that their new commander was Captain Richard Holmwood. His name was recognized as having commanded the *Philadelphia* mission, and reports of his seamanship preceded him, but the crew knew little else about him. They were now strung along the yards of the *Reliant* in Boston Harbor, peering at their new commander as he came across in the long boat. First Lieutenant Joyce had been in command since Lort was relieved, and while discipline had been lax under Lort, it broke down completely under Joyce. Lort had constantly undermined Joyce's orders or overridden them in front of the crew. Lort had an unerring ability to make the wrong decision, and when it all went pear-shaped he would publicaly blame Joyce. Anytime there is a breach between the captain and his officers, the crew takes advantage and becomes insubordinate. The crew of the *Reliant* was no exception.

The naval agent in Boston told Richard that he had ordered Joyce to move the *Reliant* from the pier and out to a deeper anchorage where, "She won't be a hazard to navigation, and I won't have to smell her." There, *Reliant* had wallowed, her decks filthy, her sails ungainly, and her crew surly. She had been a problem ship for years, and there was still enough sloth and corruption on her to completely consume a freshly-minted captain like Richard Holmwood, or so the agent thought.

The crew now hung lazily on the yards with the sheets furled in ungainly humps and sags, whistling and calling to each other as the longboat approached. Richard tried not to let his horror over the ship's condition show. She was only ten years old, wasn't hogged or broke-backed, but she listed and had an abandoned appearance. He could hear the call, "*Reliant* arriving," as he climbed over the railing and observed the crew lazily mustering on deck.

The crew of one hundred fifty was a sorry lot, though Richard, as he walked among them, could see on some of their faces weariness at the lack of work and a hunger to have pride in what they did once again. He saluted the officers and then walked the length of the deck. His orders were to get the ship seaworthy and be in Gosport by the beginning of March. His orders had been delayed in reaching him and by the time Richard reached the *Reliant*, he had just three weeks to get to Portsmouth. Even that would have been a leisurely trip if the ship were ready to sail, but Richard could see at least a week's worth of repair before they could even think of weighing anchor, and that was only what he noted at a distance. He would do what he could to get moving, and they would have to do the rest as they sailed south.

After Richard was introduced to the officers he called a meeting with them and was informed that First Lieutenant Joyce, Third Lieutenant Harker, and six midshipmen were on board, but the Second Lieutenant Yancy and the sailing master were ashore and would be back by nightfall. "If they can walk," added Lieutenant Harker.

Richard wondered for a moment at the name Yancy, but knew it couldn't be the same lieutenant who had terrorized him on the *United States*. Theodore Yancy would be well into his forties now and certainly would no longer be a second lieutenant. He would be in command now, if he hadn't died in another duel. Whoever he was, Richard had too much to do to think about him now. He looked sharply at Harker and asked, "Does either have leave that extends through the night?" Harker shook his head and mumbled that they did not.

"If the two of them aren't back by nightfall, a detachment of marines will assist them," Richard said, pulling out a piece of paper to write down tasks that needed completion before sunset. Joyce and Harker exchanged glances. The wind had changed, and the forecast was indeed unpredictable and stormy.

The midshipmen were young, ranging in age from twelve to fifteen, and though they looked neglected and almost dirty, Richard took heart remembering what he had accomplished at their age. He asked each of them to report on the condition of the ship. They at first stared at him like he had asked them to strip naked, but when they found their voices, each reported that materially *Reliant's* hull was fairly sound, but since most of them had not been on a ship that was well-maintained, they could report very little else. Joyce and Harker, knowing they had the freedom now to state *Reliant's* true condition, said that her decks and rigging, guns and tackle, and holds were a mess. Richard then went on a tour of the ship himself.

In the next hour, he inspected the ship with the Chief Boatswain, Honorue, who held to the tradition of his profession in using the foulest language to describe everything they viewed from the lady's hole and bilge to the top gallant yards. Honorue, though he looked large and burly, had no trouble keeping up with Richard. The crew watched from below as Richard climbed the rigging hand over hand, not using the lubber's hole, but climbing right over the edge of the fighting platform as he ascended with a sheet of rolled paper and a pencil clamped in his teeth. More and more of the crew gathered on deck to watch him, and Richard did more to earn their respect and their obedience in that climb than if he had flogged a dozen of them. In the last six months they had rarely seen Captain Lort on deck, and none of them had ever seen him in the rigging.

The rigging was worse than Richard imagined, and several of the yards were nearly cracked through. The mizzenmast would have to be replaced, and Honorue admitted they had not flown much canvas on it for over a year. The cutter was lifted so Richard could inspect its davits and tackle, and while they were hauling on the lines, it broke loose and crashed right through a grating onto the gun deck below, scattering the boat's oars and canvas and snapping its rudder clean off. Richard motioned to Honorue, and Lieutenants Joyce and Harker, and they huddled on the quarterdeck while Richard stated quietly the first orders of his command.

The purser was sent ashore with a lengthy list of items the ship needed, from rope to pitch to gunpowder, and Richard told him he would not be allowed to sleep until he had made arrangements for procuring it all. He sent six of the larger men with the purser, and told him to come back with as much of the rigging rope as possible by afternoon. The chandler could deliver the rest in his own boats when he had it assembled.

Richard's mouth tightened when he noticed that the sand used for ballast was so foul with urine and filth that it was a health hazard. The crew began pouring vinegar on it and burning sulphur to make it less dangerous, and then he ordered them to start hauling it up and dumping it overboard while twenty or more men went with the boats to start bringing fresh ballast from shore.

There was not a fire bucket to be found anywhere that was not full of feces, urine, or tobacco spit. Richard ordered the buckets scoured with clean sand, and then filled with either dry sand or water, according to where they were located on the ship, and hung on the hooks intended for them. Fire was his worst fear, and he had nearly gone into a rage when he found the water kegs on the ceiling of the powder room empty. Empty kegs would have been no use in the magazine to fight a fire there that could vaporize every one of them in a half a second. He had witnessed firsthand what exploding powder kegs had done to the *Intrepid*, and he was not about to risk it on the *Reliant*.

The marines on board were in better shape than the crew, but only because they kept to themselves and were under the discipline of their captain. The captain of marines could do nothing about the condition of the ship, but his men and their rifles, muskets, and swords were polished and ready. Richard commended him for his readiness and then moved on, tripping over a large splinter jutting up from the deck. He pointed to it and asked the nearest sailor, "How did that happen?"

The sailor looked at Richard and then down at the splinter and said politely, "Sir, I don't rightly know. It was there when I came on board three months ago, sir, here in Boston."

Richard clenched his jaw, but said nothing. He grabbed the first bucket of sand that came aboard as ballast and handed it to a boatswain's mate. "Get to work on these decks. I want them sanded, stoned, and wiped dry before lunch."

When he came back on deck later he saw some of the crew had hauled out the holystones and attached ropes to both ends. One sailor would pull the flat, heavy stone, about the size of a bible and hence its name, across the deck and then the other would pull it back, scraping it over the wet sand they had spread. Richard watched them for a moment and then said calmly, "The ropes on the stones only work if the deck has been maintained. You need to use them the way they gained their name. Get the ropes off them, get on your hands and knees, and use your body weight to sand off the splinters. You'll need the smaller ones for around the railings and the tackle. Where are the prayer books?" Richard was referring to the smaller stones used for tight spots. The prayer books were finally located, after a desperate search below decks, and then put to use.

Richard went below and found the water from scrubbing the decks dripping through where the deck had not been caulked properly, if it had been caulked at all in years. He went down another deck and looked up. Sure enough, through the gloom in three places he could see pinpoints of light. He ordered two more groups to work, caulking the decks with oakum and then pouring pitch over them. A young sailor, eager to obey, said rather timidly to Honorue, "We have no oakum on board."

"What?" Richard spoke up. He turned to the young sailor and said, "You have miles of oakum here. You know how it is made, don't you?" The lad nodded, and Richard said, "Then get aloft and cut down the rigging on the mizzen. The whole thing has to be replaced, and from the look of it, it's fairly on its way to being oakum already." The lad climbed aloft with two others and within minutes a quarter-mile of old, tarred rigging fell out of the sky, whacking the deck as it landed. The watch ordered to caulk the decks broke into sections. Some heated pitch. Some picked the rope apart into strands to make oakum. Others began jamming the freshly made oakum into the cracks in the deck with a narrow but dull chisel and a wooden mallet. A crew then came along and carefully poured the heated pitch over the cracks full of oakum. The next time the deck was sanded, the remnants of pitch would come off, and there would be a smooth and waterproof seam between the planks.

Richard walked to the shot locker and stood staring. The locker was less than half-full, but everything in it was fuzzy with rust. "Jesus Christ," he muttered to himself. He ordered the shot be removed, scraped clean, and greased, "and grease that locker before you put them all back," he ordered, pointing to the rusty cannonballs.

"Where shall we put them while we are working in the locker, sir?" a midshipman asked.

Richard stood, staring at him in disbelief, then asked calmly, "What was your name again, sir?"

"Buckley, sir," the young man answered.

"Mr. Buckley, the companionways are surrounded by shot garlands. Fill them first, and then tack down some timbers to hold the rest on deck," he said, trying to be patient with the young man. It was not his fault he had been robbed of his nautical education by Lort, but he and the other five midshipmen would have to catch up quickly.

The *Reliant* became a noisy place. Men sat on their haunches scraping shot now on several decks, making the whole ship sound like a colossal blacksmith's shop. Added to that was the scratching of holystones on the oak planks and the pounding of caulk between the planking, and it all could be heard plainly on shore. Stout Captain Boxley, whose ship had been rammed by Lort, stood on his taffrail listening to the sounds coming from *Reliant* as she lolled at her banished mooring. Being somewhat bored and quite a bit nosey, Boxley ordered his boat lowered and had himself rowed over to her. "Captain Boxley at the quarterdeck, Captain," came the alert. Richard walked to greet the portly man.

"Permission to come aboard, Captain?" Boxley asked heartily.

Richard granted the permission that was a formality only, and the pudgy little man climbed aboard. He looked and listened and then said, "Holmwood, you drew a rotten berth, practically a quarantine berth, but I'll bet my best bottle of rum you whip this barge into shape well before you get to Portsmouth. My God, look what you have done already, and you haven't been here half a day!" They toured the ship and Boxley pulled Richard aside at one point and said, "I knew some of the ships under Portman were falling below standards, but I never dreamed to see anything like this in the Navy. You have your work cut out for you, but from what I've heard of you, you'll make it." They visited a little longer, and then Boxley said, "I must be going and let you get back to work. Good luck to you, and Godspeed." He shook Richard's hand and then, nearly splitting his tight trousers as he scrambled back into his boat, he headed back to his own ship.

Richard went now to the galley and looked over the stove and its chimney. Smoke was leaking out in two places between decks, and he ordered the cooks to get fires going in portable stoves to cook the noon meal and then to douse the fire in the galley stove. They would have to replace the chimney, and it had to be done while in port, they could not do it at sea. This alone would cost him another day at the very least, and he was not naïve enough to think this was the last delay he would encounter.

His next stop, and one that tightened his gut even more, was the sail locker. He found the sailmaker there waiting for him, and he spoke before Richard could. "They's bad, Captain. We was never allowed to get them out on the upper deck in good weather to check and dry them. I have aired them as best I can here between decks, but they need sunlight too. Cap'n Lort said they was in the way up there. He said if I made 'em right, they wouldn't rot. That ain't true, sir. It don't matter how good they are, they'll rot if they don't get some air."

"What is your name?" Richard asked the sailmaker.

"Stechart, sir. Adam Stechart," he said, knuckling his forehead. Richard saw in Stechart a craftsman robbed of the ability to do his job well and blamed when things went badly. With his Maine accent and soft eyes that missed nothing, Richard recognized in the sailmaker a valuable asset, and he said with compassion, "After we eat at noon, and when the deck is dry, take them up to see what you have and then report to me." Stechart smiled and got to work.

The crew's berthing decks were also a shambles. Wet clothes had been allowed to lie on the floor until the decks were marked with deep stains. All ships stink at times, but this one smelled almost as bad as a slaver. Richard had never been on a ship hauling slaves, but he recalled being downwind of one in a harbor in Cuba, and the smell had been as appalling as the wails coming from the ship. He had sworn right then to never have anything to do with black cargo. The smell, however, lingered sharp in his mind for years.

Some of the smells on *Reliant* had come from the fire-bucket latrines and the foul ballast, but there was something else going on to account for such a stench. He quietly walked down to the hold and then into the carpenter's walk, and there, in that narrow passage that runs the full length of the ship from bow to stern below the watermark, he found a man hunched down relieving himself. He could not believe what he was seeing, "What in the hell are you doing?" Richard bellowed. The sailor yanked up his drawers, trying to fasten them and salute while also scurrying away, but Richard caught him by the shirt and whirled him around. "Get a bucket and get this shit cleaned with vinegar and then you holystone the whole thing yourself." The sailor looked at him stunned. The carpenter's walk was one of the longest passageways on the ship, and he was getting ready to argue, but he looked at the peril in Richard's eyes and simply saluted and went to get the vinegar.

Richard searched and found feces in several other places on the ship. He ordered the lower decks be washed with vinegar and then scrubbed while he set about writing orders for cleanliness and maintenance of the ship.

He had all hands mustered and the new rules were read. It should have been done under Lort, but now each of the ship's five boats would have a coxswain who was responsible for the maintenance of that boat and its falls, no matter the conditions or the time of day. Honorue would choose the coxswains to be responsible for the jolly boat, the two long boats, cutter, and pinnace. The coxswain could in turn choose his own crew from his watch, but the boats were to be scrubbed, swabbed, and wiped dry every day when the main deck was sanded and scrubbed and this included every oar and the falls that raised and lowered the boat. When it left the ship, the same crew was also in charge of manning it.

Richard had listed items to be accomplished on a routine basis, and he stood by now as they were read aloud. "The main deck will be sanded and stoned every morning before breakfast. When that deck is dry, I expect it to look like snow. The forecastle deck and any sleeping deck will be scrubbed once a week beginning tomorrow. The sickbay, the cheese room, the galley stores, and the galley will be rinsed with vinegar and scrubbed every other day. The gun decks are to be scrubbed and stoned once a week. We will be replacing nearly all the rigging in the next month or so, and when it is replaced, I will not see another fag end. If you don't know how to knot them properly, Mr. Honorue or Mr. Stechart," he motioned to them, "will show you. There will be no more fag fluttering on this ship." Richard had been referring to the ragged trailing strands on the very ends of the lines. They were knotted to keep the ends from fraying further and also to act as a stop to keep the line from passing right through a block and whipping free out of reach. Some of the crew exchanged glances, and Richard glared at them as the recital continued, "The fire buckets, pump head, and water kegs in the magazine will be checked twice a day every single day, and kept perfectly full and ready for use. The main sea pump will work by the end of today, or no one will sleep until it does. We cannot fight fire or maintain the decks without it. It will be fixed today." Richard looked over the crew and narrowed his glance at the man he caught defecating in the carpenter's walk and said, "Uneaten food, spit, and shit will go in their proper places and no other. A fire bucket is not a latrine. There will be a spit kid behind every companionway, and it is for tobacco juice only; use it. If I see a man spit on the deck, he will drink the entire contents of the nearest spit kid before he spends time in the brig."

Richard paced back and forth, and when the regulations were read he said, "Every man, from the sailmaker to the stewards, including the cook, the doctor, and the purser, will have a place in the rigging and know what to do there. This is a ship of war; we cannot afford to specialize that much. Every man will know his regular job, will learn his place in the rigging, and will know basic gunnery. I should be able to pull the cook and put him on a gun crew, or send him up into the rigging, and he will at least know how to stay alive there and make a contribution." This caused a murmur, but it was not a murmur entirely of disagreement. "I want all hands who have some knowledge of repairing sails, or even if you can sew your clothes well, to report to Mr. Stechart. He is bringing the sails from the locker onto the main deck to see what can be salvaged, and he can use all the help you can give him."

Two hours later, the main deck was cluttered with bales of sailcloth and sails in all stages of completion. A small boy with a head of messy dark curls was punching holes in the sailcloth with a peg known as a stabber. The boy had to put his whole weight onto the stabber each time to get it to puncture the heavy sailcloth as he made hole after hole in neat little rows through which the sailmaker would insert his needle. He was nearly in tears from the work, but kept going, and Richard stood looking down at him and asked, "What is your name?"

"Ladysmith, sir. Jordan Ladysmith," the young man said, standing and quietly staring at Richard with huge brown eyes shining out of his filthy face. Richard could see bruises on his arms and legs where he had crawled around the tight spots on the ship, and his legs were a mass of scabs from scratching insect bites. They had been close enough to port to get the mosquitoes from the marshes near Boston, and Richard himself had been plagued by them at night.

"Carry on then, lad," Richard said, and Jordan quickly sat back on a pile of ropes and continued his work.

Richard found Lieutenant Joyce and asked why a child so young was on board. "He is the grandson of Old Bailey, sir." Joyce pointed the old man out to Richard and then continued, "Bailey found himself burdened with the boy after the boy's father died in a French prison, and his daughter, the lad's mother, just gave up and died a year after her husband. Old Bailey said there wasn't anyone to look after the boy, and he couldn't bear to put him in an orphanage, so Bailey just brought him along when he came on board. Captain Lort didn't object, and truthfully, I am not even sure he knew the boy was here."

Richard thought hard about what he would do with Owen if he had no wife or home or money, but he finally told Joyce, "The boy cannot stay here. He's too young. This isn't the Royal Navy where we take them at eight years old to break them in. He will have to go, soon."

Richard asked to see Bailey, and the old man came to Richard's cabin a few minutes later. When Richard asked if there weren't some relatives to look after the boy, Old Bailey shook his head and said, "No, sir. That's why he's here. There ain't none to care for him but me."

Richard went ashore that night and visited the Puppets. They were still lively and only scolded him halfheartedly for not visiting sooner, but Richard noticed some of their fire was gone, and he didn't think it was all from getting older. "Have you all been ill? You have barely ordered me around or complained about how I am keeping myself this whole evening. I'm a little alarmed," he teased.

Aunt Ruth, who of the three had actually taken a step toward matrimony, and would probably have seen it through had her fiancé not been lost at sea three months before the wedding, now looked up from her lace work and said, "Your wife is keeping you well these days, and you have no need of our advice. We are practically useless now."

Aunt Grace added, "You were much more amusing when you were a boy, Richard. You had little problems that to you seemed huge, but to us were easily remedied, and I for one miss being needed."

"I agree with sister," said Dorothy. "Time went so quickly, and you were not a boy long enough."

A sudden thought came to Richard and he said with a smile, "Would you take another boy to look after?" Before they could answer, he said, "I don't mean to live with you full time, but to come here when he is not at school. This would be his home, and he would spend his holidays with you, but he would be at school most of the year. Do you think that would help?"

"Oh, Richard, you don't have another child tucked away somewhere do you?" Aunt Ruth looked horrified.

"No," Richard assured them, "this is not my child, but one that desperately needs a home and some kindness until he's older." He then described what he knew of Jordan Ladysmith, and when he finished, he looked at the Puppets for their answer. They all began talking at once and finishing each other's sentences and then turned to Richard with their eyes alight and nodded, barely able to contain their excitement. Yes, they would take him.

Bailey had not disagreed with the arrangement, but said with as much pride as he could, "Sir, I would never have thought my girl's boy would have the chance to go to school, but I'm ashamed to say there ain't no money for schoolin."

"The late Commodore Portman left funds for just such a need, and I will arrange for the tuition to be paid from those funds," Richard offered, aware of the old man's dignity.

Bailey didn't say anything for a few minutes and then looked at Richard in wonder and said, "He could even become a gentlemen, couldn't he, my boy I mean?"

"Absolutely, but I think he has the sea in his nose, and I think the best thing he could do is attend school until he is old enough to sign on as a midshipman, and then finish his education in the Navy," Richard said and then added, "I don't think there would be any trouble getting him accepted.

"An officer? My little Jordan an officer?" Bailey smiled a toothless grin.

Two days later, Richard, Old Bailey and young Jordan Ladysmith made their way to the Puppets. When the carriage pulled up, the door swung open and all three ladies were nearly prancing on the doorstep as they watched Jordan come up the walk. They swarmed over him and plied him with cakes and other treats and assured Bailey they would make Jordan write to him at least once a week and promised that he would be fine. An hour later Jordan looked overwhelmed, but not alarmed, and he bravely wished his grandfather well as he waved to him and Richard before the Puppets closed the door behind him.

In the carriage on the way back to the ship, Old Bailey was very quiet and Richard left him alone. He thought now of how hard it must have been for his own father to allow him to go to sea when he was young. Richard had never regretted going, and Gabriel had come to realize it was for the best. Now that he had a son of his own, Richard realized what a sacrifice his father had made to let him go.

Bailey interrupted his thoughts as they neared the harbor and said, "Think on that, sir, my boy might just write to me. I wouldn't be able to read a word of it, 'cause I ain't never learned how, but I could hold it in my hand just the same."

Richard smiled and said, "I know my aunts, Bailey, and he will write to you. When that first letter arrives, I will read it to you myself. I have a personal interest in young Jordan now."

"Thank you kindly, Cap'n, thank you kindly," Bailey nodded, smiling.

It hadn't been necessary to send the marines for Yancy and the sailing master that first night on board the *Reliant*. Richard heard them coming back roaring drunk and met them at the railing. Yancy took one look at him and clutched his chest where the shiny crescent of a dirk wound reminded him of the young man who had heaped so much humiliation on him. Yancy's career had stalled while Richard's had soared, and now the boy was back, only this time a man, more confident and prettier than ever, to goad Yancy the subordinate. It was too much for Yancy, and he forgot himself and lunged at Richard, calling out drunkenly, "You little shit!" Instead of backing out of his way, Richard stayed where he was and allowed Yancy to plow into him. He really didn't hurt Richard, but it was all he needed to call over the marines on deck. Six of them escorted Yancy, not to the brig on board the ship, but to the Navy agent on shore. A discipline report of the incident and orders for Yancy to wait for the next southbound vessel were delivered to the agent an hour later. Yancy would leave a vacant second lieutenancy on the ship, but Lieutenant Harker could take billet as second lieutenant, and the senior midshipman could be promoted to third lieutenant and serve with more efficiency and diligence than Yancy had ever done. As for the sailing master, he took one look at Yancy being frog-marched ashore, and meekly asked permission to come aboard. They spoke privately and very quietly in Richard's cabin for no more than three minutes. No one overheard their conversation, but whatever was said, the sailing master of *Reliant* remained sober from that day forward.

The ship left Boston two days later, and she handled worse than Richard ever imagined. It took them nearly two hours to get the kinks out of the cobbled rigging as they sailed out into the open ocean to make their turn south. It had been Richard's plan to get out to sea and then hold gunnery practice, which he had no illusions would be just as ugly, but now that would have to be delayed as he concentrated on merely sailing the ungainly beast of a ship.

It took over a month to refit the *Reliant* at Gosport, but finally the work was finished, and after they had dropped off their harbor pilot near Point Comfort, Richard let her fully feel the wind for the first time wearing her new sails and rigging. He had made such a pest of himself with modifications that the supervisors at Gosport dreaded seeing him coming toward them. In the end he got his way, and now *Reliant* was headed into the open ocean on a course due east.

The crew hauled the huge sails up laboriously to the beat of the chantey to be secured to the yards. The chantey was being sung by an injured sailor who could not lend a hand, but could support them with his voice. As the sails came up into place, there were adjustments to the standing rigging as the tension pulled everything in different ways, but when that was done, Richard stood watching as sail after sail filled.

Reliant had the fortune to be built after shipwrights learned the value of a sharp and deep keel, and she now dug into the water using the very weight of the water to counterbalance the strain of the wind on her sails. Richard had been appalled at the condition of the ship when he first saw her, but he had never doubted she could be magnificent. She plunged into each wave like a porpoise in a bow wave. She was long and sleek without a hint of the raised quarterdeck of her ancestors. She was the same height above water at the stern as at her bow, and with her lance-like bowsprit held out in front of her she resembled a swordfish slashing along the surface.

Richard made more adjustments, some of them overruling the suggestions of the sailing master on board, and then the wind shifted just a bit and came up smartly from the west. *Reliant* ran before the wind in near perfect conditions. Richard looked around the crew on deck and in the rigging and he could see amazement, and joy, and something he had not seen in them before—pride. Now when they tied off a line, they made sure it was not just secured by the belaying pin, but that it looked right as it was wrapped around the stay.

The ship snapped and popped as her wooden skeleton took on and released tension. There was the wondrous creaking of rope and hiss of the wind against the sails that every sailor lives for. The wind began to rush through their ears from the ship's forward momentum. Richard nodded his agreement as the sailing master suggested setting out the studding sails. Wind like this was too good to waste. Richard watched as the crew slid the yard extensions out into space, locked them down, and hauled the sails up from below.

As the studding sails filled with air, *Reliant* lunged forward and put her nose into the sea, wetting her decks nearly to the mainmast. The crew on the yards began yelling first, and it was taken up by the deck crew until they were all cheering as they felt the ship shudder as she leaned into the wind. "She's gonna sing!" a crew member shouted to another from the rigging. Richard smiled. That rare combination of wind and water against the hull that creates a hum that can be both heard and felt was about to happen. The crew cheered and pounded their hands against the yards and railings as the vibration built to a crescendo and then slowly faded.

Richard had provided this extraordinary experience for them, and they looked to him now with eyes of respect and admiration. No matter how much he drove them now, they knew he had managed, through them, to create a beautiful ship that was sleek and fast and one they were now proud to be aboard.

Reliant took her place in the American fleet, now three frigates strong and numbering nearly twenty ships. She provided safety for American shipping along the west coast of Africa. When they finally engaged the enemy Richard found the *Reliant* as deadly as she was beautiful. It was two years before Richard returned home and took a long-awaited and lengthy leave to be with Lorraine and Owen and the rest of the Holmwoods in Hampton.

What started as leave turned into a change of home port for *Reliant*. She was now stationed in Norfolk as part of a general concentration of naval forces in American waters. For too long, the Navy had focused on the Barbary Pirates, but now that their menace had been extinguished, the attention of the nation could turn to trouble brewing right off the East Coast.

The British government did not give direct orders for their fleet to harass American merchants and naval vessels, yet the Royal Navy was stopping American vessels, even naval vessels, and searching for British sailors who had deserted. The war with France had depleted their crews, and as Britain was still building ships at a furious rate, it desperately needed sailors.

The American Navy was now patrolling the waters off the East

Coast and Richard's patrol took him from roughly Assateague Island on Virginia's Eastern Shore to the Florida Keys. Lorraine had commented, touching his hair, that it was a patrol guaranteed to keep him in gold, and sure enough, when he came back to Hampton Roads every three months or so, his head was covered with shiny gold curls from the southern sun.

He spent the next three years on this patrol with three small escort ships. He was home for Christmas this year, and Lorraine had an unexpected gift for him. She was pregnant. Richard was ecstatic, because Owen was now going to be twelve, and there had been no other children. He sprawled in bed next to her as she calculated the time for her confinement. Richard believed it was quite possible for him to be home then if he remained on his current patrol. Owen was less than excited about having a brother or sister, preferring not to hear about it at all.

The previous year, Richard had been informed that he was receiving two more midshipmen, but still keeping him under the ten required to get a schoolmaster. Their education fell to him, and while he didn't regret it, he did not fancy himself a schoolmaster. His charges received the finest schooling in navigation and seamanship which included mathematics, and learned a great deal about literature and even writing. As for science, history, or Latin, they would have great gaps in their education that they would be responsible for filling on their own when they could. Richard ordered them to, "Read up on them when you can." With that, he handed them a crate of books on the weaker subjects, doubting they ever cracked a cover.

One of the two charges he received was young Jordan Ladysmith. He was now twelve and had followed Richard's suggestion. There had been a tearful departure when he left the Puppets in Boston, but he was reporting to *Reliant* in high spirits, hardly believing his good luck at being stationed on Richard's ship. Jordan's delight soon turned to reality as he came to learn that his captain was as stern a taskmaster as he was good a seaman.

About six months after Jordan joined the ship, the intensity of their patrol was increased after two Americans were taken and pressed into British service while their ship was anchored in Philadelphia Harbor. Richard's orders were to allow no boarding or stopping for foreign ships that appeared hostile. If he was fired upon, he was ordered to return fire to protect his ship.

Reliant was sailing about sixty miles south of Charleston when the lookouts spotted a British ship astern. It was a good-sized frigate, and as it got closer it hailed them to heave to and be boarded. Richard had no intention of complying, so he crammed on sail and bolted south. *Reliant* pulled away from the British vessel, but now another British ship appeared out of the southeast from the open sea.

The drummer beat to quarters, and Richard now paced the deck watching everything come into order. The gun crews were ready, the lower sails had been furled to get them clear of any sparks and the ship's boats were bobbing along behind on their towlines. They were as set as they could be. As Richard paced, he overheard a few fragments of conversation among the midshipmen, and it was clear there was about to be a duel. He pulled aside Shaw, formerly the victim of the *Cumberland's* carnal female cargo and now his second lieutenant, and told him to bring the duelists to him.

He paced his cabin, and within minutes they were shown inside. Richard was furious to see the midshipmen appear. It was Jordan Ladysmith and another called Caruthers. He turned a foul eye on them both and demanded, "What is this about?"

The boys looked at each other, and Caruthers spoke up, "Sir, Mr. Ladysmith impugned my honor, sir, by purposefully ignoring me in front of the other midshipmen."

"That is not true, sir," Jordan interrupted. "My mouth was full, and I answered Mr. Caruthers when I was able."

Caruthers shot back, "Well, Mr. Ladysmith, you took too long chewing."

Richard raised his hands and roared, "Enough! We are going into a battle and you find this is the time for a duel?" He glared at them and then to their surprise, and his, he slapped them both across the cheek with the back of his hand. "There, now you're even. Your honors are pretty damned fragile to see the need for a duel just because one of you didn't answer the other fast enough." Each boy stood holding his cheek, trying valiantly not to let his eyes well up with tears. "What were you going to do, dodge cannon shot while you paced it off to shoot each other?" Richard asked.

"No, sir, we were going to use our dirks," Jordan said, and then added another, "sir," unsure if he had said it enough times, and then was sorry he had, because his voice chose then to crack.

"I need every officer I have, and I'll not lose one to stupidity. You get back to your gun crews and do your duty, and I swear if I ever hear of either of you dueling on this ship again then by God I will shoot you myself!" The boys stared at him, and he bellowed, "Go!" They jumped, saluted hastily, and ran out of the great cabin so fast they clogged in the doorway struggling to get out. Richard looked hard after them, listening to the hasty retreat of their boots, and then walked to the quarterdeck to take his place.

As he came back on deck the wind had shifted and he could smell rain. All day it had felt like a squall might come off the shore, but now it was here, and it provided the perfect cover. Richard turned and ordered the boats be brought back, and to prepare for heavy weather. They would run before the squall until they were clear of the British frigates. The storm appeared to be more than just a squall. Both British ships turned and fled before it and Richard now secured all battle gear and prepared for the onslaught of weather. Richard had always been good at judging storms, but this one had taken even him by surprise. What they had seen at first was only the leading edge of a huge line of storms shaped like a great archer's bow.

They could run before the storm, but from the look of it they would be quickly overtaken and could even be swamped from behind, so Richard chose to use what time and relatively calm seas he had to come about and face the storm. The crew furled everything except the storm jibs and waited for it.

At the height of the storm, *Reliant* took green water over the decks several times, and unrelenting sheets of rain nearly knocked sailors flat as they held on to lifelines hastily strung up along the deck. Richard also saw Ladysmith and Caruthers holding onto each other puking their guts out, once again brethren in the face of such adversity. The storm lasted nearly two hours, but when it was over there was no sign of either British ship.

On the return patrol, they sailed near the Outer Banks of North Carolina. On any chart, not even a very accurate one, the area is peppered with shipwrecks. It was full of shoals and chain islands and had been the hideout of pirates dating back to the era of Sir Walter Raleigh. If the United States was to be in an all-out war with Britain, it would be good to be familiar with the area, for British ships could hide in the many coves and inlets of the relatively uninhabited North Carolina coast just as pirates had for centuries.

Reliant cleared Ocracoke Island now and gently threaded the channel between Hatteras Island and Hatteras Shoals. With every hurricane, the shoals changed, rearranging themselves to be optimum hazards, but luckily Richard's charts had been updated since the last major blow. They moved toward Five Fathom Shoals and Richard chose the dangerous western side. He knew he could not continue north through Wimble Shoals, which alone had claimed hundreds of ships, but would have to turn around and sail back south to get to open water. Something told him, now, however, to take this jaunt. He had learned over his many years at sea to heed such little somethings when they whispered.

As they neared the end of Five Fathom Shoals, and the lead line began to bring up white sand marking the beginning of Wimble Shoals, Richard saw a large ship, listing to one side and partially buried in the shoal. The ship itself had acted like a weir and formed a sandbar, which further entrapped her, but also kept her safe from storms coming from the shoreline.

"What is that?" Richard asked, pointing to the ship aground on the rocks ahead.

"That's the wreck of the *Vindicta*, sir," the sailing master said at his elbow. He had been looking at the wreck through his glass as well. He continued as he looked, "She went aground late last year. I thought someone would salvage her, but it appears she hasn't even been stripped."

"They say she is haunted, sir, that she ran herself aground," said Glumm, his steward. The old steward, a wizened man of sixty, shielded his eyes from the sun as he stared at the ship ahead.

The *Vindicta* was heeled on her starboard side almost like she had been careened there on purpose. Richard walked along the deck as they sailed as close as they dared, and then ordered them to turn about and heave to so he could see the grounded ship better. The *Vindicta* was a beautiful ship, and he could see no obvious damage, but there was no way to see if there was damage to her hull without boarding her. He looked carefully through the glass and saw to his amazement that she still had a small swivel gun mounted near her rail, and it was pointed straight down into her hold. Surely, someone could easily have harvested that. Maybe she was haunted, but if she couldn't be salvaged, she should be stripped and burned, so as not to give a potential enemy any equipment they could use. Richard took one more look and then ordered a turn south and out to the open sea while he went to his cabin. He pulled out more charts and studied the area around where the *Vindicta* went aground. It was full of shoals and little islands barely showing above high tide and only fully visible in a gale. It would be a horrible place to work, and even then it might be impossible to get her off the sand. He had lingered long enough, so he put away the charts and returned to the deck still thinking of the *Vindicta*. She looked so... he searched for a word, and "comfortable" came to mind. She looked like she was waiting for something and had gotten herself comfortable while she did so.

They sailed north in the pleasant early May weather. Richard soon forgot the wrecked ship as he thought of the leave he was taking when he arrived in Hampton Roads and of the child Lorraine would be having soon. She had been fairly large with child when he left, but she should be nearing her confinement, if she had not already delivered.

CHAPTER 9

IT WAS THE MOST natural thing for Wrennet to move in with Richard and Lorraine when they learned she was expecting another child. Lorraine had a house full of staff for cleaning and such in her new house, but she needed a nurse, and no one could think of a better one than Wrennet, who had dropped some heavy hints that she wanted to come.

Wrennet tried now to get Lorraine's spirits up, but all she wanted to do was sit complaining about Richard being gone. It was strange, because she understood the life he led and had never expected him to stay home for long. Lately, she had been mournful and depressed, spending most of her waking time in bed.

Richard was at sea when the child was born, and the delivery was easy, almost too easy. Wrennet remembered the old wives' tale that an easy delivery leads to sorrow. Wrennet knew Lorraine had taken herbal remedies, but it was only recently that she learned some of them were abortives. Wrennet had been worried the child would be damaged in some way, but when he was born he was already crying and pink and beautiful like his mother. Lorraine took one look at the infant and absolutely refused to hold him. She asked instead for Owen, who had been banished from her chamber for the delivery. During the entire labor, Owen had pounded on the door demanding to be let in, screaming that he could help, and that it was his duty to be there. When he was finally allowed back in, Owen crawled in bed with his mother refusing to even look at the baby. Wrennet held the child out to the two of them, but Lorraine motioned with her hand and said, "Take him away. We will meet him later." Wrennet took the baby downstairs and arranged a schedule for some of the nursing neighbor women to come and feed him.

The next morning Wrennet thought Lorraine would have recovered and would want to see her baby, but she still refused. Owen pretended the baby wasn't even in the house. It was three days before Lorraine asked for the child. She and Owen were in bed and they had a roaring fire going, even though it was June and not even cold outside. Wrennet handed the baby to Lorraine and went back downstairs. Wrennet asked the maids about the fire, and they said Lorraine had insisted on it. The younger of the maids looked at Wrennet and said, "Ma'am, Mrs. Holmwood, she isn't right. I'm afraid of her."

"Oh, nonsense," Wrennet said, but she crept back upstairs and listened at the door. She heard Lorraine's voice and it sounded weird. "Do it! You must do it now, Owen. We will never be together if you don't. Throw him in!" Wrennet flung open the door and found Owen standing before the fire, crying while holding the infant in both hands. Lorraine was sitting where she had crawled to the end of the bed, urging him on. Owen sobbed as his mother screamed at him again to throw the baby in the fire. Wrennet raced into the room, grabbed the infant in one arm, and took Owen by the ear with her other and tried to leave, but Lorraine jumped on her back, knocking them all down. The baby rolled, screaming toward the door, and Lorraine grabbed Owen and dragged him back into bed with her. She hunkered over him like a starved bitch guarding a bone, and then she actually growled at Wrennet like an animal. Wrennet took the baby and ran downstairs, shutting the door behind her.

Wrennet ventured back hours later and found Lorraine and Owen sound asleep like nothing had happened. The room was stifling, and Wrennet opened a window to let out some of the heat from the fire. As she was leaving the room, Lorraine called softly to her. Lorraine looked sane then but tired and held out her hand weakly, and Wrennet took it. Lorraine begged, "Richard should never know about this. It will make him so unhappy, and I want him to be happy. He deserves to be happy." Wrennet nodded her head in agreement and then Lorraine let her hand drop and fell back asleep.

Lorraine was awake the next morning at dawn, but she looked unbalanced again, and would not let any of the maids or Wrennet touch her nor would she release her grip on Owen. He became frightened of his mother, begging her to be forgiven for not throwing the baby in the fire when she told him to and blaming himself for her sickness.

Owen was a strong twelve-year-old, but it took both Wrennet and two maids to free him from Lorraine's grip, so he could go downstairs to wash and be fed. As soon as he had eaten, Owen returned to his mother.

About midmorning, Lorraine seemed better and asked to see the baby, who had been named Edward. Wrennet didn't leave her alone with him, and Lorraine stared at him wordlessly for probably half an hour. She then handed him to back to Wrennet with the saddest eyes and said, "I have nothing for him, because he looks nothing like Richard." It was a dismissal. Wrennet tried to tell her the baby didn't look like Richard, because he looked so much like her, but she was no longer listening.

She got out of bed a few days later and managed to get dressed, but she went around in a daze calling Owen by Richard's name and completely ignoring Edward. At the end of the week her kidneys started to fail and she began to retain water. It was then that Richard arrived on leave.

He bolted into the house smiling, with his golden hair and eyes glowing, but he knew immediately something was terribly wrong. He called out for Lorraine, but Wrennet appeared at the top of the stairs. Richard bolted up the stairs and stood staring at Wrennet. "She lost the child?" he asked, but Wrennet shook her head no. Before she could say anything he gasped, "Lorraine is not dead is she?" Wrennet shook her head again, but Richard pushed past her and headed for his bedroom. He opened the door and stood staring from the doorway. The creature lying on the bed looked nothing like the woman he had left behind. She was huge, but not just her stomach. She was bloated all over. He turned back to Wrennet behind him and whispered, "She cannot possibly survive a delivery in this condition. What can you do?"

"She has already delivered the child, a boy, but she fell ill after," Wrennet said, putting her hand on his shoulder. He jerked away from her hand and moved to the edge of the bed, whispering her name. Lorraine's eyes snapped open and she looked at Richard and began to cry, begging him to forgive her. Richard tried his best to comfort her, but she slipped into unconsciousness at nightfall and only regained it once more.

It was just before dawn and Richard was where he had been since he sat on the edge of her bed the night before. Richard felt movement in the clammy and bloated hand he was holding. He noted with sorrow that her beautiful long fingers were now the size and shape of Surry sausages. Her eyes fluttered open and Richard bent down close to her. She struggled and then whispered, "You must find another person, and be happy with her. Do it for me, for Owen, and," she struggled to breathe, "and for little Edward."

Richard nodded and said, "I promise," and Lorraine closed her eyes again, and Richard continued, so she could not hear, "that I will never marry again so long as I live." Lorraine struggled harder to breathe as daylight approached, and as is the case so many times, her soul struggled through the night, so it could be taken away by the sun.

THE FUNERAL was a blur for everyone in the household, and when it was over they returned to the house. Richard made it through the wake and funeral without a tear. When everyone had left, and he had done his best to comfort Owen, he went to look at the tiny child. He so resembled Lorraine that Richard gasped. He sat next to the cradle and bowed his head to cry. His throat was on fire and his chest ached, but no tears would come. He had suppressed them for so long.

Richard paced the house all night. The next morning, looking disheveled and unshaved, he announced they were moving to Scotland

Neck. He owned a house there that had been empty for years, and they would be safe there. War with England was brewing, and he had planned to move everyone north after the child was born and strong enough to make the trip.

Wrennet started preparations and asked, "Are we leaving later in the week?"

Richard looked at her and shook his head, "We are leaving in three hours." He walked out the door and Wrennet ran behind him and grabbed his arm.

"Richard, we cannot get this house ready to leave in three hours. What about the staff? What about the children's things? Who will feed Edward if we leave?"

"Pay the staff off. I really don't care what you take with you, and as for the child, I am sure you will figure something out. Regardless of what you pack or what you do, I am taking my sons away from here. I assume you are coming, so be ready in three hours," Richard said flatly, turned on his heel, and walked out into the pouring rain.

Richard returned with a carriage and loaded it. Wrennet had managed to hire a wet nurse to come with them. Though the woman was leaving her husband and two other children behind, she would be paid more in three months for feeding her breast milk to Richard's baby than her husband could make in a year at the docks.

Richard stood on the porch with the gardener, who had earlier shuttered the house and now stood ready with a stout chain and lock. Richard closed the door behind him, and the gardener threaded the chain through the ornate brass handles and then put the huge padlock on it. He handed the key to Richard and silently walked away. Richard stepped down off the porch and looked back at the house. He stood there a long time just staring until the child began to howl as the rain fell on his uncovered face. Richard flipped the blanket back over him and got into the carriage. Edward screamed all the way to the pier, and then most of the way up the James River in one of the small ships Richard had inherited from Anthony Portman. It was sadly called *Lorraine*.

Richard deposited Wrennet, Owen, Edward, and the wet nurse, whose name he could not remember, at the house in Scotland Neck and left on the *Lorraine* two days later. He loaded haphazardly from his warehouse there and headed for Washington. He had kept both ships he had inherited from Anthony Portman busy on merchant cruises, and he had made a tidy sum over the years. It was only by chance that the *Lorraine* had been in Norfolk when Lorraine died. He didn't really care now what profit he made from the merchandise, he just needed purpose and action. He had a month's leave from the Navy, and as long as he kept going he thought he could stay ahead of the grief. He stopped in Norfolk to take on a few crew members and planned to leave the following morning for Washington. With the exception of some toast he had choked down while Wrennet glowered at him the morning he left Scotland Neck, he had not had anything to eat or drink. He was in no condition to consume alcohol when he reached for the rum, initially because he was thirsty, but later because he was needy. The alcohol seemed to dull the pain, or at least build a welcome wall.

He made it to Norfolk, but went no further. He released the crew on leave for the night, and then drank through the early evening hours, alone on the ship except for two men on watch. He drank to the point where he no longer heard the bells or the water lapping. At one point, Richard realized he had become that which he despised most, a drunken captain, and he staggered off the ship to get food and coffee to try to sober up. It would not be easy, for the talons of rum were deep in his flesh. He staggered for about two blocks and found a seedy tavern where he ordered some bread and cheese and a pot of coffee. When he was told they didn't have any coffee, he just took the food and left, giving them a stern shot for not having coffee. It started to rain, but Richard didn't feel it though it was falling on his bare head. He had long ago lost his hat. Mercifully, he was not in uniform, or he could have found himself being hauled away by a passing shore patrol. The cold of the rain, not the rain itself, drove him to find shelter, and he staggered under an awning he saw down an alley. He looked at the bread and cheese in his hand, but it turned his stomach, so he set it down on the flags and leaned his head back against the building. He closed his eyes, only for a moment he told himself, and awakened an hour later, vomiting. He had the presence of mind to roll onto his side, so he wouldn't choke to death, but not the sense to get up out of his own filth. In this manner he spent the night under a leaking awning next to a barrel of slops in a back alley with his only companions the skulking wharf rats.

Richard awakened the next morning through layers like he was ascending inside a murky well. He was aware of sounds before he could garner the strength to open his eyes, but even before he could hear, he became aware of a warm, rank, and damp smell that seemed inescapable. He managed to garble aloud, "Christ, do I smell that bad?" and tried to sit up, but there was a terrible weight on his chest, and he struggled to breathe. Suddenly the weight and its accompanying warmth rolled off him, and he opened his eyes. He was staring at what was by far the largest, ugliest dog he had ever seen. It was nearly as large as a pony and smelled worse than any goat. The brute licked his face and panted hotly. The dog's breath was only slightly less volatile than his hide, but Richard realized as he felt his pockets and found the coins and the beautiful gold watch Lorraine had given him still in place, that the monstrous dog's presence had been a deterrent to both thieves and rats. "Who the hell are you, beast?" Richard said, rubbing the dog's neck. This brought about great slobbering and licking on the dog's part, and Richard pushed him away. As he did so, his hand caught on a rag tied around the dog's neck. He untied it and found it was a sack of some sort. All that could be read of the mark originally stamped on the sack was GRB.

Richard stood and had to lean against the wall until his head stopped spinning, and then he walked hunched over back toward the *Lorraine*. He had sobered up enough by this time to care whether he was spotted in such a state, so he hurried as best he could. When he was about fifty yards from the pier, a call went up on the ship. He had been spotted. Shaw, who lived in Norfolk, and who had taken leave from the Navy only to find his room at home was given over to a cousin, had agreed to sign on with Richard for the horrible trip up the James and then to Washington. He came forward now with a blanket and wrapped it around Richard's shoulders. "Sir, glad to see you are unhurt. We have been looking for you all night," he said without any recrimination in his voice. Richard smiled weakly and with some shame. It was the first time in his career as a sailor that he had not put his ship and his crew first. There was not a man on board who would hold what he had done against him, knowing that he had just lost his wife, but even they were shocked to see him in such a state.

"Thank you, Mr. Shaw. I am in a terrible state," Richard said, hiking the blanket tighter around his shoulders.

"If I may be so uncouth, sir, you smell even worse than you look," Shaw said softly.

Richard almost smiled and cocked his head, "It's because of my bed partner." Shaw, puzzled, looked in the direction Richard had nodded and saw nothing. Richard turned and looked as well, but the dog was nowhere to be seen. Just as he was about to turn and walk away with Shaw, Richard spotted him peeking from behind a stack of barrels. He smiled, patted his leg, and whistled. The rangy, gray-red dog bounded from behind the barrels and leaped up on his hind legs, licking Richard's face. On his hind legs the brute could look Richard right in the eye, and his smell had not decreased with the new day.

Shaw fanned himself. "God, I see what you mean, sir."

Richard said, "I think it's just because he's wet. All dogs stink when they're wet. He'll be fine when he's dried off some." Richard and Shaw walked up the gangway, and GRB came along with his great ears flapping. The first order Richard gave was for a pot of coffee, strong, hot, and black. He sat sipping the coffee, looking at GRB. "You are by far the ugliest dog I have ever seen," Richard said. GRB cocked his head, listening as malodorous fumes encircled Richard and filled the great cabin. Shaw came back with some bread and ham on a small platter. Richard shook his head no, but he motioned to the dog and Shaw put the platter on the deck. "I am going to call him Grub, short for GRB," Richard said, looking at the dog bolt the food. "Any guess as to his ancestry?"

Shaw shook his head and looked at the dog. "He has bloodhound in him and some large, wire-haired sighthound, Irish wolfhound perhaps? He is an ugly devil though, that is for certain, and look how big he is!" All of it was true. Grub was ugly, and he stood nearly as high as Richard's hip. He had the stout legs, huge feet, floppy ears, and baggy, forlorn eyes of his bloodhound kin, painted with the deep, keel-like chest and long, stiff coat of his wolfhound relations. Grub's coat was reddish gray, almost what could be called liver, and over his yellow, sad eyes were magnificent gray eyebrows. A matching gray mustache and beard adorned his face. Both Richard and Shaw agreed he was a unique specimen in the canine world.

"He cared for me when I didn't even care for myself," Richard said. "I'm keeping him."

Shaw said softly, "I am sorry to hear about Mrs. Holmwood." The *Reliant* officers had attended the funeral but not the wake, and Shaw had not had a moment to speak to Richard until now.

Richard nodded and sipped his coffee, "So am I. Thanks though, just the same, Kirk." He used Shaw's Christian name for the first time ever. Richard looked away, and Shaw left him alone, but when he checked about an hour later, Shaw found Richard asleep in his chair and Grub sitting with his huge, ugly head in his new master's lap.

The trip to Washington was an easy run. While there, Richard met with several other officers, including Stephen Decatur. He was horrified to learn that American sailors were being forcibly pressed for service on British ships, and not just taken from ships at sea, but now on shore in taverns and while drunk in alleys. "This is going to lead to war," Decatur warned. "We cannot just stand by and take it. Be wary at all times, Richard. Don't let your guard down for a moment at sea."

Richard agreed, and realized how lucky he had been that he hadn't been knocked on the head in Norfolk and dragged away to awaken and find himself part of the crew of some British man o' war. There was no way to know for sure, but it was possible that the night he had tried to drink away the pain, Grub had kept him from that very fate.

Upon arrival in Scotland Neck, Richard debarked, and he and Grub made their way up the steep clay road to the house. Grub trotted along, marking every weed and post he could with a seemingly endless supply of urine. "Come on, Grub, you need to meet the family," Richard said, rubbing the dog's huge floppy ears which were stiff with salt and grime.

Richard found the door locked at home and had to stand waiting for his knock to be answered. Wrennet called from the other side, "It's nearly dark. Who is it?"

"For God's sake, Wrennet, let me in," Richard said.

The door flew open and Wrennet stood staring at him. "Oh, I am so glad you are home, Richard. I didn't know if you would come back."

She leaned forward and hugged him, shocked at how bad he looked, and overpowered by how bad he smelled. She then caught sight of Grub, screamed, and slammed the door. Richard heard a scuffle on the inside, and the door opened again. Owen was standing on the doorstep in his nightdress with a sour look on his face.

Richard realized Owen had still not forgiven him for abandoning him with Wrennet, and in hindsight, Richard realized it had been a terrible and selfish thing for him to do. Owen missed Lorraine as much as he did, yet Richard had hauled him fifty miles from his home and friends only to leave him days later. Richard had wallowed in self-pity with little regard for how Owen or Wrennet might be suffering.

Richard reached out now and touched Owen's cheek with the flat of his hand, feeling the smooth, warm skin and offered, "Come here." Owen stepped stiffly forward and then wrapped his arms around Richard. Owen didn't cry; he didn't have the tears left, and in the weeks his father had been gone he had healed somewhat. Owen stepped back from Richard's embrace and smiled weakly, and just then Grub stretched out and sniffed the boy's arm, tickling him with his whiskers. Owen stared at him and then broke into a huge grin.

"Papa, what a dog! Is he yours?" Owen asked, rubbing Grub's ears. Grub wiggled all over and whined with happiness. His old canine heart had been gladdened by Richard alone, but a boy was even better. In the back of his mind Grub recalled there had once been a small boy who rode on his back and snuck some of his dinner into his pocket to give to him later. The huge dog licked Owen's face now, saturating the side of his head with slobber.

"You can't trust a brute like that with your boys, Richard, and God, does he stink," Wrennet harped as she closed the door behind them. Grub walked straight to the kitchen and stared at the hearth. He recalled a time when he had a hearth of his own, and this one looked just as inviting. "Oh, Richard, can't you smell him?" Before Richard could answer, she added, "I don't suppose so, you both smell just as bad as the other. Which one stunk first, you or the dog?" She asked the question, but she had already softened when Grub turned his big, yellow eyes on her. She melted, saying with much less venom, "I never knew an animal could smell like that."

Richard smiled slightly, "It's probably just because he's damp. All dogs stink when they're wet."

After he had done his best to wipe down Grub, and took a bath himself, Richard sought out the baby. Edward was sleeping in the drawing room next to the fire. The dog had already taken up his station next to the cradle, and about the time it would slow down and stop its swinging, Grub would sniff the infant and begin the cradle rocking again. Richard stood and stared down at his sleeping son. He was swaddled tight in his blankets and with his little cap he looked very much like a little white grub. Richard shifted his weight and bumped the cradle. The baby started and his mouth began pumping like he was nursing. Wrennet came and stood next to Richard and whispered, "He's a beautiful child." Richard nodded and reached out his hand. He stroked the fine golden hair showing along the edge of the cap, and his throat tightened painfully. Twice in the night Richard heard Edward cry, and he started to get up, but each time he heard the nurse get up to feed him. He still could not remember her name and he felt bad. Richard had met her again last evening, and she was a rather large, round-faced, simple soul.

He looked around the bedroom, only a quarter the size of the one he and Lorraine shared in Hampton, and wondered how she would have fared at Scotland Neck. It had been his intention to move them upriver away from what he believed would be shelling and burning by the British when war came. It was no longer a matter of if war would come, it was now a matter of when.

CHAPTER 10

WAR WAS DECLARED on June 1, 1812, and the news spread quickly. Richard was offered the command of the *President*, but had heard the grumbling in Washington that it and four other frigates would more than likely be held in port to be used as a last resort. He couldn't stand the thought of sitting idly and having too much time to think about Lorraine. The *Reliant* had become such a valuable ship under him that she and her thirty guns would be held close to home until the very end as well. He hadn't quite turned down the command of the *President* when word went out that letters of marque were being issued for privateers. Richard quickly applied for and was granted a license to use the *Lorraine* as a privateer with himself as captain. As soon as he had the document in hand, he requested a leave of absence from the Navy, explaining his plan, which, to his surprise, was granted.

He needed a larger crew for the *Lorraine*, and he knew he could not look to the Navy for sailors. He had the existing merchant crew of sixty from the *Lorraine*, and he could take some from the little *Fiona* which had just come into Norfolk from Baltimore, but they would still not be enough. Richard needed to overload the ship, so he would have a crew to sail any prizes he captured. If they could get thirty more, he would feel better. There were plenty of merchant sailors out of work with the long chain of congressional acts that had crippled some merchant fleets and left their ships rotting at the pier. They were competent sailors, but Richard needed a crew that would also fight. He was looking for rough and hearty souls who would follow orders and fight like the devil.

Two weeks after war had been declared, the *Lorraine*, packed to the gunwales with enough food and water for six months, left Norfolk with its malicious looking crew, whose nasty appearance was only outdone by their smell. They had come to Richard heeding the age-old signal for a privateer crew, three musket shots fired in quick succession, preferably from the roof of a whorehouse. Richard had committed a slight breach in etiquette by firing them from the top of Abbey Tavern, so named because it hovered under the menacing glare of Freemason Abbey Chapel.

Richard had known from the time he was a boy what those three shots meant, though he never actually heard them. He had barely finished his brandy when the first batch of sailors began to congregate, and when a fair crowd had gathered, Richard smiled and stood on a barrel to address them. "I have received a letter of marque for my ship the *Lorraine*. She is fitted with twelve guns, which is all she can hold, but I hope to capture ever larger prizes as we go along. I need a crew, and I need a big one. Anyone who has experience, please step forward." The men took a step forward en masse, and Richard smiled. "I will take half of what we earn, my officers take a quarter, and the rest of the crew will split the final quarter." This was far richer fare than usually offered in prize money, and a murmur ran through those gathered. Richard continued, "You will get a berth and three squares, and as for wages, you earn them by taking prizes. Anyone still interested?" The mob nearly crushed him as they leaped to get their names or marks on the muster.

He had a surprise awaiting him as he returned to the *Lorraine*. Standing on the pier was Jordan Ladysmith, looking anxious as he nearly blubbered, "Sir, I lied. I told them you had requested me, and they gave me a leave of absence to sail with you. If you don't take me, sir, I am without a ship or pay, or anything."

"Let me see your leave chit," Richard said, holding out his hand, partially expecting that Jordan had jumped ship and was without authorization, but Jordan handed it over and it was valid. It seemed unheard of for the Navy to release a midshipman for any reason, but perhaps they thought, in some odd way, Jordan could keep an eye on Richard. At any rate, Richard now had the second officer he needed, no matter how young. His first officer was a man named Clemmings.

Lorraine rode heavy in the water, overloaded with men and armament, but even so she was still fast and very maneuverable. They captured their first prize, the British brig *Corning* with twenty guns, which had been patrolling just off the coast of Maryland. The crew was a little apprehensive that Richard would take on a much larger ship, but there wasn't much of a struggle. Richard had to admit to himself he was a little disappointed the *Corning* hadn't put up more of a fight. His gun crews, considering half of them had never loaded a gun in their lives, were just getting a nice rhythm going when the commander of the brig struck his colors.

Richard had stalked among the crew before the fight and made it absolutely clear that any prisoners taken would be treated with the utmost courtesy. He made sure everyone understood, "They are your enemy until you take their ship, then they become your prisoner. There is a vast difference between an enemy and a prisoner. You are responsible for them, and you will treat them well. Being a prisoner can be hell, but we will not make it so for them. They are doing their duty and we are doing ours. It is not our job to punish them after they surrender."

In securing the prisoners and making sure the wounded were treated, Richard found that two of the *Corning* crew were pressed American sailors. They whooped and hollered when Richard brought them back to serve in his crew until he could return them to the Navy.

Richard took three more prizes in the next week, two sloops and another brig, and they sailed with him like a mother duck and her ducklings back to Hampton Roads. The Union Jack flew beneath the Stars and Stripes on all four captured ships to designate them as prizes. Richard remembered well the need to get the American flag on the prizes as quickly as possible from an incident in the Barbary War.

He had been a young lieutenant, smug with his first captured prize, and was so excited about sailing it back to port to show it off that he forgot to run up his own colors on it. Thinking the prize was an enemy ship, another American ship twice fired on it before Richard was able to signal that they were attacking a prize.

The *Lorraine* sailed into the Chesapeake Bay and received word that the naval agent purchasing prizes was in Baltimore, and he had no choice but to sell them there. If he had been a privateer that had no duty to the Navy, he could have ignored the message and sold them in Hampton. His leave of absence to take a letter of marque had clearly stated all prizes must be first offered to the Navy.

Somehow word had spread ahead of them that an American ship was bringing in prizes, and Baltimore citizens had turned out to see for themselves, complete with picnic lunches and cowbells to ring in celebration.

Richard settled up with the naval agent in Baltimore and received a chit that he would be given twelve thousand dollars. It was less than he could have gotten if he wasn't bound to sell them to the Navy, but he didn't argue. There was rich fishing to be had by just going out again, so he paid his crew their share and they went off to celebrate. To many of the sailors it was a fortune and represented six or even eight month's work. A small family could live quite well on only seven dollars a month. He would pay the officers in full when his prize money came in, but in the event they wanted to carouse a bit before then, he advanced them three hundred dollars each against their future share.

He sat sipping brandy thinking how easy it had been, how much money he had made so quickly. When he was hunting prizes, he didn't think about Lorraine, and the game now was to hunt as much and as often as possible. He thought of how many prizes he could capture with a larger ship.

He was still thinking of a larger ship when he dozed off in his bunk. In a dream he saw a redheaded woman walking toward him down a beach. Her head was thrown back like she was feeling the wind in her hair, and she had her hands clasped behind her back as she swayed waist-deep in the breaking waves. She came closer and he could see crevasses and knots in her skin and realized she was made of painted wood. This should have frightened him, but as it is in dreams, she was not scary and seemed oddly familiar. The wooden woman never looked at him, but beckoned with her hands behind her back for him to follow. He heard himself say in the dream, "What is that?"

A disembodied voice answered, "That's the wreck of the *Vindicta*, sir. She went aground, and I thought someone would salvage her, but no one has touched her."

The crash of his brandy glass slipping from his grip to the floor snapped him awake. Richard knew exactly where he needed to go. He would take the best carpentry crew he could find to see if the *Vindicta* could be salvaged, or if she was even still there.

Richard met up with the *Fiona* and her crew and sent them on to Scotland Neck for supplies from the warehouse there. He also asked them to bring Owen back to Norfolk if he had a mind to sail with his father.

THEY ARRIVED off the North Carolina coast at the wreck of the *Vindicta*, but it was foggy. At first they couldn't make out details of her on the tiny sandbar on which she lay. As the fog dissipated, they could see she was still high and dry, as if a great wave had washed up under her and set her on the sand. There was not much information about her other than she was a British ship built in Philadelphia around the turn of the century and had run aground on her maiden voyage. One of the old sailors had heard that whenever a ship came to try to salvage her, a storm would blow up and drive it off. After several captains wasted their time with a ship that did not want to be saved, they all avoided her as if she were cursed.

Richard gazed at her through his glass and ordered a boat be lowered. He ordered Jordan, who was the officer of the watch, to stay alert for British ships. "This would be a hell of a place to get caught. There is nowhere to run, and the wind is fickle today."

He took four other men and Owen with him to the stranded ship. Richard reached the bow first, and as he walked around it, he stopped short. There, lying on her side in the sand, was the *Vindicta*'s figurehead, the same wooden, redheaded woman who had beckoned to him. She looked just as she had in his dream with her red hair flowing in carved curls, her unseeing eyes, and her hands clasped daintily behind her back. Though she was nearly double the size of a real woman, she was exactly as he had seen her in his dream right down to the carved white blouse that had slipped off her shoulders to reveal her breasts. Though she had been ripped off her support beneath the bowsprit, the figurehead was intact, and Richard took it as a sign the *Vindicta* could be saved. "I'm here," he whispered to the ship.

They started work on *Vindicta* that afternoon, and amazingly, she was in good shape having been exposed on the sand for over a year. After a week of work, the old carpenter, Lockley, came to Richard and said, "I don't know that she ain't haunted, sir, but if she is, it's by kindly spirits because she wants to be fixed." Richard looked at him puzzled, and Lockley continued, "She helps us. Let's say for instance, I need a chisel, and it's just out of reach. She will find a little swell that wasn't there a moment ago, and it will lift her bottom and the chisel will roll right into your hand."

Richard smiled at the old man's superstition, "Lockley, she's barely touched by the waves anywhere."

"You can laugh all you want, Cap'n, but more than a dozen men'll swear she's alive and helpin'. Twice now, my lamp has gone out, and each time it's as though a wave came and tilted up the gun port lettin' the light in, so I could relight my lamp. I tell you she wants to be saved, and she's helpin' all she can."

It took nearly a month, but the *Vindicta* was rebuilt as best they could with her nearly on her side. Mercifully, her masts were still in their steps but would need a good deal of repair. The standing rigging was sturdy enough, and Richard concluded he could get her back in the water without losing the masts; however, the majority of her running rigging hung in frayed tatters like Spanish moss. They made their repairs as best they could, all the while laboring to empty out her ballast.

When the repairs were as complete as possible, they dug into the sand and sank four inflatable bladders called camels and wedged them under the side of the ship that was not submerged and then pumped them full of air. They attached lines to the *Lorraine* and attempted to pull the stranded ship down to the waterline.

The *Vindicta* was about a hundred and fifty feet long, a good forty feet longer than the *Lorraine*. The first time they tried to pull the *Vindicta* free from the sand, the lines parted, nearly decapitating a sailor. Richard then had the entire off watch applying leverage with poles and pikes while the *Lorraine* was tugging at her. The *Vindicta* budged, but still did not move. He was about to try it again when a tiny hot puff of air caught Richard's attention. He looked westward, and there were no clouds, but nevertheless, he ordered the crew to stow everything and get back aboard the *Lorraine*. Unless his sixth sense for the sea had abandoned him, a squall would appear on the horizon very soon. He did not want to be caught in a storm with the coast on one side of him, Five Fathom Shoals on the other, and Wimble Shoals blocking any passage north.

Everyone had barely gotten aboard when a call came from the

rigging that there was a squall bearing down from the southwest. The *Lorraine* retreated south and then east to more open water so as not to be caught near the shoals in heavy weather.

What appeared to be a fast-moving squall was merely a foothill of a mountainous storm that pounded and pushed them eastward for two days before it finally relented. It was too wide to sail around, so they had to face into the jaws of the storm, bail water, and hang on. When the storm finally blew itself out, the wind was cool and brisk, but the sea was still angry, like a cat whipping its tail in fury, as they sailed back westward.

As they neared Wimble Shoals, hoping against hope the *Vindicta* had not been beaten to splinters, they found no sign of her except for the camels.

Richard went by boat to the little island where she had lain, half hoping to at least get a memento of the *Vindicta*. The lines anchoring the camels had been snarled and snared around some driftwood tree trunks forming almost a lattice work where the ship had been. The sand that had been under the ship was reduced by at least three feet, and Richard was kicking around in it when his boot struck something hard. He brushed away the sand with his hand and underneath was a creamy expanse of smooth stone or shell. He brushed more away to reveal a long, smooth curve. He realized with a start that it was an elephant tusk. He stared in wonder at such a thing here in North Carolina and called the other men over. They began to dig. They uncovered two more tusks right away. Richard sent some of them back to the ship to get shovels and another boat while he and the others kept digging.

As they went down a foot, they could see a dozen overlapping tusks in perfect condition. As they were unearthed, Richard had them set aside in a pile. He laughed at a young sailor who said, "Sir, this will at least compensate for the money you put out to repair the *Vindicta*."

Richard smiled and said, "More than compensate I would think."

They had stopped counting at thirty tusks, but there were at least double that. Some of them were only about twice the size of a man's arm, but some weighed nearly eighty pounds. It took several trips with the two boats to get all the ivory to the ship, but they finally got it stowed below, and were preparing to set sail, when the lookout yelled that he had spotted something strange in a cove ahead. They quickly set out to investigate.

As they sailed closer, the lookout now reported it was a ship wallowing with none of her sails set, and she appeared to be abandoned. Richard climbed into the rigging and looked at the ship through his glass. It was the *Vindicta*. She looked like she was carrying a lot of water, but she was intact, and not in much worse shape than when they abandoned her to run from the storm.

Richard and the carpenter Lockley and his mates went to see how she had fared. Miraculously her pumps worked, and crews were quickly put to emptying her of water. They lashed the ship to a towline and began working on her rigging and rudder in earnest. Two weeks later, she was in excellent shape, but they had exhausted every inch of line they had on board the *Lorraine* to repair her fore and mainmast rigging. The mizzen would just have to wait until they got to a port. Her guns needed some repair to the carriages which had banged about horribly when she rolled over, but most would be working within a few days. Until she was registered as a vessel under a letter of marque, she could only be used for defense, but Richard intended to update his letter as soon as he was sure she could sail properly. She was his to keep based on the ancient right of high-sea salvage. She was abandoned, and she belonged to anyone who took her. He was itching to use her, but he would have to wait for the letter of marque. If he hunted with her sooner than that, he would be no better than a pirate, and convicted pirates still danced from the end of a rope.

Even though *Vindicta* couldn't be used for attack, she made a great show of strength by just being there. Richard captured two British ships in the next two days, and he didn't even have to fire more than a warning shot either time. As he slipped into New York bringing the prizes with him, the people at the Navy pier cheered when they recognized the Stars and Stripes flying above the Union Jack on the prizes.

Richard quickly shed himself of the prizes and altered his letter of marque with the Navy agent to include the *Vindicta*, and then went to a coffeehouse to catch up on the war news. He learned that the very first ship captured in the war had been taken by a Revenue cutter. As Richard sat sipping his coffee he was regaled with other tales of sea battles that had occurred while he was away. A particularly remarkable one had happened the previous month which again involved a Revenue cutter. When Richard questioned him, the coffeehouse proprietor looked at him like he had grown daft. "What you mean? You ain't heard 'bout the *Eagle*? Everyone's heard tell about that, and I'll tell you, them Rev'nue cutter capt'ns got a whole smatherin' of guts they do!" Richard turned to the man next to him, who was bursting to tell the tale, and raised his eyebrows in question. The man next to him claimed he had first heard the tale from one of the actual *Eagle* crew members. He and Richard took a booth, ordered dinner, and the tale unfolded. "It's the damnedest thing you ever heard. The Revenue cutter *Eagle* was patrolling right here off Long Island when she was attacked real badly. They were about to sink right to the bottom, so their captain, Frederick Lee, ran her aground on Long Island, but they were still in range of the British guns."

Richard interrupted him at this point and asked, "Did you say

Frederick Lee?"

"That's him," the man hastily acknowledged. Eager to get back to his tale, he continued, "You'd think that beached and in range of the British, they would have rolled over and given up, but that's not what they did, no, sir. That crew hauled their guns nearly a hundred and fifty feet up to the bluff on the island and set them back up. They fired at the British ship whenever she came in range. When they ran out of cannonballs, Captain Lee told them to look around, that there was plenty. The crew gathered the shot the British had fired at them, loaded it into their own guns, and blasted the British back with their own shot. They kept firing until they ran out of wadding, and then they used their shirts, hats, trousers, and finally, Captain Lee tore up the empty pages in the back of his logbook and used it as the wad for the last shot they fired. It was only then that Captain Lee struck his colors which were pinned to a tree."

"Jesus," Richard said, shaking his head.

The man continued, "You know those British didn't have the guts to come ashore then until another ship came in to cover them. When that British captain finally got on that bluff and took a look at that naked crew, completely black from gunpowder, injured but still standing, he asked where the rest of them were hiding. Old Captain Lee said he only had a crew of twenty-five men to start with, five had been killed before they abandoned ship, and he had to do what he could with the twenty left. Lee explained this as he offered his sword to the other officer. When the British captain understood an American crew of merely twenty had held him and his crew of a hundred, with triple the American's armament, off for all that time, he sheepishly told Captain Lee to keep his sword. The British captain said he couldn't accept a sword from a man who had fought so valiantly. The British returned to their ship, put three or four broadsides into the beached *Eagle* for good measure, and sailed away."

Richard shook his head again, and then he asked, "Do you know where Captain Lee went after that?"

"Why he's right here," the man said. "He and most of his crew were injured, not badly, but certainly in need of care and rest, so they are staying at the Limner Boarding House not far from here until they get a new cutter." He looked at Richard strangely. "Do you know this Captain Lee?"

"I am proud to say I do," Richard said, smiling. "I sailed on his ship when I was just a lad. He was my first captain. Do you know if he is well enough for visitors?" Richard asked.

"The whole town has been up to visit him," the man laughed. "Why, he and his crew have been fed and petted until, just between you and me, I think they are itchin' to get back to sea where only the British will bother them."

Richard left the coffeehouse and made his way along the streets until he came to the boarding house. He stepped through the door and into the parlor and there, with his leg propped up to ease the pain of a wound to his thigh, was Captain Lee. His hair was now snowy white, but his eyes were bright, and the skin on his face amazingly firm. Richard stepped closer and stood before him, smiling. Lee looked up and racked his memory for a name. It was the eyes, those same blue-green eyes set in a boy's face, and then Lee remembered, and said with a smile, "As I live and breathe, young Mr. Holmwood! By God, Richard, how are you?" He tried to stand, but Richard stepped forward and shook his hand. Lee said, "Sit down, son, sit down. I hear tales that you have been up to mischief as a privateer these days. Tell me about it." Lee shifted his weight, getting ready to listen.

"I would rather hear about your battle on the bluff. Now that is interesting," Richard said and leaned back in his chair. The teacher and the pupil exchanged tales until Richard left shortly before midnight. Talking to Lee had been like stepping back in time, back when there was just the excitement of the day and the hope for more tomorrow, before he knew what it was to love, and before he knew what it was to lose that love, and it was a welcome respite.

THE *VINDICTA* received her letter of marque and Richard took command of her, while he left the command of the *Lorraine* to Shaw. Working together, the two ships took dozens of prizes in the next eight months. On one occasion they had captured so many prizes, and the crews were so thin, that Owen, barely fourteen, had to command a prize until they reached port.

As the captured ships were sold for cash, Richard's wealth grew, and so did his notorious reputation among the British. He sailed his tiny fleet south to Bermuda where it nearly disrupted the English sugar trade. He had become an expert at creating the impression that his ship was damaged. The British had been stung so many times by this trick that they were becoming wary. The *Lorraine* would appear to be damaged and when a British captain, overcome with greed, tried to take her, the *Vindicta*, which was waiting just over the horizon, would swiftly appear. A few escaped to tell the tale of fakery, bolstering Richard's reputation, and the British bestowed on him the highest honor they could give to an enemy, a nickname. They called him "The Killdeer" after the meadow bird who flops about so piteously dragging its broken wing that a predator can't help but follow.

The idea for the elaborate pretense came about accidentally as Richard watched two men in the crew load barrels onto the ship. They were both freed slaves and unbelievably strong. Richard quickly learned that the freed slaves were honest and loyal, fought like demons any enemy that might again oppress them, and above all, were powerful.

The *Vindicta* was provisioning and Richard watched as the chandler's cart pulled up piled high with provisions. To his amazement, two of the crew, rather than rig a block and tackle, each picked up a barrel and hoisted it onto his shoulder, carried it onboard and into the hold. The barrels had to weigh at least two hundred pounds.

Richard quietly stepped up to the two of them and asked, "How much do you think you could move with a block?"

The older of the two men, Jameson, said, "Sir, I could probably move six, seven hundred pounds, and more if I could get my back against something." The other man nodded in agreement, and this gave Richard an idea. If he could get them to extend the tackle on the guns enough to get the weight slightly off center of the ship, she would list to one side. The ship would then appear to be damaged and leaking, but when the enemy came near, the guns could be pulled back into place and begin firing upon the unsuspecting ship.

The first time he tried it, the plan worked like a charm. Jameson then took over and showed the others how to move the most weight with the least amount of leverage. From then on, Richard was on the lookout for powerful men like Jameson, and in turn those same men sought out Richard. Many times he would sail into port to find several freed slaves waiting for him.

Over time, Richard perfected the image of a wounded ship by adding a fake mast which appeared to be snapped off just below the platform, and canvas rolls would be hung over the side which looked remarkably like snapped yards and pieces of mast. A knotted web of lines hung from the snapped mast which looked just like torn rigging, and the whole affair could be jettisoned at a moment's notice. This clever fakery, along with the listing of the American privateer, was more than many British sea hunters could resist.

RICHARD HAD JUST taken a prize, a small sloop loaded with rope, food, and gunpowder intended for the British fleet. With these supplies he would be able to stay at sea another two months. The crew had just completed stowing the supplies on the *Vindicta* when they spotted another British ship. It must have seen them as well, because it awkwardly came about and began to flee, though the set of its sails was all wrong. The American ships set off after it and soon caught up. As Richard peered at the ship through his glass, he realized it was beautiful. It was long and sat low in the water, so low at first he thought it had taken on water, but as he watched it slice through the waves, he realized it was simply her hull design. He looked at her rigging and shook his head. Whoever the captain was, he needed lessons. The tension on the running rigging was all wrong, and the sails appeared to have been set at the pier and never adjusted. The *Vindicta* easily caught up with her, and Richard ordered a warning shot to be fired. It dropped into the water about twenty feet from the ship, and he now demanded surrender through a speaking trumpet. He secretly hoped the other captain would give up without a fight because the ship was too beautiful to destroy. She immediately struck her colors and sat wallowing in the waves with what appeared to be her entire crew on deck.

Richard sailed in close enough to look down at the ship's captain. He was perhaps twenty-one, and very slight, hardly bigger than Owen. As Richard stood staring, the young captain waved and smiled weakly. Richard now looked more closely at his prize, and she fit her namesake, *Draco Mare*, the sea dragon.

They lashed some lines to the *Draco Mare*, and to the crew's horror, Richard swung over alone and landed on the deck of the captured ship. He animatedly pulled the young captain about pointing out adjustments he could have made to the ship here and ways to capture more wind there. The young captain stood nodding his head, and then he finally said, "Sir, why are you telling me all this?"

"A ship like this is like a fine horse, and it needs to be given its head to find its stride. You have her cinched so tight, she barely leans. This is a magnificent ship, and if you had rigged her right, I would never have been able to catch you," Richard said, looking around smiling.

The young captain stuttered and said, "Then you are not going to take it from me?"

Richard smiled. "Oh, I'm going to take her from you, I just wanted you to know," he said, assuming that all men were interested in seamanship and its improvement. "Now," he said good-naturedly, "tell me your name, and identify your cargo."

"Benson, sir, Jonas Benson, and I don't know what my cargo is, exactly," he said, looking over at the deck of the *Vindicta*, which was crawling with curious sailors.

"How is it you don't know your own cargo?" Richard said doubtfully.

"It was already here when my father sent me aboard. I really don't sail very much," to which Richard had to refrain from saying no kidding, but the young man continued explaining, "and my father said it would make a man of me, and that I had spent too much time on books and numbers." Benson looked about the deck and then at Richard and added, "He is going to be very angry at me for losing this ship."

Richard nodded and then said, "Sorry about that, but war is war."

"Are we prisoners now?" Benson asked, almost like a child.

Richard shook his head, "We are about thirty miles from shore, and I don't see any foul weather about, so I will put you and your crew into a cutter and you can head for land."

Benson looked horrified and backed away saying, "Sir, I would rather be your prisoner, than to get into the cutter. Please, set my crew free, but don't make me go, not in that little boat. My background is in accounts and ledgers, not sailing. I hate the sea."

Richard stared at him confused and then looked around at Benson's crew. He could tell they did not choose captivity over escape, so he ordered up the cutter, supplied them well, and pointed them in the direction of the shoreline. Without a backward glance, the crew steered the cutter for shore leaving Jonas Benson to his fate with the Americans. Jonas could offer no information as to who had built the *Draco Mare*, only that he had been told by his father to sail her to Jamaica, deliver her cargo safely, and not to come home until he did so. Benson was no sailor, and it is a wonder his crew hadn't mutinied before he managed to get separated from the small convoy with which he was sailing.

The *Draco Mare* was indeed a stunning ship. At nearly two hundred forty feet and with a beam of only thirty-two feet, she was long and lean and sat low in the water, but her depth below the waterline was deceptive. With a draft of twenty-four feet, she was not the vessel to cruise in shallow coastal waters. *Draco Mare* was black as liquid pitch and built for blue water. She carried as much sail as a large frigate on her three steeply raked masts, and her combination of fore-and-aft and square rigged sails made her fast, but still extremely maneuverable. In the right hands and properly armed, she could turn quickly, sting with her guns, and then sprint away.

It wasn't just that *Draco Mare* was fast, she was also beautiful. Whoever had built her had an artist's bent. The theme of the dragon was carried throughout the ship. The gunwales were patterned in scales depicting dragon skin, her cleats were open claws, and every belaying pin was topped by a carved dragon's head. She was black and gold and she gleamed. The binnacle posts were each a dragon's arm and the ship's bell hung from a curled dragon tail. It should all have combined to look ridiculous, but it did not. The final stroke to the *Draco Mare's* beauty was her figurehead. It was a woman, naked to the waist, with the lower half of her body a curling dragon's tail. She was covered from the waist down with carved intricate scales painted gleaming black. Her head, arms, and torso were glimmering gold, almost like gold foil, and her full, carved breasts were studded with pointed claw-like nipples while carved locks of black hair coursed down her back. Her arms were held at her sides with the tip of her tail curled around one wrist. Her eyes were closed and her head thrown back as if she were sniffing the wind for quarry. She wore a menacingly erotic smile which exposed her gleaming black fangs. There was something perilous yet attractive about her.

They set about getting her ready to sail with a prize crew and performed some routine maintenance that had been abandoned since the *Draco Mare* was separated from her convoy. Some of this repair involved touching the figurehead as they cleaned and adjusted rigging to the bowsprit. More than one sailor who laid hands on the figurehead confessed to having erotic and disturbing dreams for several nights after having touched her.

The cargo was also something of a puzzle. When Richard went through the hold, he found it loaded with crates and barrels filled with nothing but sand. Owen had grown increasingly angry as each one was opened, and he finally stalked off to sulk. When Richard questioned Jonas, he swore he knew nothing of it, and, if anything, seemed hurt his father had him risk his life to transport such useless cargo.

They used the sand to replace the ship's ballast, which had become rather foul, and broke down the empty barrels and crates. The only thing of value, other than the ship itself, was found in the great cabin in a locked cabinet for which even Jonas didn't have a key. Wrapped in layers of straw were several rhinoceros horns. Richard only knew of them from pictures, but he had read that they could be traded like gold in the Orient. In the bottom of the cabinet in a small leather bag were about a dozen medium-sized cut emeralds which Richard locked in his cabin. They transferred the horns to the *Lorraine* and set sail for home to cash in their prize. It was a cold February day with a chilly wind, and they all wanted to get home and rest if the harbor was not still blockaded.

As the little squadron was approaching Charleston to take on food and water, they were hailed by a passing ship. Richard received the astounding news that the war was over. The treaty with England had been signed on Christmas Eve, but word had not reached America until the latter part of February. There was a general shout of relief from the crews of the three ships, and when they finally found berths in the crowded harbor, Richard granted his sailors a long and deserved liberty.

He sought out the Navy agent in Charleston, and was told there was no money to pay him for the *Draco Mare*, but he could keep her and sell her in any market he chose. Richard was almost relieved. He had quickly become fond of the beautiful black ship, and had dreaded parting with her. She would now be the fastest ship he owned, not much on comfort, but stiff, sleek, and made for speed.

When they reached Norfolk, Richard and Owen set out for Scotland Neck. He had been home only twice in the last several years, and he wondered now if Edward would even know him. He felt guilty that he had not really thought about him very much, and knew in his heart they were practically strangers.

Richard and Owen made it halfway up the long drive to the house before Grub spotted them, and he came barking and whining, trying to lick them both as he squirmed like a puppy. "Well, old boy, at least you don't smell any differently," Richard said, laughing at the odiferous beast.

Wrennet had come to the door to investigate Grub's barking, and when she saw them she wrapped them both in a vice-like hug and did not let them go until they reached the house. As they entered, Edward ran and hid behind Wrennet's skirts.

Richard squatted down and called to him. Edward stepped out from behind Wrennet, and both Owen and Richard gasped. He looked just like his mother. "Come here, son," Richard called to him. Edward looked at Wrennet, who nodded smiling, and he came forward. Richard waited, holding out his hands, and with a final look back at Wrennet, Edward launched himself into his father's arms. Richard stood laughing and patting Edward's back, but Owen did not smile. Looking at Edward brought back painful memories of his mother, and it also reminded him of why she was not alive. If it had not been for Edward, she would still be with him, so he turned on his heel and climbed the stairs to his room.

Richard stayed two weeks in Scotland Neck and then left for Washington to see what was in store for him. He was still commissioned, and, as such, required to report. There was a general homecoming of many of Preble's Boys, and they traded stories and news, and time wore on as he awaited orders. Finally, near the end of September, Richard found out what the Navy had in mind for him.

He met with a Commodore Perkins, who reminded him of the latitude the Navy had extended when he requested a leave of absence to act as a privateer. The Navy now was calling in that favor. Commodore Perkins, who looked perpetually tired and put-upon, said, "This peace with the British is very fresh, and I am not sure it will take. Both sides agreed in the treaty, but these things have a way of going bad. We were caught with our proverbial pants down on the Great Lakes, and we don't want to be there again, at least in the short haul with this new peace. What we are asking you to do is to go to Mackinac Island, located in the Straits of Mackinac between Lake Michigan and Lake Huron, under the guise of supporting the American Fur Company which has its headquarters there. You are known as a merchant as much as a naval officer, so it will not seem as odd for you to go there now to seek new trade. What you will be in reality is an armed force in the event the British do not keep their word. You will be required to remain there for approximately five years."

"Five years?" Richard said almost as if he had heard incorrectly.

Perkins nodded. "That should be sufficient to make sure this peace will stick. I would encourage you to take your family. The government is anxious to settle the area more, and you could hasten that end. There is a treaty with the native population there, and, frankly, I have more confidence in that treaty than the one with the British. I know for a fact my ships are too large to make it through the Welland Rapids up the St. Lawrence River."

"Are you providing me with ships already there?" Richard asked.

"You will have the use of the ships left from Commodore Perry's fleet. I have reports that they are in good order, though as you know, they were not made to last long term, but for the battle only, but they should last as long as you need them. You will transfer from your own ships at Welland, where it will be necessary to portage and to load onto the fleet ships on the other side of the rapids," Perkins explained.

"When do you expect me to report?" Richard asked.

"At this juncture, and we do understand there will be some preparations you will need to make to be away for five years, you will be expected to arrive in Welland to relieve the fleet there by June. If you were to leave now you would arrive in the worst of the Great Lakes' weather conditions and would not have time to make proper preparations for your fleet before the lakes froze over." Perkins continued to talk, but Richard's mind was abuzz with thoughts of being away from his own ships and saltwater for five years. He came back into the conversation as Perkins was saying, "Of course it may be necessary for you to return to the East Coast once or twice, but you are expected to remain there as a defense if needed. You will also be taking two cartographers who will spend their time increasing the accuracy of the lake charts. Don't let the word "lake" fool you, the water may be sweet there, but it is an inland ocean in all other respects. I understand the weather is extremely changeable there and the storms legendary, but you come recommended to me as the seaman of your age by men who should know such things, so I don't think you will find it too difficult to adjust to sweet water sailing."

They talked for nearly two hours more, and Richard finally left, orders in hand, to begin preparations to be away from Scotland Neck. As he walked back to the ship, he thought about how his business would carry on without him. Shaw was a capable captain, and had spoken about resigning his naval commission to sail merchantmen for Richard. Owen was nearly eighteen, and though young, he was an excellent sailor, and even Jordan Ladysmith, young as he was, would be valuable. Jordan had already resigned as a midshipman, against Richard's advice, and signed on with him. There were two other captains Richard employed, but what he needed was a controller, one who was good with inventory, and above all one who would be honest. Richard arrived back in Scotland Neck and broke the news to his family. Owen was excited at the prospect of commanding his own ship, but Wrennet just shook her head. Richard said he had no intention of taking Edward with him to the Northern Territory; he felt it was too dangerous. Edward would stay home with Wrennet and go to school, but Wrennet's head-shaking told him otherwise. Wrennet explained, "I am too old to take care of him by myself. Lately, I have felt poorly and don't know what strength I would have left in five years. I love Edward too much to say I can take care of him when I don't think I can. You will have to leave him with your father, or your aunts in Boston." "I can't leave him with my father. He is weaker than you, and Edward wouldn't be a good fit for the Puppets." "Well then, you'll do what you should have done already," Wrennet said, looking at him over her spectacles, "get yourself a wife."

"That is the last thing I want, and you know it," Richard said sourly and left. He walked down to the ship and stood staring out over the water. He could take Edward with him if he was a little older, but as it was, he was too young. He would think about it later, but for now he congratulated himself on solving the problem of the controller. It turned out that when he returned from Washington and stopped in Hampton, Jonas Benson was still on board the *Vindicta*. He explained that he thought he was a part of the crew now, or at the very least a prisoner. Richard explained that he was free to go back to England, and the little man nearly broke into tears. It turned out that Benson was as good at accounting as he was bad at sailing, and Richard trusted his gut feeling and hired him to stay in Hampton and run the shore operation and keep the books. It was a risk since Benson had been an enemy only months before, but Richard sensed in him an honest spirit. A month went by, and with the problem of a controller solved, Richard was still forced to make a decision about Edward. He was still pondering it when a small ship arrived. Richard walked over and greeted Jacob Spencer, a merchant sailor who, like Gabriel Holmwood, stayed within the bounds of the Chesapeake Bay.

"Richard, good to see you home safe through the war," Jacob said, shaking Richard's hand. They settled in the warehouse for a drink and caught up. They drank more than they had intended as tale upon tale unfolded, and before he knew it, Richard had divulged his need for a wife. "Well, what kind of woman are you looking for?" Jacob asked as if they were talking about purchasing boots or a coat. "I want someone settled, someone who will be good to Edward, and can take care of the house." Richard thought a moment. "A widow would probably be best," he said, not believing he was saying it. He had sworn to himself he would never sully Lorraine's memory by remarrying, and here he was actively discussing a future wife like it was of no consequence.

"Well, you might try Widow Duggan. She ain't too bad, and she's a jolly good housekeeper," Jacob said. Richard nodded, not having the least intention of considering her, and the conversation turned to other things.

A week went by and Wrennet prodded him for what he intended to do about Edward, reiterating again she could not take care of him alone. There had been times when Richard was away during the war, when she had panicked about what would happen to Edward if she got ill.

Richard couldn't believe he was doing it, but at Jacob Spencer's advice he sought out Mrs. Duggan, a widow of his age, perhaps thirty-five, who ran a boarding house in Surry three miles away. He concocted some tale of why he had to stay at her place rather than at his own house or on his ship, but in the end he got a room for two nights.

The first night he looked her over carefully as she moved about the sitting room, and she didn't seem too bad. She was tall and stout, and had as serviceable a prow as any of his ships, and she ran a spotless house. He thought she might be worth pursuing for Edward's sake. He polished off the baked chicken and blackberry pie she served and was even more convinced she would fit the bill, if she was willing.

Richard retired to his room. He attempted to imagine the widow in his own kitchen, or his sitting room, and furthermore without her linen dress, but he couldn't. Every time he tried, Mrs. Duggan transformed into a vision of his mother, and it turned his stomach. Still, he didn't really need to like her, she just needed to be good to Edward.

There was a knock at the door, and just as he was about to answer it Mrs. Duggan strode in. She held out her hand and said, "I need that shirt, Captain Holmwood. The prices here include washing and pressing clothes. Nanny, the washerwoman, likes to get an early start on things, and she'll want them soaking overnight, so let's get that shirt off." Richard stood staring at her as though nailed to the floor. The Widow Duggan looked him up and down and then pointed to his pants. "Oh, and you've gone and gotten berry on those britches. That will have to soak as well, or that stain will set permanent like. There's not much more stubborn than blackberry. Give them to me as well." Richard looked trapped, but he turned and obediently unbuttoned his shirt and put it on the bed. Widow Duggan snatched it away and said again, "Get those pants off, too." Richard was certain that he had been transported back to his childhood. He was sure that if he but turned his head he would see his mother standing there with a switch at the ready. Widow Duggan snorted as he hesitated, "Modesty, Captain? Goodness! I've had three husbands and nine sons, and you don't have anything in those drawers that hasn't been seen by these eyes before. Give me the pants." Richard obeyed, slipped off his pants, and handed them to her. He stood in nothing but his drawers trying to resist the urge to cup himself with his hands for protection. Widow Duggan snatched the pants and breezed out the door shaking her head. Richard stood staring after her.

It didn't matter how good of a cook she was, or how well she kept house, he couldn't muster the courage to stay around her another night, and he certainly wouldn't subject Edward to her dominance. Now that he had been around her, she looked to be the type of woman who would inspect the back of your neck after you washed it and who would be overly interested in the movement of your bowels, so, no, she definitely would not do.

It was now back to Jacob Spencer, and the next woman he suggested was not at all dominant, but plump and chipper. Dolly Basser was the widow of Norman Basser, who had died some years before. She had two teenage daughters just as plump as she, and Richard thought it might be nice for Edward to have sisters.

Richard rarely attended church, but Jacob Spencer said the Bassers attended every Sunday, so there he sat watching them like a predator on the hunt. His opportunity to meet them came just as he was leaving the church. When he stepped outside, he found it was beginning to rain. The Basser women had walked to church, so taking them home in his carriage provided the perfect excuse to get to know Dolly. Richard told Wrennet and Edward to wait at the church, and he would come back for them as soon as he dropped off Mrs. Basser and her girls.

The Bassers piled into the carriage barely leaving room for Richard among their wide backsides and prominent breasts. They started off and though Dolly was right next to him, she yelled, "Oh, Captain, this is most kind," as she jogged his arm in jolly fashion. She then craned around to look at her daughters, who giggled, and she said to them for Richard's benefit, "And we thought we would have to walk home in the rain. Remember the last time we did that? We all fell in the mud right there by the river!" She snorted and laughed aloud and continued, "Remember girls? Remember how we looked like red-skinned hostiles with that mud all over us?" She punctuated this with a snort and punched Richard in the ribs. The girls tried to tell the rest of the story of the red mud, but they couldn't stop laughing long enough. Finally exhausted, Mrs. Basser stopped to wipe her eyes, but she still jiggled with mirth on the seat beside Richard. He smiled down at her, sizing her up. She had a jolly face with an overly pink complexion, and she was not what he could call pretty, but she only needed to be good to Edward until he got back. What he would do then he didn't know, but by then Edward would be old enough to go to sea with him, and they could spend most of their time away from home.

One of the horses snorted just then, and Dolly looked over at Richard and burst out laughing again. Between guffaws she got out, "Oh, Captain Holmwood, this reminds me of the time, back when my dear Mr. Basser was still with us, when our horse got into the oat barrel. He was so bloated that he made oat-music all the way to town!" She looked at Richard's startled face and added, "Oh, no, Captain, not Mr. Basser, it was the horse what made the music." She turned to the girls and laughed, "Oh, girls, he thought I meant Papa made the oat noises!" At this, all three women commenced imitating a flatulent horse, and they laughed until Richard thought they would faint. When they finally calmed down some, he tried turning the conversation to the weather and the condition of the road, but no matter what he said, it caused nothing but giggles from the lot. If he even looked at them, they started snickering, and it was a relief to finally drop them off at their doorstep. He was practically rude declining the offer of tea as he climbed back into the carriage to flee. Richard looked back over his shoulder as he left, but even that caused howls and snorts. He rode away knowing he had failed to find a mother for Edward, but also knew that in doing so he had saved his own life. If he married Dolly Basser, he would be hanged, for he knew with absolute certainty he would strangle her within a week.

Richard saw Jacob Spencer and reported his most recent failure to locate a suitable wife. "Perhaps you are looking at women too settled," Jacob said. "I know you said you don't want to saddle a young woman with running your house, but you might take a look at my daughter, Mary Margaret. She is pretty and clean, nearly as good a housekeeper as her mother, and I have never had to raise my hand to her in her life." Richard began to shake his head, but Jacob spoke for him, "I'll tell my wife you are coming for dinner tomorrow. You meet my Mary, and then see what you think."

As Jacob was about to leave, Richard stopped him and asked, "She isn't soft on someone else is she?" He then clarified, "I wouldn't want her to say yes to me because the man she wants hasn't yet asked her."

Jacob smiled and shook his head, "There have been a few young toms sniffing around, but she doesn't seem to show much interest in them, or certainly not to one in particular." Richard shook his head uneasily, but agreed to the dinner. He was running out of time.

Richard arrived at the Spencer house the following evening a few minutes early and was shown into the parlor by a woman about twenty years old. She was large and course and had a simple, not overly bright look about her. Arla Spencer, Jacob's wife, came into the room just then and greeted him, then said, "Thank you, Mary, I will take care of Captain Holmwood. " Richard looked at the girl as she left the room, wondering how old Spencer could ever stretch her into any category of prettiness. Jacob entered a moment later followed by his two eldest sons, Adrian and Ben. Both men lived at home with their wives and children in the spacious Spencer house onto which they had built additions as their families grew. Jacob and Arla Spencer had six sons ranging in age from nineteen to thirty, but only one daughter, Mary, who was also the baby of the family.

Jacob offered Richard a drink, and he accepted with perhaps a bit more enthusiasm than he intended, but it was going to be a long night, and it would do to take off the edge. He sat sipping his wine while the others filed into the parlor waiting for dinner. "Where's the baby, mother?" Jacob asked Arla, looking around the room for his daughter.

"Oh, she was just here a moment ago, but if she has gone wandering by the river again, she'll catch it from me even if she is eighteen," Arla said tartly, pursing her lips. Just then the large girl, Mary, appeared again, and Arla said to her, "Mary, where is that girl?" She just shook her head and Richard looked from her to Arla confused. If she wasn't Mary, then who was?

The clock struck seven and Arla looked at Jacob, and he shook his head. They entered the dining room, and as they were milling around finding their places, Richard saw a girl nip in through the side door to the dining room and take her seat. She unfolded her napkin and looked around as though she had been there all along. He gave her a light nod, and she grinned back exposing dimples in both of her cheeks. Jacob caught sight of her and said, "There's Marget. Your mother said we would not hold dinner for you if you were out walking again, but now that you are here, let me introduce you. Captain Holmwood, may I introduce my daughter, Mary Margaret, whom we call Marget." They bowed to each other, and as everyone was settling, Richard took the opportunity to look at her closely. She was absolutely tiny. If she stood in front of him, he doubted she would come above the center of his chest. Her skin was a creamy pink, and her dark eyes sparkled under long, thick lashes which matched her curly hair piled on her head in a saucy way. He also noted as she leaned forward to adjust her chair that she possessed a lovely and shockingly healthy bust line.

Richard was caught between two brewing conversations on either side of him. As he looked across the table at Mary, she smiled back almost in sympathy. The Spencers were a lively lot with big appetites and the table was fairly groaning with food. Richard was not used to such fabulous fare and he did his part in making it disappear. As the meal progressed, Richard looked around the table at the Spencer clan. They were all dark-haired with rosy cheeks. He was just thinking what pleasant manners they all had when his eyes found Emma, Ben Spencer's wife. She was sizing him up as if she would eat him alive given half a chance. Richard had seen that hungry look before, and he suspected it might be for this very reason that Ben kept Emma at his family's home rather than give her one of her own.

Richard had been raised in a large family of boys, and it was comfortable now to return to the loud and strident table conversations he recalled from the first half of his life. The Spencers were a merry lot, well-educated and warm-hearted. He could marry into a much worse family. He looked at Mary trying to picture her as a wife, and it dawned on him she was the same age as Owen. While the Spencers had been breeding up Mary in Scotland Neck, he and Lorraine had been rolling around in Rosalind Cottage building Owen. It seemed almost wrong to marry someone so young, though men did it all the time. He thought with a pang that perhaps if Lorraine hadn't been so much older than him, Mary wouldn't then seem so much younger.

They finished dinner and the ladies departed to the sitting room. Emma and Diana had barely made it through the door before they asked, "What is he doing here?" Arla Spencer said honestly that she didn't know. Jacob had prudently kept her in the dark not wanting her to do any obvious matchmaking that might scare Richard off.

When the men joined them in the drawing room, they all sat around talking. There were a few games of cards before Richard departed. As he rode home, he remembered pleasantly being married, but it just seemed wrong to be with anyone but Lorraine. He had promised himself he would never marry again, and now he was actively working to break that promise. Mary Spencer was the first one he had come across who did not absolutely repel him, so he decided he would keep an open mind about her. She was the exact opposite of Lorraine. In some way, that was comforting. He would just wait and see what happened, but he didn't have forever. He would join the Spencers for tea the following Tuesday.

Jacob confided in Arla Spencer later that night the reason for Richard's visit, admonishing her to keep it to herself. Of course, the first thing Arla did the next morning was tell Emma and Diana. "Can you imagine little Marget catching a husband like Captain Holmwood? He is certainly handsome, and he has that nice house on the hill. They say he was devoted to his first wife, moved here heartbroken," she gushed, "and has never shown the slightest interest in any lady." Arla smiled and added, "Now he may be after our little princess." She sipped her breakfast tea and continued, "Of course that house will need a little fixing up after having only the Captain and his boys living there with old Wrennet and those two lazy girls she keeps on hand." Arla poured more tea and then added, "Little Marget will have her own house. I can hardly believe it."

"Will she set up housekeeping right away, mother?" Emma asked with an edge to her voice. There was a vast difference between getting married and setting up housekeeping, and one didn't necessarily bring about the other. Many young women lived with their families after they were married. The husband would come and go from the house, but they would not have their own home for a while. Many times they did not have the money, or the house was not ready, or the woman was pregnant and wanted to be with her own mother when the child was born. It was not totally unheard of for a woman to be several months pregnant when they got married, and, in fact, Emma had been just such a case. She and Ben had gotten married very quickly and Ben stayed with Emma's family when he was ashore for nearly a year. After that year he had decided to build onto the Spencer home. The addition was completed before he ever checked with Emma, who wanted a home built. She was furious, but obedient. It turned out that living at the Spencers was pleasant. No mother-in-law could be kinder than Arla Spencer, nor did one ever have a sharper eye.

When Adrian, the eldest brother, married his wife Diana, they too joined the Spencer household. Emma and Diana quickly each produced two boys, adding four more people to the already large household. Both women would have killed for their own home and to finally be out from under the keen eye of Arla Spencer. They now stared silently at her, unable to trust what they might say, as she advised them that Marget, the princess, would indeed have her own house if and when she and Captain Holmwood were married.

Mary was the baby of the family, and the only girl, so the Spencers made no bones about it that she was their princess. Both Emma and Diana envied the freedom Mary would have once she left home. She could indulge in a harmless little flirt if she felt like it or could take a day and decide not to get up until noon. They were even more envious that Mary would have a husband who was away for years. After breakfast they slipped out of the house and began to plot their revenge.

That same day, Jacob called Mary into his study. She was a little confused as she closed the door quietly behind her. She had many times wandered into her father's study to sit by the fireplace and read, but she had never been summoned there like her brothers. Adrian and Ben and the middle twins, Lawrence and James, were older and practically grown men when Mary was born, but her youngest brothers, Joshua and William, had been close enough in age that Mary could remember them being summoned into their father's study, and it was not a summons they relished. The whole house would wait, pretending not to listen, but unable to shut out the sound of Jacob Spencer dispensing justice behind the closed door.

Mary now stood before her father, racking her brain for anything she had done wrong. He smiled up at her and motioned for her to sit down. She sat on the very edge of her chair and waited to hear what he had to say. He cleared his throat and said, "What did you think of Captain Holmwood?"

Mary looked at him and shrugged, "I didn't really think anything of him. He was polite, and he's handsome, but other than that, I really didn't think about him." She said after a moment, "I really have never seen him about here much. Isn't he away most of the time?"

Jacob nodded, "Yes, he's away much of the time. You know his son, Owen, don't you?"

Mary nodded, not giving voice to how much she did not like Owen Holmwood, or rather how much she did not trust him. She had danced with him a few times, but he had been too free with his hands. When she tried to pull away, he had glared at her reminding her of a cat with a mouse, a cat which isn't hungry but still enjoys the kill. "Why do you ask, Papa?" Mary said.

Jacob came right to the point, "What kind of a husband do you think he would make?"

"Owen or Captain Holmwood, sir?" Mary asked, dreading that her father and Captain Holmwood were conspiring for her to marry Owen.

"The Captain, of course, what kind of a husband do you think he would make for you?" Jacob said, watching carefully for her reaction.

"For me?" Mary asked surprised. "Why?"

"He has expressed an interest in you, that is why. He's coming to tea on Tuesday, and I would like you to speak to him with this in mind," Jacob said softly.

"Do you think I should marry him, Papa, if he should ask?" Mary questioned.

"Yes, Marget, I think you should." Jacob smiled at his only daughter. "He would be a very good catch for any woman." Secretly, Jacob could not overlook the fact that between his shipping company and Richard's they would be a formidable force of trade in the Chesapeake Bay, but instead he said, "I have never heard anything but good about him."

"Do you know him very well?" Mary asked.

"Not extremely well, but what I know is very good. Child, say yes if he asks."

"If he asks, Papa. If he asks."

On Tuesday, Richard arrived at tea time to find the entire household waiting. This only confirmed his suspicion that they all now knew his mission. Emma and Diana stared openly at him, trying to work out how Marget had done it. How had prissy little Marget attracted the attention of this handsome and confirmed widower? This was a man who had shown no interest in any other women, even in those who had tried openly to capture him. What was her secret?

Mary looked more closely at Richard while he spoke with her father. She had not paid much attention to him that first night at dinner, but she looked carefully at him now. He was tall, much taller than Jacob Spencer, and very broad through the shoulders. His hair was light brown and cropped very close to his head. He had no facial hair and had even done away with the sideburns so many men were sporting these days. His eyes were a strange mixture of blue and green, and oddly but interestingly shaped. The lids were slightly heavy on the outer edge causing his eyes to seem almost triangular. Richard Holmwood looked like a man who could take care of himself, which meant, Mary thought, he could take care of her.

Richard sat sipping his tea and sneaking glances at Mary while Jacob rattled on about the weather. She was even tinier than he remembered, but she was very well shaped, and Richard realized with a jolt of shame that he had not been paying any attention when Jacob spoke to him. Jacob then repeated his request that Richard give Mary a turn in the garden which still had something to offer even this late in the year. Richard rose rather abruptly and offered his arm to Mary who took it gingerly as they walked toward the rear of the house.

They walked for about fifty yards while Mary stiffly pointed out what flowers were where when they were in season, but there was nothing in bloom except a few wild asters, and even they looked a little leggy and tired. They reached a stone bench where Richard motioned for her to sit. On the bench they stared ahead silently. Richard finally cleared his throat and said, "Miss Spencer, I am not one for small talk or hinting about things. May I speak plainly to you?"

"Please do, sir," Mary said, waiting.

Richard took a deep breath to begin what was undoubtedly the most awkward conversation of his life, "Miss Spencer, your family has no doubt spoken to you about why I am here?" Mary nodded, and he continued, "I have been a widower now for nearly six years, and I swore to myself I would never marry again, but I have to leave on a mission that will last about five years. My son Edward is not yet six and needs a mother to look after him. If he were a few years older, I would take him with me, but he is too young, and his nurse is too old to keep him. So here I am, though I am ashamed to admit it, shopping for a wife. When your father knew my predicament, he suggested I meet you."

"Why me?" Mary asked curiously.

"Why not you?" Richard shifted uneasily. "I will not lie to you and tell you something trifling about my heart being captured. Even though Scotland Neck is a small place, and though I am familiar with your father and brothers, I don't think I have ever been introduced to you before a few days ago." He turned to look at Mary and added, "It would not be a lie though for me to tell you I will do whatever is in my power to make your life with me as pleasant as possible. As I said, I am away a great deal of the time, and that should sweeten the prospect for you." Richard smiled, then added, "Miss Spencer, I am willing to marry you if you will have me, but you must know without any doubt that I don't love you, nor would I ever. You must make no mistake about this point."

Mary looked at him and then said quietly, "I understand, sir, and to be honest, I don't love you either. As to whether I ever could or would, how can I possibly know? I think though we could at least be friends and be kind to each other, couldn't we?" Richard nodded. He was awed at this refreshing view from a woman, and listened carefully as Mary continued, "If I were to say yes, you must understand why I would do so." It seemed important for Mary to explain herself, and Richard nodded for her to continue. She said, "I want to be out from under my mother's thumb. It's not because I want to run wild, but that I want to be able to breathe freely. My mother is wonderful, but she has a way of taking up all the air in the room and then convincing you that you didn't need to breathe in the first place." She looked at Richard and said, "Sir, you need a mother for your son. I want a way out of my parent's house. We can provide this to each other, and if you were to ask me, I would say yes."

Richard smiled at her frankness, and rose offering his arm to Mary, saying, "Perhaps we should go and tell your family."

Mary looked at him, but she refused to move. She said with a little grin, "Captain Holmwood, I said I would say yes if you asked me. You have not asked."

Richard chuckled and sat back down on the bench. He cleared his throat and said softly, "Will you marry me, Miss Spencer, and be my friend?"

"Yes," she smiled, and finally took the arm he offered. She glanced toward the house and added, "And I think we should tell my family right away, if only to save them from themselves. Look." She pointed to where the whole Spencer family was crowded into the dining room pressing their faces against the windows. By the time Richard and Mary reached the house, the family had abandoned the windows and adopted poses of intense relaxation in the sitting room. Richard looked down at Mary as they entered the sitting room and gave her a quick wink, and then he asked if he might speak with Jacob in private. As the two men left, the women swarmed around Mary asking her questions all at once.

Mary put her hand up to silence them. "Yes, Captain Holmwood asked me to marry him, and, yes, I told him I would. He is speaking to Papa about it now." Arla Spencer threw up her hands and squealed with delight. Diana smiled weakly, but Emma looked daggers at Mary, still trying to comprehend how this little mite had garnered the likes of Richard Holmwood.

RICHARD TOLD HIS SONS at dinner. He simply said, "I am getting married right after the new year."

Both boys stared at him with forks halfway to their mouths, and then Owen said, "Do you have a bride in mind, or are you starting your search now?

Richard laughed and said, "I have one in mind, and she and her Papa have already said yes. The date has been set as well!" He tipped his glass toward Owen and drank deeply.

"Do you plan to tell us who our stepmother will be, or do we have to see her at the wedding?" Owen asked and then said to Edward in a wicked tone, "I'll bet she is some old widow who will thrash you before and after she drinks all the rum Papa has put aside!" Owen leered at Edward, and Edward looked to his father, silently pleading with him to deny this horror.

"She is no old widow," Richard laughed and added, "I think you know her, Owen. She is about your age. Mary Spencer, Old Jacob Spencer's daughter."

Owen's face turned hard. He knew Mary Spencer all right, but she would barely give him the time of day. She danced with him once at a party, but pulled away as soon as the music stopped and refused to dance with him again, and it enraged him. It was easy for Owen to disarm most girls with big talk and his pretty looks. Many times with a flash of his bright smile, they would come undone, dropping their reserve as well as their drawers. Mary Spencer, though, had been immune to his charms, sweetening the quest for her all the more. He said now with an edge to his voice, "Mary Spencer has agreed to marry you?"

"She has, son, just over two months from tomorrow to be exact. It'll be right after the beginning of the new year." Richard smiled and drank from his wine glass again, and then turned to Edward and asked, "Well, son, you will finally have someone to call mother. What do you think of that?"

Edward didn't know what to say having no recollection of his own mother. He had always dreamed of having one, but he was nervous because he had caught the tone in Owen's voice and said, "Will she like me?"

"Of course she will like you! She's only about twelve years older than you, so you might be more like a little brother to her," Richard laughed and looked to Owen for a laugh, but it wasn't there. Richard had had a bit too much wine, or he would have caught Owen's vicious look.

The next day, Owen carefully washed and shaved and went to find Jacob Spencer to speak to him about Mary. Spencer welcomed him and even offered him wine, but Owen declined and came right to the point. "Sir, if you really must see Mary wed, why not let her marry me? I am more her age, and will certainly make her happier than an old man will."

Jacob Spencer looked at him and said, "Well, I certainly don't see your father as an old man, Owen, but let's come right to the point, shall we? Please bear in mind I mean this in the kindest way, but why would Mary settle for the cub when she could get the lion? Son, she is spoken for, and she will marry your father."

Owen left the Spencer house with his rage barely concealed. How could Mary possibly favor him less? He was younger and set to inherit a healthy fortune when his father died. Cub indeed! She would regret this.

Owen went that night into Williamsburg and found a small dark-haired prostitute who resembled Mary enough to be a target for the beating he was itching to inflict. He knocked her around until she had a bloody lip and then paid the madam triple the rate to hush her up. Even after that exertion, he was still angry, but he got some relief when he tripped Edward the next morning in the kitchen and watched him fall, skinning his chin on the flags.

Richard left Scotland Neck two days later on a run to Philadelphia and had several meetings scheduled in Washington. He took Owen with him and left without seeing Mary. The pending marriage had been checked off his mental list. Mary, on the other hand, took her new role seriously.

It was about a week after Richard left that Mary sent a note asking if Edward would like to go fishing with her. The note was returned with YES scrawled in large block letters.

William brought Mary the next morning and she and Edward walked the easy few miles to a pond north of Surry. Mary was so engaging and sweet that Edward's initial shyness was overcome. They fished until they could barely carry their catch home on stringers they made from forked sticks. Edward stayed with them that evening for the fish dinner, and it was so late when they finished that Arla sent a note to Wrennet saying Edward would spend the night.

Mary and Edward became almost inseparable. He was a guest at the Spencer home most of the time, often spending the night. Arla fussed over Edward, making him blush as she patted his curls and remarked on his blue eyes. "My beauties all have hair and eyes dark as night, but you are like a little angel topped with gold."

It was the first of December when Richard returned and found the house empty except for Wrennet. He asked, "Where is Edward?"

"Oh, off with Miss Spencer again," Wrennet said, folding a shirt. "She's had him near steady since you went. Good to him too she is, so that's where you'll find him, at the Spencer house. They sent me a note saying he would not be home until nearly bedtime, but that will only be if he comes at all. They keep him over there quite a bit." Richard was a little surprised but pleased, and said he would clean up and go check on him.

Richard arrived at the Spencer house about half an hour before dinner. Big Mary, as Richard referred to the maid he had mistaken originally for Mary Margaret, saw him coming and alerted Arla, who came right out the front door to greet him. "Captain Holmwood, what a pleasant surprise. We were not expecting you."

Richard dismounted and then said, "I don't mean to impose, but do you have my son?"

"Yes, we do, and what a darling boy," Arla smiled and gestured toward the door. "Please join us for dinner." Richard tried to decline, but refusing Arla Spencer was like trying to hold back the seasons, and he gave in, understanding just why Mary might want to escape this house.

Richard was ushered into the sitting room where the family was gathered while Arla went to see that another place was laid at the table. Richard spotted Mary and Edward sitting on the floor playing checkers. Both looked up at him and stood at once. Richard motioned for Edward to come to him, and he ran forward and then stopped hesitantly a few feet from his father. "I told Wrennet where I was, Papa. She knows," Edward said, fearing he was in trouble for not being at home.

"I know. She told me," Richard said, squatting down. He smiled and said, "Come here, son." Edward ran to him. Richard picked Edward up and tickled his belly.

They settled in to dinner a few minutes later and Big Mary entered carrying a huge platter of fried fish, which she set down on the table with a flourish. "Mary and Edward caught these, Captain," Arla announced. Richard smiled and looked across the table at Mary helping Edward with his napkin. Richard ate dinner and shared the news he had brought from Philadelphia and Washington. He had seen Adrian in port in Washington, and Adrian asked him to deliver his best to Diana and the family. Arla, taking no chances that Richard might back down on his marriage proposal, made a show of pointing out to him the dishes Mary had prepared. "Mary put up these cucumber pickles and this elderberry wine last year."

After dinner Richard and Mary moved to an alcove at the edge of the room, and he nudged her softly. "So, not only did you put up the pickles and wine, but you can fish as well."

Mary shook her head, "My mother was just making sure you weren't going to change your mind. If she keeps this up, she'll be having you check my hooves and teeth to make sure you aren't getting inferior stock."

Richard chuckled and shook his head, "No, Miss Spencer, I'm not changing my mind, and, as a matter of fact, I need something from you." Richard produced a small piece of thread from his pocket, and said, "Let me see your hand." Mary held out her right hand. Richard shook his head and clarified, "Your left hand." He wrapped the thread around her ring finger as a measure and knotted the length carefully. Her finger was even smaller than he estimated, but he said with a smile, "I need it for your ring." There was a silversmith in Williamsburg who also did gold work on commission and would make the ring if Richard brought him the measurement.

ANGLICAN WEDDING SERVICES are not known for their length, and the ceremony was a brief blur to both Mary and Richard. He escorted her to the reception where it seemed every resident living on the banks of the James River, from Hampton to Richmond and fifty miles inland on either side, was in attendance.

They had survived dinner, the cake, the blessings, and the toasts, and now the reception was in full swing. The noise of the crowd was almost overwhelming, and to make matters worse, the newlyweds were the target of a continual stream of bawdy jokes. Richard looked at Mary, and she didn't seem to be enjoying it much either, so he leaned down and whispered in her ear, "Are you holding up?"

She nodded bravely, but didn't look at him as she eyed the crowd and whispered back, "Do we have to stay here until all these people leave?" The crowd was getting rowdier, fueled by alcohol, rich food, and lust.

"We've gone through all the rituals, so we can leave anytime," Richard said and smiled softly.

"Please, let's go away from here," Mary put her hand on his arm, almost pleading.

Richard stood and helped Mary from her chair. People saw them leaving and began to hoot and holler. On their way out they were stopped by Adrian Spencer, who stooped and kissed Mary on the cheek and then said in Richard's ear, "Take care of her, Richard, she's our princess." Richard nodded.

Richard now helped Mary into the carriage and drove the mile from the parish hall to his house. Richard glanced over at her on the seat next to him, and her head barely came to his shoulders. She was staring intently ahead, and when Richard patted her hand, it made her jump. "Are you all right?" he asked softly, leaning down for her answer. Mary only nodded yes and kept staring ahead.

They rode in silence until they pulled up to the front door of the house. A young man came out from the barn and held the horses while Richard helped Mary down. Richard thanked the lad and then added, "When you have the horses put away, you should go down to the dance. You won't be needed here today, so go enjoy yourself."

The youngster's eyes lit up, and he tipped his hat, "Thank you, Captain!"

Richard turned to Mary and held out his arm for her. She smiled weakly up at him and clung to his arm, and they went into the house.

Mary looked around. She had only been in the sitting room on a few occasions when she came for Edward. The house itself was nice, but it suffered from a lack of attention. She walked from room to room exploring what would now be her home.

No one saw Owen dragging Edward across the field from the wedding dance toward the house. "You are going to watch this, you little shit!" Owen hissed at Edward who was trying to keep up with him. One hand dug mercilessly into Edward's thin little arm while Owen dragged him by the collar with the other. At times Edward's feet were not even touching the ground. "Come on! I don't want you to miss it!" Owen yelled in Edward's ear, urging him on faster as they covered the mile to the house. Owen slowed the last fifty yards so their breathing would return to normal and not give them away as they neared the wood pile in the back of the house.

It was Owen's job to bring in fire wood twice a day, and he had noticed a few weeks before that a crack nearly an inch wide had opened during a January thaw. The crack ran down the wall of the house near the wood pile, which was under a little lean-to near the back of the house.

The house was two stories, but as it was built into the hill, the second story was easily accessible from the ground. Owen had stuffed the crack with straw until it could be fixed in the spring, but it would now prove handy, because it ran right down the wall of their father's bed chamber.

RICHARD SHOWED MARY through the house, and her estimation of forgotten and neglected dinginess was reinforced. There were beautiful things, but they were dusty or simply piled among the detritus of the passing years. All the windows on the front of the house looked out over the river. At Scotland Neck, the James River is a mile wide, so the house had a fantastic view, but it could barely be seen through the dingy windows. Richard showed Mary both floors of the house, and they finally ended up at a room on the far end. She stopped at the doorway and asked, "Is this your room?"

Richard smiled and said, "Well, ours actually, Mary, at least until I leave." He looked at her in her creamy silk dress with the flowers and ribbons in her hair, and she was very lovely, if a man preferred dark-haired, dark-eyed women.

He had determined at first that he would not touch her. He was marrying her for Edward's sake, but he came to realize she would expect it, and the more he thought about it the more he wanted to be with a woman. He looked down at her and she smiled bravely pulling the shawl from her shoulders. She shivered, but not from being chilled, and Richard said softly, "Mary, that can wait. It doesn't have to be now; all I wanted was to get away from the crowd."

Mary shook her head and said quietly, "There will be people here tonight, won't there?" Richard nodded, and she continued, "I don't want anyone here, um, at first. Won't they all be at the dance for several more hours?" Richard nodded they would. "Please? While we are alone," Mary said and turned her back to him. Richard looked almost reluctant, but then he carefully unlaced the back of her dress. It fell whispering to the ground, and he picked it up when she stepped out of it. He draped the dress over a chair near the bed. Grief had kept his lust at bay all these years, and he had secretly wondered if he could still conjure any desire, but to his surprise, it had returned with a vengeance a few weeks before the wedding.

Mary turned to face him now, and he reached with unsteady hands to unhook her corset. He released the first hook, and it was like opening a dam. Mary spilled out, and though she had looked busty under her clothes, this was true bounty beyond what Richard ever anticipated. Mary was just shy of being plump though she had a very small waist and tiny hands and feet.

Without taking his eyes off her, Richard released the last of the hooks and placed the corset on the chair over her dress. She was standing now facing him in only her long white chemise, sky-blue stockings, and little slippers of white shot through with gold embroidery. Richard picked her up like a child and set her on the edge of the high bed. He carefully lifted her foot and took off each shoe. As he set them aside, he noted the shoes looked about the same size as Edward's. He pulled the ribbons on the garters above her knee, and the bows came loose, allowing him to slide the stocking off her legs. Mary's skin was creamy pink and the softest he had ever felt. Her ankles were tiny, but her calf muscles were strong and curved from walking.

He stood looking at her and said honestly, "You are lovely, Mary." He unbuttoned her chemise, and it fell back off her shoulders and settled at her waist. Even the thin fabric of the chemise had been a governor of sorts, but now her large and very lovely breasts were released, and Richard's breath caught in his chest. He kissed her neck softly and felt her hands fumble with the buttons on his shirt. He pulled back and watched her work to get the buttons through the stiff fabric. She struggled, and finally gave up after getting only two of them undone. Richard smiled and unknotted his tie and dropped it to the floor. He kicked off his shoes and pulled off his trousers and stockings together. He stood before her now in his partially unbuttoned shirt and nothing else, trying to calm his breathing.

Mary reached through the unbuttoned section of his shirt and put her hand on his chest. She said in nearly a whisper, "I'm so glad you are not too hairy. I have seen my brothers washing at the pump, and they are horribly hairy, almost like animals!" Richard chuckled, but his laugh was cut short, because at that moment and to his utter amazement, Mary reached down and wrapped both her hands around him through his shirt. "Please don't wait!" she said breathlessly. Richard stared at her, and she tugged at him again and said, "Please, please don't make me wait." She was sitting on the very edge of the bed, and Richard was standing in front of her stunned as she gave one more begging tug, "Please?"

Richard had rehearsed in his mind how gentle and patient he would be with her. She was the only virgin he had ever known in his life, and he was going to be a gentleman, but Mary it seemed was not the princess the Spencers had thought her to be. With a touch of anger at being deceived, and a good six years of dormant lust building, Richard grabbed Mary by the hips and pulled her toward him. As he wrenched her legs apart, she fell back onto the bed, and he shoved himself inside her. All the gentle steps he had rehearsed were abandoned, and all the care he intended to take this first time evaporated as years of repressed desire roared out of him as he grasped Mary under the buttocks and slammed into her.

OWEN HAD WARNED Edward as they got close to the house, "If you cry out or reveal we are here, I will kill you! You know I will too, don't you?" Edward shook his head yes, quite certain Owen would kill him if he could. He stood at the crack in the wall of the house, now in terror of Owen behind him and in horror at the scene before him. Even though his father still had on his shirt and it hung halfway to his knees, Edward knew vaguely what he was seeing. He had seen dogs and bulls, but this was much more fascinatingly frightening, and he could not close his eyes to block it out though every instinct told him to do so.

Owen crammed Edward's head further into the crack in the wall, seething as he watched Richard with Mary. The old goat must be deaf if he couldn't tell from the way she cried out that he was killing her, but he just kept bulling away. Edward tried to struggle to get away, but Owen held his head, crushed cruelly against the stone wall, and forced him to watch as he hissed, "Open your eyes, damn you, or I'll crush your head against the wall."

Owen and Edward watched their father give one final horrendous thrust, and then Mary's legs draped limply over the edge of the bed on each side of his thighs. Owen took one last look and hauled Edward backwards with his hand clamped over his mouth, so he couldn't cry out. Owen hissed at him, "Get going, you little turd. Get back to the dance!" Edward stumbled away from him and Owen took a stone from the drive and threw it, catching Edward between the shoulder blades as he ran sobbing back toward the village hall.

Owen followed him and then slipped behind a small hill. His anger and lust at what he had witnessed was overpowering, and he tore at himself until he felt relief. When he calmed down he said disgustedly, "You should have married me, Mary. I could have treated you better than that old bastard just did!" Owen wiped himself off with his handkerchief and buttoned his trousers. He then slowly followed Edward's trail back to the village hall where the wedding dance was still going strong.

RICHARD STOOD next to where Mary lay on the bed. He had pulled away from her, but was still holding her by the hips. He relaxed his hold now and stepped back. She involuntarily curled onto her side and held herself, trying to ease the pain. Richard looked hard at her and then softened when he saw her eyes were tightly shut and her lower lip quivering. He wiped himself off with the long front tail of his shirt. Watery blood soaked through. He looked at the blood and then reached and gently moved Mary's hand from where she was holding herself. The chemise had bunched between her legs when she curled up on her side, and as he pulled it away from her he noted it was also marked with the same stains. Richard said with some dread, "Mary, were you a virgin?"

Her eyes were closed, but her bottom lip quivered even more, and she nodded as she cried, "Of course I was. What did you think?"

"Oh! God!" Richard exhaled and pulled her to a sitting position to hold her close as he tried to explain, "Mary, I am so sorry. I didn't know. I mean you grabbed me, and I thought you knew what you wanted. I would never have treated you that way except I thought you had done all this before."

Mary spoke from where her face was buried in his shirtfront. "I have never done anything like this before. I have never even seen a man," she searched for a word and mumbled, "there." She explained, trying to keep from crying, "I was only doing what my sisters-in-law told me to do." She couldn't help it and was sobbing hard now, "They told me that I should grab you there as soon as you took off your trou-trousers, and that if I told you not to wait you would be kind to me!" She was crying hard and stuttering. Richard stroked her back trying to sooth her. She finally calmed a bit, and he leaned back and lifted her chin to see her face. It was all blotchy, and her eyes were red and full of tears. He wiped them away with the end of a ribbon in her hair and said, "That was a very cruel trick they played on you Mary, and I am sorry I did my part. I can never take this back. I can never make your first time other than the way it was, but, I promise, I will try to make this up to you." He kissed her forehead and held her for a few more moments, and then he sat to put on his stockings and pants. He tucked in the stained shirt then stood next to her.

"Do you want me to help you get dressed?" he asked softly.

She looked at the heaped clothing and nodded, her head whispering, "I can't get into the dress alone, so you will have to help me." Richard lifted her down from the bed and handed her the corset, and she quickly hooked it down the front over her stained chemise. She then sat on the floor like a child as she put on her stockings and retied the ribbon garters above each knee. She slid on the shoes Richard handed her and then stood and pulled the dress over her head. She turned for Richard to lace her up the back, and when he finished, he patted her shoulder.

Mary looked around the room. Richard noticed and asked, "What are you looking for?"

"A mirror so I can arrange my hair," Mary said, still looking.

Richard pulled open one of the doors of a large wardrobe. On the back was a fairly good-sized mirror. Mary looked at herself and pulled the ribbons from her hair, which wasn't mussed as badly as she thought it would be, smoothing it with her fingers. Richard stood behind her and said to her reflection in the mirror, "How about some wine, Mary? Then you can tell me what other sage advice your sisters gave you." He smiled sadly, and added, "Perhaps then we can avert another disaster." He caught her wounded expression and turned her around to look at him and added, "Not on your part, Mary. The disaster was of my making alone, though you paid the price." He smiled and led her downstairs to the sitting room where he poured them both large glasses of wine.

Their conversation began in a stilted manner, but eventually it eased as Mary revealed to him what her sisters-in-law had said. "They said that if I was ever angry with you, I should always tell you about it over dinner. They said that you would appreciate it more if I told you in the middle of dinner rather than before or after." Richard shook his head and nodded for her to continue. She took a breath and said, "They said I should invite as many of my relations as possible to come and stay for as long as possible, because new husbands like to show off by feeding as many people as they can." Mary looked up at Richard, and he smiled without comment, but motioned for her to continue. "They said I should always do my laundry on a rainy day. They said you would secretly appreciate seeing the laundry hanging all over indoors to dry, especially sheets, as they reminded you of bed. I was told that bed was what men thought about most."

Richard laughed out loud. "That one may be true, not about hanging the sheets, but it's true that most men's thoughts don't stray far from a bed." Mary blushed, and he said, still chuckling, "Did they have any more pearls of wisdom?"

Mary's face went even redder, and she whispered, "They told me three things I should do to you, but the one I tried seemed the least frightening of the three, so I know I couldn't do the others. Anyway, their advice didn't help, so I think I will forget the other things."

Richard was dying to know what they had told her, but knew he wouldn't get it from her, so he let it go. He patted her hand and said, "Mary, think on it this way: Things between us can only go uphill from here." He raised his glass and she did the same. They continued talking until the house began to fill with merrymakers returning from the wedding reception in varying states of indigestion, inebriation, or both.

Edward was suddenly shy with Mary as his view of her as a comrade had changed. He now stared at her from the doorway wondering how she could just sit and drink wine after what he had seen her doing. Richard finally said to him, "Edward, either come in and sit down, or leave the room, but don't stand there and stare, son." Edward walked in, wary of his father and unsure of Mary, and sat on the edge of a chair by the fireplace. Owen sat next to Mary's chair waiting to see how she walked when she rose. He was convinced she would limp, and the thought gave him another spasm in his groin.

Richard spoke to Owen and Edward. "We left right after dinner before they started dancing, so, gentlemen, how was the dance?" Neither of them answered and he glanced at Edward, who jumped when he asked, "Edward did you dance with anyone?"

Edward shook his head and said in a small voice, "I didn't dance with no one, Papa." He could barely look at his father.

"I didn't dance with anyone, Edward," Richard corrected him, and then continued teasingly, "Why didn't you dance? Were there no pretty girls there?" Edward shook his head no. In truth he had gone back to the village hall, vomited behind the building, and then sat outside on the cold steps until he heard Owen calling for him to go home. Richard turned now to Owen. "How about you, Owen, did you see anything that interested you?"

Owen gave him a sly look, and then glanced at Edward who looked like he was about to vomit again, and said, "I saw something interesting, but she didn't seem like she was having much fun."

Richard went on sipping his wine, "That's too bad, son, most girls like to dance."

"I guess it all depends on the skill of their partner, doesn't it?" Owen added, shooting a glance at Mary. Richard didn't catch Owen's look and nodded in agreement. They sat listening to Owen's desultory description of the reception until Wrennet came in and told Edward it was time for bed. Mary got up to help them, and Owen looked her over, disappointed that she walked normally.

After they put Edward to bed, Wrennet pulled Mary aside and handed her a small ceramic pot about the size of an egg. "This is a soothing ointment for brides. You use it where it will do the most good both before and after, and it will help. You can't use it too often, and if he is like other men, you will need to use it frequently here for a while." Mary stood staring at Wrennet, shocked at the calm way she covered the topic, but she took the ointment and thanked her.

Mary returned to the sitting room and Richard had refilled her glass. She took the glass and looked at it, not wanting to make eye contact with either Richard or Owen. The men talked a bit longer and finally Richard said, "It's been a long day, and I think we should all retire."

Richard led Mary to their room and said, "I'll be right back, but turn around, so I can unlace you." Richard deftly undid her dress and then closed the door softly behind him as he left. Mary resisted the urge to lock him out of the room and began to dig through the trunk of her things that had been delivered the day before the wedding until she found a nightdress. She yanked off the rest of her clothes, pulled the nightdress over her head, quickly applied Wrennet's salve, and jumped into bed yanking the covers up so tightly under her chin she was barely able to breathe. She had been prepared for Richard to be gruff or even indifferent toward her, but she had not been prepared for the violence he had shown her, and it was only her pride now that kept her from running out into the night when he suggested they go to bed.

Mary clung to the quilt under her chin, not even aware of the stench of Grub, who until tonight had been Richard's bed partner, as she strained to hear Richard's boots on the stairs. She tried to steady herself with the thought that soon he would be gone for years, and if she could just get through the next few months she would have the house to herself. She assured herself that whatever was to come, it probably couldn't be any worse than the first time.

Richard came back a few minutes later with more wine and sat on the side of the bed. Mary sat up, and he handed her a glass, saying softly as they clinked their glasses, "To better days ahead."

They quickly finished their wine, and then Richard puffed out the lamp, undressed, and crawled into bed next to Mary who stared straight ahead in the dark trying not to make a sound. Richard was silent for what seemed an eternity, but Mary could feel the heat radiating from his body into the bedding. He finally said in almost a whisper, "Mary, I am not a monster. You have no idea how differently I planned to be with you. Please let me try again, and I will prove to you I am not a beast. May I?"

Mary spoke in a whisper, "I thought you owned me now, my body, I mean. I didn't know I had a choice."

"This isn't slavery. I'm responsible for you now, but I don't own you," Richard explained. He pulled the covers down slightly from her face and said in a silvery voice, "Wouldn't you like to know that it can be nice between us?" He moved closer, "Aren't you at least curious?" he whispered. It could have been the soothing ointment, or it could have been Richard's enticing tone, but Mary nodded her head silently, and Richard reached for her.

A SOUND WOKE MARY in the night, and for a second she didn't know where she was. When Richard stirred next to her, she remembered. He had been kind and patient, and to her surprise, she found she rather liked their second encounter. She thought about it now as she carefully rolled over toward him. She had never slept in the same bed with anyone and it was wonderful to have the whole thing warm with no cold spots for her legs and arms to wander into. She looked at Richard sleeping on his side and with the moon shining through the window beyond him, his shoulders and back looked like a great, dark wall next to her. She remembered how gentle he had been with her and how afterward he had smoothed her nightdress back down from where it was bunched at her waist. Mary could not pick out his features in the darkness, but she could feel the warmth from his body. She snuggled closer, nearly touching him, then fell asleep.

The next morning Mary rolled over to see Richard standing beside the bed, buttoning his trousers. He walked to the washstand, unaware she was watching him, and quickly shaved. He then rinsed his face, puffing and snorting and splashing as she had seen her brothers and father do. Mary could wash her entire body from a washbasin and not spill a drop of water on the floor. Up until today she assumed it was only the Spencer men who made such a wet mess.

Richard was about to pull his shirt over his head when he saw her looking at him, and he stopped and turned to her. His voice was hoarse and sounded deeper than she remembered. He greeted her softly, "Good morning." He watched her carefully for a reaction, and then smiled as he remembered how rewarding it had been late last night to hear the prim and prissy princess Mary beg him not to stop when he offered to do so.

Mary greeted him and sat up self-consciously wrapping the sheet around her. She looked at the heavy muscles on Richard's chest and arms, and her eyes followed the hair on his chest downward across his abdomen where it disappeared into his trousers. Thinking aloud, she said in a tone of surprise, "You're not old!"

"No, Mary," he said, laughing softly. "Did you think I was?"

"No!" She was scrambling now for words. "It's just that I think of my big brothers as, well, they seem so much older than me, but you are older even than Adrian, so I . . ." She stopped, totally flustered and Richard chuckled.

"I suppose to you I am old. You may well wish you married someone your own age," Richard said with a wink, and Mary felt the blood burn in her cheeks as she vehemently shook her head no.

He tucked his shirt into his trousers and gently moved her wedding dress from the chair to sit down and put on his stockings and boots. He looked up at her when he finished, and said almost as an apology, "I'm headed to the ship right after breakfast. There's a great deal of work to do there." He stood and smiled again. "So what is your plan for the day? Are you going to try to settle in here?" Mary nodded her head, and though she didn't say it, the first thing she was going to do was clean the place from top to bottom. If nothing else, she would take the edge off the smell of Grub, which she now realized was everywhere.

Breakfast was strange with both Owen and Edward staring at her as she tried to eat, but Mary got through it by making a mental list of what she was going to do to the house. She decided to start with her own room, and tackled it right after Richard and Owen left for the ship.

Mary stripped the bed of its rather oily-looking sheets, which were now lightly stained with blood. When she went to the linen cupboard for fresh ones, she found that changing sheets was not a common occurrence. Even those in the cupboard were far from fresh. Mary took down the bedroom curtains, which were fuzzy with dust, and carried them into the laundry-mud room attached to the kitchen. She built a fire under one of the large copper pots and started hauling water. Edward showed up soon after, and she was able to enlist his help. She began furiously washing all the linen in the house as well as the curtains.

A few hours later, the two house girls Wrennet employed arrived and sat loafing on the steps. Mary introduced herself and put one girl to work immediately on the laundry while she started cleaning in the bedroom with the other one.

Mary moved all the bedroom furniture to one side of the room, so the floors could be scrubbed. When that side was finished, they moved the furniture onto the clean side and scrubbed the other one. The windowsills were scrubbed and then rubbed with fresh rosemary. Unlike the walls at the Spencer home, which were made of painted paneling, these were made of stone which had not seen a coat of whitewash in years. She sent a young boy she found lounging by the barn to town for whitewash and then paid him to coat the walls. When the walls had dried, she and one of the house girls named Abby waxed the floor until it shone. The rug next to the bed was so tattered, Mary just threw it into the fire making a mental note to replace it.

When they stopped for the noon meal, Mary went to check on the laundry, which was drying on the line. She watched the linens billow in the cold sunshine which reminded her summer was still a long ways off.

Mary tackled the kitchen next. She pulled everything away from the walls and had them whitewashed as well. She had the flags scrubbed until they gleamed, and put down some rushes on the floor until they could weave some rugs. Ashes were emptied from the fireplace and the hearth scrubbed. All the dishes came down from the walls and out of cupboards and were washed and dried. Some of the dishes on the walls had a thick coating of dust that looked like peach fuzz. There was some good silver around the place, but it was black with tarnish, so Mary set the two house girls to work on it with polish and a heap of rags. They whined, but Mary simply turned her back on them and began scrubbing the large pine table that took up much of the kitchen. When she was finished, she rubbed the surface with fresh rosemary and the rich resinous smell filled the kitchen.

Mary put Wrennet to work on dinner, leaving the menu up to her. Later in the afternoon, Mary set one of the girls to work ironing linens. She grumbled the whole time, but in the end all the beds in the house were fitted with fresh sheets, and those in the cupboard were fresh and white. Little Edward had never felt ironed sheets, and he couldn't get over how smooth they were as he helped Mary tuck them around the mattresses.

Mary had checked the dining room, and it didn't look too bad, most likely because it was rarely used. When she polished the big walnut table and put clean linens and the silver on it, the whole room gleamed. She corrected one of the girls on how to set the table, and then left to see what Wrennet had planned for dinner. She was not disappointed to see two large chickens turning on a spit over the fire. The fat from the birds dripped, then hissed and flared deliciously, and Mary could see peeled potatoes waiting in a bowl of water to be cooked. There was a pile of endive that Wrennet had been growing in a cold frame over the winter that would now be transformed into salad. Wrennet had caught the spirit of this new domestic frenzy and made a pie from dried apples. The smell was just beginning to escape the crust. She smiled at Mary, who peeked at it in the oven.

When Richard came home around seven, he was alarmed to see the two house girls stretched on the doorsteps in various poses of exhaustion. As Richard approached, the older one said, "She is a demon, sir, your new Mrs. Captain. She worked us all day long, cleaning, scrubbing, and carrying things! We snuck out here to get a little rest before we have to walk home." Richard smiled, glad they were finally earning their keep, and stepped gingerly across them and through the door where he stopped and stared, unable to believe what he was seeing. The difference Mary had made in just one day was inconceivable. The dining room table was gleaming and lit up with candles in polished silver candlesticks, and everything smelled fresh. He stepped into the kitchen where Wrennet was working on dinner, which smelled delicious, and though she looked exhausted, she reported happily, "She is a worker. I don't think she let those girls stop once except for a bite at noon, and even then only for about a quarter of an hour." Wrennet looked at him with a spoon in her hand, waving it as she spoke, "But as hard as she worked them, Mary worked twice as hard herself. I have never seen so much energy from such a little person. She was like a little whirlwind around this house!"

"She must have been," Richard said, looking around again. "Where is she?" Richard asked, marveling at the change in the kitchen. It looked brighter and somehow even larger than he remembered.

"She is in the mud room, bathing I believe. She captured poor Edward about twenty minutes ago and scrubbed him good, and then said she was going to bathe before dinner," Wrennet said as she basted the birds over the fire. Richard nodded and walked through the kitchen to the back where Mary had set up her laundry operation. He found her sitting in a large copper tub, rubbing her arms with soft soap. Her large breasts joggled as she washed. Richard eased back against the door jam and watched. Mary was oblivious to him as she stood to rinse off. She then reached for a towel, and wrapped it around her tiny body.

Richard said softly, "So it isn't just the house that's getting scrubbed I see." Mary whirled on him, startled, her eyes huge. He said softly, "I didn't mean to frighten you." Richard moved forward and tucked a strand of hair behind her ear, then said, "The house looks wonderful and everything smells fantastic. I didn't know the dining room could look that nice, but how did you manage it all in one day?"

"We just started after breakfast and kept going," Mary said, looking for her shoes. She stood on a clean board, and said, "There is still a lot of cleaning to do around here, but we can start again tomorrow. "

"As bad as that, ma'am?" Richard looked amused.

"There are a lot of things around here that need a good scrubbing," Mary said, trying to sound more sure of herself than she was as she looked Richard up and down.

"Are you saying I should jump in the tub as well?" Richard said.

"We'll get you fresh water if you like," Mary said.

"Who has been in here besides you and Edward?" Richard said, taking off his jacket.

"Just the two of us," Mary said, wiping the water from her eyes with the corner of the towel.

Richard looked at the bathwater. He had undoubtedly had to drink water on shipboard that was dirtier than her bathwater, so he said, "This will do fine for me." He took off his waistcoat and began to unbutton his trousers when he caught Mary's trapped look. It amused him that she would still be shy, but he said, "Do you want me to carry you into the house, so you don't get your feet dirty?" Mary nodded, relieved, and gathered her clothes and shoes. Richard bent and picked her up effortlessly. She thought he would put her down in the kitchen, but he carried her all the way to their room. He looked at her for a moment, almost amused, and then went to take his bath.

As he soaked, Richard began thinking of Lorraine, which quickly turned to comparing her to Mary. He knew deep in his heart that he had chosen Mary because she was completely different in looks and temperament. He could not have tolerated a woman who gave Lorraine's memory competition. He shook his head, driving away the thoughts, trying his best to live where he was now. Mary was sweet, and there was no question she was efficient. She didn't appear the type to make many demands on him, and if she started to, it didn't matter anyway, because he was leaving in a short while and would be gone five years. He knew Edward would be in good hands with Mary, and that is what she was there for anyway.

After they married, Richard made two short trips up the James River to Dutch Gap in Richmond. As he arrived at the pier in Scotland Neck from the second trip, he saw the house lights gleaming on the hill. Mary had finally brought it to life.

Mary took after her mother, Arla, the daughter of a prosperous Pennsylvania farmer. Arla had gone with her father to Philadelphia one fall where she met a dashing junior officer serving in the Continental Navy named Jacob Spencer. They eventually married, and when he brought her to Scotland Neck to set up housekeeping, Arla carried that almost legendary Pennsylvania Dutch efficiency and tidiness with her to Virginia.

As efficient as Mary was, there were things at the house over which she had no control, things that marred an otherwise peaceful household. The family had just finished one of Mary's superb Sunday meals, and Owen had disappeared toward town while Edward was playing outside with some boys his age. The boys were going down by the river, and Richard told him as he left, "Edward, you listen to the church clock, and be in this house before the clock finishes striking eight. Do you understand?" Edward shook his head quickly and scampered off.

The late afternoon deepened into dusk, and when the church clock struck seven forty-five, Mary started listening for Edward's return. It was a cloudy evening and the sun had set early, so it was now nearly dark and rather chilly. She went to the door to listen for his feet on the gravel but heard nothing and went back inside. The church clock started its chime melody, then it began to strike. . .five, six, seven, eight. Richard now went out on the front steps and stood listening. The last bell rang out and died on the night air. In the distance they could hear small feet flying over the gravel as Edward came running and sobbing into the circle of light thrown by the open doorway. Mary grabbed Richard's arm and pulled him back, "No, Richard, find out why he was late. Maybe he has a good reason."

Richard turned and gently shook her off. "It doesn't matter the reason. I told him to be here by eight, and he disobeyed me." Richard didn't say a word to Edward, but took him by the collar and led him up the stairs. Mary listened from the foot of the stairs, wincing as Edward was punished. Owen came into the house just then and looked at Mary. He nodded his head toward Edward's room and said flatly, "I told him he would never make it home in time. I told him Pa was going to trounce him, and it sounds like I was right." Owen turned and walked into the kitchen and began to slice a piece of pie.

Richard came downstairs looking sour, and flung himself into a chair in the sitting room staring straight ahead. Mary stood in the door looking at him and then walked back out the front door and stood staring into the dark. She could hear Edward sobbing even through the closed windows of his room. After it became silent again, Mary walked back into the house. Richard was in his study with the door closed, so Mary left him alone and went to bed. She was asleep when he came into their room after midnight. He reached for her as soon as he got into bed and hissed in a whisper, "Don't interfere again, Mary." She didn't resist him, but he was still almost rough with her. When it was over, Richard simply rolled over on his side, pulling her with him, and was asleep within minutes. Mary lay curled on her side, with Richard's heavy arm across her, as a single tear of confusion rolled across her cheek and disappeared into the pillow. Her mother had told her men were unpredictable, especially in the dark, and there were times she was just going to have to overlook things that happened there. Richard moved, pulling her closer, so her body was pressed against him full length. She could feel him breathing gently into her hair, and thought perhaps this was one of those times.

Richard awakened before Mary. As he was getting out of bed, he found the nightdress he had practically ripped off her in the darkness the night before. He ran his hand along the smooth satin ribbons that gathered the neckline and thought how different it was having her in the house. It wasn't just the addition of ribbons around the place that was different. It was more. The house had come to life since Mary moved in, perhaps for the first time since it was built. Uncle Micah, for whom Richard's eldest brother had been named, was elderly when he built the house. He moved in and suffered with poor health for a dozen years, trying any and all remedies for his ailments. It therefore must have come as an insulting blow that he finally succumbed to something as inglorious as blood poisoning from a nick he got while sharpening a knife. Richard had purchased the house, mainly for its river frontage, while Uncle Micah was still living, giving the old man in essence a life lease on the house. Soon after he bought it, Richard built the warehouse and the piers and began his river trade. Richard already had the house in Hampton for Lorraine and himself, so when Uncle Micah died, the Scotland Neck house sat empty for years until Richard limped up the James with what remained of his tattered family. The house was now, for its first time, a home.

After breakfast Mary was sorting through some linens that were so tattered they were good only for rags or bandages when Owen came into the room. He stood leaning against the doorway, watching her. She said, "I thought you went with your father."

Owen cocked his head to one side and looked Mary up and down as he said, "I did, but I came back, and I thought I would see what you were up to." Mary had been working hard and some of the hair near her face had escaped its combs and hung down. Owen let his eyes follow one tendril down until he came to the curve of Mary's breasts. He lingered there, staring wickedly, and then said, "I'll just watch if you don't mind, unless you need me for something." He raised his eyebrows, his meaning clear.

Mary looked at him and said more casually than she felt, "It was your house long before it was mine, so stay if you like." She put the old linens in a basket and started through the door, but Owen put his leg across the doorway and rested it against the jamb, blocking her way. He stared down from his vantage point at her plump cleavage and then carefully picked up the tendril of hair from off her collarbone, letting his fingers linger. She tried to pull away from him, but he held her firmly by the arm and slowly tucked the hair behind her ear.

"I was just helping you, Mary. Your hands were full," Owen sneered and lowered his foot so she could pass. She scurried through the door, her heart pounding, but he grabbed her by the arm and pulled her close so he could whisper, "You are going to come to rely on my help, Mary, once my father leaves. You may even beg me for it before he gets back!" He coughed out an evil chuckle deep in his throat and then turned and walked away. Mary stood with her heart pounding until she heard him leave and then she sat down, breathless.   The next morning after Richard left, and while Wrennet and Edward were walking to Surry, Owen approached Mary again while she was alone in the house. He caught her in the upstairs hallway and whispered in an evil tone, "Just wait, Mary, I won't be at sea all the time, and you will be under my say soon enough." Mary wrenched away from him and ran into her bedroom and locked the door, and she did not come out until she heard Wrennet's voice in the kitchen.

Mary went through her tasks for the day, but decided to walk down the drive before dinner to meet Richard coming home. If she was lucky, Owen would be off with his friends as he was several days a week, and she could talk to Richard alone. If not, she would confront Owen with Richard there.

Mary set out late that afternoon, and she rehearsed what she would say to Richard as she walked down the long drive. She was still mulling it over when she came around the sharp corner at the bottom of the hill and was nearly run over by Richard's horse.

"Whoa, there!" Richard reined the horse to the side to miss her. "Mary, are you all right?" She nodded her head and then he asked, "Is something wrong?"

Mary looked up at him, shielding her eyes from the setting sun with her hand. "I was hoping to talk to you," she swallowed, and then added, "alone."

Richard dismounted and stood looking at her, concerned. "What is it?"

She blurted it out, "It's Owen. He said some things to me that were improper, and he frightened me." Richard looked at her for a moment, and then he started walking forward and offered his arm.

"What did he say to you?" Richard said.

"It was more the way he said it than what he said," Mary explained, already stumbling on her words as she added, "and he touched me here." She brushed her hand across her collarbone where Owen had picked up the tress of hair. She looked at Richard, and he was staring at her.

He repeated calmly, "Tell me exactly what he said to you and how he touched you."

Mary repeated the conversation as best she could, trying to put the right emphasis on what Owen had said, but even as she said it, Mary knew it sounded silly and childish. Richard hid a smile and then said, "I'll talk to Owen, all right? I'm sure he didn't mean anything by it, but if he frightened you, I'll make sure he doesn't do it again." Mary nodded and they walked a ways further, but she had trouble keeping up with his long strides, so Richard finally scooped her up and put her on his horse where she sat sideways clinging to the pommel. He jumped up behind her and held her around the waist. He said, "Turn around and put your legs across his back." Mary looked at him shocked, and he said chuckling, "There is no one to see you ride astride, so just do it. I need room for my legs." Mary hiked her dress and turned to straddle the horse. Then Richard reached around her and urged the horse forward. She clung to his arms terrified he would urge the horse into a gallop, but he trotted slowly all the way home.

After dinner, Richard called Owen into his study. Owen closed the door behind him, and Mary stood in the kitchen holding her breath trying to hear what was being said. Owen must have fed Richard a good line, probably about the excitability of women, because they were both laughing within five minutes while in the kitchen Mary's face burned with shame and anger.

Richard must have believed Owen's explanation, and the matter was dropped. At any rate, Owen didn't bother Mary again because he left a few days later on a run to Washington. It was peaceful without him in the house, and on Sunday they picnicked after church. They stuffed themselves on a chicken pie wrapped in kitchen towels and still piping hot, ham biscuits, boiled eggs, various pickles and preserves, endive in vinegar, and a caramel cake with icing. After they ate, Richard leaned back on his elbow on the blanket and tickled Edward under the chin with a long stalk of grass. Edward erupted in giggles and then curled up next to Mary, and she stroked his curls. Richard smiled and said, "That was a fine meal, but it's a good thing I'm going to sea soon. If I stayed here any longer, I would weigh three hundred pounds." He sat back up then and said, "Just so you know, I'm leaving Wednesday week for Jamaica. I'll be gone about two months, and then when I return, I will head for the territories shortly after." He looked across the river and added, "And then I'll be out of your hair for good." Mary nodded slowly but didn't say anything.

Richard left for his run to Jamaica a week later. He told Mary two months, but he couldn't be absolutely sure of the length of the voyage. Mary watched him walk away, but having grown up with the tradition, she did not wave, and he did not turn around.

CHAPTER 11

RICHARD WAS GONE three months rather than two, and Mary had certainly kept herself busy while he was away. Richard barely recognized the house with its new coat of whitewash. The shrubs had been trimmed, there were bulbs coming up by the doorstep, and he could see where Mary even had the beginnings of a small garden plowed. The house glowed in the afternoon light and looked welcoming.

Richard walked through to the kitchen. He saw Mary with her back to him folding table linens, and he crept up behind her and whispered in her ear, "What a hard worker you are." She turned and stared at him and then bolted out the door, running like a scared rabbit. "What in hell!" Richard said, then ran after her. Mary was already over the crest of the hill behind the house and running down the backside before Richard cleared the peak. She was moving quickly and didn't look back. Richard took off after her and only gained on her when she slipped on some loose stones. "Mary! Stop running! It's me, Richard!" he called to her, and she turned and stared.

She was breathless, but managed to yell back, "No, sir, you are not! My husband does not have yellow hair!" She turned and ran again. Richard's hair had been cropped close and he had not been to sea in months when she first met him, so there was no way for poor Mary to know that this big, blonde man now pursuing her was indeed Richard. She turned and hauled herself through the long weeds trying to get away from him. Richard watched her fall again and ran to try to help her, but she jumped up while he was still about twenty feet away, and screamed, "You stay away from me, sir." Richard chuckled at the use of sir to an assailant and started forward again, but quick as if blasted by gunpowder, Mary let loose with a stone the size of a hen's egg and caught him just above his right eye. The impact sent him reeling, and he staggered to stay on his feet. The stone cut a short but deep gash in his forehead, and he caught the blood in his hand as it ran down his face. He fumbled for his handkerchief, holding his bleeding head as he yelled to Mary who had fled again, "Mary Margaret Spencer Holmwood, stop running!" Mary stopped and turned to stare at him.

"Say again, sir." Mary stood panting and poised to run.

"For God's sake, Mary, don't you even know me?"

His voice sounded familiar. "Richard, is that really you?" She moved forward slowly, like a doe entering a field at dusk. When she got within ten feet she gasped, "Oh, Richard! I didn't know it was you. Your hair is yellow, and you have a beard, and it's yellow too!"

"My hair's blond from the sun. I have a beard because we had bad weather the whole way back and it's bad luck to shave in a storm, but no worse than coming home to you, I guess." Mary looked like she would cry, but he winked with his good eye, then teased, "Some greeting for a man away months at sea!" He looked at her again and chuckled, "What a throw! I could have used you in a boarding party." Mary came forward to pull back the handkerchief, and blood oozed from the wound.

"I think that will need to be stitched," Mary said and touched his cheek. "I am so sorry, Richard." He smiled and offered his free arm and then they walked back to the house.

Wrennet and Edward had just returned to the house from the Spencers and stood waiting to greet Mary and Richard. When Wrennet saw the blood on the handkerchief she said, "Good Lord, what happened to you? You haven't had time to be in a tavern brawl."

"I'll tell you how it happened," Richard said with a wink, "I came into my own house, took one look at my bride, and what did she do? She fired a stone right at my head."

Wrennet carefully took away the cloth. "You will need one, no, two stitches I think. Do you want me to do them or does Mary want to take a stab at it?"

They both turned to Mary, who backed away stammering, "Wrennet knows what she's doing, so she better do it this time."

Wrennet piped up, "This time? How many times are you going to split his head open?" Richard smiled, but Mary kept quiet and stood off to one side where she watched, sickly fascinated, as Wrennet threaded a needle and waxed the thread by dragging it several times through the liquid wax at the top of a burning candle. Wrennet bent Richard's head toward the lamp and said to him, "Hang on to something now."

Mary spoke in a wavering voice, "I should leave."

"No, stay, but get Edward out of here," Richard hissed as Wrennet dumped rum into the wound without any warning for him to close his eyes. Wrennet pinched the sides of the wound together with her fingers and pushed the needle through with a thimble on her thumb. Using pliers, she pulled the needle through the other side. Richard sat grunting and clutching the arm of his chair. Wrennet deftly made one stitch and then another, then stood back and looked at her handiwork. Seeing no scissors close by, she leaned in and sheared off the thread ends with her teeth.

"Close your eyes," Wrennet commanded, remembering to warn him this time, and dumped more rum on the stitches. She patted Richard's shoulder. "There you go. One week and we'll take them out! You're lucky she didn't hit you with the full force of the rock, or there'd be terrible swelling. It must have just grazed you as it passed." Wrennet stood with her arms crossed on her drooping bosom. "Now I bet you have a few things to say to this little one, don't you?"

Richard turned to Mary, who stood gripping the back of a kitchen chair, her brown eyes huge, and said, "That was a marvelous toss! Who taught you to throw like that?"

Mary caught his wink and said smiling, "Adrian, but he would be disappointed."

"Why is that?" asked Richard.

"I was aiming for your eye!" Mary said, smiling as she came forward to look closely at Richard's wound. She asked quietly, "Will it be all right now?"

"This is nothing. Wrennet has stitched up much worse, haven't you?" Richard said, turning to Wrennet.

"Oh, heavens yes, much deeper, longer." Then she added with relish, "Even punctures. Now, you have to keep your eye on those. A man can be dead in two days with the right type of puncture. You can never let your guard down." She continued, lost in ghoulish memory of past wounds. Richard slipped away to bathe, and Mary retreated to the sitting room, not wanting to hear any more details.

Later that evening the family was sitting next to the fire and Richard came in with three packages. He handed one to Wrennet which contained a shawl. He handed the smaller of the remaining packages to Owen. It contained a beautiful brass sextant. Owen held it up almost reverently as he removed it from its ornate wooden box. Richard smiled, watching Owen with his gift, and said fondly, "You can't use my old one the rest of your life, son, you need one of your own." Owen thanked him and then watched while Edward opened his gift, which was a square wooden box also beautifully carved. He placed it on the floor and opened the lid. Inside was a carved ark. His eyes lit up as he set it on the floor and reached for one of several dozen small paper-wrapped packages inside the ark. He tried to break the strings on the little packages, but could not. He handed one to Mary, and she could not get it to budge, either. She looked at Richard and said, "I think they are tied with silk." She marveled at the waste of such a commodity. Richard cut the strand with a pen knife and handed it to Mary, who handed it back to Edward. As he unwound the paper, a tiny, intricately carved and painted elephant slipped into his palm. He stared at it, smiling, and then put it down next to the ark and reached for another packet. This one was a leopard with spots and gleaming eyes. Edward sat up on his knees and handed the whole box to Mary. She passed it to Richard, and they worked like a brigade with Richard clipping, Mary passing, and Edward opening. Mary was nearly as excited as Edward as they revealed the mates to the elephant and the leopard, and then pairs of crocodiles, camels, wolves, bears, monkeys, oxen, hedgehogs, and others, and finally even old Noah with his shaggy beard. Mary reached her hand up to Richard for the next package, but he put a small velvet bag in her hand instead. She automatically started to hand it to Edward, but when she felt the fabric, she looked over her shoulder at him.

"That one is for you, Mary," Richard said. The bag was tied with gold cord. She quickly slipped the knot and gingerly poured the contents into her tiny hand. There, coiled in her palm like a jeweled snake, was a braided gold necklace with a locket. She pulled up the chain and found the matching bracelet still in her hand.

"Oh, Richard, they're beautiful! Thank you!" she exclaimed.

Richard nodded. The necklace had not been his idea. As a matter of fact, he hadn't even thought to get her a gift until Shaw asked what he was getting for his new bride. The first nice thing Richard saw when he went ashore was the necklace and matching bracelet. He looked down now to where she was sitting on the floor and said, "I'm glad you like them. I was worried. I've never seen you wear jewelry."

"I don't have any to wear," Mary explained. "My Papa said I had to wait until I had a husband to buy it for me." Richard fastened the necklace at the nape of Mary's tiny neck. It settled just above the curve of her breasts where the locket rested very fetchingly. "You didn't have to get me anything."

"I know I didn't have to, but that's what made it fun," Richard replied. Nothing is easier to give than jewelry, Richard thought. All it takes is money and requires very little time or thought.

RICHARD HAD BEEN HOME only a week when he started feeling ill. A sailor at sea eats the same thing every day. After the fresh meat, fruit, and vegetables are gone, it is a monotony of dried peas, oatmeal, and salted meat. As an officer, Richard may have gotten a few raisins in his pudding or a lemon sauce now and then, but it was the legacy of Edward Preble that in the American Navy, unlike the Royal Navy, its officers and crew ate the same food. If the officers got fresh meat, then so did the crew. If the crew went without, then so did everyone else. Even though Richard had been in essence a merchant sailor for the last several years, he still stuck to the same policy on board the ship.

Monotony kept their digestive tracts remarkably regular. As long as they got fresh fruit or vegetables now and then, they could sustain on dried foods and salted meat. Any sailor from the highest officer to the lowest crew member who is turned loose ashore, will eat until he nearly bursts, gorging on slabs of dripping fresh meat, pastries, sweets, cheeses, and fresh fruit. He steers clear of anything resembling peas and oatmeal. This avoidance of roughage coupled with an abundance of rich food invariably leads to either raging diarrhea or cement-like constipation. Richard, partaking of Mary's rich food, found himself burdened with the latter. Wrennet noticed he was looking "peaky" and suggested he take a tonic. She offered to whip one up for him, but he declined. Two days later, however, with still no improvement, his gut began to bloat, forcing Richard to seek out Wrennet

She mixed up a "black slider" which she swore was just the thing he needed. Richard looked at the foul brew in the mug and sloshed it around a bit. The concoction gave off a nasty odor similar to bilge water, was about the same color, and contained enough senna to dose a horse. Richard trustingly drank it and the effects were virtually instantaneous. Within minutes Richard was clenching his jaw trying to cope with the spasms in his abdomen. Mary came and felt his forehead and announced he had no fever. She suggested that Wrennet give him something to perk him up, but Richard gasped, "No, she has already given me more than I think I need." In twenty minutes, he was enthroned in the privy in agony. The slider was working, but he feared he might actually pass his guts out along with everything else.

When a full hour had passed, Mary walked carefully down to the outhouse and listened. Hearing nothing, she softly called his name. He answered in a mumble, asking to be left alone.

Richard remained in there for the better part of the day, drinking the pitchers of water set outside the door. When he finally emerged, he looked like a plague victim. He walked, listing heavily, into the house and flopped down in a chair in the kitchen, resting his head on the table. His face was dripping with sweat from the exertion of walking, and he was breathing heavily. When he had recovered enough to talk, he sat up and locked a malevolent eye on Wrennet and said barely above a whisper, "Don't you ever give that to anyone in this family again. Do you understand me?" Wrennet shook her head solemnly. It took both Mary and Wrennet to get him upstairs to bed where he slept until midmorning the next day.

He started off eating broth and toast, but worked his way back up to fabulous victuals by the second day, though this time he ate them in moderation. Four days later he was headed for Norfolk to make some final preparations before heading north. He planned to go back to Scotland Neck only once more before casting off. Owen had already left on a run to Charleston, but they planned to meet in Washington, if possible, before Richard left for good.

JORDAN LADYSMITH woke from a dream, not sweating and clawing himself back to consciousness to escape it, but lingering with all his might in that misty world. No matter how he tried to stay in the dream, it slowly faded around him like fog in the sunshine. He stared desperately at the woman's face before him as she vanished like steam. He sighed with disappointment, but he would see her again in his dreams just as he had for a decade. The woman, whoever she was, seemed about eighteen and had not aged a day since he first conjured her. She had haunted him since he was eight years old. She came to him first while he was living in Boston with the Holmwood sisters and then in every distant port he travelled to. Now she came to him in his bunk on the *Vindicta*. He had no idea who the dark-haired woman was as she loomed before him with her sparkling eyes. When Jordan first saw her he thought she was an angel or some benevolent older sister watching over him, but as he caught up to her in age, he saw her differently. She was beautiful, she had come for him, she was waiting, and she would be his when he finally found her. Jordan had no doubt that she was real.

RICHARD WAS SITTING in the little cordoned section that served as an office in the big double warehouse he owned in Norfolk. He owned other warehouses in Washington and Boston. Some were stocked with agricultural stores such as tobacco, grain, and, of course, rum, while others were stocked with a bounty of tea, silk, spices, and fine glassware. He had to thank Anthony Portman for the seed capital to start his little shipping venture. He had made wise choices in the commodities he shipped and where he shipped them, and he had wisely invested the money he earned on prizes. Richard sat now, comparing inventory to receipt logs, mainly to reassure himself Jonas Benson was trustworthy before he left the whole thing in his hands for five years. There was a soft knock on the door. "Come," he said without looking up from the papers before him. When he finished, he looked up and there stood Jordan Ladysmith. Jordan was only a year younger than Owen, and they were both about the same height, but Owen was bulky with muscles where Jordan was lean and elegant and had not yet filled out. Richard said, "I thought you and some of the others were tapping a keg this evening."

"We were, but I need to talk to you," Jordan said vaguely.

"Talk," Richard said, pushing a chair over toward him with his foot and putting down his pen.

Jordan looked unsettled, and he said softly, "Before I start, please know, I have nothing against Owen. He is almost like family, but I have been with you long enough that my loyalty must fall to you over Owen."

Jordan looked steadily at Richard and continued, "I was in Nattie's Tavern." Jordan was referring to a tavern run by Nattie Tate, a captain's widow who turned the family house into a tavern and was celebrated as the worst cook in Hampton Roads. She shoveled out the largest portions for the money though, and the place was always packed. Jordan continued, "I was in a rear booth eating one of those gristly meat pies when Owen came in with two other men that I didn't know. Owen was paying for the others to drink, so they clung to him like loyal dogs, and they settled in the booth right behind me. At first I didn't pay much attention to their talk, but when I heard your name and that of your wife, I listened more closely." Jordan looked down at his hands and shook his head.

"Tell me what he said, Jordan," Richard urged.

"You are not going to like what I have to say," Jordan looked at him sadly.

"Just tell me," Richard said, leaning forward.

"Owen was bragging that once you left for the territories, he would be in charge of the house. He said there were going to be changes, and that you had no right to wed this Miss Spencer you married. He assured the others he would turn her against you before you got back." Jordan looked miserable, but Richard nodded for him to continue. Jordan swallowed, and said, "He said that he had already gotten even with you some." Jordan looked up pained and when he saw the puzzled look on Richard's face, asked, "Did you and Mrs. Holmwood leave the wedding reception early?"

"Yes. We left to get away from the noise and the crowd. Why?" Richard answered.

"Owen saw you leave, and he followed you." Jordan looked embarrassed. "He watched you with your new wife at the house that afternoon." Jordan stopped and watched for Richard's reaction, and then added, "And he made Edward watch."

"Jesus!" Richard said, "but I don't understand. The house was empty. There was no way they could have. . ."

Jordan cut him off and added softly, "Apparently, there is a large crack in the back of the house, one that you told Owen to fix. He claims to have just stuffed it with straw, and his laziness came in handy, because it was from there that they watched you."

Richard sat stunned, humiliated by the fact that not only had his sons watched him consummate his marriage, but by how he had conducted himself doing it. "How could he do something like that to me?" Richard said, horrified.

"There's more, Richard, and it's worse," Jordan added gently. Richard clenched his jaw and motioned for Jordan to continue. Jordan took a deep breath and said, "Owen claims he has sabotaged Edward several times and gotten him in trouble with you. He only mentioned the most recent, where Edward was to be home by eight o'clock." Richard nodded, acknowledging the incident, and Jordan continued, "Well, Owen claims he held Edward at the foot of the drive until the clock started to strike eight, and then let him go to try to get home before it stopped striking. His exact words were, 'The little shit ran like hell, and I was worried he was actually going to make it on time, but he didn't, and my Pa laced him good,' or something very close to that." Jordan then added, "It was strange, Richard, he didn't say our Pa, or Pa, but my Pa, like Edward wasn't even his brother." Richard shook his head sadly as he remembered thrashing Edward that night because he was late, and how Mary had tried to stop him, begging him to find out why Edward was late before he punished him.

There was a soft knock on the door, and Shaw walked in looking distinctly uncomfortable. He saw Jordan and said, "I think I may be here for the same thing as Jordan. I was sitting a few tables from Owen, though Jordan didn't see me, and I heard what was said too. It just took me longer to get here." Richard nodded and Shaw pulled over a short keg and sat on top of it.

Richard leaned back in his chair, his face stricken, "I think Jordan has told me already, but thank you for coming."

Jordan took a deep breath and said, "I'm sorry, Richard, but there is more."

"Oh, hell," Richard exhaled and then said wearily, "What is it?'

Jordan began again, "Owen said that he will rid himself of Edward while you are away, and it will look like an accident. No one will ever know. "

Shaw spoke up, "Owen will kill the boy. I saw it on his face. He looked strange, like a madman, and then said something I didn't understand. He said, 'I should have burned him when I had the chance. He and my father killed my mother. He has ruined my life, and I will make him pay for it before I end him.'" Shaw looked ill and added in a whisper, "It made my blood run cold to hear him say it."

Richard looked to Jordan though he already knew it was true, and Jordan confirmed it with a nod saying, "It's true. Owen will kill him if he has the chance. Of that I am absolutely certain. You must not leave him in that house."

Richard pushed his blond hair back and then ran his hands over his face. He had not shaved, and the stubble scratched loudly in the quiet office. The only other sound was the hiss of the oil lamp. Richard finally said softly, "Mary asked me to let her live with her parents when I left. She said she thought there would be more for Edward to do there and that her brothers would be a good model for him while I was gone. I thought it was odd since she was itching to get out of her parent's house, and I told her no." He shook his head and added, "Hell, I went so far as to tell her Owen was a good role model and when he wasn't at sea, he would be the one to help Edward." Richard looked at both men and smiled sadly, "I guess she will get her way after all and live with her parents. I should have known something was afoot for her to want to go back, but I never dreamed it was this driving her back there." Richard shook his head, "I should have paid more. . ."

"No," Shaw said flatly, interrupting him. "The boy cannot stay here. He must go with you. Owen will do away with him if he is anywhere around, on that I would bet my life."

"Mr. Shaw is right," Jordan said. "Edward cannot stay here, and," he said, dreading it, "there is more."

"How can there be more? How can one man do so much wrong? He is eighteen years old for God's sake!" Richard exclaimed. Jordan and Shaw exchanged glances, and Shaw took over the telling.

He took a deep breath and began without looking at Richard, "Owen said that you stole Mary from him, that he had wanted her but was biding his time."

"That's a lie! He was hell bent on getting into Marjorie Allspat's drawers all summer, but she wouldn't do anything but dance with him. He never even once mentioned Mary Spencer. I know he's lying," Richard said.

"We don't believe it either, but Owen made himself believe it, and he wants revenge for a thousand injuries he seems to have imagined over the years," Shaw said, waiting until Richard looked at him again and added, "and he will have his revenge if you don't protect your wife."

"What do you mean?" Richard said.

"I am going to say it in Owen's words, so there is no chance of a misinterpretation," Shaw said, "and Jordan can correct me if I'm wrong." Shaw quoted Owen, "'She comes into my house all tight and prissy, but she likes it rough. You should have seen what the old man did to her, and the next day she is all smiling and sweet. If she thinks she likes being bulled by that old goat, wait until I get a turn at her. She'll learn what a real man is like. Old Pappy will come back after five years and think he planted a seed before he left. He will go prancing around showing off his spawn, and I will laugh, knowing what he is really showing off is his own grandchild.'" Richard looked horrified and started to speak, but Shaw put up his hand, "Let me finish, please. This is difficult enough. One of the men who was with Owen must at least have known of your wife, because he said, 'Mary Spencer would never do that. You are talking nonsense, Holmwood.'" Shaw added, "Owen just laughed and said, 'I didn't say she would come to me willingly. Taking her will make the conquest all the more sweet. Then I will convince her that she was to blame, and she won't dare tell my Pa. She will hold her tongue and raise that kid, and I will have gotten my bastard on my own father's wife. Won't that be sweet?'"

Richard sat stunned for several minutes, unable to speak, and then he cleared his throat and said, "Is there any more?" Jordan shook his head, and Shaw bowed that mercifully there was no more. "Holy Christ, what is he thinking? I'm going over there right now to wring his neck!" Richard rose and started for the door, but Shaw stopped him.

"He's long gone. He was boarding when I left to come over here. He would have dropped his harbor pilot off by now and be headed for Charleston. You'll have to catch him in Washington."

Richard said, "I'm headed back upriver the day after tomorrow to make my final preparations, and I'll ask about this. I'll have to make other arrangements now for Mary and Edward because they wouldn't be able to avoid Owen completely even if they lived at the Spencer's house, not if Owen is truly out to harm them."

"I agree," Shaw said sadly. Their talk eventually turned from Owen's sedition to the logistics of the Great Lakes trip. After Jordan and Shaw left about an hour later, Richard sat staring at the wall, not really thinking and not really feeling. It was still incomprehensible that Owen fostered this kind of hatred toward him. What had he ever done to deserve his ire? He moved numbly toward the door and walked out leaving the lamp burning. He found his way to the pier and climbed aboard the *Fiona.* He groped his way to his cabin and crawled into his hammock without undressing or even finding a blanket. Richard lay staring at the ceiling in the darkness, glad for once that Lorraine was not there to see the failure he had made of the beautiful son she had given him.

Richard arrived at Scotland Neck just before dinner, but he did not go to the house. Still on board the ship, he read the mail, made lists of things he would need, and he spent a great deal of time simply thinking. That night, about two hours after dark, he went to the house. As always, Mary was awake and still working, and she looked startled as he came through the door. She ran to him and took his coat, asking if he would like tea or something to eat. Richard shook his head and said solemnly, "I'm not really hungry." Without anything further, he walked to his study and shut the door. Mary stood looking after him confused, and then went back into the kitchen.

Wrennet came into the kitchen and said, "Did I hear Richard's voice?"

Mary nodded and said, "Yes, he came in and went right to his study. What do you think is wrong?"

Wrennet shook her head, "Perhaps nothing, but I'm sure he'll tell you if it concerns you or Edward." Wrennet touched Mary's arm and said, "I'm going to bed, and whatever it is that's wrong will look better after a night's sleep. You should go too." Mary nodded and bid Wrennet good night. She continued tidying up the kitchen, and looked up from wiping the harvest table to see Richard standing in the doorway.

He said quietly, "I need to speak with you, Mary. Please come to my study when you finish."

"I'm finished now," Mary said, putting down the cloth. She followed Richard into his study where he eased her down into the large chair at his desk and squatted in front of her with his hands on her knees. She stared at him tense and unsure, but she knew that whatever he had to say was important, as he had worked himself up to it. Richard cleared his throat, "Mary, I want an honest answer from you." Mary nodded her head, and then he asked, "You came to me once and told me Owen had touched you, and I dismissed that as nonsense, but it wasn't nonsense was it?" Mary shook her head ever so slightly, no. Richard continued, "The night I punished Edward for coming home late, Owen made him late on purpose. Do you believe that?" Mary shook her head yes. Richard asked softly, "Has Owen ever threatened you?" A huge tear brimmed on Mary's lower lid and then slid down her cheek and off her jaw where it splashed onto her dress, leaving a dark spot on the dove-colored wool. "Tell me Mary, please," Richard urged gently.

She said barely above a whisper, "Owen hasn't said anything that he couldn't turn around and say I took the wrong way, but I know what he means. I will not be safe when you are gone. He keeps reminding me that when you are gone, I will be under his rule." Mary gulped and added, "Richard, I am afraid of him. Please let me stay with my family when you are gone, please." Mary was sobbing now, and Richard patted her leg until she sniffed and stopped crying. She stared at Richard, waiting for him to speak. He looked down at the floor for a long time.

In the months they had been married she had always had to look up at him because she was so short, but now she looked down to him where he was squatting and noticed for the first time that his eyelashes were long. It was an odd thing to notice at such a time. They seemed almost out of place on this large and serious man. Richard looked back up at her, touched her face and asked, "He has threatened Edward as well, hasn't he?"

Mary nodded and then said in a flat voice, "He will kill Edward. I am certain he will. I don't know why, but he hates him, Richard." She then added in a softer voice, "I am so afraid for that little boy."

Richard sat back on the floor and exhaled. He looked at Mary seriously and then said, "Well, you don't need to worry about Edward, because I've decided to take him with me when I go."

Mary's eyes lit up. "Oh! I am so glad. He'll be safe with you and . . ." Mary stopped, her eyes got huge, and she burst into tears. Richard looked confused and asked what was wrong, and she sobbed, "Then you won't need me for Edward, and I won't have anywhere to go but back to my family!"

Richard shook his head and stood up. He pulled Mary to her feet and said, "Mary, no, you have it all wrong. I plan to take both you and Edward with me. That is, unless you would rather return to your mother."

"No!" Mary almost yelled. "I'll go with you and Edward!" she said and lunged at Richard, hugging him around the waist, both laughing and crying. Richard smiled and then looked up to see Wrennet standing in the door in her nightdress. She tilted her head inquiringly, and Richard nodded, mouthing later. Wrennet withdrew, casting a worried look at Mary.

Richard pulled Mary back so he could see her face and said, "I have always believed women are bad luck on a ship, and I am certain before this is over you will wish I had found a different solution for you, but I see no other way than to take both of you along." Mary smiled, and he warned her further, "You have never been on a ship, and I doubt you will like it or where we are going, but you have five days to get ready. Can you do it?" Mary nodded eagerly.

Richard assumed Mary would begin packing and gathering what she planned to take in the morning, but he was wrong. She started that very night, and it was nearly ten before he insisted she stop and get some sleep. She protested, and he finally just picked her up and carried her to their room.

The next morning she was up bright and early. Richard looked at the open cupboards and warned her, "You have limited room. I'll send some crates up here for the housekeeping things, and you and Edward can take a chest each, but that's all we'll have room for when we leave here. We'll transfer to another ship in Norfolk, and you'll have more room once we get there. You can buy whatever you need in Hampton or when we get to Washington and Boston, so pack light."

"We're stopping in all those places?" Mary asked, and her eyes lit up when Richard nodded. When he left her she was scurrying around like mad. He left before Edward was even awake, leaving it to Mary to break the news to him when he woke up.

Edward was at first excited about the trip and then uneasy until he asked, "Mary, is Owen going too?"

Mary looked at him and smiled, "No, just you, me, and your papa." Then Mary quickly added, "And Wrennet, of course."

Once Wrennet heard they were leaving, she was determined to go, and had exclaimed, "I'm going too, even if it kills me!" Richard just shook his head. If Wrennet would have gone with him in the first place to take care of Edward, he could have avoided getting married altogether.

Edward's eyes brightened at the thought of being free of Owen's torment, and he hurried to get dressed. As he ran by, Grub jumped up from the hearth and followed him up the stairs.

Mary could hear his little feet pounding up the stairs and then they suddenly stopped. He very slowly came back down into the kitchen with Grub in tow and stood looking at Mary. She raised her eyebrows at him, and he asked very softly. "Grub is going too, isn't he?"

"Of course he's going. We wouldn't leave him behind," Mary said smiling. Edward's eyes lit up, and he raced back upstairs. He got dressed and then walked with Mary to the Spencer's house to tell them the news and to enlist Arla's help.

When Richard came back to eat at noon, the house was in an uproar. Arla was there along with Diana and Emma Spencer and all of their children. Wrennet and the two house girls were busy packing, and Mary looked ruffled. Eight large crates had been delivered to the house earlier that morning, and three of them were already full. Richard looked at the chaos and was about to step back out and try to scavenge some lunch on the ship when Mary saw him. "Don't worry. Big Mary," she said, using Richard's name for her, "is bringing lunch for all of us from home. She'll be here in a quarter of an hour or so." Mary turned and pointed to a high shelf. "Could you reach that bowl down for me?" Richard took it down and handed it to Mary. He quickly retreated to the shelter of his study, but he could still hear Mary and her mother and sisters packing in the kitchen and Edward and the Spencer grandchildren playing in the drive. He buried himself in some crude charts of Lake Huron he had received while in Hampton, and it was about twenty minutes later that a cheer went up from the children. He looked out the window to see Big Mary and two other helpers arriving with the food in a small handcart. The mob in the kitchen now moved into the dining room, and Richard could hear bumping and thumping as chairs and stools were brought in for everyone. Added to this was the wailing of the children getting their hands and faces washed. He thought about going to see if he could be of help, but he couldn't summon the courage and thought if they needed him they would come and ask. Richard had seen the Spencer women in action before, and he gave them, especially Arla, the "gun captain," plenty of room. Mary finally came about ten minutes later and knocked softly on the door to call him to lunch.

Richard looked around the dining room and noted it was the first time the big table had ever been crowded. A sea of faces turned to him as he entered. The children were all red-faced and subdued from the scrubbing Big Mary had given them, but they waited eagerly for him to sit down, so they could tuck in. There was enough food to feed the crew of a frigate, and it was delicious to boot. Richard ate his fill, knowing before long they would be living on what the ship's cook could conjure. Grub, having already thoroughly licked the bed of the handcart clean, was now circling the table as he scrounged for bits of food dropped by the children.

Throughout the meal, Arla or Wrennet would remember something Mary would need to take. They would shout it out, and Arla would record it on the running list she had at her elbow. Richard was not part of the planning. His advice was not heeded or welcomed, so he finished as quickly as possible and left the table.

Richard stepped out onto the front steps to get some air, and Arla caught up with him there. She looked at him anxiously and said, "Mary has never been away from home, and I know she will try, but there is so much she doesn't know about keeping house. I thought she would be around where I could help her, so please, Captain Holmwood, be patient with her. I do feel better that Wrennet is going. She will be such a help to Mary, but you must promise to take care of my baby. She is our princess, you know."

He looked at Arla, "I promise she'll be fine." He walked down the long drive back to the ship feeling ineffective and somewhat overwhelmed, and detesting, like any sailor, having to walk. Before he left on the previous voyage, he had taken his beautiful gray gelding to the Spencers where someone could feed and ride him for the next several years. They were only too happy to have another mount, and such a splendid one at that.

Richard loaded tons of supplies from the warehouse on board the ship. Included in the inventory were five tons of salt beef and pork, and five tons of pure salt which could be used for trade. He also packed for their own use barrels of pickles, flour, oatmeal, ship's biscuits, pickled cabbage, sugar, tea, wine, beer, rum, dried peas and beans, dried apples, and spices, not to mention Mary's crates of miscellany to set up housekeeping. Mary had scoured Surry and Williamsburg and brought along enough wool to make socks for every man on the ship, and she was still looking for more when Richard reminded her that yarn was available along the East Coast too.

Later that night in the devastated kitchen, Mary was going over her list one more time when Richard stuck his head in and smiled at her. She was chewing the end of the quill as she worked, and had somehow gotten a spray of ink, like freckles, over her cheeks. She looked up as he said, "You can also shop at the chandler's in Norfolk. They have a good variety. After all, it's where the Navy shops."

"Will we see any naval officers there?" Mary asked, suddenly interested.

"Norfolk is teeming with them, so there is a better than average chance that you will," Richard said. "Why do you ask?"

"Last spring Papa took me with him into Williamsburg, and while I was there I saw four lieutenants," Mary said, smiling.

"Four of them. Oh, my," Richard said teasing her, but she didn't seem to notice.

"Oh, Richard, you should have seen them in their uniforms. They looked so handsome," Mary gushed, and Richard smiled to himself. At times he forgot just how young she was. No doubt less than a year ago she was probably entranced in a girlish way by the young officers. They probably did look fine in their blue and white uniforms, and all the more attractive because they represented something outside her little world.

"So you find naval uniforms attractive?" Richard asked, teasing her.

She still didn't catch his tone, and looked at him, nodding her head seriously, as she said in an almost reverent voice, "There isn't any man that wouldn't look better in a naval uniform." Richard smiled indulgently at her and returned to his own list making. They were leaving in two days, and he still had a great deal to do himself.

It rained the rest of the time they were getting ready and packing, but finally it was the day of departure. Mary had been up since before dawn, and she paced the floor now with excitement. They wouldn't be on Mackinac Island for months, but at least their journey was beginning in a few hours. Richard was trying to get another few minutes of sleep in a real bed, but Mary made so much noise trying to be quiet, that Richard finally got up and joined her.

Mary had been intent on cleaning the house one more time before they left, but Richard explained, "Mary, it doesn't really matter. In five years it will be dirty again, and I doubt strongly Owen will do much to keep it up. There will be plenty of dust waiting for you when you get back!"

They were leaving Scotland Neck on the little *Fiona*, and the plan was to transfer in Norfolk to the *Lorraine* already waiting for them. They would then sail up the Chesapeake Bay and into the Potomac River to rendezvous with and go aboard the *Vindicta* in Washington. From there they would sail back down the Chesapeake Bay and out into the open ocean toward their next destination, Boston. Richard hoped that Owen would be at the Boston warehouse as planned, as Richard intended to confront him as soon as he got there. The *Vindicta*, *Draco Mare*, and *Lorraine* would then travel to Halifax, Nova Scotia, then west on the St. Lawrence River until they reached the impassable rapids at Welland. At Welland, they would transfer their tons of cargo by barge, cart, or on foot to the ships waiting on the other side. They would then sail through Lake Ontario, Lake Erie, tiny Lake St. Clair, and into Lake Huron. Three hundred miles north from there lay the Straits of Mackinac and tiny Mackinac Island stood there between the upper and lower peninsulas of the Michigan territory. He had pointed all this out to Mary on the charts and she said aloud "Mackinac Island," but Richard corrected her and said it was pronounced "Mackinaw." The three ships they would board at Welland were survivors of the great Battle of Lake Erie. They were small, only twelve guns each and had not been built very well, but they would serve for the few years Richard and his crew would be in the Great Lakes.

Mary and Edward now stood on the deck of the *Fiona* at her pier in Scotland Neck looking around at the activity on deck and up in the rigging. They were both trembling with excitement despite the damp and cold, gray morning. Wrennet sought the shelter of the cabin she would share with Edward, but Mary stood holding Edward's hand and they watched the men turn the capstan bringing in the anchor. Even though they were securely tied to the pier, Richard had always insisted they drop at least one anchor. They were in a river after all, and if their lines should fail at the pier, they could find themselves aground or ramming another craft miles downstream.

Mary and Edward smiled as the wind and the current caught the *Fiona*. They ran to the rail to watch the anchor being grabbed with the tackle and secured to the cathead. The weather was cold and their cheeks flushed. Richard watched them dash here and there and they reminded him of Grub after a bath, bursting with pent up energy. They ran from rail to rail and bow to stern, and Richard was certain if he grabbed one of them they would be panting.

There had been heavy rains the previous week, and the sandbars on the western side of the river are notorious for shifting, so Richard ordered regular soundings as they made their way downstream. Mary and Edward leaned far over the rail to watch this new activity. As the lead line was dropped, the depth was relayed back to Richard, and he nodded. The line was pulled up and another call of "regular gray" was relayed. Mary walked closer and asked to see it. The sailor who was now winding up the line showed her the bottom of the heavy lead cylinder which was holding a small gob of mud in a hole in the bottom. Mary looked puzzled, and he smiled and showed her and Edward the piece of wax that had been jammed into the hole which would bring up whatever was on the bottom as the weight plunged it downward. Mary thanked him with a beaming smile, and then she and Edward ran to where men were heaving on a line. Mary darted forward as the sail went up, and Richard gasped as a huge block coming down barely missed her head. The block weighed at least thirty pounds and could easily have crushed her skull. Much as he had promised otherwise, he would have lost the Spencer's princess in the very first hour of their trip.

Richard scolded Mary and Edward and banished them to the signal flag locker in the stern of the ship, but they were not the least put out as they pointed and cheered while the ship gained speed and settled well into the wind. Richard shook his head as he looked at them sitting in the weak sunshine, grinning. Both were swinging their feet back and forth, neither having legs long enough to touch the deck.

Mary watched Richard from her perch and at times had to remind herself this was the same man she married. The transformation was incredible. On the ship he was alert, in control, and absolutely sure of what he was doing. Mary couldn't imagine making sense of the cat's cradle of lines and rigging above her head, but to Richard it was second nature. After an hour sitting on the signal locker, Mary and Edward went below to find some tea and biscuits. Mary had assured Richard that Edward's lessons would not go astray while they were sailing, and they tackled them now.

Mary and Edward were intent on his lesson when a young crew member entered with a tightly folded note from Richard. She thanked him and carefully unfolded the tiny piece of paper which said,

M,
You are now eleven miles from home.
     R

Mary smiled and tucked the paper into her pocket. They had been at Edward's lessons long enough, so she walked slowly around the ship until she located Richard in his day cabin bent over a chart. It seemed for the past month he had spent most of his time studying a chart or going over supply lists. The cabin door was open, and Mary knocked on the doorjamb. "Thank you for the note," she said, smiling as he looked up at her. She added, "Somehow, I thought it would feel different when I got beyond ten miles, but I don't feel any different at all." Richard smiled at her and motioned for her to come and look at the chart he was holding.

"Do you want to see where we're going first?" Richard asked. Mary nodded her head eagerly as she went to stand beside him. "First, we will stop in Hampton Roads. I promised my father I would bring you and Edward to see him before we left for the territory. We will stop in Hampton and Norfolk for supplies, and there we will transfer to the *Lorraine*, which will take us to Washington until we finally board the *Vindicta*," he pointed to Boston, "there." Mary looked at him with huge eyes. To her the little *Fiona* was enormous, and it was difficult to imagine larger ships.

"Will we see very large ships in Hampton Roads?" Mary asked excitedly.

"Absolutely. We will see ships there as large as they come. Don't worry," Richard said, smiling at her enthusiasm. He pulled out chart after chart showing her how they would progress up the coast and into the St. Lawrence. He was pleasantly surprised she could follow the map, and she even asked questions about some of the features she saw.

As they entered the Chesapeake Bay, Richard sent for Mary. She would certainly want to see the ships and they were everywhere. He watched her as she came on deck and had to smile at her excitement. He remembered coming down with his father and seeing this same sight. It had made an impression on him that hadn't worn off. Mary, beside him now, kept pointing and exclaiming as they saw larger and larger ships.

They finally tied up at the warehouse pier in Norfolk, and the *Lorraine* was already there, loaded and waiting. They stayed at an inn in Norfolk, and about midafternoon Richard announced, "I think it is time you met my family." He had avoided his family after Lorraine's death for no other reason than that it was easier not having to deal with their sincere but suffocating attempts to console him. As his second marriage was more or less a business affair, he felt it would have been hypocritical to invite them all to it. He did advise his father by letter, but had not actually seen any of them in Hampton in several years.

Richard, Mary, Edward, and Wrennet were bombarded, as soon as they alighted from the carriage, by children of all ages. Some, Adrian and Thomas' eldest children, were almost Mary's age, and the others ranged down to slightly younger than Edward.

Lydia was still besotted with her Thomas, while Micah's Margery, no less dominating with the passage of time, saw Mary and Edward as just two more souls to boss around, and she began joyously flinging orders as soon as she set eyes on them. Margery was pressed to get dinner on the table in time. The cook/housekeeper that lived with them was down with a bout of rheumatism, and it had been up to Margery and Lydia to get the huge meal ready. While Margery tossed many orders, she really had no idea what she was doing, and it wasn't until Mary quietly took over that it appeared they would actually eat that night. Old Gabriel was in his element with all his living family, save Owen, under one roof. When dinner was ready, he ate until he thought he would burst, drank brandy until his face was red, and got more than just a little tipsy. With his tongue well-lubricated with brandy, Gabriel told Mary in a whisper that could be heard down the entire table, that she was just the wife Richard needed. Mary looked uncomfortable at being publicly praised, but she gave the old man a smile that exposed her dimples anyway.

When Richard and Mary finally extricated themselves from the house, they fairly bolted to the carriage with Edward and Wrennet, eager to put its closed doors between them and the extended Holmwood family. Mary had won them over, but even she had her fill of them.

Mary and Edward had spent much of their five days in Norfolk visiting with Richard's family, and Richard had been able to acquire some of the items on Mary's list. The *Lorraine* seemed immense compared to the *Fiona*, and Mary settled into their cabin, happily noting a writing desk and more storage. When they arrived in Washington, Mary was surprised to see a pier and warehouse with the same large black "H" on a white background as she had seen in Norfolk and in Scotland Neck. Mary turned to Richard and asked, "Is this yours too?" Richard confirmed it was, and Mary stood looking at it as they approached. Suddenly the warehouse paled in comparison to the ship moored before it. She pointed, "Richard, look at that ship. It's beautiful! Is it yours?"

"Yes, ma'am. That's the *Draco Mare*, the Sea Dragon," Richard said with pride.

"Oh, I want to go on that one!" Mary said, leaning over the rail.

"No, I really don't think you do," Richard chuckled. "The *Draco* is built for speed, not comfort. You would be miserable on her in no time."

The *Draco Mare* was fast; there was no question about it, and she maneuvered like a dream. The only problem with her was that she was a wet ship. She ripped through the water with her mound of sails, but stuck her head into every wave, trying to sever them with her bow. Although her aft cabins stayed dry, the over wash made her foredecks constantly wet all the way back to the main companionway, and that was in good weather. Comfort was not an offering of the *Draco Mare*, but if you didn't mind sacrificing some dry clothing, she would get you where you were going faster than any ship Richard had ever seen. He had already made a small fortune on her transporting important correspondence and items of a perishable nature. Occasionally, they would transport passengers who needed to be somewhere in a hurry, and Richard charged them a king's ransom for the trip. One man, a diplomat from Spain travelling from Baltimore to Charleston, claimed his feet would never be anything but white and wrinkled again after travelling on her, but that aside, it was the quickest trip he had ever made. One old sailor in her crew, after just being soaked with green water as he stood well back from her bow, was reported to have said with a lewd wink, "Fast women is always wet, and this bitch ain't no dif'rent."

As they arrived in Washington, Mary and Edward were gawking from the rail of the *Lorraine* at what for them was the largest city they had ever seen. Richard again settled them at an inn, thinking they would be cramped in ship's cabins enough in the near future. After breakfast the next morning, he told Mary he was going to the Navy Bureau. "I'm going to look up an old friend, Stephen Decatur."

"You know Stephen Decatur?" Mary asked, breathless.

"You know him?" Richard asked startled.

"No, but I have heard of him. Everyone has heard of him. He is a great hero," Mary exclaimed. She was still lauding Stephen as Richard walked out the door.

Richard intended to look Stephen up after he met again with Commodore Perkins, but when Stephen heard Richard was in the building, he hunted him down and crushed him in a hug. Several young officers stood dumbfounded to see their great hero with his arms wrapped around another man in a boisterous hug, both of them slapping each other on the back and grinning like kids. Stephen insisted Richard dine with them that very night, especially when he learned Richard had remarried and had Edward with him. Stephen sent a quick note to his wife, Susan.

Mary tried not to stare over dinner at the handsome Stephen Decatur and his truly beautiful wife. She listened to the men catch up and was fascinated by the change in Richard. He laughed and teased and told animated stories. Susan asked Mary questions to make sure she was not left out of the conversation, but Mary was more interested in what the others had to say.

Toward the end of the evening, Stephen mentioned the ball they were hosting on Saturday and added, "I assume you will be attending since you are in town." Richard tried to decline, but Mary jumped at the suggestion, and Richard had no choice but to take her.

The following evening after dinner at the inn, Mary and Richard strolled down a line of closed shops, peering in the windows. It was nearly nine o'clock, but there were still many people about. Richard turned as a man called his name, and his face broke into a grin as he shook hands warmly, exclaiming, "My God! Patrick, how have you been?"

"Fine," the man smiled. "I couldn't believe my eyes. I thought you had vanished." He shook Richard's hand then turned to the woman next to him. "May I introduce my wife, Helen?" Richard bowed.

He turned to Mary and said, "I would like you to meet my wife, Mary."

Mary bowed to them shyly.

Patrick Somers, the younger brother of Richard Somers, who had been commanding the *Intrepid* when she exploded in Tripoli Harbor, looked at Mary and said, "When did you and Richard get married?"

Mary said quietly, "In January of this year."

Helen Somers smiled and said, "You are not a wife yet, dear. You still get to call yourself a bride."

"And a lovely one at that," Patrick said, bowing again. He and Richard caught up a bit, while Mary ran her eyes over Helen Somers' attire, trying not to be obvious. Mrs. Somers was dressed in deep-green silk with cream lace and ribbons. She was not overly beautiful, but with her hair and her clothes, and more importantly her expertly bared bosom, she looked incredible. Mary twice caught Richard appraising her exposed breasts, and though it was a casual perusal, it shocked Mary nonetheless. Mary was still watching closely as they found a coffeehouse two blocks away where they could talk.

As soon as they entered, they were greeted by two couples seated at a table. More chairs were called for, and the four couples squeezed around the tiny table which was no bigger than a barrelhead. Introductions were made all around, and the names began to swim in Mary's head, though she could tell the men had known each other through their early days in the Navy. The other two were men who had grown up with Richard and Patrick Somers. As the topics turned to ships and battles and people she didn't know, Mary looked around the room. It was full of the well-to-do of Washington. The lower classes enjoyed themselves at a tavern, leaving the coffeehouses to the better-heeled. She noted all the ladies were wearing magnificent gowns with seemingly miles of cleavage. Surprisingly, the men escorting these women knew the other men were looking, but were not offended, and further seemed almost proud.

Mary had more tucked away in her bodice than these ladies combined, though she had never thought to show it off. She recalled Emma telling her once that married ladies were allowed to show their bosoms in eveningwear. Living in the backwater of Scotland Neck, she had never seen it done nor even thought to do so.

The following morning, after Richard had left for his meetings and she had made sure Edward was doing his lessons, Mary locked the door to her room and put on her wedding dress. She stood in front of the mirror and looked critically at the gown. It was made of the most exquisite silk which, at Wrennet's suggestion, Richard had given her before the wedding. After they were engaged, Richard had Shaw pick some cream silk out of the warehouse and deliver it to her at home in Scotland Neck as a Christmas present. The wedding gown had been made from the material, and the cut of the waist made it flow beautifully, but it came up over her collarbone at the neckline. Mary rolled the collar down, exposing the top of her breasts to where she normally wore her gowns, and then rolled it down another inch or two. She looked at herself, and, daringly, rolled it down another inch. It was still far from the cut of Mrs. Somers' dress, so she rolled it even lower. Inch by inch she moved the dress down until it looked like the gowns she had seen. Mary felt practically naked, but she also felt a bit daring. Armed with stout shears, she cut inch after inch off the dress until it was just above what she considered indecent. She was afraid that if she stumbled she would cascade over the top of the dress.

It would be impossible to wear any type of corset with the dress as it would show above the bodice, so she cut a shift low and gathered it in at the top in an attempt to corral her considerable bust, which now threatened to swell up out of the dress. Mary edged the collar with very transparent netting, which she thought might give her a little more confidence but actually accentuated her bounty. She had two days to worry about wearing it in public and hoped she wouldn't lose her courage.

The Decaturs had insisted the Holmwoods spend the afternoon with them and then dress for the ball from their house. It seemed a silly thing to do, but Mary was excited, and besides, Richard wanted to talk to Stephen alone. On the day of the ball they arrived with Edward, whom the Decaturs insisted they bring, and the women immediately disappeared to conspire while the men retreated to Stephen's study.

Edward was left in the care of Susan Decatur's nieces, who immediately set upon his golden curls with combs and vigor. He was like a doll that could move and talk, and even Edward had to admit it was better than doing his lessons.

Richard and Stephen discussed the logistics of the trip to the Northern Territory and the political implications it held. Stephen smiled and said, "You know, when this trip is over you could come here and make your mark in politics. Washington loves a hero."

"I am no hero, Stephen, nor have I ever wanted to be," Richard said.

"Don't you want to scorch your name into history forever?" Stephen asked, smiling.

Richard put down his glass and said, "Stephen, I am just as good a warrior as you, and I am a better seaman. You know it, and I know it. I don't need for the world to know. As a matter of fact, I spent a great deal of effort in the past few years making sure I wasn't noticed, and I like it that way."

Stephen smiled softly, "You're right. You are the best seaman I know or probably will ever know, but don't you ever want to be a part of the action here in Washington? To be where the decisions are made?"

"Good God, no! Stephen I hate politics, you know that. I always have. I am a sailor, not a statesman, and I would miss not being on a ship. Be truthful Stephen, when was the last time you were at sea, and don't you miss it?" Stephen didn't answer, but he nodded solemnly.

Richard left the discussion there and changed the subject. "I saw James Barron in Norfolk. I don't know what he was doing there, but he actually walked to the other side of the street when he recognized me. Have you spoken to him since the court-martial hearing?"

Stephen shook his head. The topic of James Barron was a sad one. James Barron was in command of the *Chesapeake* when she was attacked by the British early on in the recent war. Barron was so unprepared and had so much personal paraphernalia cluttering the deck that it was impossible for him to fire a single gun in defense. This lack of preparation cost the lives of several crew members, and forced the United States to bear the indignity of having one of its ships searched for alleged British deserters. This affair contributed to the war with England that followed. Stephen Decatur was a member of Barron's court-martial. Barron was convicted of negligence and was suspended from the Navy for five years without pay. This caused great financial hardship for Barron and his family. Barron never forgave Stephen for voting against him, but in truth Decatur could not have done otherwise. Barron returned to the Navy after five years, nearly a broken man. Stephen Decatur had been like a son to James Barron before the court-martial, and this relationship made the outcome all the more heart wrenching. Stephen shook his head sadly now and said, "James and I continue to exchange heated letters. He still claims I went out of my way to have him discharged. This is the gist of his letters in the past, but lately he has attacked my personal life. He goads me about dropping Anna and marrying Susan." Stephen referred to a girl in Philadelphia that he had been very close to marrying. "How could James possibly understand that once I met Susan, Anna was eclipsed and didn't really even exist for me anymore. Anna and I were never actually engaged, though I have to admit, if Susan and her father hadn't come sightseeing aboard my ship in Norfolk, I probably would have asked Anna to marry me. Mercifully, I met Susan when I did."

"Mercifully and fortunately," said Richard, tipping his glass to Stephen.

"You know, your name comes up at times in Barron's letters. He was good friends with Anthony Portman, and I don't think Barron ever quite forgave you for marrying Lorraine. You stole her right out from under his and his wife's noses. I think he thought perhaps he and his missus could soothe Lorraine's wounds and be there for her in her time of grief, gradually pulling her back into society. Of course they had no idea the upstart Richard Holmwood had already made great inroads into her heart. I think more than anything Barron doesn't like you because he never saw it coming. You were a marriage thief."

"Marriage thief? What the hell is that?" Richard said with a snort.

"I don't know," Stephen said exasperatedly. He took a great swallow of his brandy. "Speaking of marriage, when did you decide to have another go, and where did you meet the lovely Mary?"

Richard held out his glass and Stephen topped it off. Then he filled Stephen in on the details of his recent marriage.

ON HIS LAST TRIP to Washington, Richard had purchased a new uniform. He had not worn his old one since before Lorraine's death, and it was fairly old even then. The Navy specifications for captain's uniforms had changed. In addition to the gold epaulets on each shoulder, there was a good deal of gold trim around the collar, lapels, and cuffs. When Richard first saw the uniform at the tailor's he thought it was a joke, but the tailor had the particulars right there, and the uniform was accurate to the buttonhole. When Richard came downstairs and Stephen saw him, he said, "You know Richard, I was always envious of you. No one looks better in that uniform than you. I almost wish I didn't have to stand next to you tonight."

Many of the guests had arrived and Stephen greeted them cheerfully, sending them in search of Richard. He had been out of circulation for years and they all wanted to catch up with him. After the commotion settled a bit, Richard stood waiting for Mary at the foot of the stairs with Stephen, William Bainbridge, and another officer he did not know personally, but who had been introduced as Commodore Aldridge. Stephen leaned over and said to all of them, "You know Susan! Her entrance will be a grand one, and she'll make sure she is last."

Richard had taken an instant dislike to Aldridge, who had spent the time since he arrived assessing all the women as they walked by him, deeming them too old, too fat, not padded well-enough, padded in all the wrong places, and so forth. Aldridge leaned back now and said of a passing woman, "She would do for a toss, but I'll bet you my best buttons, she's a nag and wouldn't shut up unless you gagged her. She's good for one thing and that's in the dark, but then again, women are good for little else."

Richard and Decatur exchanged glances, and then the three of them, including Bainbridge, stepped away to distance themselves from Aldridge. Richard said, "What an ass that man is, but I have to admit I sort of see what he means." Richard looked across the crowd at the ball and then back at Decatur and Bainbridge, who were both looking at him aghast. He quickly explained, "I mean that, when I came back into society, I thought I would see a change from Scotland Neck, but I see none. What happened to all the beautiful women? Was it the war?" He looked at Stephen and Bainbridge, and added, "Look around. With the exception of a very few, these women all look coarse and dumpy, even the young ones." Stephen didn't answer, and Richard looked over to see if they agreed, but both men were just smiling and shaking their heads.

"You are jaded, Richard. You are jaded by what's on your arm, and these women don't measure up," Stephen said, smiling.

Richard now understood his meaning and shook his head, "No. Mary is very sweet, but, well, let's just leave it at that. She's sweet."

He had no more said it when Mary appeared at the top of the stairs. Aldridge saw her too, and moved over toward them to ask, "Well, whose little bird is this? I might have to teach this one a trick or two before she would be any fun, but she sure is a looker."

Richard didn't dignify Aldridge's comment, but instead stepped forward to meet Mary who was now descending the stairs. He had hardly recognized her. Her hair was stacked in a mass of curls, and she was wearing her wedding gown, but it certainly looked nothing like it did the day he married her. She had not spotted him, and he stood watching her as she searched the crowd for him.

Mary saw a knot of naval officers standing together, but Richard wouldn't be among them. She didn't see Richard edging over to intercept her at the foot of the stairs and nearly ran into him saying, "Sir, I'm so sorry, I wasn't watching where. . ." but she never finished. She just stared at Richard with her eyes huge and her jaw slightly ajar.

Richard reached out a finger and pushed her jaw shut. He held his arms out to his sides, "Alas, Mrs. Holmwood, not a lieutenant."

Mary touched the gold-trimmed lapels of his coat. His curls were like a gold crown that set off the dark uniform jacket, and he looked simply magnificent. Mary was tempted to touch his cheek to make sure he was real.

She finally spoke in fragments, "Oh, Richard. . .the Navy, how did you? Why?" Mary couldn't put enough thoughts into words. Standing in front of her was her girlish fantasy magnified to the power of ten, and she was almost speechless. She finally found her voice and said, "I didn't know you were still in the Navy. I thought you were like my Papa. I mean, people call him captain, but you are a real captain."

Richard stepped forward, grinning, and said, "Mary, the Navy has owned me since I was thirteen years old. I never resigned my commission. I simply took a long leave of absence."

Mary said, smiling, "You mean when you were a pirate?"

Richard laughed out loud. "I was never a pirate. I was a privateer, and there is a vast difference." He took her arm and put it through his, and as he led her to the salon he said, "It may be only ink and paper, but there is a difference between a pirate and me." Mary smiled up at him admiringly.

William Bainbridge nudged Stephen and said almost sadly, "I shudder to think what I would be willing to give to have a woman look at me once the way she just looked at him." He cleared his throat and added, "Richard has a knack for marrying the most beautiful women, doesn't he?" Stephen smiled and nodded.

Later, the Decaturs and the Holmwoods were watching people dance and during a break in the music, Stephen asked, "Whatever happened to your earring, Richard?"

Richard coughed on his wine and then laughed. He looked at Stephen and said, "I still have it around somewhere, and thanks to you, I still have the scar on my ear."

Mary looked from one to the other confused, and Richard quickly related the story of the spicy food and native clothing that accompanied the burning of the *Philadelphia*, but now he told about his earring. "We were supposed to look native, and Stephen took a dirk, one that undoubtedly had been used for fouler things, and pierced my ear with the point of it. He then crammed this thin gold bar through it, and crushed it closed with his teeth. I had to have it filed out of my ear when it was all over, and it left this scar." Richard pointed to his left earlobe which was slightly misshapen and bore a crescent-shaped scar.

Mary listened, entranced, as tale after tale was traded between the men. She hated to miss any of them, but she had not seen Edward for a while so she whispered to Richard that she was going to check on him. There were several more boys his age at the ball, and they were all staying overnight at the Decaturs. Edward had asked if he might stay with them, and though she and Richard had agreed, Mary was still worried about him. Susan Decatur saw her leave the group, and she asked if something was wrong. Richard explained where she was going, and added, "She has been very good for Edward."

Susan smiled and added, "I wager Edward is not the only one she has been good for." Richard started to comment, but sipped his wine instead and just winked at her. He chatted with Susan until he saw Mary return, and then excused himself to join her.

Mary was standing next to him, tapping her feet in a snappy manner, and Richard asked, "Dance, Mary?" Mary's eyes lit up and she nodded eagerly. Richard loved to dance.

They took the floor just as the music was starting and quickly found their places. Mary was good in her efficient, bouncy little way, and she seemed surprised he knew the steps. "I didn't know you knew this dance."

Richard chuckled, and the next time they came together in the dance, he said, "Mary, this dance was around when I was a boy." The music suddenly changed, and the head musician announced loudly, "The Slipper!" Several couples left the floor, and Mary looked at Richard shocked.

"Shall we give it a go?" Richard asked. Mary nodded eagerly.

The Slipper consisted of music and dance steps inserted into another piece of music already being played. The partners alternated between the original dance and the Slipper. As the music got faster the steps became more elaborate. When couples fumbled in their steps, they left the dance floor until only one pair remained.

Twice Richard had to adjust his stride when Mary moved backward so as not to trample her, but they managed to keep going. They reached a point where only Richard and Mary and another couple were left on the floor. They proceeded into the most complicated and final part of the dance where the music no longer alternated but stayed only on the Slipper. Both couples moved around the floor equally matched, but they were now required to cross each other in an elaborate twirling move. Just as the other couple gave up, Richard overstepped, and his boot came down on Mary's dress. She came up short and stumbled, but before she could fall, Richard picked her up in his arms and twirled her around laughing as they exited the floor. "Did I tear your pretty dress?" he asked, and Mary shook her head no. The contest was called a draw with neither couple actually claiming victory, though for Richard and Mary it certainly was one.

They moved toward the buffet, and Richard leaned down to Mary's ear and whispered, "Eat the oysters, Mary, if only for self-defense." She looked at him shocked, but smiled. Even in her protected life, she had heard whisperings of the aphrodisiac quality of oysters, and she blushed now that Richard would mention it. She picked up the shell containing a plump raw oyster and held it out for Richard to squeeze a lemon slice over it. He winked at her as she tipped the oyster into her mouth to catch all the rich liquid on her tongue before daintily wiping her mouth. "We will miss these where we're going," Richard said as he downed several more oysters before escorting her back to the dance floor.

The dinner portion of the ball was now over, and many people had finished their dessert and moved to other tables for after-dinner conversations. Stephen stood on the platform on which the quartet had been playing and motioned for everyone's attention. He smiled and said loudly, "We honor tonight a man who has been like a father to us. The first time we met him, he called us a pack of boys, actually a pack of schoolboys, and with regard to our brashness and hubris, he was probably correct. However, he molded us into the men we are today, so I say please raise your glass to the late Commodore Edward Preble!" Everyone cheered and drank from their glasses. Stephen loved an audience, and the stage had truly missed a fantastic performer when he chose the Navy as a career. He warmed up to his audience now by introducing all the men present who had served under Preble, complete with a little biography for each man.

Mary turned her chair so she could see better, and Richard had scooted his around behind her. Stephen told of the accomplishments of each man, and Mary found it a little game to try to guess who Stephen was talking about before he announced them. Each man stood when his name was finally called and raised his glass to Commodore Preble. Stephen was now introducing another man, and Mary listened as many of the same deeds were repeated, which since they had all served together was not unusual, and she let her thoughts stray. She began to pay attention when the feats Stephen was reciting changed from what she had already heard to, "It was his great talent and seamanship that brought our little sloop to safety after the burning of the *Philadelphia*. Through his brave actions in the recent war, over two hundred pressed sailors were freed from forced service in the Royal Navy. He destroyed more than twenty British ships, and captured thirty-three more as prizes. When other ships were finding safety from a snowstorm, thunderstorm, or fog, this man was quietly slipping out of blockaded harbors to hunt for the enemy." Stephen paused for a moment and then said, "He was in his youth, far and away the worst prankster in the U.S. Navy, and, yet, I admit without reservation, he is the finest seaman I have ever known. Please welcome back to us after a long absence, Captain Richard Holmwood."

Mary's mouth dropped, and she could feel Richard pulling his legs back from around her chair as he stood to raise his glass to Edward Preble. She looked over her shoulder to where he stood and simply stared. How could this serious man whom she had never heard do more than a good chuckle, be a notorious prankster and a naval hero? She felt as though she were married to two different men: the Richard she lived with and the Richard who had been.

When he sat back down, she whispered, "Did you really do all those things?"

He nodded quietly, "The good and the bad."

"You played tricks?" Mary said without thinking. It was so far removed to think of him as having a sense of humor that she still couldn't believe it.

"More tricks than I want to remember, and some of them were pretty rotten," Richard said, chuckling. Mary caught herself staring at him through the rest of the evening. Several times he saw her and grinned broadly back.

The ball was winding down. Most of the attendees had already left, and those who remained were the naval officers and their wives. They dragged some tables together, and then the tales really started.

Mary had consumed a considerable amount of punch, which, for her was four or five glasses, and her face and neck were flushed as Richard helped her with her shawl. After a dozen false starts where they were waylaid with goodbyes, Richard finally extricated Mary from the house. While they waited for their carriage, she rocked from foot to foot humming. She was still full of energy as they pulled away in the carriage. Richard squeezed Mary's arm and asked, "Did you have a good time?"

Mary gushed, "Oh, yes! I've never had so much fun in my life. And you, you looked so handsome." She looked at Richard and said almost sagely, "You were even more handsome than Stephen Decatur."

Richard burst out laughing and said, "He must be losing his looks here in Washington if I look better than him!"

Mary just smiled and then looked at his splendid uniform and said, "I still can't believe this is you. I mean, I never knew."

"Thank you," Richard accepted her compliment and then said, "I'll tell you one thing, Mrs. Holmwood. You have set a high watermark for the ladies at the next ball." Richard ran his finger down her neck, stopping at the netting at the edge of her bodice.

"Do you really like my dress? I mean, it's only my wedding dress made over, but I thought it was all right," Mary said anxiously.

"All right?" Richard said as much for himself as for Mary. "You really have no idea how nice you look, do you?" Mary shook her head no, and Richard smiled and ran his finger gently across the square edge of the bodice running low across her breasts. The opening was pushed forward by her bust, and it had reminded Richard all night of a treasure chest with the lid off, bursting with loot. He smiled wickedly and said, "Did you eat more oysters?" Mary nodded and he continued, "Good, because you are going to need every one of them." Mary pretended to look shocked, and then cut her eyes at him grinning. Richard grabbed her and pulled her over on his lap. She swayed a bit and supported herself against his chest, yet even through the heavy jacket and waistcoat, she could feel the muscles ripple in his chest. He ran his hand down her leg, pulling her dress up as he retracted his arm. Suddenly he said, "You naughty thing! You're not even wearing drawers!" Mary proceeded to tell him about how it was necessary earlier to abandon her drawers because the lace on them kept catching and pulling her dress awkwardly. Richard wasn't really listening. He was grinning so much.

They arrived at the inn, and Richard helped Mary out and paid the driver. They crossed the public area of the inn with as much decorum as possible, but at the first turn in the stairs they simultaneously broke into a trot. Richard suddenly picked Mary up, and she squealed with laughter as he jogged the last few steps to the door of their room. While he held her, Mary fumbled through his waistcoat pockets and finally found the key. She missed the lock twice but finally managed to drive it home and then twisted the large key with both hands. Richard kicked the door open softly with his boot and strode into the room. Still laughing, he dumped Mary onto the bed. They both tried to shush each other, but it only made them laugh more, and finally to keep quiet, Mary held her hands over her mouth while Richard went to shut the door. She took her hands away and tried to look serious, but in trying so hard not to laugh, she snorted instead. Richard turned at the noise and burst out laughing. God, it felt good to laugh. It had been years since he laughed. He shrugged out of his magnificent jacket and tossed it into a chair then moved toward Mary smiling, but she ducked around him, grabbed her nightgown and nipped into the dressing room. Richard's mouth tightened for a second, disappointed she had broken the spell, but he finished undressing and climbed under the covers leaving the lamp burning low.

Mary came out a few minutes later and crawled into bed, her weight barely even tipping the mattress. She had taken her hair down and braided it, and she was wearing a rather pretty but severe nightgown. She started to get back out to douse the lamp, but Richard stopped her. "Leave it, Mary." She looked at him alarmed, and he said without thinking, "For God's sake, Mary, give me something. Can't this ever be fun?"

Mary looked wounded and said, "I don't understand. I never deny you anything."

Richard looked at her and smiled softly, "I know Mary, but there is a difference between accepting and offering." He touched her face and asked softly, "Come on, haven't you ever wanted to be naughty?" She shook her head, and he said quizzically, "You, a rabid novel reader, tell me you have never in your life wanted to be a little bit bad?"

Mary didn't answer, more shocked that he knew about her stash of novels than what he said, and she looked at him steadily and then bit her lower lip. "Well, yes, but I don't know how. If there is something that you want me to do, then please, tell me."

Richard looked at her again and said as he gently pulled at the thick braid of her hair, "Take this down, please."

Mary started to argue. "But, I always braid it, so it won't..." but Richard put his hand gently over her mouth.

"You asked me to tell you, and I'm telling you. I've been married to you for months, and I have never seen you with your hair down. Do it for me," Richard said, tugging gently again at the braid. Mary sat up and pulled her hair forward and untied the ribbon. When she shook her head, the tresses unwound and settled in dark curls well below her tiny waist. Richard gathered the hair in his hands and ran his fingers through it, smiling. "That's better," he tugged at her nightgown, "and now, how about this?" Mary looked worried, and Richard said gently, pointing toward the door, "Once that door is shut, Mary, I would like it very much if you weren't a lady. There is no one here except me. Whatever happens in this room is between you and me; no one else will ever know." Mary smiled at him weakly, but she pulled the gown over her head and tossed it aside. Richard looked at her and smiled, "Very nice." He pulled her closer and whispered, "Now be a bit bad for both of us."

The next morning, Mary woke to find Richard dressing next to the bed. He was nearly finished, and when she sat up to speak to him, her head spun for a moment as she pulled her tangled tresses from her face.

Richard saw her and said, "You had too much of a good time last night." Mary smiled, remembering the ball and also that being a bit naughty was not a such a bad thing after all. Richard winked at her and said, "You'd better rest while I go fetch Edward."

"Edward? What time is it?" Mary asked, sitting up with the sheets bunched around her waist.

"It's only ten. You stay here, and I'll be back with him soon," Richard said, sitting on the side of the bed to put on his boots. Mary reached past him for a glass of last night's wine to wash the dryness out of her mouth. Richard rose to leave and smiled back down at her as she leaned up on one elbow. "What?" Richard asked puzzled by the look on her face.

Mary smiled, "I wish you weren't already out of bed."

"Really?" he asked, raising his eyebrows at her offer. He was certainly willing if that's what she meant. "Are you sure?" he asked again, and Mary nodded her head. It took Richard all of twenty seconds to strip his clothes and get back into bed, and from that point on they lost any sense of time as they romped with the hard morning light trying its best to push through the gaps around the curtains.

It was past noon before Richard left to retrieve poor Edward, and as he rode in the carriage to the Decatur's house, he took a rather wicked pleasure in having coaxed from the prim and proper Mary Spencer

Holmwood the frantic request, "Don't stop. Oh, God, please don't stop!"

Mary was still sprawled in the bed, which looked like it had been raided by looters, when she heard a gentle knock on the door. She jolted up, modestly pulling the sheet around her, and a young girl entered with tea on a tray.

The girl, about Mary's age, set the tray on a table near the bed and said quietly, "Captain Holmwood asked that you be brought tea and then hot water for washing. Do you need anything else?" Mary shook her head. "The hot water will be up in a few minutes," the girl said, looking around at the disheveled bed, cast off clothing, and Mary's snarled hair. She had witnessed dozens of scenes like this since she began working at the inn, and it made little impression on her, but Mary's face burned as she thanked the maid for the tea. After she left, Mary sipped her tea and smiled secretly. She had been ravished. It had been just like what happened to the women in her novels, though the words only hinted at the real thing.

Richard brought Edward back and they ate their noon meal together. After that, Richard set off for several meetings saying, "I'm getting a late start, so I will be back a bit later today, but in time to take you all to dinner." After Richard left, Mary and Edward set off for the shops while Wrennet stayed behind at the inn. Mary had twelve dollars in her reticule bag. It was all the money she had in the world, her life savings, but she soon found that the fabrics and wools alone that she would need for five years would eat up more than what she had, and there was still so much to buy. She and Edward wandered around most of the afternoon and then returned to the inn for tea.

Richard returned in time to dress for dinner, and asked to see what Mary had bought. When she explained she had nothing, he asked, "How can you shop half the day and have nothing to show for it?" He took off his coat and tossed it in a chair, saying gently, "Mary, I have a hundred things to do before we leave. I can't do this shopping. You are going to have to find the gumption to do it yourself." He was surprised as fat tears welled up in her eyes. "Why are you crying?" he demanded, and then Edward began to cry as well. He walked over and stood staring down at her, "Answer me. Why are you crying?"

Mary sniffed and then blurted out, "I couldn't buy anything, because I don't have enough money. All I have is twelve dollars I got from my father, and that isn't even enough to buy the wool I need." She stood staring at Richard with tears running down her face.

Richard's anger vanished, "Oh, Mary, I never even thought about that." He touched her cheek and shook his head. She had no way to know the merchants in any of those shops would have given her credit if they had known who she was, but they didn't know, and she didn't introduce herself.

Lorraine had always maintained accounts set up with merchants all over Hampton, and Wrennet had a small stash that Richard replenished, so it never even entered Richard's mind that Mary would need money to do her shopping. He told her not to give it another thought, but to get dressed for dinner, and they would take care of the money issue first thing in the morning. "We'll get your name on the accounts, and then you can get what you need," he smiled at her and added, "or if you see something you want, but you don't need, get that too."

RICHARD TRIED TO locate Owen in Washington but learned he had taken a smaller boat up the Potomac to pick up tobacco. Richard didn't have much time to follow up on the matter of Owen, for he had learned in his meeting earlier in the day that he would be taking on passengers in Boston. Douglas Deems would accompany them to the Northern Territory. Douglas Deems was very senior in the American Fur Company founded by John Jacob Astor. Deems would be travelling with his wife, and it was pressed heavily upon Richard to take good care of them. Astor was influential, both politically and financially in Washington and it would do to take care of his staff. Richard told Mary as they left the harbor, "We will have to double up a bit, but we have three ships. We should be able to accommodate everyone."

Mary's shopping successes disappeared into the hold of the *Vindicta*. Mary and Edward came aboard and swarmed over the ship, exploring as they prepared to set sail on this much larger ship. Once they left Washington they would make their way down the Potomac and into the Chesapeake Bay. They had been sailing in protected waters since they left Scotland Neck, but now for the first time Mary and Edward would enter the open ocean.

CHAPTER 12

NIGHT AFTER NIGHT, as he slept in his bunk on the *Vindicta* making her way to rendezvous with Richard and the *Lorraine*, Jordan Ladysmith had the recurring dream of the beautiful woman. She had never visited his dreams more than once a month in the past, but she had been at him relentlessly every night now for a week.

The *Vindicta*'s cargo was offloaded in Washington, and she was reloaded with food stores and crate after crate of household items which Jordan was told had been purchased by the new Mrs. Holmwood. Jordan was somewhat curious about her. The last time he saw Richard was the night he and Shaw had informed him about Owen's treachery, but when he had seen Richard just a few days ago, Richard had looked calm and relaxed. His marriage to this woman must then be agreeable.

Jordan took a walk to pick up some last minute things for himself before they left for Boston. He quickly obtained his parcels and then walked along the cobbled path of a nearby park. He could smell that winter had finally lost its battle and spring had arrived. Jordan had no destination in mind but was just wandering to kill time before returning to the ship. He came around a curve in the path and stopped dead in his tracks. There before him was the woman from his dreams. She was walking toward him with a small boy who now ran off the path to look at something. Jordan thought he would suffocate, his chest was so tight, but he finally managed to breathe and stood staring at her as she approached. In his early dreams as an eight-year-old, the woman seemed tall and stately, but now Jordan saw she was very small, tiny in fact. When she was about ten feet away she looked directly at him and responded to the grin on his face by smiling back. The smile created dimples on either side of her mouth, just as in the dream. She lacked the small red scar that was just under her chin, and her face was a little rounder. In his dreams Jordan thought her eyes were light, but now he saw they were dark brown. As she came abreast of him, Jordan extended his hand, "It's you. I wondered when we would finally meet."

The woman extended her hand, puzzled, but was disarmed by the smile of recognition on his face. Jordan took her hand, raised it to his lips, and kissed it while closing his eyes in both joy and relief. Over the years Jordan had dismissed a half-dozen girls as unworthy, and in doing so had cut himself off from wonderful female company, but even those half-dozen paled next to the woman standing before him.

The woman remained perplexed, waiting for an explanation or a reminder of who he was. She still smiled, but only to be polite. Jordan took her other hand, and said it again, "You must know me."

Just then he heard a voice behind him say, "I am so glad you two met." Jordan turned and saw Richard standing behind him. Richard stepped forward and added, "Jordan, this is my wife, Mary Holmwood."

Jordan gasped like he had been stabbed. Of all the men in the world who could have claimed her, it had to be Richard, and it cut Jordan to the soul.

Mary spoke now, moving her hand down from Jordan's lips to shake his hand. "It is such a pleasure to meet you Mr. Ladysmith. Edward has been so excited about seeing you again. It is all he has talked about."

That was it. No recognition, no joy at meeting him finally, nothing. Jordan's head pounded with a silent scream that he feared would blast through his forehead. He was certain Richard and Mary could hear it, but they just smiled politely and stood waiting for him to speak. He finally found his voice, and said, "No, ma'am, it's my pleasure." Just then Edward flung himself at Jordan, and he caught him as he sailed into his arms, "Edward! How are you?" Jordan asked, still caught in a vice of emotion.

"We were just returning to the ship to go aboard," Richard said, "but I wanted them to take one more nice walk before we did. Other than Boston, it will be a long time before they see a park again. Are you headed that way?" Jordan didn't answer, he just stared at Mary, and Richard said again, "Jordan, are you headed that way?" Jordan snapped out of his trance and mumbled no, he had a few errands to run, but that he would be aboard soon. "Then we will see you on board, shortly," Richard said, and put his hand in the small of Mary's back. She nodded goodbye as he led her away. Edward untangled himself from Jordan and followed them. As Jordan stared, Mary looked back over her shoulder at him and then cut her eyes away when she realized he was looking. Jordan moaned. It was the same gesture he had seen in his dreams a hundred times or more since he was a small boy. He watched Mary's back as she faded into the distance, taking all his dreams and hopes with her, and his heart froze over.

THERE WAS A FINE BREEZE and the waves were three to four feet. Richard watched Mary and Edward closely, expecting them to start feeling ill. Instead they both moved about the deck like they were still in port, though Richard noticed Mary kept one of Edward's hands tightly clamped in hers at all times. They seemed impervious to the motion of the sea, and Richard even saw Mary about an hour later, nibbling on a biscuit as she stood looking back at the shoreline. He paused beside her and she said, "Poor Wrennet. She is not feeling well." He nodded in sympathy and Mary then asked him, "Will we get out where we can no longer see the shore?"

"When we leave Boston, we'll head northeast for Halifax, and the shoreline will disappear then for a while. Does that frighten you?" Richard asked.

"No, I want to know just once what it's like to see only ocean everywhere," Mary said. Richard smiled at her thinking she was braver in this than many men he knew, including his own father.

"You'll get your wish soon enough, but not before we spend some time in Boston. Are you excited?" Richard asked. Mary nodded, her eyes sparkling as she took another bite of biscuit and jam. She saw Jordan Ladysmith on board just then and waved, but he seemed aloof, totally unlike the man they had met in the park. Mary attributed it to his shipboard duties.

The *Vindicta* arrived in Boston on a warm Thursday afternoon, and Richard regretted they would only be there a week. He and Jordan had mourned the last of the Puppets, who died several years earlier. Even though there was no family to visit, Richard retained a soft spot for the city.

They moored the *Vindicta* and Mary asked if she might walk along the pier until he was ready to go ashore. Richard nodded his head but warned her, "Be careful, that pier is going to feel mighty hard underfoot after being at sea." Mary looked at him like he was crazy and walked down the steps of the gangway.

Richard could hear the odd, repetitive, sucking, and heaving sound of the bilge pumps. The sound always reminded Richard of a dog about to be sick. Once primed, the pumps dumped their load into the dales to be carried away from the ship. The *Vindicta* virtually did not leak, which meant that the water in her bilge was not diluted by seawater. All the water there came from the decks above, and it carried down with it rainwater, seawater from over wash, the inevitable slopped urine, dropped food, sweat, and animal droppings, all of which fermented to incredible ripeness. Old salts said the horrid smell was like perfume, because the tighter the bilge the safer the ship. Richard knew the air around the ship would be pungent and he watched for Mary's reaction as she stepped onto the pier. She staggered a bit and then walked with that ungainly wide-legged stride, which is the trademark of a sailor first ashore. Richard knew from experience that it always felt like the ground came up to meet your foot before you expected it, almost like expecting one more step to be there at the bottom of a stairway. Mary looked up at Richard as she walked and she grinned at the sensation. "I told you," he called down to her.

Richard could hear the pump shafts were now nearly full and soon the bilge water would be flowing over the side just a few feet from where Mary was walking. She stood, letting the breeze run through her hair. Richard called to her to move a few feet ahead, trying to get her upwind of the exiting bilge water.

She looked up at him and shook her head, "I'm fine right here, I don't need to go any farther." Richard tried again, but Mary just shooed him off. He stood, watching her smile up at him, and he could tell the exact moment the stench hit her. She exhaled in a blast of disgust. He motioned again for her to move upwind and this time she stumbled forward until she could catch her breath. Richard loped down the gangway and joined her on the pier.

"What? Were we sailing with whatever is making that smell?" Mary said with disgust.

"They're pumping the bilges. The smell's not too bad. You should be along in the tropics. In that heat, the smell can actually make your eyes water."

"No thank you!" Mary said, still looking disgusted.

RICHARD DISAPPEARED in the dawn hours leaving Mary with Wrennet and Edward. As soon as the shops opened, Mary ventured out, armed with her procurement list and Edward for support. In Washington, she had seen a woman in a red cape and she wanted one with a hood. A cape, in scarlet no less, would be decadent beyond anything she had ever owned, and she was certain it was a sin simply to desire one. She found the fabric at a dry goods shop, and also a woman who would make it for her. Mary stood for the measurements and was told it would be ready in three days.

She bought cooking kettles, baking dishes, and all that she could think of to keep a kitchen in order, do laundry, put up preserves, sew clothing, and knit socks and gloves. After they left the dry goods shop, they found a cobbler and ordered shoes and boots for everyone. Edward was fascinated by the last, the form created to copy the exact size of his feet.

At an apothecary Mary bought herbs and powders for stomachache, headache, to stop bleeding, draw slivers, and a cure for her worst fear, lethargy. Idleness, her mother told her, was such a close cousin to sin it might as well be one. There was framed in the upstairs hallway back in the Spencer home an embroidered sampler that said "If the devil can't make you bad, he will keep you busy." Mary was confused by the saying as a child, and finally asked Arla what it meant. Her mother had said in her all-knowing way, "Even if the devil has a hard time getting you to be sinful, he will be keeping you busy thinking about it, so you don't have time for God." The sampler terrified Mary when she was little, and she would run past it absolutely convinced the devil himself, bedecked in horns and pitchfork, was going to leap out and snag her. She smiled now at her childish fear, but bought the lethargy cures anyway.

That night at dinner Mary tasted champagne. There had been some at the Decatur ball, but Mary hadn't been brave enough to try it. The bubbles tickled her tongue, so she had more than a few of the chilled, innocent-looking glasses.

The merriment brought about by champagne was only equaled by the headache it left Mary with the following morning. Even Richard was concerned when she couldn't get out of bed. Wrennet deemed her fine other than suffering from her first hangover. "What did you give her to drink?" she asked.

"Champagne," Richard replied looking at Mary, who had managed to prop herself up on pillows.

"You know nothing is worse the next day than champagne. You have practically poisoned her," Wrennet scolded.

"It's not like I held her down and poured it down her throat," Richard grumbled. "She asked me twice to get her more."

"Since when have you had trouble saying no? You could at least have warned her," Wrennet snapped as she put a cold cloth on Mary's forehead and shooed Richard from the room. There would be no shopping for Mary today.

The following morning she was much better. It had been three days since she ordered the cape. Mary told Richard all about it, praising it to the moon, pestering him, and finally begging him to be there for its unveiling. He reluctantly accompanied her to the shop, and sat as the seamstress fetched it.

The seamstress fastened it under Mary's chin. Smiling, she turned toward Richard, but quickly deflated at his reaction. She demanded a mirror.

She stood staring at herself. She looked nothing like she had imagined, nor did she look like the woman she had seen in the red cape. Mary had no way to know that capes are for tall women who have little or no breasts. On her, the cape jutted out and then hung straight down like a tablecloth making her look like a red tree stump. She began to sob, and Richard tried to comfort her. He looked at her in the mirror and whispered in her ear, "Have it made into a coat, and I think it will look very nice. A coat will serve you better where we are going anyway." Mary looked at the seamstress, who had heard what Richard said and nodded encouragingly. Richard added, trying to sooth the pain, "And while you are at it, why don't you have her make you a matching bonnet."

They had spent their week in Boston, but as their passengers were due to arrive the next day, they came back aboard the ship. Richard made alterations in berthing to accommodate the extra people. Jordan and Shaw were doubling up to make room. Now, on the eve of their arrival, Richard learned the Deemses were a party of five rather than two. It seemed they were bringing their three children, two daughters, and a son. Richard now had to find two more berthing areas as the daughters, he assumed, could sleep together. The other two ships had already left to rendezvous in Halifax, so there was no option of switching people around. They would just have to huddle up tight for the voyage to Halifax.

Whatever preconceived ideas Richard or Mary had about the Deemses were shattered as they watched them dismount their carriage at the pier. Douglas Deems, rather than being the broad-shouldered wilderness man Mary thought he would be, was short and portly and walked with a slight limp favoring his left leg. He, like Jacob Spencer, refused to give up his knee britches in favor of trousers, and his skinny legs poked out like sticks. He was about fifty and bald, and though he was not at all what she pictured, he at least looked like he would be jolly and kind.

His wife, Dorcas, however, was a nightmare. She was fat, not by any imaginative way still within the flexible realm of plump. She was hanging, rolling, waddling fat. Puffing from the exertion of climbing in and out of the carriage, she was red-faced and shouting as she waved at Richard and Mary on the rail of the *Vindicta*. Mary and Richard looked at each other and then back at the Deemses. Dorcas was nearly as wide as she was tall, and she had a good eight inches on Mary. She was clutching a reticule bag and a box of Turkish Delight in one hand, and had a small, nasty-looking terrier in the other. She tucked the dog under her arm as she headed for the ship, and there it yapped incessantly, but Dorcas seemed oblivious. Several of the younger officers ran to help her as she heaved herself up the gangway, stopping a few feet from Richard. In a loud nasal voice she yelled, "Permission to come aboard, Captain?" Richard forced a smile and offered his arm to help her onto the deck. She stood puffing before him while the dog continued yelping. Dorcas looked down at the dog, grabbed it and turned it around so its hindquarters were facing forward and its barking going behind. "Did I say that right, Captain? I have to ask, do I not?"

Richard peeled Dorcas Deems off his arm and helped her to a chair saying, "In port like this and with civilian passengers, it is more of a formality, especially when you are expected." He flashed a smile and then shuddered with his back to her as he returned to help the other passengers aboard. Mary stood watching as Douglas helped his children from the carriage and set about ordering his servants to bring the luggage. The two Deems daughters stood staring at the ship. They were tall and skinny and pale. Richard raised his hand in a polite wave, and they clung to each other, grinning as they bolted up the gangway. "Miss Deems," he said as he offered his hand to Stella, the eldest. She took it, blushing, and looked back at her sister, rolling her eyes. Richard helped her aboard and then reached for the younger daughter. They both stood now on either side of him with their arms firmly locked into his. He smiled and led them to their mother where the crew had hastily set up chairs.

"Captain, let me introduce my daughters. This is Stella," Dorcas gestured to the eldest girl, "and this is the baby, Cassandra. We call her Cassie."

Richard smiled and bowed to them alternately, saying, "Welcome aboard, Miss Stella, Miss Cassandra." They bowed and giggled, and Richard shuddered inwardly, reminded suddenly of the Widow Duggan and her big-butted daughters who could not stop laughing.

A young man of about sixteen loped onto the deck from the gangway and looked around. He had a most arrogant air. His hair was lank and rather greasy. He was slope-shouldered, and, for a young man, remarkably pot-gutted. His face was a veritable chart of acne, and his teeth gapped in his wide mouth. Dorcas called from her chair, "You must meet our young man, Captain." She said as if she were introducing royalty, "This is Reginald." Richard smiled and offered his hand to the young man, who had trouble making firm eye contact as he limply returned Richard's handshake. Reginald had obviously not suffered the benefit of Gabriel Holmwood's tutelage about handshaking, and Richard gave the boy's hand a slight crush of contempt.

Douglas Deems was the last to board. Dorcas had scolded the servants who were returning to the house to keep it in order while they were gone. After Douglas had given them some kinder advice, he paid off the driver and scurried up the gangway like a boy on an adventure. His life was completely ordered at home, but here, onboard, perhaps things could be different. He at least was hopeful. As a boy he had dreamed of slipping away on board a ship to avoid his mother and her two unmarried sisters, who combined forces to raise him. He had escaped the strict rule of home by marrying Dorcas, only to realize too late that she was a magnified copy of his mother. He now shook Richard's hand warmly, and smiled, his eyes crinkling with anticipation. Richard caught the smile and grinned at him.

The weather looked foul as they left Boston headed for their last real port of call, Halifax, and though it was cloudy, the wind and rain had held off. Dorcas sat on deck in a folding chair, sipping tea and eating from a platter of dainty treats she had bought at the Faneuil Market in Boston. Mary looked over the platter at the cheese-stuffed dates, candied oranges, custards in tiny individual crocks, cheeses in various shades of cream and yellow, pickled quail, smoked salmon, and colorful confections, and wondered at it. Dorcas and her girls were busy tucking into the fare, and though Mary had accepted a cup of tea, she didn't find the consumption of the rich, heavy snacks wise this early in the morning. Dorcas saw her and laughed, "My family, the Sennets, have always been sea people. We never have to worry about ill effects from the waves, but instead we soldier on as if nothing were amiss." Mary wondered if any of them had been to sea before, but she just smiled and sipped her tea, watching Dorcas and her two daughters gorge. The two daughters looked like leaner versions of their mother. They had blond hair, but instead of that shiny, glimmering gold like Edward's or even Richard's curls, their hair hung in lank and dull locks the color of greasy dishwater. They had the same wide mouth, though not as pronounced as their mother's, and each had the annoying habit of speaking with a whine. It didn't seem to matter what they were saying, the words hung in the back of their throats and then divided, so half the sound came out their mouths and the other half through their nose. They were slim, bordering on skinny, and would not have had a handful of breasts between them even if they pooled their resources.

Dorcas popped a chunk of salmon in her mouth and said while chewing, "I had heard of Captain Holmwood, and thought he might be right for one of my girls, but then we found out he had recently remarried." She shot a glance at Mary and continued, "I have to say, I was disappointed, because I think with some work he could have been brought around to meet Stella's standards, but at least we were glad to see you were so young." She picked up a piece of cheese that had dropped on her bosom and popped it in her mouth to mingle with the slurry of salmon already there.

Richard arrived just then with Reginald on his heels. Richard asked if they were all comfortable and then said, "I think you will have to move below deck soon. We have to adjust our course which will bring us closer to the wind, and it will get a bit rougher. Plus I believe we are going to have some weather, so don't wait too long to get below deck." As he walked away, Richard took note of the platter of food which Dorcas had now moved onto her lap for an easier reach.

As soon as he left, Reginald scoffed, "Storm? This is nothing. Mama, didn't you tell us the Sennets used to actually wish for this kind of weather?" Dorcas nodded, using her little finger to get the very last of the custard in a small pot. Reginald walked to the rail and planted his foot, stuck his chin out and announced, "We are of ungovernable spirit, and no skittish captain will dictate to us when we should seek shelter!" Reginald had no sooner said this than the ship shifted course and the foaming top of a swell lapped at the railing, wetting the front of Reginald's trousers so that he looked as if he had pissed himself. Mary looked away, but not before she saw several of the crew grinning.

The wind was now coming out of an unfortunate quarter, just enough to cause the ship to corkscrew a bit as it crested each wave which tossed fine spray over the side. Mary took this as her signal to get Edward below and into their cabin. Dorcas said her Sennet bloodline would see her through, "But you go ahead and seek shelter. You cannot help it if your ancestors were not a seafaring race." Just then the ship plunged downward, and an enormous wave came over the rail. Cassie Deems was washed off her chair and across the deck where she came up hard against the companionway stairs, and Mary went to help her. Dorcas took care to secure her platter and then screamed for Cassie to get up. Dorcas then turned in her chair, so her back was to the waves protecting her platter of treats, and she crouched down low over them like a cur with a bone. Mary looked at her quite certain that if anyone reached for the food, Dorcas would snap and bite. Mary helped Cassie to a chair and then took Edward by the hand and quickly led him below.

Half an hour later, the wind was stronger and the waves much larger. Mary came on deck clutching Edward's hand. The first person she saw was Jordan Ladysmith. She asked him if they would be all right in the storm. Jordan at first had tried to avoid her, thinking that would ease the pain, but he found he could not stay away. He spoke kindly to her now. "Mrs. Holmwood, this is not bad at all. The *Vindicta* has been through much worse and so has the captain. You shouldn't worry, but you should go below, because the water is coming steady over that rail," he pointed, "every third or fourth wave. You could get washed overboard! Do you want me to walk you both to your cabin?" Mary shook her head, looked at the huge waves, and darted down the companionway steps to her cabin. They encountered Richard coming up on deck as they went below.

Mary, still not sure, asked, "Richard, are we in danger?"

He grinned, enjoying the wind, and, forgetting whom he was addressing, said, "Oh, hell no, Mary. This is the kind of weather we used to hope for, so we could slip a blockade. This little blow is nothing, but I want you both below, so you don't wash overboard. The two of you together don't weigh as much as a soggy biscuit." Richard mussed Edward's hair and then added, "You take care of Mary now, all right, son?" Edward nodded and took Mary's hand again.

When they first set out from Scotland Neck on the *Fiona*, Mary had shared a rather large cabin with Richard and they even had a bed that folded out. When they transferred to the *Lorraine* and then to the *Vindicta*, they had increasingly larger cabins each time, although the ships were crowded. All three ships were sailing with a double crew. They contained one crew to continue on to Mackinac in the ships they would pick up at Welland, and one crew to sail the transport ships back to continue trading. They were all crammed tight as could be and had just enough room for Dorcas and Douglas Deems, but with the addition of three more people, they were beyond maximum capacity.

Richard's great cabin was divided with portable bulkheads similar to those used to partition off the gun deck. He had planned to split the cabin between himself and Mary on one side, and Douglas and Dorcas Deems on the other. Richard, remembering his duty to his passengers, divided his half of the cabin again, creating two cabins, one for the Deems girls and one for Reginald. Mary and Edward were given a tiny cabin with two bunks and barely enough room to stand, and Richard would hang a hammock in the tiny portion of his day cabin that remained. When Mary saw where she was to sleep, she asked softly, "Richard, am I not to sleep with you?"

Richard had just been accosted by Dorcas Deems about the need for her daughters to have separate rooms, so when Mary came to him questioning her own accommodations, his terse answer was, "Don't start, Mary." She looked at him confused, but held her tongue. She stood now in her tiny cabin, clinging to the bunk to steady herself. It was a low room with about eighteen inches of space between the ceiling and the top bunk. There was a little more, perhaps twenty-four inches between Mary's bunk and Edward's, and as for width, they were lucky if the bunks were twenty-four inches wide.

Mary tried to read to Edward in her bunk, but the lamp kept swinging, causing a shadow on the pages. She finally gave him some paper and asked him to draw her a picture. He sat cross-legged on the floor, using a book as a desk in his lap. Later, they heard someone retching in the cabin next door. The Sennet bloodline had obviously thinned somewhat over time, because there was a descendant suffering from a nasty case of *mal de mare*. There were some muffled words and then more retching, as another of the Deemses heaved up their tea snacks. Edward looked at Mary, and she asked him if he was ill. He shook his head and said, "No, Mary, I feel fine."

There was some banging and a crash and then more sounds of vomiting next door. Mary and Edward tried to ignore it, but the sound was almost steady now. The Deems children had sought shelter in their parents' cabin, and now Douglas Deems watched his entire family rolling around on the floor, fouling the cabin. They would vomit into a basin only to roll around spilling it as they heaved all over each other. Douglas, though lacking the protection of the Sennet blood, was doing remarkably well considering he was dripping with the semi-digested stomach contents of his entire family. At one point they all vomited on him simultaneously, and perhaps he could have stood that, but when he caught sight of Dorcas' wretched dog lapping at the mess, he fled the cabin for the fresh air of the deck. There he curled into a ball and clung to the davit line of one of the ship's boats, gratefully letting the waves wash over him, rinsing off some of the filth.

Richard saw Douglas and asked if he was all right. Deems nodded, but said his family was very poorly. Much as Richard didn't like them already, they were his passengers and his responsibility, so he went to check on Dorcas and her children.

He stared at the sick family for a few seconds and then he firmly closed the door on them. He had seen hundreds of cases of seasickness, but none where the victims conducted themselves quite so poorly as these, who rolled about heaving on everything including his personal furniture.

Richard now walked down the companionway dreading he would find Edward and Mary in the same condition. He gently pushed open the door to their cabin, and it stuck against an object. He craned his neck around through the restricted doorway and saw to his disappointment that it was Mary's ankle and foot blocking the door. Her dress was hiked up to where he could see the ribbons in the top of her stockings, and his heart sank to see they were no more impervious to seasickness than the hideous Deemses. Suddenly though, her foot moved, and Mary sat up from where she was helping Edward write his letters. She and Edward had stretched out on the floor on their stomachs, because there was no room for them to sit on the bunks. Richard opened the door and asked the obvious, "You two are not feeling sick from the waves?" Both Mary and Edward shook their heads no.

Mary stood up and reached for him for stability, "Richard, may we please go somewhere else? It smells so badly down here."

Richard had noted the sour smell of vomit coming from next door and said, "I can't have you on the deck, but I will let you sit in the companionway on the steps. The doors are closed, and you will still get wet there, because it is leaking when we have deck wash, but at least the air there is not so foul. Will that be all right?" Mary and Edward nodded eagerly, and as soon as they had on their coats Richard led them to the steps. They sat on the bottom two steps, one behind the other, and held onto the railing. The air smelled relatively sweet, and they breathed in great gasps of it. Richard returned to the deck while Mary and Edward waited just below.

Mary told Edward stories, and later Jordan Ladysmith came stomping down the hall. He brushed past Mary and Edward with a quick apology and shoved open the companionway doors. The water poured down the steps like a little waterfall for the few seconds the doors were open. Jordan found Richard on deck and reported to him the condition of the Deems family. "Sir, they are still vomiting something awful. "

"Jesus, their guts should be empty by now!" Richard said, clinging to a line to keep from being washed down the deck.

"They keep eating, sir," Jordan added.

"Eating! Eating what?" Richard asked, "Nothing has been served in this weather."

"They are eating all that stuff they brought with them from Boston, sir. The old lady is the worst. She insists they eat it now as it will only last a day or two before it spoils. They puke, sir, and then eat more custards and smoked fish, and then they puke that up too. It's horrible!"

"Where is all this stuff?" Richard asked.

"It's all in that little alcove just outside their door, sir," Jordan reported, noting himself he was using sir more than he ever had before.

"Come with me," Richard ordered, and started down the companionway stairs. Mary and Edward watched him pass, noting the furious look on his face.

Richard reached the alcove and saw the contents of the boxes and crates open where the Deemses had pawed through them. He looked it all over and then said to Jordan, "Throw this overboard." Jordan looked at him for a few seconds, and Richard caught the look, so he smiled and added, "Or if you know of some of the crew who will make it disappear in the next few minutes, give it to them, but I want it gone, you understand?" Jordan nodded and hurried for help to haul the boxes and crates below.

Richard stomped back to where Mary and Edward were sitting. He squatted down before them, then asked, "Are you sure you are both all right?" They nodded, and he touched Edward's gold curls and Mary's cheek before continuing back up the stairs.

The weather let up during the early evening, and Mary and Edward went up on deck and were given some bread and cheese and small glasses of wine. The wine was more than enough for Edward, and he was soon asleep in Mary's lap. She let him sleep while she listened for the ship's bell.

When she first travelled down the James on the *Fiona*, she thought the bells were like church clocks signaling the hour because she first noticed eight bells coinciding with the church at Scotland Neck ringing eight times, but before that first afternoon was over, she realized the ship's bells had nothing to do with the time of day. She asked Richard, and he rather impatiently told her the bell rang once for every half-hour of a four-hour watch and then started over. She paid attention and noticed that the crew changed at eight bells every four hours, and again she thought she understood what the bells meant, but from four in the afternoon to eight at night, crew members seemed to come and go on and off watch with no discernible pattern, so she was confused again. She overheard a man saying "dog watch" and realized something different happened around dinnertime. Not risking another of Richard's annoyed responses, she decided to just observe and see if there was a pattern. After a few days, though, she had given up. Particular men seemed to work together, but at different watches different days. She finally asked

Jordan Ladysmith, and he was pleased to explain it to her. He patiently told her that the dog watches were split to give the men time for dinner, and also to make sure that the men had a different watch each day. If it wasn't done in this manner, he explained, the same men would always have their watch at night. Even after Jordan's explanation, there seemed to Mary to still be a half hour for which there was no account.

Throughout the storm they had heard the ship's bell ringing every half-hour, and Mary finally asked Jordan, pointing to the binnacle, "Why don't they just use that clock they have?"

Jordan laughed. "That is a chronometer, Mrs. Holmwood. It tells the time in Greenwich, England. If we know the time there, we can tell where we are on the charts."

"By knowing what time it is in England?" Mary asked with interest, and Jordan nodded. She then asked, "Anywhere on the earth?"

"Well, anywhere that has been charted. There are still areas that are not charted as accurately as others," Jordan said. He would have stayed and talked to Mary forever, but he was called to the helm, so he smiled at her enthusiasm and then took his leave.

The first watch was now coming on deck, and Mary decided it was time to put Edward to bed. She struggled to lift him, and Richard came over and picked him up effortlessly. He carried Edward while Mary followed him back to their cabin. Richard put Edward on the bunk and then watched while Mary undressed him and tucked him under the covers. "You are very good with him, Mary," Richard said, looking at her.

"That's what I'm here for, remember," she smiled softly, and squeezed past him to put Edward's clothes on a small shelf near the door. When she stood, Richard pulled her by the arm closer to him. He looked at her carefully and then said, "I'm sorry I snapped at you, and I regret these sleeping arrangements. Deems and his horrible wife would have been bad enough, but I had no idea they were bringing their spawn too. What a hideous family!" Richard started to leave and then said again, "You really do take great care of Edward. I want you to know I appreciate it." He cleared his throat several times and then said, "This arrangement," he waved his arm around the cabin, "it is not done by choice. You should know that." He looked at her for another moment and then quickly left the cabin. Mary, finding she was as tired as Edward, slowly undressed and crawled into bed, dousing the light as she went. She was asleep within minutes.

The next day Reginald and Cassie Deems ventured onto the deck. Cassie's hair was crusted with dried vomit, and her dress was filthy. The only reason Reginald looked any better was because his hair was short. They had the complexion of an old rag left in the bucket too long, and they both looked like they had been squeezed dry. Mary approached them and asked if there was anything they needed. Both shook their heads and sat down on the chairs Mary had pulled up for them. "Would you be able to drink some tea?" Mary asked carefully, not wanting to mention food if they were still queasy. They both nodded weakly, and Mary went to get it for them.

On the fifth night out of Boston, Mary scrubbed Edward as best she could in a basin and then put him to bed. She washed herself and then doused the light as she crawled into her tiny bunk. About an hour later she was awakened by the covers being pulled down off her shoulder. "Mary, are you awake?" She heard Richard's voice very softly. She whispered she was. "Good," he chuckled deep in this throat.

Mary knew that chuckle and said, laughing softly, "Richard, you will never fit in this bunk with me, and besides, Edward will hear us."

"Edward is asleep," Richard said, and Mary could hear him taking off his clothes. In no time he climbed into the bunk on top of her, resting his weight on his elbows. He rocked on his side, pulling her hair as he did so, and she cried out still laughing, as he got her cradled in his arms with his weight balanced on his forearms. Twice his back actually banged against the bottom of Edward's bunk, and each time they waited for him to stir, but he did not. Richard started to extricate himself from the tiny bunk and when he put his foot on the floor Mary heard his boot thump on the deck.

Teasing him, she hissed, "You didn't even take off your boots."

He chuckled and whispered back, "Desperate times, ma'am." Richard dressed quickly, and stood next to the door. As he opened it to leave, he heard a sound in the corridor and shut it again, not wanting to face a crew member in such a disheveled state.

Edward thought Richard had left and called out in a small voice, "Mary?"

"Yes, Edward," Mary said, trying to hide her alarm.

"Did my Papa hurt you?" he asked concerned.

Mary tried to sound soothing. "No, sweetheart, he didn't hurt me. Go back to sleep now." Richard waited a few minutes and then slipped out through the door and back up on deck.

Mary awakened before Edward the next morning and quickly washed and dressed and went to find Richard. He was drinking tea and looking up into the rigging. Mary asked alarmed, "What is wrong up there?"

He smiled down at her, "Nothing really, but we will have to make some repairs before we get into heavy weather." Mary looked at him in alarm, and he added, "That weather we had really wasn't much. We'll go through much worse than that little storm before we get to Mackinac, I am certain of that!" Mary reached for his tea, and he handed it to her, saying, "Careful now, it's piping hot."

Mary sipped the tea and leaning closer said, "Richard, Edward was awake when you were in our cabin last night."

Richard took back the tea and sipped it saying, "I know. I was still there when he spoke to you." He looked down at her and smiled, "Don't worry, we'll find a better arrangement." Mary started to walk away, and he pulled gently at her arm and added, "Because I don't intend to stay away." Mary blushed and went to check on Edward, but she was smiling as she went.

Jordan had been watching Richard and Mary talking on the deck and his gut tightened as he saw Mary blush. He couldn't hear what they were saying, but it seemed playful, and he choked on jealousy like it was bile.

The *Vindicta* arrived in Halifax in the afternoon, and awaiting them were two cartographers who had been hired by the Navy to create the most detailed charts of the Great Lakes to date. One, Sebastian, had served with Commodore Oliver Perry on Lake Erie, but had then gone on to explore and sail all the Great Lakes.

The *Fiona* and the *Lorraine* were moored waiting for the *Vindicta*. They could now redistribute some passengers and make at least Mary and Richard more comfortable. The Deemses were moved to the *Lorraine*, where they could bother someone else for a while, but where they still had fairly easy access to Richard if they needed him. As soon as they entered the St. Lawrence, all three ships would always be within hailing distance.

The mess the Deemses made in Richard's great cabin was finally cleaned up, and then Mary had a go at it until it met her standards before they moved back. Redistributing passengers required the shifting of cargo, and this required that the two stern chasers, which had been out of sight until now, be moved back into Richard's great cabin. As soon as Mary saw them she stopped dead in her tracks.

Richard came forward and pulled her face up toward him. "Mary?"

"How can you just stand next to that," she said, pointing to the gun. "Aren't you afraid it will explode?"

He laughed. "It can't go off," Richard tried to assure her. "It isn't even loaded."

She looked up at him and asked, "Why is it on this ship? Is this a ship of war?" She fired her questions so quickly, he didn't have time to answer.

Richard looked at her carefully. "Yes, but so were the other ships you have been travelling on."

Mary looked at the gun. "They didn't have things like this on them."

"They certainly did, but you didn't go where they were," Richard said.

The war is over though, isn't it?" Mary asked, confused and

frightened.

"The war is over, and we are at peace with England, but things can change." He caught her look and quickly added, "I don't think we will ever be at war with England again. I think they will leave us alone now, but it would certainly do to be prepared just in case, wouldn't it?" Mary still looked frightened, but she nodded her head yes, and he continued. "These are a precaution, only."

"You told my family you were extending your trade up into the territories!" Mary said, looking back at the gun.

"And I am, but I am also serving the Navy by being there just in case. We are doing both at once. This peace with England is less than a year old. We are here in case it doesn't stick. I already told you I don't think we will ever have to fire these guns other than to stay in practice, but we'll be ready just in case," Richard smiled at her, hoping she would understand.

"Guns? There are more?" Mary asked, her voice catching on the last word.

Richard looked at her a long time before he said, "There are five more this size, and fourteen that are smaller."

"Can't you get a room without one?" Mary asked, looking frightened.

Richard stood and sat her down in his chair. "On a ship of war, everyone eats, sleeps, and lives with the guns, even the captain. These are stern chasers, and they fire at what is behind. On some ships they are in the same cabin as well as the port and starboard guns, so there might even be a total of four in a cabin. I can't move this one into the hold. It has been out of sight until now."

Mary looked around the room, "But where will we sleep in here with this in the way?"

He smiled and said, "We'll sleep like most sailors sleep, in a hammock. Ours will be a bit more glorious than the average jack's hammock, but it will still hang from that beam." He pointed toward the ceiling and Mary noted two large hooks embedded deeply into the oak. He continued, "I've had the ship's carpenter knock one up that is a bit larger, so we can share it, that is if you still have a mind to share." Mary ignored his comment and walked toward the cannon. She put out one finger and gingerly touched the barrel.

"It's so cold!" she exclaimed.

"It's only a twelve pounder, but that's still a lot of iron," Richard said, watching her.

Mary turned to him and said, shaking her head, "Richard, I don't know anything about naval warfare, but I can certainly tell you this thing weighs a lot more than twelve pounds!"

Richard laughed out loud, "Oh Mary, no! The cannonball it fires weighs twelve pounds. The gun itself weighs more than a ton."

"You said there is no way it can go off while we are in here?" Mary asked, still looking at the gun.

"No, Mary. It would have to be loaded with gunpowder in order to fire," Richard tried to reassure her.

Despite her fear, she had a natural fascination with the gun. "How much gunpowder would you put in it?"

"It would take five or six pounds," Richard answered her.

"Is the gunpowder on board this ship?" Mary asked, turning to Richard. He nodded that it was. "Is there enough to blow us all up?" she asked, already knowing the answer.

"Several times over, but we are in no danger. It is stored deep in the ship, and there are people whose only job is to care for it. Don't worry." Richard stood and came to where Mary was standing, looking at the gun. "So, are you going to share this cabin with me or not?"

She nodded and then agreed. "All right, I'll sleep with you and your big gun." Richard let her answer go without remark, but he chuckled thinking it left room for a great many earthy comments.

The three ships made their way slowly westward up the St. Lawrence River, and the scenery was nearly always the same. Mary and Edward were now bored and longed for the trip to be over. No matter how much she scrubbed, the ship always seemed damp and dirty, and where the dirt came from she had no idea, but she was ready to be on land again.

Mary and Edward took to bathing in the river very early in the morning, and it was in this way she taught Edward to swim. They would always get permission from the officer of the watch, because that is what Richard told them they had to do if they ever left the ship. Richard eventually heard of their morning ablutions, though, and made them stop.

At Welland there were an impassable rapids, and everything had to be portaged and transferred to the three ships waiting for them on the other side, the *Huron*, *Elsinor*, and *Chippewa*. It took three days to offload and reload everything, but then it was time to say goodbye to the *Fiona*, *Lorraine*, and *Vindicta* as well as to the second crews that would man them home. Jordan lingered saying farewell and to her surprise, kissed Mary's hand before he turned and walked to his ship.

Richard took the *Huron* as his, and they climbed aboard and spent the next two days stowing everything. If they thought they were cramped before, this was twice as bad. The ships themselves had been cobbled together from green wood in the dead of winter to fight the British fleet on the Great Lakes, and they leaked like sieves. Richard found that when he installed the additional guns he brought, he had to shore up the deck supports. Each ship handled little better than a large shoe, but together they had valiantly served their purpose.

They sailed across Lake Ontario and as they neared Lake Erie Richard explained to Mary that the *Niagara*, Commodore Perry's ship, had been purposefully scuttled in the area to be raised if ever needed again. Mary looked at him and noted the sad expression on his face as he contemplated ever having to destroy a ship that had served him so faithfully. Mary and Edward scanned the surface of the water, but there was nothing to mark the grave of the brave vessel.

They halted near Detroit to search for a milk cow. Mary had wanted to bring one from Scotland Neck, but Richard had assured her one could be found when the trip was almost over; the cow and crew would be happier if they did. When they reached Detroit there were no bovines but a few thin looking steers. Mary huffed a bit and let it be known that it was a good thing she had brought the chickens, or there would be no eggs either. Richard let her blow off steam. She had been a game traveler so far, and he knew she was getting anxious to get off the ship.

Cowless, they sailed across tiny Lake St. Clair before entering Lake Huron. Within an hour, the wind shifted completely from the east to the west. The water was confused as the wind began pushing against it from the opposite direction. Huge pyramid-shaped waves formed. The ship wallowed in, around, and over the ten-foot waves. The waves didn't have normal crests, so when each ship topped a wave, it fell sideways, corkscrewing down the steep slope of foaming, tormented water. There was no pattern to the rocking of the ship and the sailors in the rigging clung for life to the lines far above the rocking deck with the sails reefed.

Mary and Edward clung to the binnacle posts, watching the men try to carry out their duties on the flailing ship. Richard came up behind them and put his hand on Edward's shoulder as he asked, "Are you all right, son?" Edward shook his head affirmatively, not taking his eyes off three men tugging on a line to secure a boat that had torn loose. Richard said to Edward for Mary's benefit, "I'm sure Mary is fine, as she is impervious to the actions of the waves." Edward looked over his shoulder and smiled weakly, frightened by the strange waves. Richard caught his look of fear and said, "Don't you worry. We are fine. It is just the shifting of the wind. The waves will settle down soon." He squeezed Edward's shoulder and made his way further down the deck.

Rather than settle down, the wind continued to shift back and forth, first east and then west, and soon the first of the crew began to get seasick. Men who had not been seasick in decades began heaving their breakfast. Most of them had their backs to the wind, so they did not foul themselves, but there were so many men sick in the rigging that the vomit began to rain down on the deck. Mary watched horrified as the men heaved and retched and still tried to work. Richard returned a while later and stood beside Mary and Edward, but he was silent. Mary glanced up at him and saw why. He was ghastly pale, and greenish around his nose and mouth. His jaws were clenched and his lips tightly pursed as he struggled against the nausea. Mary looked away, feeling for him. It wasn't three minutes later that he mumbled, "I don't believe this," and raced for the railing where he bent over it gagging. Mary turned away and pulled Edward with her. Richard came back a few minutes later, wiping his mouth, and stood next to Mary. He said hoarsely, "I have not been sick on a ship since I was thirteen years old. I have been in storms where I didn't know which way was up. I have been in three tempests, and I didn't get sick in any of those. Here I am puking in a damned lake." Mary gingerly touched his coat sleeve, sneaking a glance at his face at the same time. He looked grim, but at least his color was better. He looked down at her and said, "If the crew and I are this sick, I wonder how that Deems witch and her brats are faring? They are fouling a cabin again no doubt. It wouldn't occur to them to find a railing."

It took another hour, but the wind finally settled in steady from the northwest returning the waves to more of an expected pattern. He had read everything he could get his hands on about navigating the Great Lakes, but there was surprisingly little in print. The waves were now between five and seven feet and very close together. Waves on the open sea are thirty or even fifty yards apart, but the waves here were no more than forty feet apart. At times Richard feared the ship would be suspended between the crests and break her back as her own weight pulled her down in the middle. Richard pointed it out to the cartographer, Sebastian, who nodded and shrugged, saying "That is just the way they are in the Great Lakes."

Richard asked, "What else is different here?"

Sebastian leaned on the rail and said, "The wave action is different, but that's something you'll get used to rather quickly, but what is strange and something I have never gotten used to is how heavy the ship feels in the water, almost like she is overloaded. I'm sure you've noticed it." Richard nodded his head, affirming that he had, and Sebastian continued. "It doesn't matter what vessel you're in, even a canoe will feel heavier in these lakes." Sebastian turned to look Richard in the eye, "But don't for a minute let the word lake mislead you. This is a sea, an inland sea, and just as you respect the salty sea, don't you underestimate these filled with sweet water. They will suck you to the bottom just as easily as the far-wide ocean. The wind blows something fierce here. It's nothing to have a fall storm with winds the strength of a tempest up here, and it might blow for three days, and to make it worse, the shoreline is absolutely laced with shoals. In the winter before the lakes freeze over, the weather is as bad as it is anywhere on earth. I have made cape crossings that were gentler than some of the sailing I have done up here. This one isn't too bad," he waved his arm, referring to Lake Huron, "and Erie and Ontario aren't bad because the weather comes the length of them and you can get out of it easier, but Lake Michigan is absolutely studded with islands, some no bigger than a drawing room, and they're made of pure stone. As bad as Michigan is though, she pales next to the conditions on Lake Superior. I've crossed the North Atlantic in foul weather with more ease."

Richard looked at him quizzically and said, "You're serious, aren't you?"

"Dead serious." Sebastian looked hard at Richard and continued, "I have seen the sky clear blue on a late October day, then the wind changes and within twenty minutes, it's coming from the exact opposite quarter and snowing like the devil with waves so confused, you can do nothing but reef everything and hang on, hoping you don't get smashed on the shoreline. At times, there is just nowhere to anchor and nowhere to run. Praying comes real natural then. You pray you find yourself in the favor of the lakes, because if you're not, you're doomed." Sebastian scratched his ear, wiped what he had mined on his pant leg, and continued, "One other thing is that it seems to freeze here at a higher temperature than in saltwater. The thermometer may read freezing at sea, but the salt keeps it from turning to ice. Here, it's frozen and clinging at thirty-two degrees. I have seen all hands on deck and in the rigging armed with hammers, picks, and pins and still barely keeping ahead of the ice coating everything." Sebastian laughed sadly, "Just when you think you have the lakes down for sure, they will come at you differently than they ever have before. You got a little taste of it earlier when it was coming from all quarters." Richard nodded and involuntarily wiped his mouth with the back of his hand. Sebastian caught the gesture and smiled, then added, "Don't feel bad. I lost my oatmeal the first time I was in a storm here too. I prefer to think of it as a rite of passage of sorts. Don't be surprised, though, if you find yourself sick the first time you get back on saltwater. It happened to me."

Richard went to his cabin to do some writing, as the Navy had been specific about extensive journals in addition to the logbook. As he was rummaging around in a letter case, he came across some buttons from his old uniform, the tang of a broken sword, and a small round object that brought a smile to his face. He found Mary and handed her a handkerchief wrapped around the object. "Here," he said, "I found something you might like to see." Mary unwrapped the handkerchief and inside was a band of gold about the thickness of a quill which had been bent into a circle. Mary looked up from it puzzled, and Richard said, chuckling, "I knew that thing was around here somewhere." Mary still did not understand, and Richard said, "The ring, the one I wore in my ear where Stephen stabbed me with the dirk! Here, I bet it will fit you as a bracelet." With that, he took the gold band and bent it into an oval. Mary held out her hand and he slipped it over her wrist and then crimped the ends by pushing them flat against the rail. It fit perfectly. The only problem was it would have to stay on her arm. Mary smiled at it thanking him, still surprised he had been involved in such daring things.

THEY HAD BEEN anchored for the night near the shore about fifty miles north of Detroit. Richard had been up since dawn and now heard the capstan turning to winch in the anchor cable. He left Mary sleeping soundly when he slipped out of their cabin. She seemed more tired than usual, and also put off by foods she had previously enjoyed. Richard was concerned she was coming down with something. He came back from the deck and was surprised to see her sitting on the floor, vomiting into a basin. "Mary!" Richard exclaimed. "You're going soft on me."

Mary lifted her head from the basin, and she looked horribly pale. She said, "I'm not seasick."

"Don't be ashamed. It happened to me too, remember," Richard laughed.

Mary grimaced, "I'm not seasick, Richard." She swallowed hard and then said, "I'm with child."

Richard's smile vanished. "What?" he said staring at her. She bent to vomit again and heard the cabin door slam as Richard left. She also heard him clearly outside the door as he hit it with his fist and cursed, "Dammit!" Mary sat up with her face all red and tears in her eyes, and she set the basin aside to roll onto her side on the floor. The deck felt cool on her face as the hot tears spilled from her eyes. She had delayed telling Richard because she wanted to be sure. That way, he wouldn't be disappointed if she was wrong. She felt stupid now to think he could ever have been excited. Mary stayed prone on the deck until her stomach settled, which is where Wrennet found her nearly an hour later. Mary confided in Wrennet that she was pregnant, and after asking half a dozen questions, Wrennet confirmed her pregnancy. Mary kept Richard's reaction, though, to herself. Mary may have held her tongue, but Richard was not finished on the subject.

Later in the morning Mary was able to choke down part of a biscuit and was sipping some lukewarm tea when a young officer whose name she could not remember arrived. He bowed and mumbled, "Excuse me, Mrs. Holmwood, but the captain would like to see you. I am to take you." Mary rose and followed him to a cabin not much larger than a closet, which served as a day cabin to maintain the log. There was no room in the cabin for Richard to pace, so instead she saw him turning from side to side with agitation. His face was red and his jacket in a heap on the desk where he had obviously thrown it. The officer delivered Mary and retreated, closing the door softly behind him.

Richard whirled on her as soon as the door was closed. "You are absolutely sure about this?" Mary nodded, fighting back tears, and he snapped at her again, "Did you know about this child when we left Scotland Neck?"

"No, I . . ." Mary whispered, but Richard cut her off.

"Don't lie to me, madam," he hissed, actually pointing his finger at her. Mary stared at him with huge eyes brimming with tears, and he screamed, "And don't you cry either!"

"I knew nothing in Scotland Neck, and I only started to wonder as we were leaving Boston, and then I wasn't sure until recently," Mary said, her chin quivering as she fought the urge to run.

Richard stood in the cramped space, clenching and unclenching his fists, and then he stopped and looked up at the ceiling as if for strength. He finally turned and motioned for Mary to sit in the chair at his desk. He stood looking down at her, and then shrugged, took a deep breath, and sat on the edge of the desk.

Without looking directly at her, he asked, "When will you be confined?"

"Toward the beginning of December," she said, looking at her hands in her lap.

"Has Wrennet confirmed this as well?" Richard asked, suddenly hoping Mary was mistaken, but Mary nodded her head without looking at him. Richard glanced at her bowed head and said quietly, "Are you still ill?"

She shook her head no, and ventured to look at him. "It seems to go away after a few hours," she said, searching his face for a reaction, but it was expressionless. "But I feel tired most of the time. Wrennet said both are normal and will pass."

Richard stood, and Mary understood the conversation was over, so she rose from her chair. He held the door for her, and then said as she passed, "Are you still able to take care of Edward?"

Mary snapped and even surprised herself, "Yes, I can still do my duty."

Richard glared at her, but said levelly, "All I was going to say is that if you need more help taking care of him, be sure to ask Wrennet."

Mary left the cabin, and as the door closed behind her it was as if a wall had come down between her and Richard. From that moment on, he barely looked at or spoke to her unless absolutely necessary, and he slept in his day cabin. Mary looked worse and worse each day, until Wrennet finally winkled out of her what the trouble was between them. Wrennet listened and then bustled off to stand in the doorway of Richard's day cabin. He was bent over a chart of the Straits of Mackinac, but looked up at her knock on the jamb. She said, "I need to speak with you, if I may." Richard pushed a stool toward her without rising, and she sat across from him.

"Now, what is this about?" Richard asked sourly, though he thought he knew.

Wrennet didn't pull any punches. She simply asked, "Why don't you want this child Mary is carrying? You barely speak to her."

Richard rubbed his hand over his chin and then his whole face, then he leaned back in his chair and said, "She took me off guard, and besides, I just didn't think it would happen."

"Well, certainly after fathering two other children you know how this comes about," Wrennet said flatly.

Richard shot her a hard glance out of the corner of his eye and said, "You know that is not what I meant, Wrennet. Don't start with me, not today. The whole thing just seems lowly somehow, how fast it happened, like farm stock."

"You have certainly become high and mighty all of a sudden, and as usual with righteous people they have a short memory. I recall you conjured up Owen in a three-week run in Boston, so I don't see how it is lowly," Wrennet said, arching her eyebrows.

Richard ignored her jab, turning in his chair. "I just didn't think I would have children with anyone but Lorraine," he said, but he didn't dare confess even to Wrennet how deep his feelings went about this. His reaction when he found Mary was pregnant had been initially disbelief, then fierce anger, and finally revulsion. He felt disbelief because in some perverse sense he considered her too young to have a child; anger because Mary had become a toy to sport with at night and this pregnancy would surely get in the way of that; and finally revulsion, which was the most unkind of all. He feared this child Mary would give him would be some kind of dark and puny thing, almost a half-breed compared to the tall, blonde children Lorraine had borne. It was a cruel thought and one that was probably beneath him, but that was how he felt. He kept his disgust to himself and only said to Wrennet, "I just didn't think it would happen, and I don't want any more children."

"Then you should have kept her out of your bed, shouldn't you?" Wrennet said sarcastically.

Richard glared at her, no longer shocked by what Wrennet might say to him. "All right, yes. Lorraine and I had Owen quickly, but it was six years later that we had Edward. Six years. I haven't been wed to Mary six months yet, and she is with child. It's like a farm animal."

Wrennet snapped, "Your precious Lorraine would have dropped babies just as fast if she didn't rid herself of them. At least Mary is doing her best to keep this one."

Richard turned slowly and leveled his gaze at her, "What did you just say?"

Wrennet looked alarmed. What she was thinking had slipped right out. One minute she was thinking it, and the next she was saying it. This seemed to be happening to her more and more lately, and she noticed she was having trouble remembering names and even words sometimes. Richard stood glowering over her now, and she tried to escape by rising and mumbling, "You are right; it's none of my business."

"What do you know, Wrennet. Tell me now." Richard took her by the shoulders and sat her down in his desk chair. Wrennet stalled and Richard insisted softly, "I'm waiting."

Wrennet looked like she was about to cry, but she started explaining, "I don't know why she did it, but I think she was very aware that she was older than you, and she thought that if she bore you child after child she would age faster, and you would leave her."

"What do you mean?" Richard asked.

"Well, I think that is what she believed," Wrennet said.

"I would never have left Lorraine. She was everything to me. If she didn't want any more children, I would have agreed to that. I would have slept somewhere else," Richard said.

Wrennet smiled wryly. "She didn't want you out of her bed, Richard. She just didn't want to grow what you planted there."

"Well, she died tending that garden anyway, didn't she?" Richard said angrily.

Wrennet snapped and said cruelly, "She didn't die because she had Edward. She died because she destroyed her kidneys trying to abort him!" Wrennet realized what she had said and clasped her hand over her mouth. Richard grabbed her wrist and squeezed it.

"Tell me now, Wrennet, or I swear." He did not finish his threat and his voice cracked.

Wrennet swallowed hard and began, "It wasn't the first time. Lorraine had taken pennyroyal on and off for years. If she found she was pregnant, she would take a tincture, and she would miscarry. I didn't catch on at first, but later I wondered, and so I began to watch her, and that's when I knew."

"All those years, she was killing my children, and you didn't tell me?" Richard said bitterly.

"You would never have heard a word against her then, and you know it," Wrennet said. She reached over and touched Richard's arm, but he pulled away. She continued softly, "Richard, Lorraine did it because she loved you. She always sobbed when it was over, but she believed it was the only way she could keep you. I think over time though the drug affected her mind. As Owen got older, and when you were away, he began to take your place." Wrennet shifted and then continued, "She loved you desperately, but she got confused at the end. You know she worshipped Owen, but when her mind began to slip, she let him take your place.

I think that if she hadn't died, her relationship with him would have been," here she faltered for a word and finally said, "unnatural." Wrennet watched, waiting for Richard to be shocked or angry, but he said nothing. He remembered well coming home from a long voyage and having to sleep in another room because Owen was sleeping with his mother and had to be convinced to sleep in his own room. Sometimes this convincing took several nights, while Richard would lie rigid elsewhere waiting his turn in Lorraine's bed. Wrennet continued, "She let him run wild with no rules or consequences. You can remember what trouble you had reining him in after she died?" Richard nodded, and Wrennet said, "I think she felt another child would have been an intruder in the triangle she had forged between the two men in her life. She found she was pregnant with Edward, and you must remember she was forty-two then, a good deal older than you are right now, she was desperate not to carry him to term, and she took the pennyroyal. I think it would have left her completely mad if she had lived. Always remember, Richard, she loved you desperately, and that is why she did it." Richard said no more, but just stood looking at the floor. Wrennet got up from her chair and quietly left him with his thoughts. Richard remembered coming back home from being at sea, and when he saw how ill she was he summoned every doctor within fifty miles. They all said the same thing, her kidneys had been irreparably damaged, and she would not survive. A few days later, she stopped passing fluid, and three days later she was dead.

Wrennet now moved astern to where Mary was sitting in her favorite spot on the signal locker. Wrennet said to herself as she looked at her, "Richard, you may think you have shut this little one out of your heart, but she is going to find her way right into your soul, and you just don't know it yet."

Richard came back to their cabin the following night, and as he lay staring into the dark, he could feel Mary was also awake. He pulled her closer, so her head rested on his chest, and he absently fingered the braid in her hair. He could feel her hot tears fall against his skin, but he offered her no words of comfort, and eventually, after a long heavy silence, they both slept.

The following day Mary heard heavy-booted steps coming toward her cabin and then a knock. At Mary's answer, the carpenter's mate popped his head inside and said, "Captain Holmwood has asked me to tell you we've raised Mackinac Island." Mary dropped the book she was reading and followed him to the deck where she caught her first view of what would be home for the next five years. Richard had given her his copy of a book describing Mackinac Island, and she had read it cover to cover. The magical limestone arch was just as she had read, but the island itself was smaller and much taller than she had expected. There were steep cliffs on the quarter of the island she could see, and as the ship came around to the western side, she saw a small pier and a few buildings. Looking further west and up on the bluff she could see Fort Holmes glittering in the afternoon sun. It had been built during the French and Indian War, was occupied by the British during the War of Independence, and had traded hands several times during the recent war. Richard had related to her the humiliation the American troops had suffered when they first lost the island to the British. It had only been delivered back into American hands by the Treaty of Ghent.

As they approached the island, she saw Richard pointing out the deadly shoals at the mouth of the harbor to the crew. Today, the shoals were capped with small waves and easily visible, but when the water was calmer, they lurked there just below the surface, waiting to take the belly out of an unsuspecting ship.

There was a small sandy beach to the west of the pier and six or seven buildings, one of which would be their home. The island was truly a gem, and Mary could see how it had given birth to so many legends among the Ojibwa, the Indians who were the original inhabitants of the area.

Richard was also struck by the island's elevation and saw now why so many nations over the years had chosen to defend it. The island rode high out of the water like a fortress, with the fort sitting like a crown on its brow. The rocky island was shaped like a turtle cruising atop the water. Richard had also lent Mary a copy of the *Schoolcraft Study of the Native Peoples of the Northern Territory*, and she raced through it in one sitting. The book contained many Ojibwa legends of the island and a good deal of its history, but it never once suggested the extent of its beauty.

The *Huron* finally cleared the shoals and moored at the tiny pier. The other two ships anchored as best they could offshore, though the current was strong. Mary heard Richard say, as he watched the two ships feel for anchorage, "This lake has a stronger current than the James River." Wordlessly, he helped Mary and Wrennet off the ship as Edward scampered ahead of them. They all walked with their legs feeling wobbly and stiff after the long voyage. They were met on the pier by Robert Stuart who had heard their gun salute while they were still a mile off. He came grinning down to the pier and shook hands with Richard.

Reginald and Douglas Deems managed to walk without too much difficulty, but Dorcas and both girls collapsed when they got on shore and sat there blubbering until they were helped up onto their feet again. Robert Stuart led the wobbly party up the hill to his warehouse and to the two cottages where the Holmwoods and the Deemses would make their homes. He suggested that after they rested and were refreshed, they join him for dinner.

The Deemses took the larger of the two cottages. The Holmwood cottage was made of square rough-hewn logs packed with moss and mud for chinking. Someone had later added a siding of sorts on the bottom half of the exterior walls, almost like wainscoting. Richard held the door for the others to enter, and they walked carefully into the one central room that served as a sitting room, dining room, and kitchen. It was dominated by an enormous fireplace that took up a good deal of the back wall and would be used for both cooking and heat. Richard looked at it and said, "We'll have to get a stove and oven in that opening, or we'll freeze to death this winter." The floor was nothing more than packed earth, and he added, "And I'll have them get right on to putting a floor in here." Off each side of the central room were tiny rooms, not much larger than good-sized wardrobes. Those would be their bedrooms, one for Edward and Wrennet to share and one for Mary and Richard. There was a small loft, but even Mary could barely stand up in it, and it would serve only for storage. Richard looked around the cottage and, for just a moment, started to panic. Living here by himself would not have been too bad, but with the others and now Mary adding a baby to the mix, it would be crowded as hell. He had lived in ship's cabins that were bigger than this cottage. His heart started to race at the thought of being snowed-in all winter. Just then, Grub burst through the door, having completed an abbreviated urination tour of the island, and he brought his stench with him.

Mary sat down on a rough-hewn bench that was the only furniture in the place and started taking stock of what needed to be done. Aside from needing everything for keeping house, the cottage needed a good cleaning. She also determined that if they could not sleep in the cottage tonight, she was not sleeping on the ship, but would rather sleep out in the open using blankets. It would be a welcome change from the stuffy air of the ship.

Richard learned that the central section of the cottage was built just after the end of the War of Independence by a fur trader, the bedrooms being added some years later. He now eyed the walls beside the fireplace, wondering if he could cut through them to add more space out back. He would ask the ship's carpenter what he thought, for if anyone knew about load-bearing timbers, Lockley certainly did. For now they would have to make do as they could with the three rooms.

After dinner with Robert Stuart, they prepared for sleep. Richard had no argument against sleeping on the beach, but there was a fairly strong breeze, and he suggested they move a bit further from the lake where they were sheltered by a small rise in the shoreline. On top of a pallet of sailcloth, they stacked blankets and sheets and settled in for the night. Richard was amazed when he checked that it was nearly ten o'clock at night. He had not really noticed the gradual lengthening of the days as they sailed west, but now it dawned on him that had they still been back in Scotland Neck, it would have been dark for an hour already.

They settled down now on their makeshift beds and snuggled under the covers. They were all nearly asleep, aided by the gentle washing of the waves on the shore, when the wind dropped. "This is peaceful, Mary. I'm glad you insisted on sleeping here," Richard whispered. He had no more than uttered the words when he heard a whining sound. The whine turned into a high-pitched hum, and he felt a sting on his cheek. He slapped at it, and shook his head to clear the insect that was trying to crawl into his ear. Wrennet and Edward were now slapping and hopping about, choking on the clouds of mosquitoes that had arrived when the wind ebbed. Richard pulled the covers over Mary's head, but it only served to trap them inside with her, and she came out kicking and slapping at her head. "Run! Run for the ship now!" he yelled at them, and they raced down the shoreline, dragging their blankets as best they could. The watch on the ship heard them coming and brought lanterns onto the deck to help them see.

The officers on board the ship had lighted shallow pots of pitch on the deck and they burned in thick, eye-watering clouds, but the smoke helped keep the bugs at bay. Mary bundled Edward down into the cabin he had shared with Wrennet and was busy slapping the mosquitoes off him. She stuffed him back into his bunk and covered his head. Richard came in then, bringing a fresh cloud of bugs, and Mary began clapping them between her hands to kill them. "Is it going to be like this every night?" Mary asked, almost in tears.

"God, I hope not," Richard mumbled, crushing a mosquito between the flat of his hands just above Mary's head.

They were still tired the next day when they began taking load after load of supplies off the ship to be stored under waxed canvas. The carpenter and his two mates quickly put in the floor, but it was still quite rough. Richard would have some of the crew run the holy stones over it, and it would soon be smooth.

After the floors were sanded, the supplies were brought into the cottage. When the loft was full, Mary stacked things along interior walls. Lockley turned some of the crates into shelves on which Mary could store her cookware and other supplies. They brought furniture off the ship, and what they didn't have Lockely made for them, including a table that would serve for both preparation and eating. Richard brought in the desk from his cabin and placed it next to the fireplace.

Mary tackled the cottage as she had the house in Scotland Neck, and soon it was clean and cozy. It was still tiny, but with open windows protected by a layer of cheesecloth to keep the bugs out and the lake breeze coming in, even Richard had to admit it was comfortable.

The Deemses, on the other hand, waged war with each other about every inconvenience, found fault with anything they could, and insisted that Robert Stuart find them a domestic workforce. He said the best he could do were some of the Ojibwa women. Dorcas screeched at the suggestion, calling the Ojibwas hostiles. With no help available that she would hire, she forced Cassie and Stella to do the chores, and this always resulted in nasty squabbles which were easily heard all over the island. Whenever there was an exceptionally wicked row, Richard would announce, "They are repelling boarders over there again."

Unlike Dorcas, Mary accepted the help of two Ojibwa women, one named Miki and the other something that sounded like Donna. They were in truth more curious about Mary than they were skilled at housekeeping, but both were hard workers. Mary offered to pay them, but what they really wanted was cotton and wool cloth, and Mary had that in abundance. Both women spoke passable English, teaching Mary a great deal about the Ojibwa way of life, both old and new.

She learned that no Ojibwa would ever have set foot on Mackinac Island if the white settlers had not first done so several hundred years before. The Ojibwa believed the island was sacred and to tread there would be to bring about terrible luck. Their ancestors first watched the French walk on the island, followed by the British, and finally the Americans. They waited for each group to be struck down, but saw that the only danger to these newcomers was each other as nation fought nation for control of the island down through the years. The Ojibwa finally would come onto the island, but refused to stay on it through the winter. The two women repeated to Mary what they had heard, "Any enemy can reach you, there is no game or fish in the deep winter, and the only water available is a small spring near the fort. Finally, and most important of all, the island likes to sleep in the winter and it should be left alone. You could awaken a Windigo."

"Windigo?" Mary asked.

The women described the malevolent spirit that overcomes some people deep in winter when the food runs low. The Windigo whispers cannibalism to them with a particular bent for the flesh of children, and one of the women added, "And some people listen." Mary nodded in horror but let the subject rest. She didn't understand why they couldn't just melt snow for water. The women explained that while snow could be melted to drink and cook with, the snow around an encampment gets fouled rather quickly with urine, human and dog waste, and refuse, and it gets very tedious to carry clean snow from so far away.

Mary was as fascinated by the Ojibwa women as they were by her and her clothing and household items. They marveled at her glassware, but most of all they were entranced by the fabrics she owned. They really began to like her, but still politely talked behind her back about her stature. They giggled as they contemplated what it must be like to be with a man so much larger.

As interested as they were in Mary, they found Edward absolutely fascinating. They had seen a few blonde men, but had not seen a blonde child before and were taken by his golden hair and blue eyes. Mary suspected the older girls were cutting off his curls as souvenirs, and confirmed her suspicions when she caught one armed with a pair of her own secateurs about to snip off a curl behind his ear.

Mary befriended the smaller Ojibwa children and they gathered around her. She bathed them and patched and washed their clothes. Dorcas Deems saw Mary sitting on a large rock with Edward and a half-dozen of his little playmates, and she pulled Richard aside saying, "Captain, I think you should keep your eyes on those hostiles. They may very well steal your boy and sell him as a slave. They could get good trade for both him and your wife, so I'll say it again, you better keep your eye on those savages. They are one step removed from cannibals." Richard looked over where Dorcas was pointing and watched as Mary walked with the children, following her like goslings.

 Over the summer she gave the Ojibwa children treats and combed their hair, taking the place of parents who were too busy. One of the Ojibwa men told Richard that the children had started to call Mary, "Dark Eyes." He said it was because she had huge eyes as dark as their own, and they also called her "Little One" because she was so tiny, really no taller than the eleven- or twelve-year-old Ojibwa girls. Over the summer the two names blended until she became known as "Little Dark Eyes."

Viewed from behind in a group of them, Mary did look very much like a little girl, but when she turned sideways her breasts and, later, her enlarging belly betrayed that image. She was no longer able to hide her belly by late summer, and the Ojibwa women were thrilled. They brought her little gifts of soft leather and freshwater snail-shell necklaces, which they swore would help her through childbirth. She asked them questions about the birth, but she placed her trust in Wrennet to deliver the child when the time came. Wrennet had acted as a midwife dozens of times back in Scotland Neck. She talked to Wrennet and the Ojibwa women about the baby constantly, but not in Richard's presence and he never mentioned it.

Everyone made preparations for winter. Mary, Wrennet, and Edward harvested blackberries and dried some and cooked the others in honey until they thickened down to a jam-like consistency, which they stored in little ceramic pots. The blueberries were pretty well past their time when they arrived on Mackinac, and they had only found enough for two small pots of jam. They had missed the strawberries and the wild plums, but they collected what they could.

As soon as the cottage was ready, no more than a week after they arrived, Richard left to explore the surrounding waters and to allow Sebastian and the other cartographer to begin improving the charts. He was gone for two weeks and when he returned he commented kindly on the improvements to the cottage, but he spoke very little to Mary. Richard spent his time ashore making sure they had enough firewood and finalizing preparations to winter over the ships.

Richard wasn't sure when they would take the three ships out of the lake, but certainly they would do so sometime in November. He had heard disturbing tales of the violent storms that raged across the lakes in late fall, and Isaac Hull had said, "If you combine a hurricane and a blizzard, you have the average fall storm on the Great Lakes." He further added, "If a man should fall overboard, his heart would only beat for about ten minutes before the cold brings it to a stop." Richard reported to Wrennet and Mary he intended to be finished sailing for the year by mid-November. Mary was relieved to hear it, because it meant Richard would be on the island when the baby was born.

The summer wore on and Mary had not even tried to plant her garden. It was too late when they arrived. By the time they could have gotten it worked up and seeded, the fall frost would have been upon them. She had to settle for some sugar peas, a few lettuces, and some onions to supplement the dried and salted food they had with them. Still, Mary managed to put on a respectable table, though it was far from the seven sweet and seven sour dishes Arla Spencer, keeping with her strict Dutch heritage, demanded at each meal.

The Deemses did little to prepare for winter. Dorcas raided Mary's pitiful garden as though it was her right, and she constantly sent the girls over to demand items such as ground sugar or oats that had been already rolled. Dorcas bossed Mary around, constantly comparing her to Stella and Cassie.

Stella Deems spent a great deal of time down by the pier. Wrennet mentioned to Mary one morning that she thought Stella had a beau. Mary snorted, "Who would want to be around her? She is so whining and snarly." Mary stated it like a fact rather than a question; nevertheless, she started to watch Stella and came to the same conclusion as Wrennet. Stella would start to walk around the side of the island, but then cut across behind the fort garrison and come out on the pier where she met a man dressed in a simple shirt and buckskin pants. They would talk and sometimes walk on the pier, but whatever they did, Stella came back to the cottage smiling and blushing. Mary wondered slyly what Dorcas would make of this get-together.

Pure nosiness drove Wrennet to find out the man was Roger Thane, a trader in one of the American Fur Company's outposts. He was on the island now, but before the snow fell he would be stationed at his outpost about fifty miles inland where the trappers brought their fur to him in trade for goods. He in turn brought the furs to the warehouse several times a year. To Wrennet he seemed nice enough and more handsome than Stella deserved, but most delicious of all, he was a quarter Ojibwa.

Wrennet whispered wickedly, "How would the old reptile like to hear that her eldest is cavorting with the hostiles, as she calls them?"

Dorcas, oblivious to the romance building right under her nose, decided they sorely lacked culture on the island and announced that Thursday evening would be one of musical entertainment. The Holmwoods and even Robert Stuart were given instructions to arrive after dinner, and Dorcas added, "Mrs. Holmwood can bring one of her nice desserts."

Mary listened to the girls practice all week, and it was torture for them as well as those within earshot, but it was Grub who suffered the most. He would be sound asleep, deep in the throes of an orgiastic, rabbit-chasing dream when the girls would start warming up next door. His feet would twitch as he chased his fantasy vermin, and he would remain asleep throughout most of their practice, but as soon as they began their final song, he would start awake, already howling. Mary had to hold his head or he would have drowned the girls out with his baleful noise. She really couldn't blame him.

Thursday arrived and after dinner everyone brought their chairs and formed a semicircle in the Deems's main room. There were about a dozen people in all, including Roger Thane. Robert and Richard looked at each other and rolled their eyes as Stuart whispered, "I should have brought something to drink stronger than Mrs. Deems's tea."

Richard nodded solemnly and whispered, "It'll be more of an execution than an exhibition, I'll wager. Have you by chance heard them?" Stuart nodded.

The girls yowled through half-a-dozen songs that bore only faint resemblance to their original melody, and at one point Richard, referring to the way the girls screwed up their faces when they sang, leaned over to Wrennet and whispered, "They look like they have gotten hold of some of your Black Slider!" Mary heard it and had to hold her mouth so she wouldn't laugh out loud.

The girls now prepared to unleash their finale: *Weep No More, Sad Fountains*. Both Richard and Stuart recognized the tune when it was announced and they shuddered. The song had a great many high notes for which to aim.

The girls now took deep breaths like fish held out of water as they prepared for their masterpiece, and Richard, though he spoke to her rarely these days, whispered to Mary, "Are you sure you're ready for this?" Mary nodded, smiling, but before she could say more, Stella and Cassie started their song. They reached the end of the first verse and both Richard and Stuart knew what was coming. Both men put their heads down and to the side as though they were facing into a sleet storm as they rode out the chorus. Cassie and Stella attacked the word joy with such vehemence it sounded like cannon fire, and though they were prepared, both Richard and Robert Stuart jumped when they hit it.

The sisters finally reached the end of the song and were about to blast the audience with a series of the word softly repeated as their cadenza when Grub let loose with an agonized howl from behind the Holmwood cottage where Mary had tied him. He bellowed in tune with them, matching each syllable as they ended their song. Richard's eyes grew wide as he recognized his own dog, and he was barely able to keep a straight face. The girls ended their song, and Grub stopped with them, but every Ojibwa dog on the island had now taken up the chant, and some forty or more inbred, rangy beasts howled into the night. It was too much for Richard, and he burst out laughing. Luckily, Roger Thane applauded and stood cheering, effectively covering Richard's laugh. To the relief of most of the audience and the chagrin of the Deems girls, the first Mackinac Island After-Dinner Musical Exhibition came to an end.

No one except Wrennet saw Roger Thane slip back later that night and stand talking to Stella through her bedroom window. Wrennet smiled wickedly as she saw Roger lean in and kiss Stella goodnight. He was leaving tomorrow to get the outpost ready for winter and would come to the island once more before the snow set in, and not return until late spring.

Mary and Wrennet were standing on the bluff when a flock of Canada geese flew overhead, honking and calling to each other, keeping their ragged V formation as they headed south. The women watched them, shielding the sun from their eyes until the geese were just specks. Then Mary said in a tiny voice, "Back in Virginia, I always liked to see the geese arriving from where it was so cold. I knew how far they had flown and liked that they found refuge with us along the river. They knew enough to leave here. Something told them it was time to go, but now I feel like they are leaving us behind." She looked at Wrennet with large eyes, "I feel a little bit frightened." Mary swallowed hard and then added, "Please don't tell Richard I said I was scared though."

The following day Wrennet watched Mary walk out the front door. She was as large with child as anyone Wrennet had ever seen. Her face was a little rounder than usual, but other than that, it was all confined to her belly. From the back she didn't look much bigger, but from the side or the front she looked ungainly and miserable. Her skin had taken on that deep glow that some women get when they are pregnant. Wrennet would catch Richard watching Mary when he thought no one was looking, and his expression was one she could only describe as wary. He now looked up from where he was writing some notes, and watched Mary leave the house with Edward behind her. "Where are they going?" Richard asked Wrennet after they had gone.

"They heard you were leaving today, and I think they are hoping if they are down there, you will take them along," Wrennet smiled, "and it will take Mary a while to get there, so she is getting a head start."

"We have stripped most of the gear off the ship, so I don't think they would find it very comfortable, and Mary has no business out in the cold," Richard said, dismissing the idea and returning to his notes.

Wrennet looked at him for a long time before she said, "I think Mary wants to go on this trip with you because she knows how much it will bother you to stop sailing all winter. I think she wants to be of help."

Richard was still bent over his notes, but he was no longer writing, and he looked up at Wrennet and asked, "How exactly does she plan to help me?"

Wrennet added, "Being herself is the only way she knows how." Wrennet stared at him for a long time, then she took a deep breath and asked, "Do you still dislike her?"

"I don't dislike her. Mary is very sweet, but the one thing I don't need is another child," Richard grumbled.

The filter between her brain and her mouth was not functioning again this morning as Wrennet blurted, "That may be good, because I don't think Mary is going to have an easy time of it. That is a very large baby she is carrying, and she is a tiny woman. You may find you don't have to worry about either of them anymore." With that, Wrennet stormed off, leaving Richard staring after her. He left without saying a word and was still not back several weeks later.

Mary stood on the doorstep trying to stretch her aching back. She was ungainly and found by the end of each day her feet were swollen. "Not long now, maybe a month," Wrennet had said at breakfast as she watched Mary trying to get comfortable on the wooden chair. Mary finally gave up and went to stand on the doorstep to eat her bread and jam. Wrennet caught her there, often, watching and waiting for Richard to return to the island. One morning Mary kept rubbing her back and Wrennet, alarmed, asked if she was all right. Mary shook her head yes, but didn't say a word. Just then a lone Canada goose flew over them, honking desperately, somehow lost from all the others that had fled earlier. Mary looked up at it and a fat tear ran down her cheek.

"I don't think it will find the others, and it will die all alone far from home," Mary's voice cracked, and she hung her head. Wrennet put her arm around Mary and held her close. Mary's spirit was finally broken, and she sobbed, "I want my Mama, and I want to go home."

Wrennet patted her and said, smiling softly, "I wondered when we were going to hear this. Of course you miss your mama, but don't you worry, I'm right here. You are just tired and worried, but everything will be all right. Is it the confinement you're worried about?" Mary shook her head no, that was not what was troubling her. "Is it Richard?" Mary sniffed now and nodded her head, allowing Wrennet to mother her a bit and ease her anxiety, and then Wrennet led her into the cottage. "What you need right now is some tea and to sit down and get the weight off those tiny feet of yours. This will all work out in the end, and he will come around. I promise you that," Wrennet said, smiling at Mary. She wasn't worried about Richard. He was being an ass, but he would fall into line. No, her worry was with Mary and the size of the baby.

Richard hadn't been gone a week when he was overcome with shame over how he treated her. He also felt guilty because he realized he cared deeply for Mary, and caring for her allowed her to intrude on his memory of Lorraine. He intended to turn around right then and go back to her and tell her how he felt, but the cartography they were doing took much longer than expected. He had never seen such an exacting man as this mapmaker, Sebastian. If one measurement was fine, then he had to take four or five and compare them to then get an average, all the while asking Richard to try to hold a position off shore without drifting. In the end, the charting of the Les Cheneaux Islands took nearly a month. In that time, Wrennet's warning words about Mary ran continually through Richard's mind.

When the ship neared the island, Richard fired a gun to let them know they were back. He watched the cliff by the house, and within minutes, Mary and Edward were standing there waving. They lowered the longboat for Richard and he came ashore while they eased their way to the pier. Edward ran down the path to meet him, but Mary stayed at the top and waited.

When Richard got to the top he found Mary sitting on a log near the path head, and he leaned down and kissed her on the top of her head and asked, "Are you well?" Mary nodded, a little unsure of what to think after he had left earlier without a word to her. "Good," Richard helped her up, but he was startled at how much her stomach had expanded in the time he had been gone, and he continually glanced at it as they walked slowly toward the house.

While they were eating, Richard explained he was making one more trip to Beaver Island, where the other two ships were wintering over. They would take the last of their supplies over and check to make sure the ships were careened properly and secured against foul weather. Edward begged to go, and Richard finally agreed. Mary noticed Richard had been staring at her all through the meal, and not in an unpleasant way, so she decided to try her luck as well. She piped up, "Please take me, too."

"I don't know. It's awfully cold for you," Richard said.

"Please, Richard, take us both. I will be confined soon, and it will be my last adventure. Please take me," Mary begged, smiling.

Richard got up from the table and came and squatted next to her, then looked at her for a long time. She sat staring back at him, and he touched her cheek. "Get what you need because we will be gone several days," Richard relented with a grin. Edward scampered away, and Richard helped Mary to her feet where she swayed as she adjusted her balance to even the pull of her great belly against her spine. Richard offered her his arm and she gratefully took it. He realized then that taking her was a mistake, but he couldn't go back on his word. Within fifteen minutes Mary had packed enough food for a fleet crew, and they were untying from the pier.

The trip to Beaver Island took most of the day. Mary and Edward stood next to Richard on the shore, and both their faces were pink from the cold as they used his body to shield them from the wind. The last of the provisions for the men who would be wintering on Beaver Island had been delivered, and the ships were already careened on the shore. Richard had spent a great deal of time looking them over and checking everything. With the whole area below the waterline visible, each ship looked twice as big on land. The ships were careened on the northeastern shore in a beautiful curved harbor which would shield them from the wind and waves and moving ice in the spring. The crew had built a few sheds, but intended to live right in the ships until spring. They had rigged some stoves so that the chimney pipes went out one of the gun ports. They had also rigged some sails to use as partitions, so that the heat from the stoves would be trapped and would keep them warm. Mary saw with alarm they had made no provision to bathe, and she certainly would have scrubbed the ships out before moving in, but she kept quiet.

The next morning while Richard was overseeing the unloading of the rest of the provisions and checking the ships once more, Mary and Edward walked a bit. Beaver Island was not rocky like Mackinac, nor did it have the tall cliffs, but it was much larger. They climbed a gentle hill which overlooked a beautiful lake, and Mary had to rest there before she could go any farther. The two of them sat looking across the still water at the perfect reflection of trees and sky. The leaves were long gone, and the gray branches and trunks reflected there looked like great roots extending into the water. When they came back to the shore and told Richard what they had seen, he said that he had walked all over the island earlier in the summer and there were actually two lakes, one in the north and another in the south. He agreed with her when she said that even though Beaver Island was not inhabited, it seemed more civilized, and did not have any of the foreboding they had both felt on Mackinac Island.

They ate their lunch on the beach, and the men were grateful for the pies and cakes Mary had brought for them in addition to the ham and cornbread that Wrennet had sent along. "We won't eat this well until next spring, and perhaps not even then. Thank you mighty, ma'am," one sailor said to Mary as she handed him a piece of cake. After lunch they loaded into the boat to return to the ship, and Mary watched the men lean into the oars, pulling the longboat swiftly through the water. Even through their heavy clothing, Mary could see the hunch and relax of their muscles as they rowed. She wondered not for the first time in her life how nice it would be to be that strong, and to have tasks she struggled with seem as easy as lifting a pillow. She saw it all the time around her. She would be struggling lifting a heavy pot or kettle, and Richard would easily lift it with one hand. Richard had been watching her carefully since they left Mackinac, but he had yet to really talk to her. The wind had now picked up considerably, and the ship rocked as the longboat came aside. Richard ordered a sling be rigged to bring Mary aboard, but she begged him not to make her use it, and though it was difficult, she finally made it up the side of the ship and then sat waiting for the contractions spurred from the exertion to pass. It had happened when she climbed the hill by the lake earlier in the day, and lately it had been happening whenever she pushed herself physically. The contractions didn't hurt and always went away quickly when she stopped moving. She asked Wrennet about them, and Wrennet told her they were nothing to worry about. She had smiled and told her, "They are just a practice for the real thing, here in a month or so, and don't you worry."

Richard helped Mary to sit in her usual place on the signal locker. He took off his heavy coat and wrapped it around her shoulders, then reached down and tilted her face up to him and grinned at her. "Did you have a nice time?" he asked. Mary smiled and nodded, then snuggled deeper into his coat. Edward was running on the deck and Richard scooped him up and held him while the crew got underway. The temperature was dropping, and the clouds on the distant horizon looked steely gray. Mary tucked her face into Richard's coat and watched the men in the rigging unfurl the sails. The wind caught the canvas and with a crack like a musket shot, the ship bolted forward. The waves were larger than they were on the way over, but still nothing to worry about. Even with a crew shortened by those staying on Beaver Island, they had no trouble handling the weather. Mary dozed as the ship rocked in time to the waves, and Richard checked on her every hour or so. As the temperature dropped, it began to snow, and Richard took her down to his cabin where she slept most of the afternoon.

Mary woke to the sound of men yelling to each other, but it wasn't the usual sound of men calling to run the ship; instead, their voices sounded alarmed. She went to look for Richard and when she came on deck he was standing about ten feet from her, looking through a glass. He didn't answer when she asked, "Richard, is something wrong?"

"Sir, she is coming straight at us. It's a British ship, sir," a young man called from the lowest yard on the mizzenmast in front of Mary. "It looks like the *Sprite*, sir," he said, referring to a British ship based on St. Joseph Island in the Canadian North Channel of Lake Huron. Mary now stood beside Richard, and she tugged on his arm, but he still did not respond.

Finally, she pushed against his chest and said, "Richard, please tell me what is happening."

He looked down at her and said, "I'm not sure. I want you and Edward to stay right here with me." He called to Edward, who scampered over. "You stay here with Mary, Edward. Stay here where I can see you."

"Sir, there is another ship coming as well! It's the big British ship sir, the *Chanticleer*," the young man on the mizzen yard called. The Americans and British still in Canadian waters had spied on each other all summer, so they knew the ships well.

Richard swung the glass to the right a bit and confirmed that the *Chanticleer* was bearing down on them as well as the *Sprite*.

"Keep a close eye on them," Richard said. He turned to Mary and Edward and said, "More than likely this is nothing. We'll know what's going on in a few minutes." They were right in the straits and so close to home, no more than five miles from Mackinac Island, but the two British ships were between them and the island. They must have come from their base on St. Joseph Island. The British had retreated there after they were forced to surrender Mackinac Island as part of the treaty.

Everyone who had a glass was now watching the two British ships. Richard had delayed in running out his guns and tried not to appear hostile, but when the two ships were about half a mile away, the lookout called to Richard, "Captain, the *Sprite* is opening her gun ports!" He then added with more alarm, "And they have run out their port battery."

Richard's jaw clenched, and he turned to Mary, "You and Edward stay here by me, and do exactly as I say."

"Richard, I thought the war was over. What is happening?" Mary said on the verge of panic.

Men were now attaching the ship's boats to the davits to get them overboard and out of the way, and Mary turned from watching them to observe the approach of the *Sprite*. Suddenly, a big puff of smoke came out of its side, and at first she thought it had caught on fire, but at the same time she saw the smoke Richard roughly pushed her and Edward to the deck. He was screaming, "Down, down!" Everyone around them fell to the deck, covering their heads. One of the shots ripped across the deck taking a chunk of the railing out, and the other slammed into the boat they were trying to lower and shattered it to kindling.

Mary heard running feet and things banging around, but she had her eyes closed as she lay on the deck. There was a sound of heavy ropes gliding across pulleys and bumping and thumping everywhere. She opened her eyes and watched as the men she thought of as just sailors began to work in unison. The *Huron* was armed with six twelve-pound guns, and four nine-pounders, but the shorthanded crew would be able to fire only six of them. Richard yelled a rudder order, and the ship swung about. Mary crawled over to shield Edward with her body, and he reached for her. Above the confusion she could hear Richard yelling, and suddenly the whole world ripped apart with noise as the *Huron* began to fire her guns. Mary didn't know such sounds could exist, and she huddled with Edward, trying to cover his ears. The ship rocked as each gun fired, and the smoke billowed out of the gun ports and drifted up and over them. "Sir, the *Chanticleer* is now opening her gun ports too!" yelled the man on the yard above them, and then he added, "And she's running out her guns." Richard gave another order and the ship swung in a tight turn and Mary could hear more running feet and clanking and banging. She lifted her head to see better and Richard pushed her back down. Just as he pulled his hand away from her there was a massive explosion just forward of where they were lying. A ball had pierced the side of the *Huron*, though no one was injured. Mary could hear Richard's voice, but couldn't tell what he was saying. The *Huron* fired her guns in quick succession, and despite all the other noise, Mary actually heard the shot strike the side of the *Sprite*. The *Huron* made a tight turn and now raked the *Sprite* with her port side guns.

Richard watched as the *Chanticleer* approached. He was outgunned and outmanned, and all the *Sprite* and the *Chanticleer* had to do was dismast him. He swiveled to see what damage he had inflicted on the *Sprite*, but to his amazement the *Chanticleer* now opened fire not on his ship but on her sister ship, the *Sprite*.

As Mary watched horrified, she noticed that not a single shot had been fired into the rigging, and it seemed the safest place for them. While Richard was looking the other way, she pulled Edward to his feet and yelled over the din, "I want you to climb up there." She pointed to the mizzenmast. "Reach down and help me, and we'll sit on that little seat up there," she pointed to the platform in the mast. When Richard noticed them, they were nearly at the top, and he watched with his heart in his mouth as Mary tried to go through the lubber's hole, but her stomach prevented it. She had to climb around the outside of the platform before she could roll onto her side next to Edward.

Richard yelled during a break in the firing, "If the mast is shot from under you, do not jump off! You must stay on top of it as it falls. It will crush you if you are under it. Do not jump! Ride it down. Mary, do you understand me? Ride it down!" Mary nodded, but her eyes were huge as she clung to Edward. They looked so small, and Mary was so ungainly, but they had made it, and for the moment they were safe.

He tore his eyes away from them on the platform as the *Huron* prepared to rake the *Sprite* again. The *Chanticleer* fired also, and the *Sprite* was caught in the fire between them. It was unclear which ship connected with the *Sprite*'s mainmast, but it swayed for a moment and then fell creaking and groaning sideways into the water. A cheer went up from the crew of the *Huron*, and Richard could hear the gun crews reloading beneath him, the solid whuff of the charge being rammed into the gun, then the padding, the clank of the shot, and then another pad. When the whole thing was jammed tight with a plunger it had taken just over a minute. Even this far removed from the ocean and with no threat of war, Richard had held gunnery practice three times a week all summer. He was glad now he had kept them in shape.

The *Sprite* was trying to return fire on her sister ship *Chanticleer*, and Richard watched amazed. Suddenly, a gun in the stern of the *Sprite* spewed a blast of fire and smoke and caught the mast on which Mary and Edward were sitting. The whole thing cracked and swayed, then broke off just below the platform. It groaned as it fell into the lake, ripping and snapping its rigging as it went. Some of the severed lines nearly decapitated the men on deck, and Richard watched in horror as Mary and Edward disappeared with the mast as it fell. He looked back over his shoulder, and saw Mary surface first and then Edward, and Mary was swimming toward Edward. He had to turn his attention then back to the *Sprite*. They raked it broadside, then suddenly the *Huron* swerved crazily to port. The sails of the mizzenmast being dragged astern had filled with water and heeled the ship as effectively as a sea anchor. The men were already hacking the mast loose as they prepared to come about again to fire on the *Sprite*. The *Huron* connected with the *Sprite* on every shot and then stood off, its maneuverability reduced greatly by the absence of the mizzen. The ship was wounded but still very dangerous. The *Chanticleer* now let fly with a broadside that slammed into the *Sprite*, downing her remaining mast. She lay rocking, her masts gone, with great holes in her sides that leaked smoke. Richard yelled for a ceasefire.

The *Chanticleer* was now hailing them, and though he was wary, Richard told his men to stand down. The *Chanticleer* sailed closer and Richard could hear the British captain yelling through a horn, "We are not at war. Repeat. We are not at war. The *Sprite* is a rogue ship. We are not at war." To further emphasize his point, the guns on the *Chanticleer* were pulled back and the ports closed. The *Chanticleer* was lowering a boat, and its captain was being loaded into it. Richard ordered the *Huron*'s remaining boats be hauled in so a crew could go find Mary and Edward and the three crew members who had also been on the rigging when it fell. They would not last long in the cold lake water. As soon as the *Chanticleer* understood what had happened, it sent out its boats as well to retrieve survivors. The *Huron*'s boats reached the wreckage of the mast, and quickly there was a call, "I got 'em, Captain." Richard sighed with relief and sat down on the signal locker.

The captain of the *Chanticleer*, now rocking alongside the *Huron* in his longboat, apologized repeatedly, trying to explain that the *Sprite* had been commandeered by a group of men disappointed in the outcome of the war and hungry for vengeance. His boat now moved aside to allow the

Huron's boat to be raised, bringing Edward and Mary back on board. The boat came up and was secured. Richard reached for Edward, checking him all over, and then handed him to a sailor who was waiting with a blanket. He then turned back for Mary, but she was not in the boat. Richard asked, "Where is Mary? Where is my wife? You said you had them!"

"No, captain, I said I had 'em, him, the boy. I didn't see Mrs. Holmwood. She wasn't on the wreckage. I looked all over," the sailor said sadly.

"We looked too, sir," one of the other survivors said. "We saw her surface and she helped the boy onto the wreckage, but then she just disappeared, almost like she dove under."

Richard stood dumbfounded. He bellowed her name over and over again across the water, "Mary! Mary!" He ordered the boat crew back to look for her again, and the captain of the *Chanticleer* ordered his boats to search for her as well. They hunted for any sign of her for nearly an hour until it was dark. Richard sent the boats back in the water. The shivering men kept searching in the waves that were getting higher as the snowfall thickened. Finally, Richard relented. He knew she could not have lasted more than fifteen or twenty minutes and nearly two hours had lapsed. If they continued to look it would not be to find her alive. For the greater good, Richard relented, and the *Huron*'s boat was hoisted aboard. The crew very quietly secured the boat, and they sailed for the island. A young sailor handed Richard Mary's dripping, red wool coat. It was all they had found of her.

The *Chanticleer* had rigged a towline on the *Sprite* and was now hauling the hulk back toward St. Joseph Island. On the *Huron*, Richard stood by the taffrail, looking back over the water, still unable to believe Mary was gone. Edward was wrapped in a blanket in his arms, and he said in a tiny voice, "Papa, we can't leave Mary out there. She's afraid of the dark."

Richard swallowed hard and held Edward close. He then spoke very gently to him, "Edward, Mary is gone. She probably drowned."

Edward tried to see his father's face in the dark, and said, "No, Papa. She swims real good. She wouldn't drown."

Richard held him close and explained, "Edward, it isn't that she couldn't swim, but the cold water would have killed her." Richard said it, trying to convince himself of the truth as well. Edward began to sob.

They sailed toward Mackinac Island and Richard stood holding Edward, who would be still for several minutes and then shudder as he sobbed again. Richard stared straight ahead as they docked at the pier. He barely waited until the ship was still before he climbed onto the pier with Edward in one arm and Mary's coat in the other. He stumbled up the hill to the house where Wrennet met him on the steps. She had heard the guns and knew something was wrong. "Richard, what is it?

Where is Mary?"

"She's gone. We were attacked, and she fell into the lake. She trusted me, and now she's dead. The mast was hit and gave under her and Edward, and we couldn't get to her in time. We got Edward, but we were too late to save Mary," Richard said flatly as he put Edward down on a chair by the fire.

Much later, after he had rubbed Edward's back as he sobbed himself to sleep, Richard slowly walked to the room he had shared with Mary and sat on the edge of the bed. From an ocean of time ago came Captain Truxton's words, "Cry all you want, but don't you ever let them see you do it." They were the words Richard had clung to and practiced all his life. Even when Lorraine died, he had not shed a tear.

He sat wearily on the bed and put his face in his hands and finally surrendered. He silently sobbed, and his stomach and chest muscles tightened like a vice. He wanted to scream, but he held the sound in, only letting out the tears as he grieved for Mary, who had trusted him, who had done everything he ever asked her to do without complaining, and who had loved him; he knew she did, and he had stubbornly refused to ever acknowledge it. Now it was too late. He grieved for Mary, cursing himself that he had not loved her openly. He sat with his head in his hands and grieved for her, and then for Lorraine, and, finally, he grieved for Owen, who he was certain was lost to him.

Richard was still sobbing when he felt Wrennet put her arms around him. He didn't try to hide from her, but let her hold him, and she folded him in her arms like she had all his life. She was sobbing too, and they held each other as she slowly rocked them back and forth. It was nearly an hour later that Richard was able to talk. He explained to Wrennet more of what had happened. "My God, Wrennet, she trusted me. I never should have taken her on that ship, but she wanted to go, and I wanted her to be with me. I was going to tell her how I really felt about her on the way back. I had actually started to go below to talk to her when we were fired on. Now I will never be able to tell her, and, God, poor Edward, Mary was the only mother he has ever known."

Richard looked at her, and she touched his cheek with her hand, saying softly, "Life is not fair, dear, not fair at all."

RICHARD WENT THROUGH the routine of living. He ate and dressed and even fed the chickens Mary had fussed over all the way from Scotland Neck, but he did this all in an effort to keep busy. One day he was going through a small basket and found an embroidered handkerchief of Mary's. He picked it up, and something rustled inside. He unfolded the handkerchief and recognized the distinct lines and margin as a page from a logbook. He unfolded the paper and there in his own writing on a corner he had torn from the back of the *Fiona's* logbook was the message, *You are now eleven miles from home.* Richard's throat tightened, and he swallowed hard. He had completely forgotten about the incident and here Mary had kept the note like it was treasure. Once again grief and guilt washed over him like cold lake water.

There had been no service for Mary because it seemed improper to do so without her body, and also because the longer he could put it off the longer he could go without admitting she was never coming back. It should have been done, and as day after day went by without a service, some of the crew began to grumble. Finally, they sent an envoy to speak to Richard.

"Captain, we are concerned about Mrs. Holmwood. She was not put to rest proper like, and she will not stay asleep. You know as well as any of us, sir, she must have the surface sealed from her, or she will rise and haunt us. The lake may keep her body, but her spirit will rise, and it will not be a happy one. None of us will be safe, and, sir, you know it." The sailor fidgeted and then added, "You must say the words to seal her under. If you can't do them, sir, we understand, but someone must to keep her away."

Richard nodded. He knew the superstition, and he knew it was time to stop delaying the inevitable and give up hope of seeing her body once more. He looked at the sailor and said, "The service will be tomorrow morning." The man visibly relaxed and left soon after to deliver the news to the others.

Sailing is a dangerous business, and sailors are the most superstitious breed alive, creating all kinds of traditions to be followed and things to be avoided. Richard, in his grief, had violated that tradition.

The service for Mary was held on the pier of the yet unfrozen lake, and it would be mercifully short for the men huddled there. Richard wrestled with the idea of whether or not to have Edward at the service, and finally decided to have Wrennet keep him at the cottage. Edward continued to insist Mary was alive, and Richard thought it best to keep him away.

Richard looked around the group of men gathered and began the words he had uttered dozens of times. Though they never came easily, the words stuck now like ashes in his throat as he uttered the prayer that had not changed in centuries, "We therefore commit his body." Richard cleared his throat and began again, "We now commit her body to the deep, looking for the general Resurrection in the last day. . ."

He continued speaking from memory, but his mind was far from the pier where flashes of Mary skipped across his memory even as his voice continued to spill the words that would seal her under the surface of the water forever, "at whose second coming in glorious majesty to judge the world, the sea shall give up her dead. . ." Mary shaking his hand at the Spencers the night he bargained for her, then grimacing in pain as he raped her the afternoon of their wedding, he saw her let fly with the stone that cut his forehead, Mary whooping with glee as he sailed with her and Edward on the James in the tiny sloop, ". . . and the corruptible bodies of those who sleep in him shall be changed, and made like unto his glorious body. . ." descending the stairs at the Decatur Ball in her lovely gown, calling him lustily back to bed the following morning, being followed by a half-dozen Ojibwa children who were smitten by her spell, sitting on the doorstep rubbing her huge belly, and finally her head popping to the surface after she fell into the lake, her first thought being for Edward, ". . .according to the mighty working whereby he is able to subdue all things unto himself." Richard ended the prayer lost in thought, not realizing he had run out of words.

There was an awkward silence as the congregation looked at each other, and then two sailors from the *Huron* stepped forward and gently tossed onto the gray waters a wreath they had made from cedar they found growing along the shoreline. The wreath bobbed on the surface for a few seconds, and then, with a collective gasp from the mourners, it disappeared under the water. One sailor turned to Richard and said, "It ain't enough, sir. She will rise again." They all looked to Richard, and he added, "We brought nothing into this world, and it is certain we can carry nothing out. The Lord gave, and the Lord hath taken away; blessed be the Name of the Lord."

There was a collective "Amen," and they dispersed, mollified. Richard stood looking out over the water, and he knew that if Mary were to come for him from the waves, no matter how corrupt she was, he would welcome her with open arms even to the destruction of them all. Having made this assessment, his thoughts turned to how she had died. What had happened to her? Had she been pulled under, or did she simply sink due to her heavy clothes? Edward said she took off her coat to stay afloat, and was even trying to wrap it around him when she simply shot under the water and was gone.

Richard prayed she had been killed quickly and had not struggled in terror until she ran out of air in her lungs. He wondered now, too, about the child. Had it died when Mary herself did? Had she perhaps even felt it die before her, or had it lived on a while longer, still warm in its mother's womb, until it too ran out of life? This led to him wondering what the child would have looked like. Would it have been blonde like him, or would it have been dark-haired like Mary?

The *Huron* was readied for winter. The crew of forty would live inside the ship, which had been beached on the rocky shore and then allowed to roll on her side. With no tide, the crew could get her no higher up the beach. The men took stoves and rigged them through the gun ports, and created a false floor to compensate for the careening slant. They had plenty of food and were welcome at the fur company warehouse, where they sometimes went to tell stories and smoke pipes. Their pipe tobacco actually aided in preserving the dried pelts.

Richard tried to keep busy, but he found himself staring at a chart, not really seeing it, or looking out the tiny window for great spans of time. He did his best with Edward, who was inconsolable, and Wrennet looked tired and afraid as the burden of the house and caring for Edward now fell to her, exactly as she said she could not do back in Scotland Neck.

Richard wandered over to the warehouse and met with Robert Stuart most nights. It was a way to pass the time, and somehow it seemed less painful to be somewhere that didn't remind him of Mary constantly. Douglas Deems escaped the turmoil at his house as often as he could and joined them, and there the three men told each other tales of their lives before coming to the island.

It was amazing to Richard the different grades of fur within the same animal species. There were six different grades of beaver, depending on size and depth of coat. Mink was divided by quality as well as color, and muskrat by its fur density. Stuart said, "The money is in beaver, but the most versatile fur in my estimation is muskrat, musquash as the English say, or wazhushk in Ojibwa. It is waterproof, warm, soft, durable, and beautiful, and I don't see why it isn't more popular. Of course, it doesn't make hats, and that is where most of this beaver goes, to make top hats for gentlemen." Stuart watched Richard looking at a pile of thin, creamy-white pelts no longer than a foot with a tail half that length. The thin tail terminated in a deep, black tip. Richard ran his hands through the sleek fur, and Stuart said, "Those, for the most part, go to European royalty for capes and stoles. It takes more than sixty weasel pelts to make just the collar trim for a short coronation cape. I have no idea how many it takes for a full-length cape. It's a sad end for such a ferocious little creature. Pound for pound, he is the meanest thing in the forest, and thank God weasels are small, or we would all be in trouble. Of course the tiny pelts are sold under the title ermine. It doesn't sound nearly so regal to say the king is wearing weasel." Richard smiled and put the fur back down and took the drink Stuart offered him. "How are you doing, Richard?" Douglas asked, taking a sip of his own whiskey.

"I'm just doing, and that is the honest truth. I get through each day, and pray the next one will be a little easier," Richard said, sipping slowly.

"I'm sorry we can't offer you a more serene escape at our house." Douglas drank deeply and then continued, "But you know what it is like over there." Richard nodded, but didn't comment.

"You've lost weight," Stuart said, "and that is a dangerous thing up here, so if you don't mind me telling you what do, I would suggest you eat whether you want to or not. You're going to need some flesh to get you through the cold this winter." Stuart said this in a kindly way. Richard nodded, finished his drink, and bid Robert and Douglas a good night.

With the ship careened, there wasn't much for Richard to do. He had cases of books with him, and there were charts to review, but he couldn't seem to do either for long. He just stared at the charts or found himself reading the same page over and over. More than anything, he longed for an escape. In the past he had run to the ocean, and though he really couldn't sail away from it, it was at least a respite from his troubles. He had taken the cutter out several times with Edward, but it wasn't the same as a ship where there was enough to keep his mind occupied.

Richard woke one morning and realized he knew more about the other islands around them than about the one on which he lived. After breakfast, he asked Wrennet to bundle Edward up and told him they would explore. Edward and Mary, even though she was pregnant, had poked around the entire island, and they had even made a crude map of their journeys. Edward proudly put the map in his father's hand, and Richard looked at it carefully. Mary's looping upright hand and Edward's fat block printing adorned the map as they marked out things like strawberry plants—check in the spring—magical arch, the crack in the world, devil's kitchen—see if it works—the single spring, Fort Holmes' garrison. Richard pointed out several places and asked Edward about them. Richard noted with a sad smile where Edward had written Holmwood Castle and where next to it Mary had marked the Deems's house ominously as Dragon's Lair.

They set out with Edward's map and walked to the limestone arch. Looking through it from above, it framed Lake Michigan, and also the way they would all eventually sail home. They moved across the island, so Edward could show him the dreaded "crack in the world." It was actually a spot where the limestone had eroded vertically, and it indeed looked like a great crack in the earth that ran across that section of the island. Edward related to Richard the fanciful stories Mary had made up for him about the enchanting world that was just inside the crack, but since they didn't have the magical phrase to open it, they could not get inside. Richard's throat tightened. He pictured Mary sitting there, conjuring these wonderful tales for Edward, and she not much more than a girl herself.

A week later they explored the Devil's Kitchen as Mary had written, and it indeed looked like a giant oven or furnace. It was another limestone formation, this time in pearly white against the grayer bluff. The more they explored, the more Richard marveled at the sheer number of geological oddities contained on one small island no larger than four square miles. He saw too why the Ojibwa had feared and revered it, and wondered if their warnings were true. Richard and his family had disturbed the island, and look at what had resulted.

CHAPTER 13

OWEN ARRIVED back in Scotland Neck a few weeks after Jordan's return from leaving Richard in Welland. Jordan was staying at the house where Richard had asked him to wait for Owen. This would be Owen's first trip alone as captain, and Richard had asked Jordan to go with him.

Owen came to the house after dark and entered very quietly, almost like he was sneaking. Jordan was sleeping in Edward's room, but heard him come in. Owen must have looked around downstairs, and when he found things deserted, he bounded up the stairway and burst into his father's room.

By this time, Jordan had gotten up and gone into the hallway to meet him. Owen came back out of the bedroom and saw him standing there, and his first question was not why Jordan was there or what had happened, but was instead, "Where is she? Where is Mary?"

Jordan said, "They have all gone with Richard to the Territory." Owen stood dumbfounded for nearly five minutes, and then he erupted. He came at Jordan demanding to know when they left. After Jordan explained, Owen stormed back into the master bedroom and drew out his sword. He stabbed the bed and pillows and slashed at the curtains until there were feathers and cloth everywhere, all the while letting fly with the most foul curses about how his father had betrayed him, and how he never could have loved him. Owen went downstairs and slashed his way around the house destroying what he could and then stopped suddenly. He came to where Jordan was now standing at the foot of the stairs and asked, "What are you doing here?"

Jordan told him Richard had asked him to stay to deliver him the orders to sail and to offer his services as second officer. Richard had said, "I know this is asking a lot of you Jordan, to take a berth below Owen, but it is only this once, and he is my son."

When Owen heard the sailing orders, his face took on the most vile look. He said, "Jordan, first mate it is, and we leave tomorrow for Norfolk to load up."

They didn't leave the next day or even the day after that. They didn't leave for nearly two weeks, because Owen kept disappearing from the house after dinner, and he always looked back over his shoulder when he left, as if to see if he was being followed. He was acting so strangely that Jordan finally followed him one night, and watched as Owen went to a large house up the river from Richard's. Owen waited for a while outside the house, and then a woman slipped out the side door and ran to him. Jordan moved closer to see who it was, but before he got ten feet closer, he realized Owen and the woman had stripped off their clothing. Jordan was trapped where he was and couldn't risk retreating for fear of being discovered, so he turned his back and waited. Jordan heard the woman mumble something, and then Owen's reply, "Yes, I find you very pretty, Emma."

On the occasions when Owen accompanied Richard and Edward to dine with the Spencers, he had caught the hungry looks Emma had given his father at the table. Richard might not have been willing, but Owen was, and it had taken him only one afternoon's visit with the Spencers to set up his rendezvous with Emma. Using Emma in this way served two purposes. First it was basic relief, but beyond that it was also a twisted form of revenge against both Richard and Mary.

Jordan stood now with his back to the couple while they had each other within the very light fall of the windows of the Spencer home. When they were finished, and Jordan observed with a smirk that it wasn't very long, Owen sent Emma scurrying back into the house with a smack on the backside to which she giggled like a girl. Jordan heard Owen finish dressing, but he jumped when Owen said aloud, "You could have joined us, Jordan. I don't think she would have minded one bit. She's rather a generous sort." Jordan stood there stunned and then followed Owen, who had started to walk home.

They left for Spain three days later.

CHAPTER 14

I T WAS GETTING DARK earlier in the evenings and light later in the mornings, and as their daylight hours dwindled, they spent more time indoors. Richard resumed Edward's lessons to keep them both busy, and Wrennet worked as best she could around them. It had now been six weeks since Mary was lost, and every morning when he woke, Richard felt the crushing pain return. It took a second longer each day for it to hit, and Richard knew the pain would ease over time, leaving a fierce ache, just as it had with Lorraine.

After the noon meal, Richard sat with Edward to do his lessons. Edward was very bright and excelled in mathematics, but his main pursuit was animals and plants, so to keep him interested, Richard usually saved the big illustrated books of wildlife for last. They had just finished the math portion and had opened the wildlife book, when there was a knock on the door. A young British officer stood on his doorstep and behind him was the captain of the *Chanticleer*. The young officer asked if Richard would meet with his captain. Richard nodded and welcomed him inside. The younger man stood outside the door as if on guard.

Captain Leteauce greeted Richard in a kindly manner, but he still burned with shame that men under his command had brought about the death of this man's wife, and he declined Richard's offer of a chair. He said, still standing, "Captain Holmwood, I must again apologize for the damage to your ship and your family by these fools under my command. If it is any consolation, the last one was hanged this morning at dawn, but what I have come to see you about is another problem." Richard looked at him, wondering what else this man could possibly bring to plague him, and he was offended by Leteauce's smile as he continued, "It has come to my attention that an American woman has been living at our base. The woman somehow found her way to the island and has been living secretly in the bawdy house."

Richard smiled weakly, "You're civilized enough over there to have a whorehouse?"

Leteauce smiled back, "It is a rather small one, and does as much clothes washing for trade as whoring, but at any rate, this woman came ashore and was living among the women there until she sought me out to bring her back. She claims she is your wife."

Richard stared at Leteauce, unblinking. He shook his head and said, "My wife is dead. She fell in the water, and we could not get her out."

Leteauce interrupted, raising his voice above Richard's protests, "She claims she kept quiet before now because she thought Britain was again at war with the United States. She says her name is Mary Margaret Holmwood. Do you know this woman?"

Richard smiled sadly, "That is my wife's name, but it isn't her." He looked at the floor and then back up, "My wife was with child, very heavy with child when she was lost, so it isn't her."

Leteauce smiled coaxingly, "This woman was delivered of a boy child in the bawdy house about six weeks ago."

For the first time Richard dared to hope Mary was alive. He rose from his chair and told Leteauce, "Please take me to her. Whoever she is, if she is an American, she should be here with us."

Leteauce smiled again. "I would have brought her up here with me when I came, but after seeing her in action, I wasn't absolutely sure you hadn't jettisoned her on purpose. What a powder keg!" Richard smiled sadly, knowing then Leteauce could not be describing mild and pliant Mary, but he walked toward the door anyway. Edward had heard all this, and he ran to get his coat, but Richard stopped him.

"Papa, please take me with you. I want to see if it's Mary!" Edward looked close to tears, and he was clinging to Richard's sleeve.

Richard bent down to Edward's level and put his hands on his small shoulders. "Edward, it's not Mary, so don't get your hopes up." Edward backed away with tears in his eyes, and Richard said as Edward ran into Wrennet's arms for comfort, "Wait for me here, and I'll be right back." Richard mussed the blond curls on his small son's head, then added, "And I'll read you a story."

On the way to the pier, Leteauce explained more of what he knew about the woman and her child. Leteauce was jocular and talkative, but Richard's head was swirling so that he barely listened as Leteauce rattled on like a gossipy old woman. "The child was born right in the bawdy house. Now you know with their line of commerce there, a baby is a liability, but since they didn't give birth to him, he doesn't get in the way of trade. I tell you when they are not working, they mother him something awful. This little fellow is the darling of them all! I don't believe the child has been put down since he was born. When his mother isn't feeding him, the women nearly come to blows over who will hold him next." Leteauce added with a chuckle, "That boy has nuzzled more décolletage in the few weeks of his life than most of us will in a lifetime!" Richard smiled, but his thoughts were bitter. Damn this woman! To come now and dig open a wound that had yet to scab over. Damn her to hell!

As they neared the wharf where Leteauce's cutter was moored, Richard could hear a woman fussing. Her voice was loud and strident, and Richard confirmed his conviction it couldn't be Mary, not from the way she was berating the men keeping her. As he got closer, he saw two young officers standing with the woman between them, holding her gently but securely by her arms. The woman was pitching a fit and accusing them of every conceivable sin as she demanded to be turned loose. Richard's heart sank further, as he realized she was at least a foot too tall to be Mary. The woman was wearing a dark-hooded cloak, and her face was turned toward the taller of the two British officers holding her. Richard heard the woman scream, "That is my house right there. You take your filthy hands off me. I bet you haven't taken a bath since you left England." She then turned to a third young man standing beside the other officers holding her and fussed at him as he adjusted a bundle in his arms. Richard saw a tiny foot and leg pop out of the bundle as the young man struggled to rewrap the infant. The woman stomped in anger, and Richard looked down at her foot. His heart thudded as he saw her do it, for she was not tall at all, but instead was standing on the seat of the cutter. Her words became clearer now, "If you are going to take my son from me, the least you can do is keep him covered. You have no right to hold me here. Let me go!" With that, she turned her face toward the other officer to tear into him, and Richard gasped. It *was* Mary!

Richard climbed down into the British cutter, and the men released Mary. She saw Richard, and without missing a beat in her attack, turned on him instead. "You! You left me there like trash tossed overboard." She now mocked his deep voice, "'Climb into the rigging Mary, and whatever you do don't let go of it! Ride it down, Mary!'" She tossed up her hands. "Great good it did me!" Richard grinned and pulled her close, oblivious to anything she said, and he took her face in both his hands and kissed her hard on the mouth. She stopped struggling immediately.

He finally pulled back from her and whispered close to her mouth, "Hush." She stood smiling, dazed, and, most importantly, silent.

Leteauce cleared his throat. "I assume Captain Holmwood that this is your wife. We have had some trouble getting her to calm down, but alas, we didn't think to try that."

Richard stood with Mary still in his arms and grinned, "Yes, Captain Leteauce, this is my wife, Mary. Thank you for returning her to me." Mary stood staring at Richard, speechless. The two officers who had been holding her now helped her onto the pier, and then retreated back to the cutter, glad to be rid of her. Richard leaned over to the young man holding the infant and said smiling, "I believe this is mine as well."

"Good luck to you, sir," he said, and then whispered low enough that he thought Richard couldn't hear, "You are going to need it."

"Damn right I am!" Richard said with a smile. The young man smiled back sheepishly as Richard climbed out of the cutter holding the baby in one arm. He joined Mary on the pier and again thanked Leteauce. He nudged Mary, and she grudgingly thanked him as well.

It was beginning to snow and Leteauce and his men would have to scramble to get back to St. Joseph Island. Richard and Mary stood watching as they rowed clear of the pier and then hoisted the single sail. The wind quickly filled it, and the cutter moved out into the harbor and was swallowed up in the snow flurry. Richard turned and looked down at Mary. He touched her face and then kissed her. "I never thought to see you again. I thought you were dead." Richard stared at her, marveling, and then cried, "Oh, God, come here." He held her tight for a long time, taking care not to crush the infant, and then he finally pulled back from her and asked, "Can you walk to the house all right?"

"Richard, I'm fine!" Mary laughed, though her eyes were filled with tears. She tucked her arm through his and whispered, "Please take me home." They walked up from the pier, and despite being dressed in hemmed-up, taken in, whore's hand-me-downs, Mary moved like a diminutive queen.

Edward was standing on a chair peering out the tiny front window, and when he saw them he came running out, "Mary! Mary! Oh, Mary!" Wrennet was with him and she hugged Mary as Edward buried his head in her chest, sobbing, and kept it there while they walked the rest of the way to the house.

They struggled, still clinging, through the small, low door and Richard stood looking at Mary holding Wrennet's hand and kissing Edward's cheeks as all three were laughing and crying at the same time. He then heard a little squeak from the blanket in his arm, and he gently uncovered his son. The tiny boy was sucking his lower lip, but stared at him steadily. "Hello, little one," he bent down close and took the baby's hand, and the child clamped down on his finger with surprising strength.

Richard hadn't seen Owen until he was nearly three years old, and even then he was still practically bald, and Edward had been born nearly hairless with only a little white tuft on his head and virtually no eyebrows. This child's head was covered with lush black hair, and he had tiny arched brows that gave him a serious and wise expression.

Edward was squeezing Mary and then pulled back from her with his hands on her abdomen. "Mary! Where is your baby?" He was too busy looking at Mary to have noticed the bundle his father was carrying. She smiled and pointed to Richard who was now sitting in a chair holding the child. Edward stared at them both.

"Come and see your little brother," Richard said.

Edward walked over, almost afraid, and peered down. After a

minute his face broke into a big smile, and he said, "I'm gonna teach him to fish and throw stones!" He edged closer, and Richard helped him up on his lap with his free arm. Mary and Wrennet came and stood next to Richard's chair, and they all looked at the new baby.

Grub had been off circling the island on one of his legendary urinating trips, but he now burst into the house through the open door no one had bothered to close and ran in circles around Mary, whimpering and crying to be petted. He greeted the child with a big lick that slicked the infant's hair straight up with saliva, and then tried to crawl onto Richard's lap to see him better. Everyone was laughing and crying and it was a while before any of them settled down.

Later, when they were finally able to get Edward to sleep, Mary and Richard were in their room propped up on pillows looking at the child. "He really is a handsome boy, Mary." They watched the baby, and he started to curl his mouth to the side. Mary smiled, "He's hungry. I fed him just before we left in the boat, but he needs to eat every two or three hours. It is actually past when he should eat, and I'm surprised he's not howling."

"Does he howl?" Richard asked, remembering Edward having no trouble making himself heard.

"Oh, yes! Have no fear he would ever be overlooked and starve!" Mary, who had changed into a simple nightdress earlier, sat up straighter and motioned for Richard to move closer behind her for support.

"May I stay?" Richard asked, not wanting to be banished. Mary smiled, and he watched silently over her shoulder as she loosened the ribbon on the front of her gown and lifted out her breasts. She had been very busty before the baby, but these were now formidable. The baby's head was dwarfed by them, and Richard thought the little guy might suffocate, but he latched right on and after a minute was in a steady rhythm of sucking and swallowing.

Richard watched contentedly. He had never seen a woman nurse an infant, and he found a deep, settled peace in this timeless act which of all things on earth cannot be rushed. He stroked Mary's hair and leaned close to her ear. "Mary, I love you. I should have told you that earlier, but I'm telling you now. God help me, but I love you so much." Mary didn't say anything, but Richard saw a tear run down her cheek. He moved around, so he could see her face better as the tear ran off her jaw and dropped onto the baby's head. Richard gently wiped it away, and then pulled her chin up so he could see her face. "Mary, what's wrong?"

Her voice cracked as she said, "I thought you didn't care. I know I wasn't supposed to, but I fell in love with you a long time ago. I thought you didn't care what happened when you left me out there. I only told them who I was so they would bring me back for Edward because I promised I would take care of him."

Richard cupped her face in his hands and said softly, "Don't ever think that again. I love you as much as I have ever loved anything, and I aim to spend the rest of my life proving it to you." He kissed her and then settled some pillows behind her to support her back while he stretched out on the bed facing her and watched.

After a long silence Mary said, "Why didn't you kiss me before? I wanted you to."

Richard said softly, "I know you did, but I was stubborn, and I didn't want to relinquish the past. Don't think I didn't want to, Mary. I was just being stupid."

"Are you going to say and do what you mean from now on?" Mary asked frankly. Richard looked a bit taken aback, but he nodded yes, and Mary said, "Good." She looked seriously at Richard and said, "I came close enough to dying out there that now I intend to say what I feel and ask for what I want. I am not going to wait for things to happen to me, because I am going to make them happen. You may think that is wrong or improper, but the woman that fell into that lake is not the same one that crawled out again."

"Nor would I want her to be," Richard said softly and kissed her cheek. "I like what came back to me."

Mary smiled and said, "You might want to reserve your judgment." She then stood with the child and said, "I'm going to change him, so he will wake up and take the other breast. If he does, then he will sleep for a few hours." Mary tucked herself into the gown and placed the child on the bed. Richard was amazed at how good she was with him, and he nodded when she said, "Stay with him, while I get a clean nappy," and then she left the room. Richard unwound the blanket and then took the clothes off the little boy. They were made from thin cotton and appeared to be sewed from a petticoat, probably Mary's. He untied the knot on the nappy and pulled it down just as Mary returned. She ran to stop him, but was too late. The baby kicked and then sent an arc of urine right up into his own little face. Richard looked stunned as he tried to catch the urine in his cupped hands. Mary quickly pushed back the old nappy, and it caught the rest of the flow.

Richard looked sheepish. "I had no idea that would happen." Mary smiled and shook her head while she cleaned the baby. Richard grinned at her and then said rather proudly, "You have to admit, though, he does have quite a gun on him, doesn't he?"

"He came by it honestly," Mary said, smiling wickedly as she sat back down to finish nursing. Richard smiled at her curiously. This new Mary was full of surprises, some of which would prove to be delightful, but others he reckoned would keep him well in line. He sat silently, watching as the baby nursed until he simply passed out like a sailor drunk on leave. He just stopped sucking and every muscle in his body relaxed.

A tiny stream of milk ran from the corner of his mouth, and Richard reached over and wiped it away with his finger. He put the finger in his mouth and his eyes opened wide.

"It's so sweet! I didn't think it would be sweet at all!" Richard whispered and held the baby while Mary put herself back into her gown.

Mary smiled at him and whispered back, "I was curious too, and tasted it. My reaction was the same as yours. No wonder they grow so fast!" She looked around the room. "Where is the cradle Mr. Lockley made?"

Richard looked hard at her for a moment, and then said, "Mary, I thought I had lost you both, and I burned it in the stove. I'm sorry."

Mary looked at him, realizing for the first time what he had gone through. She put her hand on his cheek and said, "Richard, it's all right. We'll find a place for him tonight and then have another cradle made. You told me a ship's carpenter can make anything. He can certainly make us another." Richard smiled, and they ended up putting the baby in a basket next to their bed where they stood looking down at him.

Richard said softly, "What an auspicious beginning for him." Mary looked puzzled at Richard, and he explained, "Being born right in a bawdy house."

Mary turned her head to look at him and then said, "Those women were very kind to me. You know, I was wrong about what they are. I thought they did what they did because they wanted to, but after talking with them, many have no other way to live. They make their living as best they can. Some of them followed their husbands here, and then the husbands died or abandoned them. They do what they do to keep from starving. I misjudged them completely."

"If they helped you, then they are angels," Richard said as he reached over and pulled her close and buried his face in her hair which smelled of roses. Even in a whorehouse, she had managed to keep scrupulously clean. He held her close and kissed her again and was a little shocked when she pulled his shirt up out of his trousers and said, "Take this off, please." He pulled the shirt over his head and tossed it aside, missing the baby's basket by inches. Mary unlaced her gown and let it drop it to the floor.

"Mary, are you sure? I mean, can you?" Richard asked tentatively but breathing hard.

"It's been six weeks since he was born, and yes, I'm sure!" she chuckled as she puffed out the light, and jumped into bed. Richard was right behind her. This new Mary was exciting. "Hey, Mary?" Richard asked in jest, "You didn't work while you were in that house did you?"

She punched him gently in the side. "No, I didn't work there," she said, then hissed wickedly, "but I certainly did pay attention!" Richard laughed out loud.

RICHARD BEGAN TO WAKE the next morning just as the sun was rising, and he smiled recalling the night as he reached over for Mary to pull her close. His hand fell on an empty bed, and he jolted awake. He looked around the dim room, but it was empty—no Mary, no basket, nothing. Oh, God, this can't be just a dream! He leaped out of bed and pulled on his trousers, then flung open the door and stumbled into the main room of the cottage, nearly sobbing. Mary's head snapped up, and she startled the baby who began to cry. Richard gasped with relief, "I thought it was a dream. I woke up and you and the baby were gone, and I thought I had been dreaming!"

The relief flooded over his face, and Mary said softly, "It was not a dream. We're here. You can't get rid of us that easily." She held her hand out and Richard took it as she explained, "I didn't want to wake you, so I brought him out here when he started to fuss." She smiled at Richard as she soothed the child again with her breast. "Put on some more clothes and come join us."

Richard, now dressed, took the sated child from Mary and looked down at him and asked, "Did you give him a name?"

"Oh, yes, I gave him your favorite name. I called him Jack," Mary said proudly.

"My favorite name?" Richard asked confused.

"Yes! You always are saying how some man or the other is the finest Jack you have ever known, how you wished you had more Jacks like him, or why can't they all be Jacks like that one. It's your favorite name!" Richard didn't have the heart to tell her jack was slang for any common sailor, short for jack-tar, referring to the stains on their hands from the tarred rigging, but the name Jack wasn't the worst thing that could befall a baby boy, so he held his tongue.

"I'll put it in the Bible right now," he said as he walked over to the desk and hauled out the huge Bible Arla Spencer had pressed on them before they left Scotland Neck. He added Jack's name to the front page.

As he was putting the Bible back in the desk, a letter slid onto the floor. He picked it up and realized he had never finished his letter to the Spencer family advising them of Mary's death. He had dreaded writing the letter, and had given up each time he tried because Jacob Spencer's last words kept ringing in his ears, "Take care of her, Richard; she is our princess." The letter, had he written it, would not have reached the Spencers until next summer. He crumpled it in his hand and gratefully burned it in the stove.

It wasn't until after breakfast that Mary recited the tale of what had happened to her after the mast fell. She sat sipping her coffee, and started her long and uninterrupted account of that horrid night and ensuing days:

"Edward and I could feel the mast get hit, because the impact ran through it and made our hands sting. At first I thought we were all right, that the mast would hold, but then it started to snap and groan, and I knew we were going to fall. We hung on and rode it like you said. We were thrown off when it hit the water. It was so cold." Mary shivered as she remembered, "I had to clench my jaw to keep from gasping and pulling water into my lungs.

"Edward must have surfaced about the same time as I did, because he was about ten yards away when I came up. I swam to him, but my coat kept pulling me down, so when I got where I could hold onto some of the wreckage, I took off my coat, and tried to put it around him. Some other men had been on the mast too and they swam over to help. I was treading water looking at Edward and trying to keep him away from one of the men who couldn't swim well and who kept panicking and grabbing at anything he could. The other two men got him onto some of the wreckage, and he clung there.

"I was watching all this when something grabbed my ankle and pulled me under. I know there are none here, but my first thought was of a shark or something big like that, and I tried to fight, but whatever it was, it was hauling me along under water so fast that I couldn't reach down to it. Once the tension was released, I gasped for air at the surface and realized it was rope around my ankle, but the rope was nearly as big as my wrist, and I couldn't pull it loose. I tried to look around, but there was so much smoke on the water that I could barely see before I was dragged down again. I did see your ship turn like you were going to fire and then I was pulled under again. I thought I would drown this time. My lungs were stinging so badly. Then I shot to the surface and was pulled along there for a ways until everything suddenly just stopped. The rope pulling me went slack and started to sink, pulling me under again, but with the tension gone I was able to wiggle my foot loose.

"I have never been so cold in my life, and my hands would barely work. If I didn't get out of the water soon, I would die, I knew that. Just then something passed me and I screamed. It looked like a snake in the water, but it was a rope trailing behind something. I grabbed it and held on, not knowing who was pulling me or where I was going, but I held on. My hands were so cold and locked into place that once I latched on, I don't think I could have let go if I wanted to. I saw a ship ahead of me through the smoke and realized it was the one that had fired on us first. I couldn't see your ship anywhere, but once the smoke cleared, I saw a boat pick up Edward and the others on the wreckage, so I knew he was safe. No one seemed to be looking for me, so I pulled myself along the rope until I was next to the ship. It wasn't moving, but it was really rocking in the waves, and I was afraid to get too close for fear the ship would come down on top of me. I saw the other British ship come up then and the crew attached some towlines to the ship I was clinging to. I thought of trying to get their attention, but I believed we were at war again, so I kept quiet. I managed to get my foot on those little steps that stick out from the side of the ship, and there were a lot of lines and stuff hanging there, too, and I climbed as high as I could and crouched in one of the gun ports. The cover was gone, so I just huddled in the opening. There was sailcloth hanging there as well, and I pulled it as close to me as I could. The galley fire was burning, and a bit of heat came out the gun port to me, but I had no coat and was dressed in only my wool dress, and I started to panic when I realized the hem of my dress was frozen. It's a good thing I was wearing wool, because it keeps you warm even when it's wet. If I had been wearing cotton or linen, I would never have made it.

"I crawled further inside the ship, and hid behind the nearest gun. I had watched the original crew being led away by men with muskets, and now there were only a few men still on the deck. I hid where I was until we got to the pier, and then I heard the anchor drop. Rather than tie up at the pier, they anchored the ship and everyone left. I crouched by the galley fire, and heard a man say as he got into the boat that they would come back in the morning. I knew I had to get off the ship before then.

"The lights from buildings shone on the water, and I could see it was only about fifty yards to shore, but I was so tired, I didn't think I could swim that far on my own. There was a lot of debris still hanging on the ship, and I noticed one of those things that hold the sail to the mast was there being held by only two lines. I found a knife in the galley, and started to cut through the rope. I took me nearly an hour, and I had to keep letting my hands rest, and besides I was having contractions again, and they didn't seem to be going away when I rested like they always did before. They were different this time too, because they hurt. Finally, I cut through the last strands of the line, and the piece of wood fell into the lake with a huge splash. I waited, but no one responded to the sound, and during that time the contractions came twice again, and the last thing I wanted to do was get back in that water. It looked like a fairly large establishment there on St. Joseph Island, and I figured there must be someplace I could hide on shore if I could just get there. I climbed as low as I could on the side of the ship, and then dropped into the water. It was even colder than I imagined, but this time I was waiting for it, and I started to kick my way to shore trying to be as quiet as possible. Every kick seemed harder and harder, but finally my feet struck the rocks near the shore, and I climbed out and sat on a rock letting the water drain from my dress so I could walk, and then I hid along the shore near some barrels. I heard women's voices close by, and laughter. Any thoughts I had of hiding alone vanished, and I wanted some women around me to help me deliver my baby. I tried to stand up to walk to them, but I couldn't. My feet and legs were so cold I could not stand, so I started to crawl, but because my stomach was so large, I had to do it on my side, and it was slowgoing. I pulled myself along on the ground, pushing as best I could with my numb legs until finally I was only about ten yards from the house where the women were, but I couldn't go any further. The ground was covered with small, flat stones, the kind you use for skipping on the water, and I picked one up and threw it at the house. I had to throw several more, but finally a woman came to the door. When she saw no one was there, she stepped out on the porch, and I called out to her, and she came running. I told her I had been in the water and that I thought I was having a baby. She ran back inside the house and three others came back with her and they took me inside.

"They were alarmed when I told them the war was back on, because they hadn't heard anything about it, but, nevertheless, they took care of me. The woman who first found me seemed to be in charge, and they stripped off my wet clothes and put me to bed. I think I passed out for a little while, but the pain woke me up again. I seemed to remember only pain, but I think I was actually sleeping between contractions until they became steady. Jack was born just as dawn was breaking. He was so tiny. Poor thing, he wasn't due for another month, but the ladies told me he was fine and healthy. I think I slept again or at least I lost consciousness, because I woke up straining again, and felt something slip out of my body which the women took away in a cloth. I cried because I forgot I had already had Jack, and I thought I had lost the baby and that was what they carried away, but they showed me Jack again, and I relaxed. I don't remember much after that, but they must have taken care of him until he needed to nurse. Several of the women had children, and they showed me how to feed him. I didn't know what to do, but he sure didn't have any trouble, and he tucked right in. I slept the rest of that day only waking to feed him, but the next day, I was able to sit up and talk to the women who had saved me.

"They asked around, and found there had indeed been a battle, and they assumed as I did that America and Britain were at war. It was weeks and weeks later that one of them confirmed there was no war, so I asked to see whoever was in charge on the island. He didn't believe me at first, but when I told him what had happened to me and who I was, he started yelling orders. Several men came and they discussed what to do, and for a while they were going to keep me there until spring, but I really pitched a fit, and they finally decided to bring me home."

Richard looked at Mary and touched her cheek, "I have always heard of the hidden strength of women, but I had never really witnessed it until now. Thank God you're safe."

They sat talking more and at one point he smiled and added, "You know, we actually had a service to commit your body to the deep, so I would suggest you let word get around to the crew that you are alive before they actually see you, or some of them might drop dead from the shock." Mary looked confused, but Richard was right. Several of the crew came up nosing for information after having seen the British cutter the night before. They knocked on the door, and Wrennet opened it with Mary behind her. They stared at her like she was a ghost, and though she greeted them and offered coffee or tea and biscuits, they politely declined and sat looking terrified at her as Richard explained what had happened. They nodded as the tale unfolded, but all the while they kept a wary eye on Mary. After they left, Richard told her, "They think you have come back from the dead. Be prepared when you ask Lockley to build you a new cradle because he is the worst of the lot when it comes to superstition. Even though I will explain more than once to them how you survived, some of them, especially the older ones, will always fear you."

CHAPTER 15

STARING OUT THE WINDOW now at the snowfall, Mary and Richard wondered if this was the one that would lock them permanently into winter for the year. They had both listened to tales of storms that created drifts thirty-feet tall, but they couldn't imagine weather like that. Richard had been in horrible storms at sea, and many had involved snow and freezing rain that threatened to pile up on the decks and rigging to capsize the ship. Those had been short-lived situations, and they soon sailed out of the bad weather and the snow melted.

As they watched out of the windows, two figures approached. They came from the warehouse and kept well in the lee of the Holmwood cottage. Mary and Richard could tell it was a man and a woman, but only when they were within about ten feet of the house did they recognize Roger Thane and Stella Deems. Richard greeted them at the door, and they came in stomping the snow from their shoes. "Rough weather for a stroll isn't it?" Richard said in jest.

"It's lovely," Stella said a little breathy.

"Captain Holmwood, this is not a social call," Roger said seriously. "We are hoping you can marry us. A captain can do that, can't he?"

"Well, yes, at sea he can, but I don't know if it counts on land," Richard said, eyeing them both.

"It will have to count for us. I am leaving later today, and Stella is coming with me. We can go without the benefit of marriage, or you can marry us, but we are going together," Roger said with his arm securely around Stella's waist.

Richard nodded and then asked the obvious, "You haven't told Douglas and Dorcas about this have you?" Roger nodded and Richard added, "I can't really say that I blame you, but I think in the end, Douglas at least, would have come around to the idea."

"We are leaving them a letter," Stella said, "explaining that we are married and that we will see them again in the spring."

"You two may get away, but I will have to live with the wrath all winter. Do you wish that on me?" Richard said, smiling.

Roger smiled back relieved and said, "With all my hostile little heart."

Richard turned and Mary was standing holding the prayer book out for him, already open to the celebration of a marriage, and they took their places by the fire. The service took only minutes, and then Richard said to them kindly, "May I be the first to congratulate you, Mr. and Mrs. Thane."

"You have to kiss your bride," Mary said, grinning. "Richard didn't kiss me, but he didn't really like me then!" Roger bent and kissed Stella tenderly, and Mary could feel Richard's arm steal around her waist as they watched the newlyweds.

They hauled out the huge family Bible, and Stella and Roger signed their names to the front adding the date, and Richard and Mary signed after them. "You don't plan to leave in this weather, do you?" Richard asked, jerking his head toward the window.

"This? Oh, this will stop in an hour or so, you just wait. By the time we get the rest of our things loaded in the canoe, it will have let up and we can leave. There isn't a breath of wind with it, and we can get to the encampment near St. Ignace by nightfall," Roger said, referring to the camp where the Ojibwa who traded on the island spent the winter.

They made their farewells and Stella hugged Mary tightly. Roger handed Richard a letter addressed to Douglas Deems and asked one final favor, "Could you not give this to them until tomorrow morning? That will give us time to get away from the encampment." Richard nodded and shook Roger's hand, wishing him luck.

The fit that Dorcas pitched exceeded even Richard's estimation. They heard her first and then saw her coming like a low squall line across the snowy space between her house and theirs. She stood pounding on the door until they answered it. "Come out here where I can see you!" she demanded. Richard and Mary came outside and saw Dorcas panting. "You did this," she said, shaking with rage and waving Roger's letter at Richard and Mary. "You married my girl off to that, that," she struggled for a fierce enough word but came up short with, "trapper!" Douglas had joined her by now, and he stood looking at Richard and Mary, slowly shaking his head.

Richard finally spoke, "They were going to leave one way or the other. They came asking me to marry them so they had the benefit of marriage rather than live in sin. Would you rather I just let them go?"

Douglas started to talk, but Dorcas waved him off and bellowed, "I would rather you had not let them go at all! You have ruined her. Stella was a diamond in the rough, and with a few more years with me, she could have had her choice of men, but now, they would not even wipe their feet on her if she were fallen in the street."

Douglas ignored this outburst from Dorcas and thanked Richard for delivering the letter and doing what he could to make Stella happy. He added sadly, "I hope she knows her mind. She will be a long way from family if she changes her tune." Dorcas looked defeated, and Douglas guided her back to their house. Mary stood watching them leave and suddenly realized she was shivering. Richard pulled her close to him and they squeezed through the tiny, low door of the cottage to get warm.

Mary had purchased the warmest clothes she could find in Boston but still feared even those would not be enough to insulate against the sub-freezing temperatures on Mackinac. Mary leaned against Richard, and he put his arm around her waist to reassure her. They still had hundreds of pounds of salted pork and beef, barrels of pickled cabbage and cucumber pickles, about two hundred fifty pounds of both ship biscuits and oatmeal, and thirty barrels of beer as barest supplies, not to mention cheese, beans and peas, vinegar, sugar, tea, and the like. They could last all winter and on into fall if needed.

Wrennet seemed at peace, but Mary recalled tales of people going crazy after they had spent the winter in the Northern Territory, and she prayed she would not be one of them. The word Windigo kept creeping into her mind, but she tried to push it away.

This fear ate away at her until she mentioned it to Richard. He reassured her that those men she had heard tales of had been alone, or were not really stable in the first place. He reminded her there were five Holmwoods, five Deemses, Robert Stuart, and a shipload of sailors, not to mention the garrison skeleton crew.

Even though Richard reassured Mary, he had his own dark fears about facing winter. Since he was thirteen, he had never been off a ship for more than three or four months at a time. They might be in port longer than that, but he was still on the ship. He wondered if it would be him that went mad cooped up not only in a house, but on an island in a sea of ice. Richard had lost count of the times so far he had crossed the rocky hill on the island to look at the ship lying on her side like some enormous sea beast stranded and cold. He often walked down and talked to the men, but each time before he left, he touched the thick timbers of the ship, whispering softly, "Hold fast there. It can't last forever." But it already felt like forever, and it was only December.

It snowed all night and was still snowing when they woke the next morning. They ate breakfast and even after the dishes were put away, the snow still sifted down silently on them. It finally stopped just before noon, when the sun came out. The snow lay sparkling in the sunshine, but the temperature was still low. It seemed odd to Mary that the sun could still contain its dazzling light but not retain its warmth. The snow did not melt that afternoon in the sunshine, and when the dawn came the next morning it rose pink and gray on a snowy landscape. It snowed again the next day and the day after that, and they realized finally the snow was there to stay. Richard shoveled a path out the door and connected with the paths from the Deems's and the Stuart warehouse.

The first time he shoveled, Richard used his back, but after awakening with it aching, he learned to use the power in his legs and arms rather that his spine. At first Mary swept the entire dooryard free of snow with a broom every time it snowed, but as it became a continual job to keep it clear, she finally had to give up and let the snow close in around them, only sweeping the steps themselves.

They had their first blizzard just after Christmas. The day started with some light snow, and the temperature warmed up from around twenty to just below freezing. The wind shifted and was coming from the northeast, and the barometer mounted by the fireplace, which had risen all morning, began to plummet just after the noon meal. There was a rushing uneasiness to the wind, and it came in swirling gusts like alarming whispers as it passed. Twice Richard went outside and looked at the sky. It felt like a storm, but all the markers he had for testing the weather were a thousand miles away. He brought in extra wood and made sure the lean-to on the back of the house containing more wood was as secure as possible. They had draped sailcloth over the whole thing, but a violent wind could easily tear it to tatters. He checked on the men in the ship, and they too felt the change in the weather. "Once it starts, don't leave the ship unless you have a lifeline. Otherwise, we may not find you until spring," Richard said only half in jest.

The storm itself arrived in the late afternoon heralded by a wind high in the leafless trees. They could hear the wind slapping the bare branches together before it actually reached them. Just like a heavy squall sweeps over the land, so now did the wind and snow. Richard and Mary heard it and walked outside the door to look. It came across the water from the mainland like a wall and swallowed the tiny island. As it arrived, Richard closed and bolted the door against the wind before he stoked the fire. There was nothing more they could do now but ride it out. It felt almost strange to him to have the wind whipping around him but to be still rather than lurching and heaving on the waves. It was still snowing and blowing when they ate dinner and when they went to bed. Richard woke in the night to stoke the fire, and the wind was still sucking fiercely at the chimney.

Edward slipped into the room looking frightened from the howling outside. Richard held the quilt open, and Edward crawled over him to settle next to Mary and Jack. He snuggled down deep in the covers and Richard patted his side. "It's only the wind, son, don't worry." A few minutes later, Grub, having been abandoned by Edward, joined them and crawled onto the foot of the bed to circle and settle in an amazingly small ball for such a huge dog. Richard nudged Mary and whispered, "I wonder if Wrennet will be coming too?" Jack woke them before dawn, and they realized that at some point in the night the storm had stopped. Richard stoked the stove and noticed the cottage felt warmer. They would find when they went outside later that morning that the storm had filled every little chink and crack in the logs of the cottage with snow that acted like insulation, making the cottage snug and toasty.

When they opened the door, they found a drift nearly two feet high across the doorstep and up against the jamb. Grub leaped over the drift like it was a fence and explored outside for the perfect place, somewhere worthy in all the whiteness, to unload his bladder. After breakfast, Richard shoveled them out, swearing that in the next storm he would periodically shovel the door clear throughout the storm and not wait until it was over to tackle it. Mary bundled up Edward and they both came outside to witness how like magic the landscape had been transformed by the snow. Everything was drifted and there were places where the wind had swirled making peaks like those in meringue. The lake, still cloudy from being churned up the night before, lapped dark and cold at the shore. Windblown ice had formed where the waves were tossed on the shore overnight, and they resembled nothing so much as clear and sparkling lady's shawls layered one atop the other. With no breeze, it seemed eerily still after the rage of last night. While Edward and Mary were standing in the yard, the sun came out, and they both gasped at the beauty around them. They had both been in snow before, but that was wet Tidewater snow. This was the dry, magnificent artwork of the North Wind.

They had survived what they believed to be nature's wrath, and it was perhaps best then that they didn't know that this storm was a mere blown kiss compared to what would be hurled at them before spring.

The lakes, cold as they already were, did not freeze until January. When they did submit to the Arctic blasts they remained restless under their ice cap. Huge ridges formed in the ice to the accompaniment of bangs that sounded like musket shots or even distant cannon fire. The water swirled slowly under the ice pushing here and there, the way a caged animal checks its enclosure for a weak spot. Its movement caused the ice to hum and moan or even to twang like some great stringed instrument, but oddest of all was the long, mournful lament that could be heard by placing an ear on the ice, and which Richard assured Mary sounded exactly the way whale song reverberates through the timbers of a ship.

One night in mid-January they noticed a flickering in the sky, which they first thought was lightning. Mary had read that on rare occasions there were thunderstorms in the winter, and she wanted to see one, so she persuaded Richard to come out with her. As soon as they were outside they knew it wasn't lightning because the flicker was too

slow and it was also a bluish-green. The strange flickering light hung like
a great curtain stretched across the sky, and it would shimmer and ripple
like some huge hand had shaken a rug. It seemed there should have been
a sound to accompany the movement, but there was none, and Mary
stared at it, fascinated. "What is it, Richard?"

"Aurora Borealis, the Northern Lights. I have seen them before at
sea when I was crossing to England," he whispered almost as if to speak
aloud would drive the beautiful lights away.

"I read about them, but I never saw them before. This is beautiful,"
Mary whispered back.

"I understand the further you get north, the brighter they are,"
Richard said, draping his arm across Mary's shoulder. They watched for
a few minutes longer, but as neither had put on a coat, they were soon
driven in by the cold.

The snow was relentless as it piled up sometimes a few inches or
sometimes a few feet a day. The sun might shine and pack the surface
down a bit by its radiant heat, but it could not keep ahead of the snow,
and everyone felt, though no one admitted, that they were being buried
alive. The wind screamed and raced across the island at hurricane speeds,
but like a tight ship, their cottage repelled the weather. The Holmwoods
made the best of their time together, and Richard continually updated
his charts with new information he had gathered during the summer.
Wrennet went about the tasks of home, and Mary, when she wasn't
cleaning and caring for the children, made curtains and rugs for the
house which only made it snugger. They all read whatever they could get
into their hands, even young Edward.

Mary and Edward, and at times Richard and Edward, explored
and updated their map of the island which changed as it wore a
new winter coat after each storm. The household settled in and the
claustrophobia Richard had feared never appeared. As a matter of fact,
he was very content.

Any man can have a wife, and any man can have a lover, and many
men have both at the same time, but it is only the luckiest of men whose
wife is also their lover. At some point in that long, dark, and cold winter,
Mary became both.

The Deemses on the other hand fought like rats in a sack. Dorcas
and her children complained about the cold, the snow, the wind, the food,
and the company. Often Douglas would escape on the pretext of business
to the Holmwoods, or he might go to the warehouse to visit with Robert
Stuart, or even up to the garrison to visit the soldiers. Douglas didn't
really have much to say once he got there but just enjoyed the peace that
was nonexistent at home.

By March the harshest part of winter relented as the snow began
to recede. There would be an occasional snow shower, but the sun was

warmer now, and for at least a few hours in the middle of the day the sound of dripping from melting ice and snow was everywhere and little rivulets of water ran downhill. The cold at night would petrify them again, but by the middle of the next day the rivulets would be dripping. The snow itself was no longer clean and white but had a brown-gray, old, and used-up appearance, and it was especially shaggy looking near the houses, rife with tossed dish water, dog urine, and human tracks. Nothing other than the conifers showed green, but the brown grass and last year's leaves peeked out from under the snow.

The lake ice was beginning to look dark in patches, and around the shoreline there was a tiny margin of open water. The crew had kept the inside of the ship fairly neat, but they had done so by jettisoning everything they no longer needed into the snow. It was all Mary could do to restrain herself from going down and clearing the pile of litter, though Grub scavenged successfully through it several times a day.

The rising meltwater in the lake was lifting the beached ship, so Richard had his crew caulk and paint her, and they then pulled the planks that were keeping her from floating away. Once she was in the water, they refit her rigging. There were a hundred other chores to get her in shape for sailing, but everyone seemed eager to do them. Months from now the same tasks would again be drudgery, but they represented a step toward the freedom of the waves and everyone went about them with alacrity. The decks were sanded, and the fag ends on the new lines tied up into neat monkey's paw knots, then they sailed her around to the west side of the island and moored her at the pier.

There was still ice in patches, but it was melting quickly now, and Richard believed he would soon be leaving for his first voyage of the year. He figured he had probably put the ship in the water earlier than they really should have, but he was eager to sail to Beaver Island and see how the others had fared over the winter. Thinking he may have rushed it, he was doubly surprised then when both the Beaver Island ships sailed through the straits and fired their guns in greeting.

There was a jolly mob as the men from the three ships sought out old friends and greeted each other. Somewhere along the way, the other ships had stopped to hunt and they soon had fires burning and three large deer turning on spits over the fire. The men on Beaver Island had actually fared better than Richard and his crew. Their island provided game to supplement their salt pork, and they had even collected maple sap a few weeks before and boiled it down to a smoky, ashy sugar which they dumped on everything.

Robert Stuart and the Deemses came down to the beach. Richard, Mary, and the rest of the family stood sniffing, trying not to drool at the smell of the fresh meat cooking. The sailors from Beaver Island didn't know the story of Mary coming back from the dead, and since they had not been there to witness it, they did not fear her. They made a fuss over Jack, passing the six-month-old around like the last bottle of rum on a desert island. Richard just smiled and nodded to Mary that it was all right.

When the meat was cooked, they all settled on blankets and stools and stuffed themselves on venison and the other fare wrangled up by Mary and Wrennet. After dinner Richard broke out a barrel or two of rum, and Robert brought down a barrel of whiskey. While the men on the Beaver Island ships had better food all winter, they had run low on spirits and partook with gusto. They gathered around the fires, full and slightly drunk, and began to sing songs of the girl back home and the lovely life of the sea. It wasn't long before Richard escorted Mary, Wrennet, and the children back to their cottage where distance made it a little more difficult to make out the increasingly vile lyrics. The Deemses had already fled indoors, securely locking the door behind them, all except Douglas, who was waiting eagerly for Richard by the door path, hoping he too was going to go back down toward the beach. Richard looked at Mary, questioning if she would be all right, and she smiled and pushed his chest gently, "Oh, go back down there and have some fun. We'll be fine here." He grinned and kissed her cheek and then trotted back down with Douglas right beside him where they joined Robert Stuart and howled until the wee hours of the morning.

Richard came in a few hours after midnight, and he was startled to see Mary sitting by the fire. At first he thought she had waited up and was angry, but as he came further into the room he realized she was nursing Jack. She smiled, and he came and sat beside her. She looked at him and said, almost amused, "Richard, are you drunk?"

He smiled sheepishly and said, "A little." He was certainly not drunk by a sailor's standards, but he had had enough to loosen his tongue. He pulled his chair closer to Mary and whispered in her ear rather raunchy favors.

When Jack was finished she put him in his cradle and turned to Richard, saying in mocking sternness, "Your clothes smell like smoke."

"Then I'd best shed them," he said, grinning wickedly.

The next morning, Mary rose before Richard and fed Jack and Edward. Edward wanted to go back toward the beach, and Mary had to admit she was curious too, so they slipped down that way and stood at the crest of the hill and stared at the carnage. Most of the fires had burned down to ashes, and men lay sprawled about them in various poses of stupor. Some of them were wrapped in blankets, and some were huddled like kittens for warmth. The officers had retreated to the ships, leaving the regular crew scattered. It looked more than anything like a battlefield sunrise the morning after. "Good Christ, look at them," came a voice from behind, and Mary and Edward whirled to see Richard in his shirtsleeves. He looked clear-eyed, and except for the fact that he had not washed or shaved, he didn't look too bad for wear. "They must have really carried on after I left," he said, shaking his head. "I'll let them sleep it off. It has been a long winter." They turned back to the cottage where they could smell Wrennet cooking the first of the day's salt pork, but at least they had eggs and biscuits to go with it.

CHAPTER 16

ALL BUSINESS ran on credit or barter in the Northern Territory because there was so little currency in that remote part of the country. The Ojibwa and white trappers traded fur for blankets, gunpowder, whiskey, tools, fabric, and the like, while the fur was stored until it could be shipped to the Atlantic Coast. Some of the cash from the fur sales was used to buy goods, which were then transported back to the various outposts of the American Fur Company. Some of these posts were nearly a hundred miles inland, and the men who lived on them were completely cut off from the world except when a trapper came in with fur. At those times, the trapper was shown splendid hospitality with food and a warm bed and plenty of whiskey. The outpost keeper's wages were usually held at the company headquarters and sent only when the keeper asked. There was nothing to buy, and having it on hand was only asking to be robbed. It was safer to barter. Everyone charged in the winter, and come spring, the tallies were swept clean against wages or items collected. The Navy permitted Richard to trade all he wanted as a private citizen, as long as he kept naval accounts separate and provided the security he was sent there to maintain. He had done both with gusto. He found that in the territory, as in Biblical times, salt was one of the most precious commodities, and he knew he could easily lay his hands on a hundred tons of it and triple the price charged in Detroit, where it was abundant. The last word he sent in the fall to the ship stationed on the east side of Welland was to gather as much salt, salted pork, and beef as possible to be shipped farther north. The message would not reach the ships at Welland until spring, and by then the trade routes would again be passable.

Richard's four ships were trading all over the Atlantic and parts of Africa while he was away, and he looked forward to seeing the figures.

Summer came and with it a profit even he could not believe. Richard settled into the following fall with expectation for the same the following summer. Everything was looking bright and prosperous until a small sloop arrived unexpectedly from Welland in late April.

Shaw had arrived in Welland on the *Lorraine* after being denied harbor privileges in Halifax. Shaw could get no details from the harbormaster other than the port did not deal with pirates. In the broad view, this was incorrect, as Halifax had long shielded and spawned pirates. Shaw was perplexed but had no choice but to sail west into the St. Lawrence without stopping. Luckily, the *Lorraine* was loaded with foodstuffs from the warehouse in Norfolk, so the crew would not go hungry, and there were plenty of small creeks that flowed into the main river to supply fresh water if needed. The *Lorraine* was denied docking privileges in Welland as well, and Shaw was forced to anchor downstream to the east.

Shaw managed to rent a small, retired sloop of war west of Welland where they weren't so particular, and he set out immediately to find Richard. The *Huron* had not yet sailed, but she was ready at the pier at Mackinac Island, and Richard was actually standing on the pier holding Jack when Shaw hailed him. When he recognized Shaw, Richard knew right away that something was very wrong. Richard led Shaw to the house as soon as the sloop was moored, and they sat down at the table. Shaw began, "Richard, we have been denied credit everywhere we have been, even in Welland. I met up with the *Fiona* in Norfolk, and she was just in from Charleston with the same problem. Her captain said the word was you were to be given no credit anywhere. We cannot take cargo on credit, and your entire fleet has been denied even entrance to some of the ports, and there is talk of a charge of piracy."

"Piracy? I was a privateer. What the hell are you talking about?" Richard stood dumbfounded. Shaw looked haggard, and Richard got him a drink, then said as calmly as he could, "Tell me everything you know."

"Well," Shaw took a long pull, "the charge of piracy is technically for dealing in slaves."

"Slaves, like hell! I have never dealt in black cargo in my life!" Richard yelled, trying his best not to shoot the messenger. He stood up and paced the floor, then turned to Shaw and said, "When was this supposed to have happened?"

"All I know is what I have heard, and that is second or thirdhand, but I am told that the *Vindicta* was impounded in Washington and the charge of piracy, as a result of importing slaves, was leveled against its captain, one Richard Holmwood. Sir, I don't see how this is possible either, but the charge is there, and others have picked up on it. Also," Shaw looked sheepish, "there are large debts that have not been paid."

"I trusted my instinct on Jonas Benson, and I have been a fool," Richard hissed.

"No, it is not him. Jonas is doing his best to keep everything afloat, but there are debts all over for luxurious things like silk and gems, and these are coming in from Morocco and Spain and even a few from African ports. The charges are on the standard form we use and signed by Richard Holmwood, but they were never reported to Jonas in any manner. You can't buy silk on one continent while you're living on another. I don't understand how this can happen."

Richard's gut tightened, and he sat down heavily. He knew how it could happen, and he said aloud just above a whisper, "Owen."

"Pardon me?" Shaw said awkwardly, taken off guard by the sudden deflation of Richard's anger. "What did you say?"

"Nothing, except I have an idea who is behind this," Richard said as he got up and went to his desk. He quickly wrote out some orders and shoved them into Shaw's hand saying, "Beach the sloop where we had the *Huron* last winter, and we'll leave in two days or less from here and transfer at Welland. Go now and get started." Shaw shook his head and left the cottage. Richard turned to Mary, who had been keeping busy and out of the way during the exchange with Shaw but who had heard every word. "I have to leave. I have to find out what is going on. I think Owen is behind this, but I have to get to the bottom of it, and I can't do it from here." He saw Mary's look of protest and added, "If I don't go, we may have nothing to return to at Scotland Neck or anywhere else."

Mary nodded, "But what about what you agreed to do here? Don't you have orders to stay here?" Mary hoped she had thought of something he hadn't.

"I have to make sure it is patrolled, but I don't have to do it myself," Richard said as he put on his coat to go down to the ships at the pier. "I'll be back in a little while to pack. You and the boys may want to come too, so talk to Wrennet about it, and let me know."

TWO DAYS LATER Richard took Jack from Mary and held him tight, kissing the top of his head. He bent to Edward's eye level and said to him seriously, with a hand on each of his shoulders, "I need you to help Mary and Wrennet and to take care of your brother, all right?" Edward nodded solemnly. "Remember, son, you may be eight, but you're the man here until I return." He hugged him for a long time and then stood and hugged Wrennet, who clung to him, and finally he kissed Mary and held her tight. "I won't be back before the summer is over, but look for me when the trees turn. Are you certain you don't want to come along?"

Mary shook her head and smiled, "I only want to make that trip once with Jack." They both looked at the child. At two years he was already a stout and horribly stubborn child, who was sure of what he wanted and exactly sure of what he did not want. Travelling with him would not be a pleasure.

Jack smiled as Mary took him back from his father, and Richard touched the child's plump cheek and then said to Mary, "When the leaves turn red, sweetheart, look for me then." He turned and left them at the cottage without looking back and made his way to the pier.

Robert Stuart was travelling back with Richard to Washington. Now that he had Douglas Deems on the island, he could take a well-earned rest. Stuart had been on Mackinac since 1807, only retreating when the British took the island during the recent war, so this would be his first time east of Detroit in nearly eight years, and he was nearly giddy with anticipation.

Richard had taken all the cash and gold he had with him, so that if indeed he was denied credit, he could pay his dock fees for the sloop to leave her in Welland as they transferred to the *Lorraine*. Several weeks later, when they arrived in Welland, he found his hunch had been right. It was cash, or the sloop could not stay, and if she was not paid for she would be impounded. Though Richard expected it, this was the first taste he had of just how bad things were.

At the chandler they had used before in Halifax, he was told point-blank there would be no trade with pirates. The chandler refused to sell him any goods, and Richard was forced to seek the few supplies he needed from a rather seedy and overpriced chandler located near the mouth of the harbor. As they left Halifax, he prayed there would be no more expenses before he got to Washington, because there was no money to pay for them.

Since he was thirteen, Richard had never been completely out of money, and it galled him. He had to admit it was also frightening. Being penniless brought with it a feeling of vulnerability, almost like facing enemy ships without any ammunition.

Mercifully, the remaining voyage to Washington was without incident. Richard was in luck since the harbormaster there had known him for many years and granted him credit until the matter was sorted out. Without it, they would have had to anchor far out in the Potomac River. As soon as the ship was moored, Richard sent a message to Stephen Decatur, who arrived at the pier within half an hour of receiving it.

Stephen looked closely at Richard, shaking his head. There was no golden crown of curls, and his bright eyes looked haunted and dull. He appeared to have lost considerable weight since Stephen had seen him at the ball with Mary. Decatur listened to Richard's tale of having all his credit stopped. Richard asked if he knew why. Stephen said, "The rumor mill has you trading in black cargo and leaving huge debts from here to South Africa. I never believed it, because you have always been so adamantly against it, but I thought there must be something to it when they arrested Owen and his crew."

Richard was stunned, "Owen is here?"

Stephen nodded. "He and his entire crew were arrested and charged with piracy. You know that since 1807, trading in slaves carries a charge of piracy. If they convict him, Richard, he will be hanged."

"Take me to him, please," Richard said, his stomach in knots. With his finances in such a mess, he could not even hire an attorney for Owen unless he paid cash, and he had run out before arriving in Washington.

"Come on. I'll take you to him," Stephen said. They rode in silence, and Stephen could tell Richard was trying to digest what he had learned.

When they arrived at the jail, Stephen was surprised when Richard said, "Let me see Jordan first. I need the truth, not some story Owen has concocted to save his ass."

Five minutes later Jordan Ladysmith was led into the room where Richard was pacing. Richard barely recognized him. Jordan had lost so much weight, he looked skeletal. His dark, curly hair hung lank and long, and he had a beard of at least three inches which was neither trimmed nor clean. He eyed Richard, who looked horrified, and said, "I guess you've heard?"

Richard came closer. "I don't know anything, Jory," Richard used the endearment the Puppets had given Jordan. "You'd better tell me what's going on."

Jordan sat, or rather backed up to a chair and collapsed into it. He ran his hands, which had blue-black crescents of dirt under the nails, through his greasy and matted hair and let out a sigh. "I don't know where to begin, so I'll just start when we left Hampton Roads." Jordan settled his thin frame on the chair. He looked thirty-nine rather than his true age of nineteen. He began his harrowing tale starting with Owen's return to Scotland Neck. He related the tale of Owen and Emma Spencer, and asked Richard, "Do you know the woman?"

Richard nodded and said, "She is Mary's sister-in-law, if you can believe it."

"Oh, I can believe it," Jordan said, swallowing. "Anyway, we set sail for Spain like we were supposed to and made our crossing without any problems to deliver our cargo as planned. We were then to come back here with a load of knives, blades, and wine, but while still in Bilbao, Owen had the hold altered so that it was partitioned into cubicles. I questioned him several times on this, but he refused to give me a direct answer. The crew had been paid very well, so none of them thought of leaving even though Owen was acting more strangely every day, and, of course, most of them stayed with him due to their loyalty to you. We left Bilbao with only about half the hold full of blades and wine and headed south. We never made our turn back east to beat home. Instead, Owen set a course that sailed us right around the Cape to the east coast of Africa. We stopped several times and took on food and water, and each time Owen would leave and be gone a short while, and then we would sail into another nasty port and he would do the same again. Finally, he came back and looked like he had found what he was looking for, and that afternoon we took on a cargo of women, light-skinned black women, who had been bound for North Africa. He put one in each of the cubicles which had been outfitted with a cot and chair and fine dresses, and then he told us they were being transported to some dignitary in the north of Africa. This seemed odd, but even odder still that we didn't sail back west to deliver them. We wandered around the eastern coast of Africa, and near Madagascar we took on six more women. These women were darker-skinned and looked nearly wild with fear and rage. The youngest was about fourteen and the eldest perhaps my age. They came aboard in chains and were placed in the cubicles in the hold as well. The crew and I now both raised some questions, and Owen said it would be taken care of in three days. He told us the six new women were being taken back to their families. They ran away when each refused to marry the man to whom she had been promised, and we were being paid to bring them all back.

"The ship anchored off this small island three days later, and Owen took the six wild looking women ashore with him in the long boat. We were anchored nearly a mile out because of sandbars, but he sent the boat back to the ship rather than have the long boat crew wait for him on the shore. He said he would come back down to the beach when he was ready to leave and we should keep an eye out for him. He had been gone about three hours when we spotted him on the shore again. The boat was lowered, and he was brought back aboard. As soon as his feet touched the deck, he ordered a new course, south and west to round the Cape again. As Owen passed me, something fell from his jacket pocket. I didn't say anything to him but retrieved it when he left the deck. It was a small, carved-wooden ring which was unremarkable, except for the fact that the girl's finger was still inside it. I think he took it as a memento, and knowing what I know now, Richard, he didn't leave those girls alive on that island." Jordan looked hard at Richard, who had gone very pale.

"Someone found out about this, and that is the piracy charge?" Richard asked anxiously.

"No. I doubt anyone other than you and I and Owen know about those six women, but there is far worse to come," Jordan said flatly.

"With Owen there always seems to be another layer of shit," Richard said sadly. "Tell me the rest, and get it over with."

Jordan looked solemnly at Richard and then returned to his tale, "We turned north after the Cape and then sailed along, stopping at Owen's whim to trade or take on luxury items like silk and dates, olives, cheese, scented oils and the like, even some gems. Owen was now dressing the remaining half-dozen women he had in the hold in silk and plying them with sweets and dainty things to eat. His steward had to massage the naked girls with oil twice a day while still doing all his other duties for Owen. We all found this behavior strange, but the girls didn't seem to be captives though they only ever left the hold to spend time in Owen's cabin. Since they appeared to go there willingly, we assumed they were not being treated poorly.

"It was now six months since we picked the girls up. They were walking freely about the decks though they would not speak to anyone but Owen. He assured us they did speak some rudimentary English, but I had never heard them utter a word except to him and even that was in a whisper.

"Some of the women were now showing obvious signs of being with child, and to my disgust, Owen offered them to me while he concentrated on impregnating those who were not. I didn't take Owen up on his offer, and more than anything, I felt sorry for the women, who were really not much more than girls. I ordered the rest of the crew not to touch them no matter what Owen said.

"In another two months, all but two of the women were with child, and Owen had taken to calling them by the Christian names he had given them. Every single name was a derivative of Mary, so there was Marianne, Marilyn, Margeaux, Mary Sue, Mary Jane, and so forth. He used their names more than was really necessary, like he enjoyed saying them in a mocking tone.

"Owen rarely took part in sailing the ship anymore but gave orders from his cabin, which was tricked out like a bordello. One night when I was on duty, I found one of the girls hiding behind the stays and I asked her what was wrong. She was sobbing and shaking her head frantically from side to side. She kept repeating something, but I couldn't understand her. Owen came on deck then and saw her, and she looked at me in terror and started to run. Owen caught her by the arm and pulled her up tight. He said, 'There you are, Margeaux. I have warned you about leaving my cabin until I am finished with you.'"

Jordan drank the water the jailor had provided and continued, "The poor girl nodded frantically and tried to smile, but Owen roughly hauled her back to his cabin, and I didn't see or hear anything else from either of them that night. The next morning I saw her huddled against the rail and she was looking out over the water, but you could tell she was not really seeing it. I spoke to her, and when she turned, I gasped. Her eye was swollen shut, and the socket from her eyebrow to the middle of her cheekbone was an ugly bruise. Owen came up just then with a rag and very gently held it to her eye. She winced and tried to pull away, but Owen dug painfully into her shoulder with his fingers while whispering soothing and calming words to her face as he held the cloth to her eye. The whole thing was sickening.

"We continued sailing west, and we all prayed this voyage would be over. One morning I woke up though and knew it was not going to end soon. The sun was rising over the portside of the ship rather than the stern, and I knew we had turned south. If we kept this up we would be off the coast of South America before long. Owen confirmed my suspicions when he said we would sail south trading and then turn back for Hampton Roads.

"The first of the women bore her child later that month, and the others soon would follow. There was only one woman who had not become pregnant, the little Margeaux, and though Owen nearly bulled her to death, she must have been barren. Anyway, we came into Charleston Harbor and Owen went ashore with her. He returned the next morning alone, and I questioned Owen closely about her, but he shrugged and told me to keep to my own business. We headed south again toward South America, and the other children were born over a six- to eight-week period. Owen walked about with them proud as any father, sometimes carrying three or four of them at a time, or even all five at once in a basket.

"We sailed southward and eventually got into cold weather, and it became a full-time task to keep the ice off the decks and rigging. We never stopped at a port after the children were born. Rather, we would anchor offshore and fire off a few shots, and within an hour the native people would come out with food and water for which we traded knives and other blades. We never hailed another ship, and we were ordered not to answer a hail. We took no trade for profit, nor did we stop to make arrangement for future cargo. Owen just sailed south until we reached the Horn, and then he turned around. At this point we were all exhausted, mentally and physically, but the worst was yet to come.

"We had been burning the galley stoves full-on to try to keep warm and to cook as much hot food as possible, but when we turned around and headed north, the weather turned foul, and we had to douse the stove. It was four days until we could light it again and when we did, we all gratefully ate our peas, oatmeal, and boiled salt pig like it was a banquet. The fire was burning at a furious rate and Owen stoked it even more. I was afraid we were going to catch on fire, but he just kept loading in more wood and coal. The fire was really roaring and Owen came up with the babies in two large baskets. He ordered everyone away from the galley saying, 'My children need to get good and warm.' We left Owen to the fire and went about our business. As I was passing Owen's cabin to go to my own, I heard a strange noise, almost a sucking sound, like water and air struggling through a drain. I pushed open the door and found three of the women dead with their throats cut. There was a fourth one still alive struggling to breathe, but she had lost so much blood there was no way she could live. I called for the officer of the watch, and together we went to the hold where we found evidence of another attack. While we were searching for the fifth woman, she crawled out from under some blankets and fainted in front of us. We carried her to my cabin and I summoned the ship's doctor. She regained consciousness shortly after, and the first thing she said in her thick accent was 'baby'. The watch officer and I looked at each other and ran to the galley, leaving her with the doctor."

Jordan gagged and looked at Richard, dreading the end of this tale. He swallowed and then, avoiding Richard's stare, said, "We were too late. Owen had thrown all those babies in the galley fire. My God, Richard, those were his own children, and he tossed them in the fire like they were rubbish! When we got there he was just standing, rolling their bodies around in the fire with a poker with absolutely no expression on his face. What I saw in that galley will haunt me the rest of my life."

Richard sat staring at Jordan, not daring to believe it was true but knowing in his heart it had to be. He finally said in a defeated voice, "What happened then?"

"I have never, ever considered mutiny a solution to anything, but I swear to God, Richard, I lost my senses then. I bashed Owen on the back of his head with the butt of a musket while he was still slowly stirring the sizzling remains of his children. He crumpled onto the deck and we placed him in irons. He screamed and cursed and threatened, but no one listened to him.

"The stench of those burning children filled the ship and it was enough to sicken even the heartiest of the men. We discussed what to do about the bodies and finally decided to bury them at sea, wanting to get as much water between us and them as possible. We wrapped the women separately in canvas but put all the little bodies into a single sack and weighted them down. We said the prayer for burial at sea and then pushed them over the railing. As I was saying the prayer though, Owen was screaming his version of it from the brig. I said, 'We commit their bodies to the deep to be turned to corruption awaiting the day the sea shall give up her dead,' but Owen was screaming 'Commit their heathen and half-breed bodies to the deep where corruption will only improve them. The sea may give up her dead, but she'll puke these up to stink on the surface.' I ordered two men to gag him, so we could get through the burial, and then we just kept him drunk all the way back home." Jordan looked at Richard solemnly and said, "You can think of me what you will. I am now a mutineer, yet I would do the same again, and my only prayer would be to act sooner next time."

Richard shook his head, "Owen was unfit to lead. You did the right thing. Did you record it that way in the log, that he was unfit?" Jordan nodded affirmatively, and Richard added, "That will probably help."

"Apparently while we were in the south Atlantic, news of Owen's treachery spread west, so they were looking for us when we reached Hampton Roads. We had had no news or correspondence for over a year, and when we saw armed ships coming to intercept us, we fled, not waiting to see if we were back at war or not. We moved north and during the night I sent three men ashore on the Eastern Shore of Virginia near Matomkin to see what news they could gather. They came back and said there was no war brewing, but the talk was all about how Captain Richard Holmwood had turned foul and was dealing in black cargo. There was talk that when he was found he would be charged with piracy. I didn't know what to do, so I sailed north to Washington, and here we are. We turned ourselves over to the authorities, and they arrested the lot of us. Owen was masquerading as you the whole time we were in African waters, signing your name, and as you own the ship we were sailing, most people thought it was you."

Stunned, Richard stared at Jordan and finally said, "I used to overlook Owen's reckless nature, as it usually caused a local broken heart or, at its worst, a girl's reputation. But now he has cost all of us our freedom and livelihood. Even if the truth were known, and a flotilla of ships sent with no purpose but to inform people of it, there would be a lag of years before the word spread properly and there would always be those who questioned it. This time Owen has poisoned everyone around him." He touched Jordan's arm and said, "I am so sorry, Jory. I promise you, I will do everything I can to get you free. The crew will be an easier matter. They were following orders, but as officers, you and the second mate will come under harsher scrutiny. Let me see what I can do, providing they don't arrest me too."

"That is a real possibility. Everyone here thought it was you at first," Jordan said sadly. Richard squeezed his shoulder and then left the jail.

He found Stephen still waiting in the anteroom and pulled him aside, asking, "Do you know the details of what happened?"

Stephen shook his head, "I spoke with Jordan Ladysmith too. This is a bad business, Richard, and not just for Owen. I think the first thing to do is make a public statement calling for outstanding debts. Send it out on every ship that leaves here to spread it to other ships that Richard Holmwood will cover the debts his son Owen has incurred in his name. You and I know you will pay some concocted debts that Owen had no part in, but at least you will begin to clear your name and also spread the word that it was not you involved in this horrible business. Richard, you must separate yourself from Owen. It is the only way. "

"I know. He chose to separate from me long ago. I just never reciprocated, but there are others I have to think of now too," Richard said, thinking of Mary, Edward, and baby Jack.

"This is going to cost you a fortune, Richard," Stephen warned.

"The money will be the least painful part," Richard said, and then turning to the jailor's assistant, asked, "May I see my son?"

The assistant nodded and walked Richard down a narrow hallway.

The jailors were not bringing Owen to him as they had Jordan, no doubt because Owen had given them trouble already. Richard would have to visit him in his cell. They came upon him at the very back of the jail, and the assistant turned and said softly as he left, "I knowed it wasn't you, Captain, when all this talk first started. It was him what did it." He jerked his head at Owen and continued, "He's a bad'un, sir, begging my saying so." With that, the jailor left Richard with his son. Richard shivered, but it was more than just the feeling of the jail. The weather had been so foul all the way to Washington he couldn't believe it. They left Mackinac in May with frost and ice on the puddles, but it never seemed to get any warmer the further south they sailed. Once they actually sailed through snow. Snow in July! It seemed summer had abandoned them.

Owen was sitting wrapped in a thick-wool blanket with his back to the door, and Richard called his name softly. At first he didn't think Owen heard him and was about to say it again, but then Owen slowly turned on his stool and faced him. There was no remorse, no relief, nothing on Owen's face as he said, "It took you longer than I thought it would to get here. When can we leave? I am sick and tired of this place."

Richard stood holding onto the cell bars and shook his head, "Owen, you will not just walk out of here. They have charged you with piracy, and they mean to hang you. You are lucky they haven't done so already."

"I'm told that is only due to your great reputation," Owen said with the hint of a sneer.

"Is it true?" Richard asked, wanting to hear it from Owen.

"Is what true, that everyone thinks you are some hero or something?" he snapped.

"About the women and the children? Your own children, for God's sake!" Richard hissed.

"They were animals." Owen took a piece of something, a hair perhaps, off his tongue and continued, "If I fucked a goat, and then she produced a kid, would you raise it lovingly, Papa? Would you bounce it on your knee and show it off? Those women were animals, and what they produced was of even less value. Don't tell me you don't have a dozen or so of those little half-breeds scattered about."

"To my knowledge, I do not, but that is far from the point. You murdered women and children, Owen. You burned tiny babies alive!" Richard snarled.

"All right! I don't need any damned lecture from you. None of this would have happened if you had left my mother alone. She had that little bastard, Edward, and it killed her, and it's your fault." Richard stood dumbfounded, and Owen continued unabated, "Then when I wanted Mary, you stole her from me. I loved her, and you took her away. Now, make it up to me and get me out of here." Owen shifted on his stool and turned his back again. Richard stared at Owen, who added with a snarl, "And tell the assholes keeping me here that I don't like to eat pork all the time. Some chicken would be nice." At this, Richard turned and left, nearly tripping over the jailor's wife who was bringing Owen his dinner.

Richard left the jail. He and Stephen rode in silence for several minutes and finally Richard said, "He looks exactly like me, but there is nothing of me in him. How could I have fathered such an animal, Stephen? How is that possible?"

"You are looking to the wrong person to answer any questions about children. I have never been so blessed," he looked sadly at Richard and added, "or so cursed."

The trial lasted only a day, and the verdict of piracy in the form of slave transport was well-buttressed by murder charges to show Owen's lack of character. Mercifully, it was not necessary to bring out the lurid details of the incineration of the children. It was enough that he had transported at least one woman for profit. Once the *Vindicta* crew started talking, the authorities quickly dragged the truth out of the slave trader in Charleston, and he immediately betrayed Owen, telling them everything he knew about the purchase of the girl named Margeaux. It is ironic that in the hypocritical eyes of the court, Owen's mistake was not in murdering the other women, but in selling the single one.

The charges against Jordan and the other crew members were dropped. It was determined they were only following their captain's orders until he became unstable, at which time they took command from him. Since they sailed directly into port to surrender, it was viewed as less than mutiny. In the end they were all set free, and except for a handful, they all reported back to the *Vindicta* which was still covered in gore and in terrible need of maintenance. The crew was not idle as they waited in port for the outcome of the trial.

Owen's execution was delayed for three weeks, as the authorities were waiting for another felon to be transported to be executed the same day. In keeping with his already foul reputation, Owen made as much of a pest of himself as he could at the jail, all the while perfectly convinced he would walk free.

Richard continued to visit Owen in his cell, until Owen asked him to leave and not come back. Stephen had put up the money for Owen's defense, and Richard now needed to get to Norfolk to gather the funds to repay him. When this mess was cleared up, and his credit was restored, he would be fine. Any assets he had were also frozen, so he could not even get to his own money, but he needed to pay the crew of both the *Lorraine* and the *Vindicta* and begin to cover the debts Owen had incurred, which he believed would soon come crushing in on him.

Robert Stuart had stayed with Richard, lending his support through the ordeal, but now he located an office of the American Fur Company and unloaded the fur in the hold for which Richard was paid a handling fee. Richard paid the crews and with the remainder of his money paid his dock fees to date, took on what provisions he could afford and set out with the crew he had for Norfolk. About two dozen of the crew came to him and asked not to return to the Great Lakes when he went. Those men had fulfilled their duty as they had signed on to serve until the ship returned to Washington, and it had now done so. Richard relieved them with no hard feelings and sailed away. He would worry about mustering a full crew when this horrible business with Owen was over.

When he got to Norfolk, he informed his crew they were restricted to the *Lorraine* but could have liberal use of her, and he was barely out of sight before the prostitutes began making their way onto the ship. When it came time to sail, the women would be more difficult than rats to eradicate, but the crew deserved a frolic, and Richard didn't begrudge them having a good time.

He took the little jolly boat and went alone to a small warehouse lodged between several other larger ones, but this was in a seedier section of town. This warehouse did not bear the large "H" like the others he owned, and there was no sign or identification of any kind. The only thing that broke the line of the heavy stone walls was one small door containing a stout lock. Richard took a lamp from the boat and unlocked the door then shut and locked it behind him. In the gloomy, stale air of the warehouse, Richard sorted through what he had always considered to be his last-resort stash. This warehouse was not on any ledger, and the only mention of it anywhere was in his will. He first went to three small chests and took out the gold. There were assorted coins he had gathered over the years, mostly Spanish, and there was gold dust which he had found tucked away in the captain's cabin of the *Draco Mare*. Since he never turned her in for prize money, he kept the gold for himself. He remembered, though, to make a nice bonus each year to young Jonas Benson, as the gold was undoubtedly his family money. As best Richard could estimate, there was about six thousand dollars in gold, but he had no way to know the amount of the debts Owen had incurred.

He next moved on to the other items in the cramped warehouse and shone his light on the piles of ivory tusks which had been in the sand under the *Vindicta* when she was righted. He also came upon a dozen rhinoceros horns which he had found to be nearly the total cargo on the *Draco Mare*, and which would have considerable value if he could find a trader to the Orient where they believed the horns held all manner of healing properties for men who no longer had the vim and vigor of life. Over against one wall there was a small coffer containing about eight strands of pearls, a tiny leather bag of emeralds, and a wad of broken and tangled gold chains. Finally, wrapped in brown paper and stored high above everything else were two bolts of double-thick silk heavily embroidered with gold and silver. The needlework must have taken a decade or more, for the bolts weighed nearly twenty pounds each. The fabric was heavy, gaudy, and undoubtedly very valuable to someone who would care to wear such a monstrosity.

He took the gold, the pearls, one of the larger ivory tusks, which weighed about seventy pounds, and the fabric. He hesitated for a moment, thinking Mary might like the pearls, but decided against them. He had never really liked pearls on women, but as an afterthought, he put the emeralds and the broken chains in his jacket pocket and locked the door behind him.

When the watch on the ship saw the jolly boat coming, they began to clear the decks of the Norfolk whores, but Richard told them not to bother as he was leaving the ship again right away. This came as good news to the men just coming off watch, and they traded places with the men going on duty and the frolicking continued.

Richard locked everything except the tusk in the safe in his cabin. He left the tusk securely lashed to the deck, and it would not be a bad thing if word spread that he had it. If there was someone looking to buy, they might find him and make the whole thing a lot easier than him looking for a buyer. When the women aboard the ship left, they could all pass right by the tusk, and they could tell more people they had seen it than if he ran an advertisement in the paper or posted signs around the harbor.

He stepped gingerly over a sporting couple and set off for home, not the home he had shared with Lorraine, but his boyhood home. He wondered if Gabriel would welcome him as the prodigal son, or if he would be turned away as a pirate. It was nearly nine o'clock when Richard tapped on the front door of the house. There was a bumping and some shuffling, and the curtain in the window next to the door was pulled back. Richard held the lantern up next to his face to allow Gabriel to see who he was. With a mighty rattle of the latch, the door burst open, and Gabriel scampered out in his slippers to fold Richard in his arms. Prodigal it would be after all.

After feeding him until he was about to burst, plying him with several lovely wines he had set aside, and complaining about the strange cold summer, Gabriel finally asked him the question that had been brewing all night, "Micah told me he had heard about this piracy business, but I told him it was bunkum. Now, you tell me, my baby boy, what really happened?" Richard told him, not leaving anything out, and when he was finished Gabriel wiped his eyes and said, "You never know how they will turn out, but you cannot blame yourself, Richard. You must turn your attention to Edward now, and to your little wife."

Richard said, almost in a whisper as if to mention him would take him away again, "And I can't forget little Jack."

"What's this?" Gabriel's eyes lit up.

Richard forced a smile and said, "Mary had a boy back in November, and we named him Jack."

"You see, the Lord looks after you. He took one son away from you, but he gave you another," Gabriel said, patting Richard's arm.

"That is better than saying the devil claimed him," Richard said.

"Nonsense. Owen has faltered, but God loves him just as much as he ever did. It is up to Owen now to take that grace and make of it what he will in the time he has left. God never turned his back on Owen, but Owen turned his back on God. You have to look at it that way. I do. I believe God took your mother away because she was needed somewhere else. How desperate a state it must have been for her to be needed more there than here," Gabriel said, smiling.

"And David and Zanna, were they needed too?" Richard said flatly.

"I don't have all the answers, son, but I do know that God works in ways we cannot understand, and it is not our job to understand those ways but only to accept them. Can you honestly tell me you have never seen a miracle?"

Richard smiled, remembering bringing Mary home again, alive and well with Jack to boot, when his very best hope up to then had been to just find her body for burial. He said, "All right, Papa, I'll try to understand."

They talked far into the night, and finally they slept. Richard was off again at dawn to the ship to return to Washington. When he returned, he found that Shaw had cleared the decks of the tradeswomen and the crew was about their business, but he could tell by the way they moved that most of them had been going at it hammer and tongs all night long. They sailed back to Washington without incident, but Richard now needed to muster enough to make a full crew in time to sail back north after this horrible business with Owen was over. Luckily, he knew just where to go.

He went to the Tallus Tavern, which was known since colonial times as the place to muster a crew. With his recent reputation as a pirate and Owen's trial, it was unlikely he would be able to find talent or experience, but he would take whoever he could find at this point. He posted his notice and then went to set up his table and wait. He had no more than pulled up his chair when he felt a hand on his shoulder. He turned and looked into a horribly fat, reptilian face that was split with a huge grin. "As I live and breathe, it's my dear little Lieutenant Holmwood! You must remember me, Mrs. Adeline Fisk?" Richard couldn't believe it. Here was the old dragon herself, the leader of that pack of horrid girls on the *Cumberland* who had extracted young Midshipman Shaw's virginity.

Richard stood up and towered over her squat frame and said, "Mrs. Fisk, where are your next set of charges? What are you doing on this side of the Atlantic?"

"Oh, hell," she waved her hand. "I gave up on trying to help those kinds of girls. They only went from poor white trash to rich white trash, and if anything they increased their ration of trash as they went. Now I deal with honest girls. At least they know what they are, what they're for, and they don't try to be anything else."

"Do they have a choice?" Richard asked, remembering a conversation he had with Mary when she came back with Jack about how so many of those women had to be prostitutes or starve.

"I don't take no women who hate their work. Now these ain't artists, mind you, like you might find in Paris or Venice, but they like what they do, and, to be honest, their clientele ain't the most demanding, mostly young officers and such, 'bout like you was when I first met you." Mrs. Fisk said proudly. "So what are you doing here?"

"Mustering a crew."

"For yourself or someone else?"

"For myself for the Northern Territory," Richard said awkwardly.

Mrs. Fisk locked a hazel lizard's eye on him, and said, "I've heard plenty about you. Some real good and some real bad." She saw Richard's look of dismay and added, "But I never believed any but the good. A man with eyes that pretty has to have a good heart." She smiled and touched his face and then plopped down and Richard sat next to her. She patted his leg and said, "We'll cut a deal tonight that may help both of us, but let's wait until it fills up a bit more in here."

They waited another hour drinking whiskey and making small talk while Richard looked around Tallus Tavern. It was more than just a tavern, it was a compound of sorts. There was the tavern itself in the middle, and to its left, connected by a roofed walkway, was the Tallus Inn, where respectable men and women could eat and sleep as they waited for their ships to sail. To the tavern's right was another building connected by a covered walkway. This building sported a storefront but bore no sign or name except for an elegant brass letter "E" on the door. The "E" stood for the Emporium, and it was recognized on an international level as a sporting house. This establishment stocked more tradeswomen under one roof than anywhere else on earth, and it held proudly and tenaciously to that newly perfected American tradition of sheer quantity eclipsing quality. Mrs. Fisk had taken over management of the Emporium only two years before, and she decreased the size of the working rooms and increased the number of her employees and within weeks had made a small fortune. Her girls were clean and quick. There were plenty available any hour of the day or night and there were no hidden fees.

She nudged Richard's knee with hers and said, "You willin' to pay a dollar a head to get this muster roll filled?" Richard nodded eagerly, and she said with a smile, "Then listen and learn." Mrs. Fisk stood on the chair on which she had been sitting and said in a loud voice, "We need to make muster on the," she leaned down and asked Richard the name of the ship and then said, "*Lorraine* bound for," again she asked Richard and repeated, "the Northern Territory, on a three-year mission commanded by this man right here, Captain Richard Holmwood. Now, I'm telling you any man who signs this here muster," she tapped it with a surprisingly dainty booted foot, "will get a free tour of the Emporium with the guide of his choice!"

Many of the men in the room had spent all their money on liquor before they had a chance to partake of the delights the Emporium offered, and most of them needed another sailing berth. Right then one ship looked as good as another, and if a berth was coupled with a roll in the sack for free, it seemed like an attractive offer. At the conclusion of Mrs. Fisk's offer, they practically knocked their chairs backwards getting to the table to put their marks on the muster. A few fights even broke out amongst the pushing and shoving, but Richard got the crew he needed. He settled up with Mrs. Fisk for an even one hundred dollars at a dollar per head as agreed. As he was about to leave, she offered, "You wouldn't care for a jaunt yourself would you? I'll make it one on the house for old times."

Richard smiled but graciously turned down her offer. The only woman he wanted to take a jaunt with was a thousand miles away as the crow flies and over two thousand by sea. He thanked Mrs. Fisk again and set off to get some sleep. He would see about provisioning the ship tomorrow, but for now he just wanted to get warm.

Richard was in the chandler's shop wrangling for salt pork and dried peas when he heard his name mentioned. It had happened several times since his arrival, and he cringed at it. For a man who had spent his life trying to stay unnoticed, it was torture. He saw the chandler's assistant point to him, and he turned to face whatever was to come.

The man inquiring after him was middle-aged and very short. He had the most spectacular waistcoat Richard had ever seen, bursting in stripes of robin's egg blue, burgundy, and lime green. He had a pair of spectacles hanging from where they were hooked over one ear, and incredibly blue eyes that sparkled in his round, pink face. "Captain Holmwood?" he asked, rubbing his hands like he was in front of a fire.

"Yes," Richard said, towering over the man.

"Please let me introduce myself. I am Aaron Cookman, of Cookman & Conway, and we procure, oh, what should I call them?" He looked up at the ceiling as though the words were printed there and then said, "Fine niceties from around the world." He took a step closer and brought his hand up to his mouth as though he was going to say something ladies shouldn't hear and said, "I understand you have some ivory that you would like to, well, shall we say, like to move."

"It isn't stolen if that's why you are whispering," Richard said a bit amused.

"Oh!" Cookman winced as though he had been stung and said, "I certainly didn't mean to, well, I would never imply it was, Captain. Could we though find a place to talk privately?" Richard agreed to meet him at a coffeehouse across the way and then turned back to the chandler. Cookman & Conway was very well-respected and the chandler who had dealt with Richard for decades was ashamed he had treated him so poorly and even apologized. Richard concluded his business with the chandler and then went to the coffeehouse to see if he could move some ivory.

It turned out that a ship lying in Norfolk's harbor had been visited by the same professional women that plied their trade on the *Lorraine*, and news had spread of the great tusk lashed to the deck. The other ship left Norfolk for Washington prior to the *Lorraine* and arrived there in time for news of the tusk to reach the sphere of Mr. Cookman's influence. He and Richard agreed to a sale of the tusks at three times what he thought they would ever fetch. He casually mentioned to the little man that he also had some rhinoceros horns if he knew of anyone who would take them off his hands. Cookman leaped like a nun who had been goosed, and he pumped Richard's hand with glee, agreeing to pay him, ounce for ounce, more for the horns than if they were made of gold. There was now a chance Richard could clear Owen's debts and still have a little left over.

He set out the following day, glad to be moving rather than sitting and thinking about Owen's last days alive. Owen had made it clear he didn't want Richard around, and for now at least, Richard honored those wishes.

While he was in Norfolk, he met again with Jonas Benson and turned over to him the first of the receipts for Owen's debts. They reviewed the manner in which they were to be paid. When Richard returned to Washington late the following week, the next batch of Owen's debts rolled in and they were staggering, but Richard forwarded them on to Benson in Norfolk.

Richard tried to keep his mind occupied, but it kept returning to Owen's execution. He thought of all the years he had desperately wanted to be with Owen and his mother before he could morally and legally be with them. Even though Owen was a thief, a torturer, and a murderer, Richard could not help but love him. He hated what Owen had done, but he did not hate Owen. Regardless of Owen's wishes, Richard decided to spend the next two days with him. On one of those visits the jailor's wife was hanging about Owen's cell while he ate his noon meal, which Richard noted was chicken. She smiled at Richard and blushed as she left. Twice before she had been lingering around Owen's cell when Richard visited, but she always darted away when he arrived. Richard sat silently while Owen ate, but as soon as he had finished, Owen started taking inventory of all the ills that had happened to him in his life, and this time he focused on Richard's alleged cruelty to him.

Owen was twelve years old when Lorraine died, and he had received no discipline whatsoever up to that point, and in fact he had rarely ever even been told no. Richard had honored Lorraine's request that she handle Owen and to let the short time he was in port with them be peaceful. Lorraine assured Richard she would be much firmer with Owen when he was away at sea, and Richard had agreed. In truth there was no discipline from Lorraine as Owen did exactly as he pleased. To make it worse, Lorraine covered for him. When the responsibility for his discipline fell to Richard after she died, Owen's life did indeed take a sharp left turn. Richard was lenient for the first few months, allowing Owen to grieve, and he allowed a few outbursts, then he became strict with him, and it took the next six months to whip Owen into shape. Owen learned to toe the mark and be obedient, but inside he seethed with rage at the turn his life had taken. He blamed the arrival of Edward, and the cause of Edward was, of course, Richard.

Richard listened to Owen whine from his cell for about ten minutes, and then he silently turned his back and left. He had held onto some blind hope that Owen would repent, but deep down he knew it would never happen. Owen believed he had done nothing wrong with regard to the women and that if only his mother were alive, she would make it all go away.

As he walked back to the ship, Richard thought about Owen's accusation of cruelty, and his thoughts in turn went to the cruelty of burning tiny children alive. This triggered another memory.

When Owen was about nine, Richard and Lorraine gave him a kitten. He played with it constantly, and the kitten followed him devotedly. One day Richard heard a strange noise in his study where he found Owen with a fireplace poker in his hand, grinning as he repeatedly shoved the screaming kitten back into the fire as it desperately tried to crawl out. Richard yelled and grabbed the poker from Owen, but it was too late to save the kitten. Richard shook him, and Owen's grin immediately changed to crocodile tears as he howled that his kitten was dead. "I was just trying to get him warm," Owen lied. Lorraine arrived then and began scolding Richard for speaking harshly to Owen. She glared at Richard as she soothed Owen and promised him they would get him another kitten right away.

"You didn't see the look on his face, Lorraine. He did this on purpose," Richard tried to explain, but Lorraine told him that was nonsense.

"Richard, dearest," she cooed, "do you honestly think he would put a kitten in the fire on purpose? Look at this face and tell me that."

Lorraine turned Owen's face away from her and toward Richard and Owen gave him a sly, gloating smirk from where he was tucked in his mother's arms. Richard stormed out of the house and walked for miles to cool off.

When he returned, Owen crawled into his lap and whispered innocently, "Papa, I love you. Hold me." Richard held him, pushing what he knew to be the truth to the very back of his mind where it gathered dust.

Richard thought about the children Owen had murdered, and he realized they meant no more to Owen than the kitten.

The execution was scheduled for eight the next morning, and though he knew it was useless, Richard tried to sleep. He pushed with his leg against a deck timber above him and swung in his hanging bunk. The ceiling swayed back and forth overhead, and though this movement had given him peace for over a quarter of a century, there was none to be had now. The only thing he could do was convince himself he had done everything possible he could for Owen. Richard had even requested a priest, but when the old man hobbled to the jail with his arthritic hips and knees screaming, Owen had only cursed and spit at him. Richard started to apologize, but the priest stopped him, saying, "I will pray for his soul, but I can do nothing if he keeps himself from the Lord. God is ready whenever Owen is ready." The ancient Episcopal cleric patted Richard's arm and left, but not before saying, "I will also say a prayer for you, my son."

Around midnight and still unable to sleep, Richard heard a commotion on the pier near the ship. He found the local constable and four armed men standing at the end of the gangway. Their breath steaming in the strangely cold summer air was illuminated by the lanterns they carried, and it made them appear as if in a cloud. When the constable saw Richard he said, "I know he's your son, but it will go better for both of you if you give him up, Captain Holmwood."

"What are you talking about?" Richard asked.

"Owen Holmwood escaped not more than an hour ago. Apparently, the jailor's wife was rather taken with him, and she smuggled in clothes and weapons, and tonight she left her home and her children to help him escape," the constable said, shaking his head. "One witness said she even shot her own husband to help your son, and the two of them were last seen running in this direction. There was some confusion in the scuffle, and we lost them, but we know he would come to you for help, so please hand him over."

"I haven't seen my son since before seven o'clock when I was at the jail with a priest," said Richard.

"Oh, come now, Captain. We can take him by force if need be, but why do that if he will give himself up?" the constable asked, and Richard walked down the gangway and leveled his gaze at him. The constable said, a little less sure of himself, "He is on this ship, correct?"

"There hasn't been anyone on or off the ship since well before midnight." Richard thought for a moment and then said, "Other than my steward, who took some tea to the harbormaster around eight o'clock, but he came right back after delivering it."

"Why would your steward be taking tea to the harbormaster?" the constable asked suspiciously.

Richard shot him a nasty glance and said, "Because when I got here, I didn't have a fucking penny to my name, and the harbormaster let me ride on my credit—something others around here have been less than willing to do for me."

"Captain Holmwood, that matter has been cleared up, and you shouldn't worry about anyone's confidence in you," the constable said quickly.

"Yet you come to me to see if I am harboring a convicted pirate?" Richard said sourly, then added, "You are welcome to search the ship all you like, but he is not here, and you will simply be wasting your time." The constable was about to speak again when a lad came running up with the message that Owen had been cornered in a barn trying to steal a horse. As the constable turned to leave, Richard said, "I'm coming with you."

They ran to a stable about a quarter mile from the jail where a crowd with lanterns and torches was already gathering. The torches lent a medieval air to the scene, and the constable yelled for Owen to give himself up peacefully. There was a commotion near a second-story double door that was used to load grain and hay, and the door opened. The jailor's wife appeared in the opening and she looked terrified. She struggled a bit and looked behind her and screamed. Her scream was cut short, and then she fell from the open doorway clutching tightly at her neck. Richard could see spurts of blood glistening black in the torchlight as it gushed between her fingers where her throat had been cut.

Everyone rushed toward where she landed, and in the commotion Owen slipped out the side of the barn and joined the onlookers dressed in the clothes the woman had brought to the jail for him. No one saw him as he moved quietly with his head down through the pushing crowd. He ducked behind a house and groped his way along until he was well away from the crowd.

Back at the barn, Richard helped carry the woman's body to her home where the undertaker was already at work on the husband. Richard looked around at the three small children huddling with their grandmother, and he was overwhelmed with guilt. Owen had sweet-talked this poor woman into abandoning everything and everyone, undoubtedly with the promise of an easy life.   The grandmother was doing her best to soothe the children, who had been robbed of both their parents in less than three hours, and Richard left her to her pitiful duty, promising himself he would do something to make amends. He kept seeing their faces as he wandered back to the ship, yet even through that image seeped the question of what he would have done had Owen come to him, and it bothered him that he couldn't say with absolute certainty that he would have turned him away.

Richard would not have to make that choice, because Owen was already riding hell for leather toward Baltimore on a horse he had finally managed to steal. In Baltimore, he would take on a new identity and debark on an outbound ship. Before the sun set the following day, he would be headed out to sea.

RICHARD WAITED a week for news of Owen, but there was none. He had settled huge chunks of Owen's debts, and he had already left instructions for the remainder to be forwarded to Jonas Benson in Norfolk. The largest of the debts, according to what Jordan could remember, had already surfaced, but Richard knew others would roll in for years, and he prayed that when his fleet was released, they would again be profitable. He had an idea of how he might achieve it.

Some of the evidence presented at the trial had a side effect Richard had not expected. The silks which had originated in the Orient and the jewelry were of a quality rarely seen in Washington, and they were the talk of the city. Little rotund Aaron Cookman, who had kindly taken the tusks off his hands, rather coyly suggested that if Richard could get his hands on more of the silk and the jewelry, he had a market for them that was, in his words, bottomless.

Richard spoke with Jordan about a voyage back to eastern Africa to trace the origin of the goods, but before he could suggest it, he realized Jordan was in no shape physically or mentally to command the trip. He had Jordan instead give Shaw directions as best he could remember. Armed with the logbook of that horrible trip, Shaw agreed to return to Africa in the *Vindicta* and purchase the goods. He would also carry documentation proving Owen had acted without authority, and in time perhaps, this would clear up Richard's reputation in the area. Shaw readily agreed to the voyage and departed with the *Vindicta* and a good many of the original crew. The voyage was estimated to last two years.

Shaw had the more difficult voyage ahead of him, so Richard had provisioned the *Vindicta* with the better victuals available. He then attempted to provision the *Lorraine*, but it seems the terribly cold weather they had experienced in Washington and Norfolk was not isolated. The cold was felt much wider, and the entire East Coast froze repeatedly, killing crops. In many areas there was no harvest at all. The price of flour and oats was seventy-five times higher than it had been the previous year, and what he could get was of poor quality. Since there was no grain to feed livestock over the winter, farmers had sent their animals to slaughter early, and salted pork and beef were in abundance. Even though there was plenty of the meat available, it was little better than salted shoe leather.

Richard returned to Norfolk one last time to stock up on tea, sugar, cheese, vinegar, and rum from the warehouse there, and he also grabbed a small crock of olives and a barrel of molasses. He tucked in a few bolts of green silk for Mary, even though he knew they were impractical, but he wanted her to have them all the same. He wanted her to know how beautiful she had looked the last time she wore silk, the night of the Decatur Ball, and just in case he hadn't told her how beautiful he thought she was, he would tell her again. While he was in Washington, he had had the emeralds and gold chain made into a necklace and earbobs for Mary, and they were magnificent. He wanted to court her like he never did before they were married.

Before he left Washington, Richard anonymously set up a pension for the jailor's children that would feed and clothe them and help Richard assuage his guilt.

It was now late summer, and in Norfolk it should have been crowding the one hundred degree mark, but Richard stood huddled on the deck of the *Lorraine* in a wool coat with the thermometer barely registering forty degrees. With everything done he could think of, he headed to the open sea to begin the long journey to Halifax. Winter had barely relaxed its grip all summer, so it had a very good head start on Richard, but he hoped the bizarre weather had been isolated to just the coast. He had no idea how Mary had fared over the summer and was anxious to be back with her and the children. Every day he sailed north was a day closer to embracing her, and he didn't hold back on the canvas.

By the time Richard reached Halifax, the St. Lawrence was freezing along the edges. The volume of water passing out of the river should have kept it free of ice much later in the year, but the weather had been so cold that winter was already striding forward, ready to lock them in ice until spring. Richard entered the river, determined to go as far as he could in open water, but a cold feeling in his gut told him he would not make it.

CHAPTER 17

AFTER RICHARD and his crew left the island for the East Coast, Mary and the children spent more and more time outdoors as the days warmed. They had to go out in the afternoons though, as Mary was again coping with morning sickness. She had no idea she was pregnant when Richard left and now smiled as she stroked her stomach, thinking what a shock he would have when he saw her on his return in the fall.

The Ojibwas returned to the island with their late-winter furs a few weeks after Richard left, and Mary's housekeeper of sorts, Mikwaniwum, also returned. Miki, as Mary called her, was so named because she was born during a hailstorm. Even though she retained a bit of that storm's fury in her dealings with other people, she made a fuss over little Jack as Mary proudly showed him off. Miki spread the word among the other Ojibwa women who gathered to see the child. They had ignored him last spring, as infant mortality is so high among them they really did not want to get attached to a child until it had survived its first year. They looked Jack over excitedly now and brought little bundles of plants and packets of herbs wrapped in bark, which Mary was to place where he slept to ward off evil and sickness. A few days after they saw Jack again, the women named him Ahsin, which means rock. Mary was at first a bit hurt they would call him dumb like a rock, but she quickly learned they were not referring to his intellect, but to his temperament, and they meant he would be stubborn and strong as a rock.

The Ojibwa women told Mary the wise elders predicted a cold summer and a winter colder than anything they could remember. The oldest women were warning to keep more muskrat fur for shoes and clothes, rather than trading them. Three of the eldest women had had the same dream: The great wolf of winter had devoured the hare of spring along with all her young, except one tiny female kit. After great discussion, the dreams were interpreted to mean winter would hold sway this year. The younger people in the group, although they respected the elder women above all others, also doubted winter had any muscle left as the trees and plants were in bloom and the temperature was rising by the week, but as is custom, they followed the advice of the maternal elders and kept back a little less than a quarter of their catch.

June arrived with warmer temperatures, and some of the young Ojibwa men grumbled that they had worked so hard to trap the fur, only to have it stored away unused for trade. Mary and Miki planted a little garden with peas and carrots and onions, but it had not come up yet, and though there was still plenty of food at the house, they were all aching for something that was not salted, pickled, or dried.

On one of their excursions, Mary exclaimed and dropped to the ground on her knees. Wrennet rushed over, certain something was wrong, only to find Mary grinning. She had found some wild strawberries, and she, Edward and Wrennet ate them, reveling in the taste of fresh fruit after nearly a year without. Each of them crushed the berries with their tongue against the roof of their mouths, chewing them slowly to get every morsel of flavor. Their jaws ached from the gush of saliva, and their eyes stung from tears of pleasure.

Through the ages in the English speaking parts of the world, the strawberry has held a place of honor. Side by side, it is not as tangy as the raspberry or as rich as the gooseberry, but it is the first of the season, and therefore is remembered fondly. Mary now smashed a berry and put the juice in Jack's mouth, which he opened like a bird in a nest as soon as the fruit touched his lips. His eyes opened wider, and he grimaced at the new taste, then opened his mouth again, reaching this time with his hands. Wrennet saw it and said, "I wouldn't give him very much of that, or he'll have the squirts." Mary nodded and gave him a few more berries and then stood up, but Jack howled, being cut off so soon from his newly discovered treat.

The middle of June was wonderful. The days became full of warmth, and they ate peas from the garden to go with the perch Mary and Edward caught in a little rocky cove on the northwest side of the island. While they were poking around the cove they also discovered a small type of crab darting for cover under the large, loose rocks. They were not the round, dinner-plate wide blue-crabs harvested from the Chesapeake Bay that they were used to, but were instead a drab golden brown and shaped more like their North Atlantic cousin, the lobster. Mary pointed one out to Edward saying, "Look at these. I bet if we could catch them, they would be good to eat." Mary and Edward proceeded to catch several dozen a week later, and her suggestion was correct—the little crayfish did taste deliciously like little lobsters.

Mary woke up cold one morning about a week later. This seemed odd as the days and nights were generally getting warmer. The nights were still cool, but they had always been that way on the island even in summer. The house was actually cold enough for an early fire before they even started cooking. As she stepped outside to get more wood, Mary could actually see her breath puffing in great clouds. With every step she fought the nausea of morning sickness. Once the fire took hold, she stoked it well and looked at the gray morning clouds. The Ojibwa elders' warning of a relentless winter ran through her mind, but she dismissed it as nonsense. Summer always followed spring as it was in turn followed by fall; the world didn't just skip a season now and then. They had had surprisingly cold days in summer on the island compared to Scotland Neck, and as she stoked the fire, she reassured herself it was nothing.

Mary had Edward help her and they brought in enough wood for the rest of the day and the night, and then she sat down to do some sewing before dinner. The temperature had dropped dramatically, and the air had the feel of fall or early winter. She heard an odd noise and opened the door. She stood staring at sleet bouncing in the yard.

Mary shut the door and stoked the fire, then went about her work. She noticed the sleet had stopped about an hour later, but when she checked outside, her breath caught in her chest. The sleet had stopped, but it had given way to something even more frightening—a gentle wet snow. She stood staring at the snow falling, then closed the door and locked it, as if throwing the bolt could somehow keep the weather away.

When they awakened the next morning the wind was blowing, and it was still snowing. Miki came stomping into the house from her tent near the shore, and she said the Ojibwa were meeting to see what they needed to do to drive the Wolf away. "Have you ever seen snow like this in the summer?" Mary asked anxiously.

"No," Miki shook her head, "never. There is always cold weather in the summer, but only once did I see it snow, and that was only a few flakes for a short time, and then it was warm again a few days later."

"Do the elders think this is the winter in summer they predicted?" Mary asked, hoping the answer was yes.

"No," Miki looked at her solemnly, "they say this is only the tip of the wolf's nose."

The snow stopped during the following night, and dawn rose on an accumulation of about three inches. Mary walked down the rows of her garden looking brokenhearted at the frozen and limp plants. She pulled the pea vines and took them inside to harvest what pods there were, and then she did the same with the carrots and onions.

The garden was replanted after the snow melted, and it grew for nearly a month in the unusually cold July weather, until one afternoon a dry bitter wind drove Mary indoors from tending it. She went to sleep dreading what the dawn would bring. She woke once in the night to the sound of rain on the roof. When she awakened there was no sound from outside. She opened the door unprepared for the cheerless inch of snow waiting there. Once again the icy breath of the Wolf had taken the life of her garden. She planted twice more that summer, but each time her vegetables were killed by the freezing temperatures, and she finally gave up in August knowing that even if the plants survived another month, it was too late in the year for them to ripen. There were no berries or wild fruit due to a late frost in May, and now they faced winter relying only on the pickled vegetables they had on hand to ward off scurvy.

The Ojibwa blamed the unappeased Wolf for the cold, and while Mary knew it was not some mythical lupine beast, she had no way to know that it was really the effect of a hundred cubic miles of ash belched into the atmosphere by the volcano sleeping under Mt. Tambora. The volcano, on the far side of the world, had come roaring to life the same day they left Scotland Neck, and all over the world, the weather was now deadly cold. The volcano pumped clouds of ash into the sky, which blocked sunlight. Crops failed everywhere and farmers were having trouble feeding their fowl and livestock. The six chickens Mary had transferred from ship to ship all the way from Virginia had thrived and with the help of the vicious red rooster had produced another dozen chicks. She had only allowed one chicken to raise a brood, as they had eaten the other eggs, but now Mary worried about getting what birds she had through the winter. They could eat the young birds when they matured, but Mary hoped the mother hens and the cock could exist on oatmeal and crumbled ship biscuits, both of which they had in abundance.

While Mary and the others suffered with the cold on Mackinac Island, the conditions were even worse along the North Atlantic on both sides of the ocean. The Thames River froze in May, something it usually didn't do even in winter, and the snow piled up to sixteen inches in Philadelphia in July. All over the world, but especially in the northeastern United States, people were staggering under loads of June and July snow. They dreaded even more what the winter would bring.

The other two ships which had wintered on Beaver Island came for supplies in the fall. The crews believed Richard would bring more supplies back from the East Coast or with him from Welland when he came. Mary had to explain that he was not back yet, but she gave them most of the supplies she had, knowing Richard could only be weeks or a month at most away, and they would have more supplies than they could store on the island. Dorcas kept a watchful eye on what was taken and what was left. Four families could have lived well for six months on what they still had on Mackinac, but Dorcas begrudged the crews of the ships every barrel, bag, keg, and crock they took with them.

October arrived with the same flaming leaves Mary recalled from last year, and even though the leaves on some of the trees had frozen and had to re-bud again, the color was still magnificent. She began to look for Richard.

October turned to November, and twice they had snowstorms

that approached the caliber of a blizzard. Mary was truly worried now about what had happened to Richard, and as she watched the waves of the latest storm batter the shore by the pier, she began to doubt he would make it before winter. The waves crashed on the crude breakwater that had been erected last summer, throwing the spray thirty feet in the air. Unable to help herself, Mary bundled up and walked the short distance to the top of the bluff where the waves came unhindered by the artificial shoal. They beat against the stone wall so hard, Mary could feel the concussion in her feet. The waves retreated with a hungry, sucking sound before coming in again and again. She shuddered at the thought of Richard trying to get back to them through a storm like this. Back indoors, Wrennet scolded her and held her hands against Mary's icy and wind-blasted cheeks to warm them. "I know Richard is out in this," Mary whispered, almost sobbing.

Wrennet shook her head, "You know nothing of the sort. He might be on his ship, but he will be safe and snug somewhere riding it out. You just wait and see." Wrennet had smiled, but it was insincere, for she had had a nagging feeling for the last few days that she would never see Richard again. It could be due to the fact that she was feeling the weight of her years, or just the strange weather, but she was certain she would not lay eyes on him again.

The two other ships in the small fleet from Beaver Island came again to check for supplies, and they were alarmed that Richard was not back. The captain in charge suggested Mary, her family, and the Deemses come with them to stay on Beaver Island, but when she refused, fearing Richard would not know where they were, he set men to work chopping and piling wood for them for the winter. Mary assured the captain that Richard couldn't be much longer now, and besides there was Douglas Deems and the men at the garrison if she needed help, though she knew she would only go to the garrison as a last resort. Those were rough-talking men, not overly clean, who had made lewd comments under their breath but loud enough so she could hear and they had even made them when she was heavily pregnant.

It was almost as if the commander at the garrison had waited for Mary to say no to the Beaver Island fleet, because less than a week later he came to tell her and Douglas that the garrison was relocating to Fort Michilimackinac on the southern mainland where they would rebuild some of the old shore defenses over the winter. He asked if any of them would like to winter-over with them, but Douglas declined, and when he asked Mary if she wanted to go, she adamantly shook her head no.

Winter set in for good on a Sunday, and the only reason Mary knew the day of the week for sure was that they had to cut short their makeshift church service because Wrennet nearly fell from her chair in the middle of it. Mary helped her to bed and shuttered the window because Wrennet said the light hurt her eyes. Mary sat with her and though Wrennet had no fever, her pulse raced, and it reminded Mary of a small bird that had gotten trapped in the house which she had caught with her hands, its tiny heart fluttering in its chest so fast it was almost a vibration. Wrennet's pulse was like that now, as she dozed on and off the rest of the day and mumbled through the night. It snowed heavily all night, and just before dawn Wrennet fell into a deep sleep, and Mary left her to try to get some sleep herself. She had just drifted off when Jack came to her wanting to be fed. She stumbled back awake like she was crawling out of a well. She tried to find something for him to eat without waking the others. As she fed him at the table, she noticed through the small windows in the main room that she had forgotten to shutter, that it was still snowing.

Wrennet woke later in the day having no memory of what had happened. She was very groggy, but she needed desperately to speak with Mary. Mary sat on the edge of the bed. Wrennet took a deep breath and began, "Did you know I have been with Richard since he was just days old?" Mary nodded her head. She knew Wrennet had been with the family a long time, but she didn't know it was that long. Wrennet continued, "I came after Catherine Holmwood delivered Richard. She was very ill, and had no milk, and needed a wet nurse. My husband had been lost at sea not two months before, and my baby was born the same night as Richard, but he only breathed for a few hours and died. I came to the Holmwood house as a wet nurse. I was so alone and in so much sorrow, I didn't think I could go on, but I took one look at Richard in his little cradle, and he gave me a reason to live. He even looked like my little boy, and once I began to feed him and care for him, I couldn't help but love him like he was my own. I never left the Holmwoods after that. I cared for all the Holmwood children, and I loved them all, but none of them that touched me like Richard." Wrennet held Mary's hand and tried to smile, and then continued, "When he married Lorraine there was a lot of scandal in Boston, and none of her staff would come with her when she moved to Hampton, so I moved in with them and took care of her and Richard and Owen. Owen was a beautiful child. He looked just like Richard had when he was little, and I took to him right away. As time went on though I found out he was nothing like his father. Owen was sneaky and cruel and he saw the world only in how it would be best for him. Richard was oblivious to it, and I didn't want to risk being sent away, so I kept my mouth shut and put up with Owen. Then when Lorraine died, Richard was lost. The very same day, right after the funeral, he took us to Scotland Neck. Oh, Mary, I will never forget that trip up the James River with Edward screaming and Richard with a face of stone. I stayed on in Scotland Neck, but when Richard said he was to leave for five years, and I would have to watch Edward, I knew I couldn't do it. Edward is the sweetest child, much like his father was when he wasn't pulling a prank, and I could not risk having something happen to me while Richard was gone and having Edward left in Owen's hands. You see, I knew I couldn't last the five years to take care of Edward, but the thought of never seeing Richard again before I died was too much for me, so I decided to come along with all of you here." She took Mary's hand again and smiled, "I do not regret coming here. I have been able to see Richard happy again after so many years." She chuckled, "I told him to be careful shutting you out of his heart, because you would simply get right into his soul instead." Wrennet smiled and added, "And you did." She sighed and patted Mary's hand, then fell into a deep sleep, and Mary left her after a few minutes.

It snowed that entire day and the following day, and this was the snow that did not melt. Weeks later it was still there, only now several more inches had been added to it. Mary wept silently knowing there was little chance of Richard getting to them before the lakes froze over. She hadn't seen a ship in over a month, and if he was going to make it in time, he needed to come in the next week or two.

As the snow locked them in for their second winter, a change came over Dorcas Deems. She had been an unparalleled trencher since Mary first met her, but now her appetite took on a totally different quality. Dorcas no longer tucked in with gusto at mealtime, but food came to dominate all her waking hours. The more it appeared likely they would have no more food delivered until spring, the hungrier she became. The only people now left on the island were those in the cottages occupied by the Deemses and the Holmwoods, but there was enough food to last them and several more families until well after spring, if they were careful. Douglas mentioned to Mary in an aside that he was worried about Dorcas, but Mary didn't really think much of it until Dorcas told Mary she would have to get rid of Grub. Dorcas insisted, "That dog will eat food that our families are going to need to stay alive over the winter. You must put him down. If you can't shoot him, I will have Reggie do it for you." Mary was stunned, but what was worse was that Edward had overheard the conversation and ran crying into their cottage, dragging Grub along by the collar.

Mary stood there stiffly and told Dorcas she would do no such thing, nor was Reggie to harm a hair on that smelly dog's head. Douglas had come upon them outside just then and asked what the trouble was. Normally, Mary would have held her tongue, but this time she told Douglas exactly what Dorcas had said, and while she did, Dorcas locked her nasty toad-like eyes on her. Douglas looked shocked and assured Mary no one would touch the dog. He bid her good day and escorted Dorcas into the cottage, but even through the closed door of their house, Mary heard the shouting and screaming.

If Mary could trust the calendar she was keeping, it was now the middle of December. She walked down to the pier to look once more for

Richard's ship and was alarmed to see slush forming in the water nearly ten feet out from shore. It had not frozen until after the new year last winter. When she came to check it again the next morning, it was a solid, clear sheet, almost eerie to look at. She could see rocks along the bottom of the lake through the clear ice and the clear water below, but she was not brave enough to walk on it.

When the lakes first freeze, and then it snows shortly thereafter, the snow insulates the ice, and it does not freeze very thick. Now with three days of bitter cold, the ice froze downward until it was nearly two feet thick. It would then support a man or could have easily supported a four-horse carriage fully-loaded.

Mary stared at the ice and looked across the lake hoping to see open water, but there was none. Richard, wherever he was, would not join them now until spring. Once again she would bear him a child while he was miles away, only this time he had no idea there was even one coming.

Dorcas was cold and distant for a week or so, but since Mary held the bulk of the stored food at her cottage, Dorcas soon warmed to her again, at least as much as her cold-blooded nature would allow. After a few days Douglas came knocking at the door looking rather shamefaced as he asked, "Is there any way you would consider splitting the food we have on hand and allowing my wife to keep our half?" Mary looked puzzled, and he added, "Dorcas is losing sleep over this, and my life would be so much more comfortable if she could see and touch the food." Mary nodded slowly, seeing how haggard Douglas looked, and quickly agreed. The stores were split equally, and Reggie and Douglas came and took their half, Douglas again apologizing as they left with the final load.

Two days before Christmas, Mary went over to ask if the Deemses would join them for Christmas dinner, and she found Dorcas sitting on a chair in front of a barrel of sugar, cupping it with her hands like it was water and eating it. Mary stared transfixed at the sight and realized that Dorcas was dipping deeply into the barrel and that she had eaten pounds of it since they divided it only a week or so ago.

Douglas looked at Dorcas and then back at Mary, and then he spoke for them. They would be happy to come for dinner. Mary hurried back to her cottage where she tried to put the horrid picture of Dorcas eating sugar from her mind.

Two weeks later, Mary saw Douglas and Reggie hauling kegs and barrels from Robert Stuart's house over to theirs. Douglas apologized to Mary for making so much noise, but said that they were running low on food and that Dorcas would feel better if they got what was at the warehouse and brought it to theirs. Mary could not see how they were low on food, as she had barely put a dent in what was stored in her cottage.

That same evening, Cassie appeared at the door of the cottage begging Wrennet to come and look at her Papa. "He just collapsed, and he looks so gray and his face is covered with sweat." Wrennet quickly went over, and by the time Mary got the children settled so she could run over, it was obvious Douglas was in a bad way. He was barely breathing and every so often would dig at his chest with his fingers and struggle to breathe. Wrennet pulled Mary and Dorcas aside and told them she thought it was his heart, especially after all the exertion of moving the food to the cottage.

Dorcas looked at Wrennet and said, almost relieved, "Well, at least he got the food moved here before he took sick. We can all be glad for that." Wrennet again explained to Dorcas that Douglas was very ill and there was a strong chance he would not survive the night. Dorcas nodded her head that she understood and pulled a chair up to the sugar barrel where she began dipping handfuls of it into her mouth. She alternated between bites of cooked salt pork and handfuls of sugar, and in this rotating feeding pattern, passed the last hours of Douglas's life. He died around two o'clock in the morning. Mary and Wrennet comforted Cassie, but Reggie just wailed with his head in his mother's lap as she stared straight ahead, shoving food into her mouth that neither Mary nor Wrennet believed she even tasted.

The ground was frozen solid, so they wrapped Douglas in some sailcloth Mary found in her loft, and they piled snow and wood over his body. They would not be able to bury him properly until spring, but this way he was protected from the elements and possible scavengers.

Reggie came a week later and asked if Mary would split her food with them, admitting they were again out. It seemed impossible, but Dorcas had eaten all the food they brought from the warehouse in addition to that which Mary had earlier split with her. Mary divided the food, and Reggie took it back to their cottage. After he left, Mary went to check on her chickens which she had placed in a small coop near the wood pile in the lee of the house. She carefully removed the wool cover over them and stood stunned. They were gone, all of them, the hens, the half-grown chicks, and the rooster. By feeding them carefully, they could have provided them eggs to last the winter, but now they were gone. There was a trail of feathers and drops of blood, which led to the Deems's cottage. Mary was so angry she didn't know what to do, but without Douglas there as a governor of sorts to Dorcas's temper, Mary was afraid to confront her.

Mary returned to the house and took some of the oatmeal and a small keg of the salt pork and moved them to her bedroom. She was certain this would not be the last time Reggie came begging for food, and after finding the chickens gone, she wanted something held back that didn't have to be divided.

About a week later, during the height of a terrible snowstorm, Dorcas herself waded over through the snow to speak to Mary. She demanded half of what food there was in the cottage, and furthermore, suggested it was a good thing the dog had not been destroyed because he would provide meat after the salted stuff they had was gone. Mary argued that there was plenty of food to last until spring if they were careful. At this, Dorcas pulled her lips back from her teeth in a snarl and she shoved past Mary to stand staring at Jack who was sitting by the fire playing with a carved wooden horse. "I have heard that in extreme conditions people have selected a member of the party to be eaten. I think in this case it should be him," she jerked a thumb at Jack, "because the one you are carrying won't provide enough meat at first, but later we can use it." She glanced around the room and her gaze fell on Edward. She didn't say anything, but it was obvious she was calculating how much meat he would supply as well.

Mary was stunned at what Dorcas had said, and she shoved her toward the door like a mouse trying to move a sow. When she touched her, Mary finally realized how much weight Dorcas had gained. She was doughy and soft, and as Mary shoved her, Dorcas lurched out the door, was pulled over by her top-heavy load, poorly balanced on her tiny feet, and fell into the snow. Mary screamed at her, "I will divide what I have left with you, but don't you ever come here again!" With that, she shut and bolted the door. Dorcas lay sprawled in the snow, unable to get up no matter how much she rolled from side to side, but within less than a minute Reggie came and got her and helped her home. He shot one last vicious glance at the Holmwood cottage and then slammed the door shut behind him.

To add to the horror of the evening, Wrennet collapsed just before bedtime. Mary and Edward helped her to her bed, and she tried to talk several times, but her words were gibberish and the whole side of her face sagged. It was obvious to Mary that Wrennet had suffered a stroke. Mary sat with her and tried to comfort her, but about an hour later Wrennet suddenly took in a shuddering breath and went limp. Mary shakily checked for a pulse, but there was none. Wrennet was gone, and Mary was now truly alone to care for Edward and Jack. As she sat sobbing next to Wrennet's body, the child in her abdomen kicked hard, reminding her of another thing she would have to handle on her own.

Mary and Edward wrapped Wrennet's body in a sheet and pulled her to the door. They were able to get her outside and next to the house, where they shoveled snow on top of her, and then hauled the canoe which had been resting behind the house and placed it upside down on her snowy grave. It would have to do until spring. The only animal on the island large enough to disturb her grave was Grub, but Mary would watch him closely. Grub? Mary realized she had not seen him since morning when she let him out to go on one of his legendary urination tours of the island, and she wondered now what had become of him. She sat waiting for the contractions to subside, which had sprung up from moving Wrennet's body, and she glanced in the direction of the Deems's cottage. Did Dorcas have Grub killed? She couldn't picture Dorcas doing the deed herself, but certainly her loyal minion Reggie was up to the task. Reggie wouldn't have the courage to kill Grub with a knife—he would have to shoot him with Douglas' pistol, but she had not heard a shot and was fairly sure she would on the tiny island.

Mary didn't realize through all her complaining about his stench and his great muddy tracks on the floor just how much she liked Grub and how much security he provided. She sat now feeling about as alone as she had ever felt in her life, and the child in her belly kicked and brought her back to reality. She needed to get off the island and away from these people but had no idea how she could do it.

Rather than risk Dorcas and Reggie taking all the food by force, she twice divided what she had left and placed it on their doorstep. She was down now to a rack of salt pork and some bread she had made. There was nothing left to be divided, and even the stash she had kept in her room had gone to appease Reggie and feed the monstrous eating machine that Dorcas had become. She made up her mind that she would leave the island the following night. She would take Edward and Jack in the canoe and pull them across the ice to the Ojibwa encampment. They might all freeze to death on the ice, but it was better than being murdered by Dorcas and Reggie.

Mary packed warm clothes and took the large, beaver fur blankets they had been given by Robert Stuart. There was even a bear skin rug, but it was so heavy Mary didn't want to try to take it with them. She thought it best they leave at night so they would have some chance of getting away undetected. Travelling on the ice at night was really no more dangerous than in the day. Open pressure cracks covered by a skiff of snow would be no easier to see in the daylight, so she determined she would leave just after dark the following day. It was storming great sheets of snow, but she hoped it would let up by morning. She was busy packing when she heard a tapping at the window. She looked up and saw Cassie's pale face framed there. Cassie looked scared, and Mary feared it was a trick, but she softened to the girl's weak call for help. She opened the door and Cassie leaped inside and slammed and locked the door behind her. She was bundled in the heaviest clothes she had and was breathing very hard, "You have to leave! You have to leave this island tonight. My mother is sending Reggie to get Jack. Mary, they said they will eat him! It's like they don't even know who they are anymore. All they care about is eating. Please leave, and take me with you," she broke down and sobbed.

"Are you sure?" Mary pulled Cassie's chin up to see her face, still wondering if this was some kind of trick, and she said harshly, "Cassie, answer me. Are you sure they are coming tonight?" Cassie didn't answer, but nodded her head vehemently. Mary nearly panicked then and more so because she had felt for the past several hours the gradually increasing contractions of true labor. Cassie looked up now, and Mary said, "All right. You have to help me get the children ready, and we'll leave in a half-hour." Mary's hope was to get across the ice where the Ojibwa women could help her when she delivered. She was in labor with Jack the better part of twelve hours, and it was only four miles to the encampment. If they couldn't make it in eight hours or so, they probably wouldn't make it at all.

The storm had not abated since earlier in the day, and, if anything, it was worse than before. The wind seemed to suck the air from their lungs as they prepared the canoe to leave the island. They pulled it around to the opposite side of the house where it was shielded from the wind and away from view of the Deems's cottage, but unfortunately also furthest from the door. Mary placed her bundles of clothes and what food they had in the canoe and put Edward inside with Jack in his lap. She and Cassie had rigged some crude manropes and now, bundled in all the clothes they could wear, they started out across the lawn toward the pier. It was the closest place to get down on the water and one of only two places that did not involve going over a bluff. It was easier to pull the canoe than Mary thought, but they were on a gentle downhill incline, and she feared it would be much harder out on the open ice. As she neared the water, Mary had another contraction and this one took her breath away. She stopped and sat on the gunwale of the canoe, breathing slowly until it passed. When it was over they started again, but within five minutes she had to stop again. They were making their way along the southeast side of the island when Mary realized she would never make it to the encampment before she gave birth. The wind was blowing so hard, she had trouble making herself heard, so she just took Cassie's coat sleeve and pulled her toward the beached sloop and motioned for her to climb inside. She then helped Edward and Jack into the small ship as well. They huddled under blankets while Mary made what preparations she could to give birth.

She had Cassie place two crates on end and drape a blanket over them. She told Edward and Jack to crawl under and to sit one on each side, looking at her face. In this way they could all share body heat, but by facing away the boys would be shielded from the worst of the gore. She then crawled under the blanket herself and got on top of a sheet hastily spread over a blanket on the deck. Cassie crawled under the blanket as well and they crouched in their little fort, staring at each other, doing their best to keep their hair and clothing away from the lantern. "Don't let anything near the light, or it will catch on fire," Mary warned Cassie.

Edward stared straight ahead, terrified of leaving the house, terrified of the Deemses, and terrified of what was happening to Mary.

When the contractions were so close Mary felt the urge to push, she leaned back so that Edward and Jack were near her shoulder, but still facing her so that they could not see the bottom half of her. Jack was terrified of his mother's straining and grimacing, and he added to the confusion by sobbing quietly. Cassie had now maneuvered around until she was where she could help catch the child as it was born. Mary writhed in pain and fear, expecting at any minute for Reggie to burst in on them and try to take Jack.

The child was born after only two tremendous shoves by Mary, and Cassie did her best to dry it off and wrap it in the loose folds of the sheet. She had tried to hand the baby to Mary, but the umbilical cord was not long enough, and Mary had screamed for her to just hold the child herself. It was a girl, born early like Jack, only even smaller, but she was already breathing and howling at being shoved into this frigid world from where she had been warm and cozy. Cassie wrapped her in a little coat of Jack's that Mary had brought in from the canoe, and they waited for the afterbirth to emerge.

Mary recalled hazily how the women had tied off Jack's umbilical cord and then cut it, and she directed Cassie as best she could to do the same. Cassie never once grimaced or turned up her nose, but instead went about her work as gently as possible. As Mary lay propped up on her elbows, the placenta slipped from her body and she picked it up herself. She had Cassie tear a piece of the sheet off and she wrapped the foul-looking, blue-black organ in it. As she sat up, Mary lurched sideways and braced herself against the deck, leaving a perfect handprint outlined in blood.

She sat holding the tiny girl in her lap on her crossed knees, and only then let Jack and Edward look at her. Mary reached her hand out, and Cassie took it gingerly, and she said, sobbing, "Thank you, Cassie. I could never have done this without you." Mary sat holding the child and said, "We can't stay here for long, but I can't move yet, so let's rest here for a while, and then we'll move out onto the lake." Cassie nodded and then looked in the direction of the cottages as if she could somehow see her mother and brother through the oak hull, the snow, and the solid stone bluff that shielded them from the wind. She knew as Mary did that when Dorcas and Reggie found her missing from home they would look in Mary's cottage. When it was discovered they all had fled, Dorcas and Reggie would begin hunting them down. Mary wondered, as she held her baby, what could have happened in only a few months to drive Dorcas from a haughty snob to the verge of cannibalism.

Mary actually slept with the child on her chest, and Edward and Jack dozed next to her. Only Cassie was awake, as she listened for the sounds of her approaching brother through the howl of the wind and the hiss of the lantern. It was fairly comfortable under the blanket with the warmth of their breath and the heat from the lantern, but the deck under them was cold like stone, and it seeped into their bones.

The crack of a musket or pistol woke Mary, and she stared at Cassie who had heard it too. Mary scrambled to get herself done back up, and as she stood she realized her clothes were now hanging on her from where she had loosened them as much as possible while she was still pregnant. She had no time to cinch them now, but hurried to wrap the baby in the blanket and furs and to get her, Edward, and Jack inside the canoe and under cover.

They hauled the canoe back onto the ice, using only the shadowy bulk of the island as a guide as they moved slowly up its east side. They dared not light the lantern again, so they would have to travel the whole length of the island before they could turn north to head for the encampment. They would have to do it in the dark, but every step was one farther away from Dorcas and Reggie.

After many stops to rest, they reached the end of the island and there met a piled ridge of ice. The wind was blowing the snow so hard they could only see in patches. Mary and Cassie struggled to get the canoe over the ice pile, but they could not. Mary was spent, and she could also feel that she was passing huge clots of blood. "We will have to stay here for the night. I wanted to get on the other side of the ice pile so the wind would be blocked a bit, but we just can't make it tonight," Mary said, looking wearily at Cassie. She wanted to say that she would feel better if they were out of sight from the island and crazy Dorcas, but she held her tongue. They got the children nestled into the canoe and covered with blankets and some fur. Mary handed both boys the last of the bread she had made, and they nibbled on it as best they could with nothing to drink. It was the only other thing they had to eat except the sides of salt pork Mary had brought with them.

Mary planned that she and Cassie would sleep at either end of the canoe with the boys between their legs. "You get in," she said, holding up the blanket to cover Cassie, "and I will cover you up."

Cassie started to get into the canoe, and then stood back up. "I have to relieve myself," she blurted out.

Mary looked toward her and said, "You will have to go right here next to the canoe; you can't wander off, and we can't have a light to guide you." Cassie nodded, and mustering all the dignity she could, she squatted next to the canoe trying her best to keep her skirts up out of the streaming liquid.

Mary patted her face as she tucked her into the canoe and said again, "Thank you."

Mary started to climb into the canoe, but a movement registered in her peripheral vision within the swirling snow, and she froze. She turned and looked into the dark, and something was moving to the right, something blacker than the darkness. She stared hoping she was mistaken, but again she saw movement. It was something large, but it didn't look like a man, and it was making horrid snarling noises. As she stared into the darkness with her eyes straining to see, Mary wondered if it was some large animal attracted to the blood that was everywhere on her and Cassie. She was staring, still trying to see when she heard a muffled growl right next to her. The thing lunged at her. Mary put up her hands to protect her face and felt its hot jaws filled with a massive tongue and huge teeth. She didn't even have time to warn the others, she just closed her eyes and waited for the fangs to close on her hand, but there was no pain. She gasped and opened her eyes, but even before that she recognized her attacker by its smell alone. It was Grub. He was whining and licking her face at the same time. She hugged him and ran her fingers through his wiry coat, sobbing with relief, "Oh, Grub, it's you. I'm so glad to see you!" Mary stroked him and then carefully pulled back the fur cover on the boys and whispered to Edward and Jack. "Give me the baby, Edward, I have something for you." Edward held up the baby and Grub sniffed her and whined with excitement as Mary took her. "Move over to the side, Grub is here with us. He will keep you warm." Edward gasped and held out his hands. Grub licked his face and climbed into the canoe, circled six or eight times, only stepping on the boys twice, and settled in for the night. Mary shook her head, climbed under her covers, and gently eased down on her back with the infant on her chest. She waited until her body heat warmed up the space a little and then nursed her as best she could. A short while later they both passed out from exhaustion, one from the ordeal of being born, and the other from that of cheating death.

Mary woke once in the night to feed the baby, but she was still exhausted and stiff from lying on her back. She had purposefully put a package on either side of her, so she couldn't roll over in her sleep and crush the tiny child. She shifted her weight now to give her back some relief and then fell back to sleep. When Mary awakened next, she peeked out from under the fur, and the eastern sky was slightly lighter. She was still weak, but much better than she had been last night. She changed the baby as best she could and woke the others. She wanted to get over the ice ridge before daylight.

It took them about fifteen minutes to unload the canoe, and when it was empty they hauled it over the heaved ice then reloaded it again. Mary, her head spinning and dark spots clouding her vision, sat for nearly half an hour once they got the canoe to the other side. Edward insisted he be allowed to help. "Papa told me to help you," he said. Mary agreed to let him walk along and help pull on the ropes attached to the canoe.

They had only cleared the island by about a mile though they had

walked nearly four miles from where the ship was careened. If they could
cover that same distance today, they would be nearly to the shoreline.
Everyone seemed invigorated by the rest. The wind had subsided, so the
sun felt warm on their faces. For the first time Mary thought they just
might make it. Grub bounded ahead, running back and forth across his
tracks from the night before but returning to the family again and again
to make sure they were following. His muzzle and eyebrows were covered
with snow and his huge feet acted like snowshoes as he padded along.
Once they had to stop because the baby was screaming and she looked
blue. When Mary picked her up, she gasped and then howled again.
Mary squatted down by Jack and said again softly, "Jack, you must hold
her loosely, now. Remember, loosely." Jack nodded solemnly. While they
were stopped, she nursed the baby, and then handed her back to Jack,
and he said in his tiny voice, "loosely," but it sounded like "Lucy" when
he said it. They had to stop every eighth of a mile or so for Mary to rest,
and each time, Jack again assured her, "Hold Lucy." Before the morning
was over, they all referred to the baby as Lucy.

By late afternoon, they were close to the shore. About three
hundred yards from where the ice was piled, they sat on the gunwales
of the canoe to rest. Mary was nearly done in, and they still had to get
over the huge slabs of ice piled twenty feet high like blue-green building
bricks at the shoreline. They could easily miss the Ojibwa encampment
and wander a half-mile off course, but Mary kept hearing the crying
of an infant, and whether it was real or fantasy, she had followed the
sound toward shore.

As Mary rested, she heard different noises from the shore and
looked up at the ice ridge there. Dogs of every size, color, and build had
swarmed to the top of the heaved ice and stared at Mary and her small
entourage. They started to bark and howl, and she looked down the row
of dogs terrified at the horror that would ensue when they attacked.
The dogs would tear her and the children apart and then fight over the
scraps. The only evidence for all they had struggled would be a patch
of blood-stained snow. Cassie saw the dogs now, and she stood next to
Mary staring, not even daring to breathe. There had to be at least forty
of them, and suddenly, as if by some signal only they could hear, they
bolted, scrabbling and clawing their way down the ice toward the canoe.
Mary and Cassie both gasped, and at the same time Grub took off toward
the pack to defend them. He would be the first to die. Mary pulled Cassie
closer, and they gathered the children in their arms as she whispered,
"Turn your back. Don't watch them come." Though Cassie took the advice,
Mary found she could not look away herself, and she watched the dogs
close in on Grub. They swarmed around him, howling and yapping, and
then everything changed. The same dogs that had been streaking forward
with fangs exposed and tongues lapping, now eagerly fell, groveling and

whimpering at Grub's feet, exposing their belly and neck areas to him in submission. Mary smiled and started to laugh. Cassie turned and realized too that the dogs were not going to kill them, but that Grub was the king, and these were his people. He had only disappeared in order to find help and was returning for Mary and the children the night she met him on the ice.

The Indian encampment had followed the dogs to see what was going on, and they now topped the ice pile and stared silently at Mary and the others. One old woman made a harsh cry and three men leaped down and hurried toward Mary. They took the canoe from her and Cassie and pulled it back toward the camp. Mary and Cassie followed as best they could through the throng of barking, sniffing dogs who found it necessary to christen the canoe as they hopped along on three legs, spraying it with urine. Mary began to lag and at the command of the same old woman, one of the men carried her. She could hear people greeting her with the phrase "Little Dark Eyes." Cassie clung to Mary's arm, terrified and speechless, as she loped along next to the man carrying Mary.

The tall Ojibwa man carried Mary effortlessly, as if she were a twig, all the way to the ice ridge and into the encampment. Miki came running, shocked at Mary's appearance, asking when she had given birth.
Now that she was safe, Mary started to tremble and her lip quivered as she answered, "Last night. I had her during the storm on that ship that is pulled up on the shore." Mary nodded toward Cassie and said, "She helped me, and then we started walking toward your camp." Miki exchanged glances with old Zagaswe, the eldest of the elders, who had arrived in time to hear Mary's answer.

Zagaswe mumbled something to one of the older men. Then he approached Mary and asked respectfully, "How is it that the woman of the great Captain is brought to this?" He wasn't condescending at all, but he asked it out of concern, knowing that something very bad must have happened for her to leave the island.

"He never came back in the fall, and we..." she shot a glance at Cassie, and then said, "we ran out of food, and things got very bad. May we please stay with you?"

Zagaswe spoke aloud now, "You will stay with us. Our camp is not easy to find, and you could have wandered on the ice and become lost. You were fortunate."

Mary smiled and said, "I kept hearing a baby crying, and I just followed the sound." The Ojibwa all exchanged glances and then Zagaswe turned and barked an order. One of the young girls ran to a nearby lodge and came back with an infant about two months old. As she handed it to Zagaswe, Mary could see the child was not Ojibwa but white.

Zagaswe spoke now, "The child has called you and saved your life, and now you must save hers. She was left with us, but the woman nursing her fell ill and has no milk. You must help her." She handed the baby to Mary who shifted Lucy, so she could take the infant in her other arm. She looked down at the child and gasped. It looked just like Dorcas. Mary and Cassie exchanged glances and then Zagaswe confirmed their suspicions. "You hold the child of Roger Thane." She looked at Cassie and said solemnly, "This child is your blood. You will care for her as well."

"Why isn't she with Stella and Roger?" Cassie blurted out.

"She was born just before they were to travel back to the outpost, and Stella didn't think the child would survive the trip, so she was to stay with us until spring. There is no other woman in the camp that can feed the baby. We have fed the child from our mouths what we eat, but she is wasting. She would have died in another week, but now you have come and can feed her." Mary nodded and looked carefully at both infants. Lucy was born only last night, but she looked stronger and fuller faced than Stella's baby even though she was only half her size.

"What is she called?" Mary asked, holding the babies tighter.

Zagaswe smiled and said, "She is Rose."

Mary, Cassie, and the boys were led to a lodge that was vacated for them. It had been one of two lodges for the adolescent boys in the camp, and they simply huddled up into one lodge and gave the other to Mary and her family. They left piles of fur in the lodge to sleep on, and Mary and the others collapsed on them and sighed with relief. They were unwashed, their hair like haystacks, and Mary was still crusted with the blood of delivering Lucy, but they were safe and alive and, for now at least, that was all that mattered. Cassie reached out her bloodstained hands to Mary, and they held each other tightly.

CHAPTER 18

JORDAN LADYSMITH tossed and sweated in his bunk like a man burning with fever even though the cabin was nearly freezing. Since he had learned her identity, Mary had abandoned his dreams, almost as though she had only been interested in the quest for him to find her. Since he was a boy, she had called to him often across both time and space. He had dreamed of her when he was ten thousand miles from home. She had been absent of late, so he was unprepared when she came to him tonight.

This dream though was not like the others. In this one Mary was terrified, and he saw her raise a bloody hand to push her hair back from her face, leaving a red smear on her cheek as she struggled with something. She looked straight at him in the dream, desperately pleading and then vanished. Jordan sat up gasping and covered in sweat. He rolled out of his bunk and began to pace. He didn't care how he was going to get there, but he was going to help Mary. He grabbed a satchel and began to pack.

Richard had been able to get the *Lorraine* to Welland. East of there the river was frozen, and the ships had anchored in the mouths of steams that fed into the St. Lawrence. The ice would be thinner there. The open lakes were covered with ice. Richard and Jordan were told that all the horses in the area had been slaughtered. Due to the unusual summer, there was no grain to feed the animals through the winter. If they wanted to get to Mackinac before the ice thawed in spring, they would have to walk more than five hundred miles.

Just as Jordan finished his packing, the door flew open with Richard standing there in only his shirt and britches. Before Jordan could speak, Richard said, "I had the most horrible dream that something is wrong with Mary. I'm leaving the ship in your command."

"No, please. I saw her in my dreams too. She needs help. I'm coming with you. Orkney and Bradshaw can take care of things," Jordan said, referring to the other officers on the ship. Richard nodded once and then left to pack. He spoke briefly to the officers. The men had more than enough food, most of it actually better than what was available in Welland. Passing the winter on the ship was not the worst thing that could happen to them.

Richard and Jordan packed and set off at first light to find a guide to take them to Mackinac. They were turned away without success most of the morning, but finally lighted on a man named Reuben Hastings. He was a jolly man with the brightest red hair Richard had ever seen. Hastings looked them over from head to toe and then said, "Well, I don't think you can walk that far, but I'll take you if the price is right."

Richard didn't even wait to bargain, but said flatly, "I will give you two hundred dollars if you will take us to Mackinac Island." Hastings's eyes lit up, and a grin broke across his wide face. "You're gonna need some gear if you plan to walk that far," he said. "First off, you need something different on your feet. These Indians living here know a thing or two about footwear. You need fur moccasins, and they should be muskrat. I know where I can get you a pair for, shall we say, twenty dollars each?" Hastings arched his red eyebrows. Richard nodded and handed over the money.

Two hours later they were loaded with muskets, heavy clothes, and food. Richard brought along a compass, his sextant, and the spyglass for no other reason than he had never traveled without them. They were heavy, but he packed them all. They set out that afternoon, and Hastings began asking friendly questions before they had gone half a mile. Richard answered them as best he could, but he was already winded. Both he and Jordan had not been completely well since the whole ordeal with Owen had begun. He hoped they got to Mackinac quickly, or both he and Jordan would be suffering from scurvy. Once on the island, they had barrels of pickled cabbage, cider vinegar, and cucumber pickles, so they could cure themselves if they were weakened.

They made only ten miles that first day before it grew dark and they had to stop. They didn't bring a tent with them, but just rolled up in blankets and covered themselves with their fur coats. Both Richard and Jordan were surprised at how warm they were as they slept with their feet to the fire. They woke before dawn, and Reuben already had a pot going for tea. He broke some bread into chunks and handed them each a fistful of cheese. The bread was stale and the cheese stank, but they ate it gratefully.

They walked until noon, or at least what Reuben Hastings called noon. Richard could have gotten out the sextant to check for sure, but it really didn't matter. They ate the remainder of the cheese and some bread washed down with lukewarm tea that they had not taken the time to heat to a boil. The noon meal had taken all of ten minutes. By the time they stopped at dusk to build a fire, Richard and Jordan were bushed. Reuben had some peas and salt pork in a bag and he boiled them in a small pot on the fire. When the peas were mostly cooked, the three men simply squatted around it and dug in with their spoons. They drank some tea Reuben had sweetened with sugar almost to syrup, and then they curled into their blankets and slept.

They woke at dawn to the smell of boiled salt pork being fried, and when it was done they speared it with their knives and ate it leaning over the pan. They gnawed on more of the tough bread and after drinking more of the sickeningly sweet tea, they headed out for the day's march. In this way they walked for the next several weeks. They saw no one and very little game. Once, Reuben shot a rabbit, but it was old and tough and stuck in their teeth even though they simmered it all night in a pot on the fire.

Richard and Jordan were beginning to feel the effects of scurvy, and even Reuben said his teeth hurt, but they kept walking just as before. That afternoon Richard stumbled and fell on his side, and though he wasn't hurt, he wasn't sure about the compass and sextant. When they stopped that evening, he took them out and checked them over. When he was putting them back in place, he accidentally joggled the bag of gold coins he had sewn in his jacket and they jingled merrily. Nothing makes quite the sound of gold coins tinkling, and Reuben caught the sound and jerked his head to hear better. Richard said nothing and bedded down after dinner. Rueben bid them good night, but he sat up looking at Richard's wide back thoughtfully for a long time after Richard had fallen asleep.

It started snowing around midnight and by dawn it was a blizzard. The men could do nothing but build a shelter with some boughs and their fur blankets and hunker down until the storm blew itself out. As they sat nearly elbow-to-elbow, they talked of things they had done and places they had been. Reuben had been all over the northeast and way into eastern Canada. They discussed Richard's fears of what might have happened to his family and they discussed family itself. Reuben had never been married. "I ain't never in one place long enough to meet no women," he said with a tinge of sadness to his voice. Jordan related how Richard had sent him to school, signed him on as a midshipman, and then put him aboard his private fleet when he was eighteen. Richard, who felt he had already exposed enough about himself, just sat and listened. They finally settled into sleep and when they awoke on the third day, the storm had ended.

The ground was covered with nearly two and a half feet of snow on the level, and there were drifts everywhere six or eight feet high. Reuben directed them to take the snowshoes they had lashed as a base for their packs and strap them on. Richard thought it would be a relief to wear the snowshoes instead of carrying them. The snowshoes were about four feet and shaped like an elongated skillet. They were made of bent elm and the netting across them, which supported the boot straps, was made of dried buckskin. It took Richard and Jordan about twenty minutes to get used to walking in the snowshoes and though the wide-legged stance tired them out quicker than plain walking, hauling themselves through mid-thigh snow would have exhausted them in no time.

Richard and Jordan could stand on deck for hours in horrible, wet and stormy weather, and they could move around a pitching deck with ease, but the relentless marching day after day was taking its toll on them.

They came to a small lake. Reuben checked the ice near the edge, and it was strong enough to hold a man. They started out without any trouble, but as they neared the far shore none of them saw the little stream that flowed into the lake under a fallen log. There the ice was much thinner, and they unknowingly were heading straight for it. Reuben went first without any trouble, though there was a little snapping and cracking, and he was followed by Jordan. Richard came last, plodding along looking down at the tracks in front of him rather than ahead. Suddenly the track in front of him turned dark with slush, and he was just about to call out to Reuben and Jordan when the ice collapsed in a circle around him, and he fell through into the water below. He held his breath waiting for the icy water to close over his head, but instead stopped with it just below his armpits. He could feel his snowshoes on the bottom, and, mercifully, he had fallen through on the little sandbar created by the stream where the lake was shallow. His pack had been torn off when he went through the ice and the surge of water as he fell sucked the pack under. That was the last he saw of it. All his extra clothes and one-third of their food was gone. Reuben and Jordan turned and stared at him with just his arms and head sticking out from the ice, but at a shout from Reuben, Jordan dropped flat on the ice and lay there and watched as Reuben crawled carefully toward Richard, who was struggling to pull himself free. The ice kept breaking under his weight and he could not get his legs up out of the water while they were strapped to the snowshoes. He finally stood on one foot and reached down and took off the other snowshoe and placed it on the ice. He got out of the other one and then crawled onto them flat to distribute his weight more evenly. In this position he managed to get to shore and lay there breathing heavily. Reuben and Jordan built a fire while Richard stripped. The temperature was just above freezing, and he stood shivering in his own fur blanket while standing on Jordan's blanket. Mercifully, Jordan had been carrying them both. It would take hours for his clothes to dry, but they had no choice. Richard would freeze to death if they didn't at least get the wool clothes half dry. Wool is warm even when damp, but it cannot be dripping wet and still hold heat. Richard unloaded the pockets of his fur coat and placed the contents on the blanket next to his feet, which were now encased in Jordan's spare socks. Reuben watched as Richard frowned at the compass which was clearly broken. He took out the sextant which appeared fine and the spyglass from which a thin line of water poured as he tipped it. The glass also appeared to be ruined, but perhaps when dried it would be fine.

Reuben made the decision they would stay where they were for the night and they went about making dinner with what they had left. They had eaten a third of their food, Richard had lost a third, and they had a third left, yet they were not quite halfway to Mackinac. Reuben sat looking at them trying to decide what to do, and then he said they had to move more quickly. They would only take what was absolutely necessary. Jordan unloaded his pack and took only his knife, blankets, and what food he was carrying. Richard only had what was inside his fur coat, but he also left the sextant he had had since Lorraine gave it to him when he earned his captaincy and the spyglass. With a resigned smile he dumped out the bag of gold onto the packed snow, and nearly two hundred dollars clinked merrily in the frigid air. He also tossed down the beautiful emerald necklace and earbobs which had been made for Mary. He tossed the jewelry down now, saying, "They won't do me or her a damn bit of good if I am frozen stiff, will they?" He looked from Reuben to Jordan and then turned his steaming clothes over so the other side could dry a bit near the fire. After dinner he put on the still-damp clothes and climbed into his blanket and under his fur. He could not remember a time when he felt more miserable.

They travelled for five more days, not making the miles they needed to get there before their food ran out, but Reuben assured them they were getting into territory where they would find more game. They ate some salt pork and a few stale biscuits Jordan forgot he had, and then they turned in for the night.

Richard woke the next morning before Jordan. The camp was quiet and Reuben was nowhere to be found. Richard stood and looked around, thinking Reuben had gone to get more wood, but there was still a fair pile next to the fire which they had gathered last night. It had snowed overnight, the fire was very low, so Richard moved toward it to build it up when he noticed a carved piece of wood sticking out from the ashes. He picked it up and his throat tightened. It was what remained of a snowshoe. "Jordan, get up!" Richard kicked him and began looking frantically for the snowshoes. Jordan sat up rubbing his eyes, but he was already fully awake, something that a sailor learns to do very quickly. The snowshoes were gone. Richard scratched through the ashes and came up with the buckles that had fastened their boots to the shoes. They exchanged glances and Richard bellowed, "That bastard! He has left us here with no snowshoes, and..." he looked around, "no food or even a musket." He looked hard at Jordan and added, "He left us here to die."

They looked around the camp, and it appeared Reuben had taken everything with him that would be of any value. Jordan had his knife but only because it was inside his coat while he slept. Jordan's pack had been burned along with the snowshoes in the fire. A cold, strangled feeling settled in Richard's stomach and he nearly panicked. They were hundreds of miles from anywhere and the snow was so deep they would flounder and die of exhaustion within a few miles. They had nothing to eat, and except for a knife, nothing to use to get food. The flint and striker had been in Jordan's pack, but no matter how they scraped through the ashes, they could not find them. Richard said, "We can't stay here. If we do, we die. I don't think our chances are much better moving on, but I am not going to just wait for death. I didn't fight my way through a dozen battles and hunker down through a hundred storms at sea to sit here and freeze to death now. Gather up your stuff. We're leaving." Jordan nodded and began to roll up his fur blanket. They took a good supply of pine knots from those they had collected the night before and kept the fire burning on one at a time like a torch so that when they settled for the night they could light a fire. They found where Hastings had left camp and followed his tracks, but about an hour into tracking him, Richard noted a change in the air and mentioned it to Jordan. "The weather is changing. Can't you feel it, a close, pressing feeling like before a thunderstorm?" Jordan nodded and just then a wind whispering high in the spruce trees changed to a plaintive moan. They continued on, but within an hour it started to snow in huge, accumulated flakes the size of a half eagle coin. It was weird and beautiful and would have been wonderful if they were by a cozy fire looking out the window at them. Within another hour the snow turned to a cold rain and Richard and Jordan looked for a place to take shelter. If they got soaked through, they would be even more likely to die. They walked about a hundred yards farther and found where a large spruce tree had toppled over onto a stone bluff no more than three or four feet high. It fell in such a way that there was a dry space under the tree trunk, and if they could get some boughs to cover the places where the bluff and the trunk did not quite meet, they would be relatively snug. They could build their fire under the tree as long as they kept it small, and then hang more boughs over the front of the tree to make a lean-to of sorts.

Without an axe or anything to cut the boughs except a knife, it was slow work. After they completed their little hut, they spent the rest of the time until dark gathering wood. As they sealed themselves into their little nest, leaving a small hole where the smoke could seep out, it was raining fairly hard. Mercifully, the rain ran down behind them off the little bluff and not across where they were sitting. They huddled together like abandoned orphans wondering if they could risk sleeping.

It was still raining hard when they woke in the morning. The day turned colder and freezing rain formed a crust on the snow that would hold their weight. Dry wood was becoming more and more scarce around their camp and they settled in with what they hoped would be enough, once again cold and hungry. They stared at the fire for a long time and Richard spoke first, "God, I miss my family." Jordan smiled and nodded. He had no family living since his grandfather and the last of the Puppets died, and he almost told Richard about the dreams he had about Mary. It was a secret that might die with him in the next few days, but one he swore he would take with him to the grave.

They woke the next morning and stretched their stiff legs and backs. The rain had stopped and when they poked their heads out from their shelter they saw the world around them had been transformed to a forest of glass which gleamed in the sun. Everywhere they looked, every branch, every limb, every weed sticking out of the snow was coated with clear ice to a thickness of about half an inch. It was cold and still, but the sun was out, and at least it had stopped storming. The pine trees all around drooped under the tremendous weight of their ice-coated branches and they looked very much like a parasol that was collapsed but not yet closed tight. Richard moved from the shelter and gingerly stepped onto the snow. The coating of ice gave under him only an inch or so. He took a few more steps and then turned to Jordan, smiling. "Look, Jory, if it will hold my weight, then you certainly can walk on it." Jordan tried and was able to walk easily as well.

They agreed that backtracking Reuben Hastings was a waste of energy. "We need to turn west and try to hit the shoreline of Lake Huron. Maybe we will come across an encampment. Even if we're captured, they'll feed us. An Indian might kill you, but they would never think to let you starve," Richard said, smiling sardonically.

They set off hungrier than either of them had ever been in their lives and walked due west without speaking. A gentle breeze came up, and as it moved the tree branches, the ice broke off and fell to the crusted snow where it shattered with the same sound as glass. They had not had food now in nearly a week, and each felt stabbing pains in their abdomen as they walked with their hoods pulled up over their heads to protect them from the plummeting ice. They transferred their torch to new knots as they burned down and, in this way, bedded down again for the night.

The next day, after walking about three hours, they came across where the snow was trampled and covered with tracks and blood. They followed the trail and came across the carcass of a deer that had been killed and mostly eaten by coyotes. There was quite a bit of meat clinging to the bones and they picked up as many of the bones as they could carry and took them along until they stopped for noon. Neither said anything, but they had both listened carefully for the sound of the wild dogs that would be tracking them to retrieve the kill they had stolen.

They built a fire at noon and placed the bones over it. They didn't wait for the meat to really cook through, and as soon as it began to sizzle they stripped it with their teeth and even cracked the bones open for the marrow. Richard looked at Jordan and then back at the bone he was gnawing and said half-kidding, "Jesus, I look like Grub eating this, but it tastes about as good as anything I have ever had." Jordan nodded but didn't answer as he sucked loudly on a narrow foreleg bone.

They reached the shore two days later, and found they were farther north than they thought, almost to Georgian Bay. They headed west across the Lake Huron ice toward Cockburn Island. The island's name on the map had provided endless mirth, but now they looked forward to it eagerly. Mackinac Island was due west from Cockburn across Lake Huron and only about fifty miles away. A few days more and they could see Bois Blanc Island, and though they had veered south nearly five miles, they were very close. The memory of falling through the ice was still very fresh in Richard's mind, but they were so close now he blocked it out. They spent the night on Bois Blanc which is much larger than Mackinac, and walked nearly the full length of it the next day before starting out for Mackinac three miles away.

As they got closer, Richard recognized structures on the island, but his stomach tightened the closer he got. They staggered across the ice the last half-mile, but before he got there, Richard knew something was wrong. There was no smoke from any of the chimneys and snow had drifted inside his front door which stood wide open.

He looked at Jordan and shook his head and then waded through the snow into the house. It was nearly dark, and they were exhausted, so Richard suggested they spend the night there and then figure out what to do the next morning. They were both very weak, but Jordan started to shovel snow out of the front door so they could close it while Richard got a fire going. He then looked through the house for clues. Edward's bed was unmade which was odd, because Mary was a stickler for beds being made first thing in the morning. Wrennet's bed was made, but it was piled with crates that appeared to contain clothing Jack had outgrown. He then walked to the room he shared with Mary and stared. It was a shambles with clothing strewn over the floor and the bed not only unmade but stripped. Jack's crib was overturned and all of its bedding gone. The large, fur rug in their bedroom and the one in the main room were also missing. He returned to the center of the house. Jordan, exhausted from shoveling, collapsed into a chair and put his head on the table as he gasped for breath.

When they had both rested, they scoured the house looking for anything to eat. "I cannot believe there is absolutely no food in this house. What the hell happened here?" Richard asked. He took a lamp and went next door to the Deems's cottage, but came stumbling back moments later and stared at Jordan, his face pale and drawn.

"What is it? Richard, what's wrong?" Jordan said, jumping to his feet.

"Come with me," Richard said and walked back out the door without another word. They followed in the tracks Richard had made earlier and slipped inside the darkened Deems's cottage. "Get some lamps going. We need light to see what happened here." Richard moved forward in the dark house and then added, "And we have to make sure Mary isn't here." Jordan lit the lamp near the door and picked it up and walked to the edge of the kitchen where he stopped next to Richard and stared.

There was evidence of a pistol having been loaded and fired several times, and the bear skin rugs from Richard's house were there, and it appeared someone had actually tried to eat the hide, but even worse than the shooting damage or the gnawed hides was Dorcas Deems lying flat on her back, her arms frozen as they clutched at her throat. Her frozen eyes bulged and her skin was a horrid blue-gray. They concluded from the overturned chair that she had been eating something and apparently choked on it and then fell onto the floor. About ten feet away was Reggie's body. He had been shot in the upper chest, and one of his lower legs was missing. "Did a wild animal do this to him?" Jordan asked.

"Look at the plate," Richard said, flatly indicating now what had driven him from the room earlier. Jordan brought the lamp closer and then gasped. On the plate was the cooked and mostly eaten missing leg.

"Jesus!" Jordan said, backing away.

"If she would kill her own son and eat him, then what would she do to my family?" Richard said, and Jordan didn't answer, but he began searching frantically around the house. Richard searched too, but finally called to him, "Jordan, they are not in this house, or if they are, they are not alive. Let's check the sloop."

They waded through the snow which was not iced over as hard as it had been farther east, but as they got around to the lee of the island where the little ship was careened, it was easier going. They rested, leaning against the hull and then climbed through an open gun port. There was some snow on the floor inside, but only right near the port. Richard saw a bundle of cloth and some crates ahead and hurried over. The cloth was stained with blood and there was a clearly defined handprint on the deck, also in blood. It was small, and Jordan asked, "Is that Edward's handprint?"

Richard shook his head, and said, "It's small, but not that small. I think it's Mary's." He walked to a bundle near the companionway stairs and picked it up. It was heavy like something was inside. He set it down on the deck and gingerly unwrapped it, finding thicker blood with each layer. His heart was racing as he tugged the bloody, frozen cloth away. He finally reached the center and said, "What in God's name is this?" He tilted it toward Jordan's light, and they both stared at the thing in Richard's hands. It was about the size of a small loaf of bread and obviously some kind of organ, though whether it was human or animal they did not know. Richard looked up at Jordan and said, "In the aftermath of a battle, I have seen about every part of a man that can come out and be strewn on the deck, but I have never seen anything like this." They both looked down at the bluish-purple organ covered in a whitish membrane, almost like a leg of lamb, and Richard said, "Look at that whitish extension there, almost like a windpipe."

Jordan touched Richard's arm and said with recognition, "It's an afterbirth. I saw one once when your Aunt Grace took me with her to a farm outside Boston." Richard wrapped it back up and set it gingerly aside then said, "Come on, let's check the rest of the ship." Richard headed for the forward hold, but they were so weak they couldn't get it open. Richard said panting, "Let's check my cabin."

In the cabin they found a tin of biscuits with four left, but they could not bite into them with their weak teeth and jaws tender from over six weeks without vegetables or fruit of any kind. They sat sucking on the stale, frozen biscuits. When they finished, Richard said, "Let's go back to the house. It's going to take us a while to get there, so we better get started."

Richard had walked that path from the house to the ship dozens of times, and it usually took no more than five minutes, but tonight it took them nearly thirty minutes to stumble and tug at each other to get back up the hill. They wrapped themselves in blankets from Wrennet's bed, got as close to the fire as they could and collapsed. Richard woke once in the night and was so tired his tongue was actually hanging out. He had to work it a bit to get some saliva going before he was able to swallow. The only light in the room was the red glow from the seams in the stove. He got up and stoked the stove and then glanced at Jordan sleeping a few feet away. The gloom only tended to accentuate his sunken eyes and pale skin, the telltale signs of scurvy, and Richard was certain he didn't look much better himself.

They awoke the next morning, and Richard stoked the fire. He leaned against the mantle to calm his spinning head and to clear his vision. He looked up at the ceiling and then at the wall behind the mantle. At first he thought it was the trick of the spots dancing before his eyes, but then he realized there was writing penciled on the wall near the mantle. The message said in small, block letters, "Gone where Little Dark Eyes are welcome."

He turned to Jordan and said, "I know where they might be. Come on!" They bundled into their coats and headed out the door, making sure this time it was closed tightly behind them.

"Should we bury the others?" Jordan asked, looking at the Deems's house.

"They aren't going anywhere, and we couldn't bury them until spring." Richard said as he cut around the back of the house. He noted, but gave it no further thought then, that the canoe that usually hung there upside down on its rack was missing.

They set their sights on the Ojibwa encampment and started off across the ice. It was only about four miles, but they were so weak they could only shuffle along, resting frequently and making barely half a mile an hour. About halfway Jordan's blistered feet began to leak blood through the soles of his moccasins, but he was so tired and had so much pain in other places, he didn't notice.

CHAPTER 19

THE OLD OJIBWA WOMAN was named Iskode, which means "the fire," but over the years she came to be known as Zagaswe, which means literally "she who smokes." Zagaswe earned her name because she constantly sat in the smoke of a fire while working on animal pelts. The fire kept her warm, and the smoke drove away the biting insects.

Zagaswe now sat up from her bench where she was trimming the fat from the skin-side of a beaver pelt, scraping it clean with a knife that looked almost like a bell hook. Zagaswe scraped the bits of fat off the pelt and popped them into her mouth like jerked meat. A couple of ragged-looking dogs were at her feet and occasionally they would get a scrap or two from her work. Zagaswe suddenly looked up, hearing the sound of men's voices speaking English.

Richard and Jordan stood on the ice staring ahead, wondering if they should go into St. Ignace for help or straight into the encampment. Richard feared they had only enough strength left to make it to one or the other. Jordan was suffering the most, and at times this morning he had been staggering. Richard stomped his feet to try to get some circulation going, and at the noise Jordan looked up and then out across the ice pointing to three men who appeared to be Ojibwa. Richard looked at Jordan knowing that with the exception of a knife, they had no weapons. The Ojibwa had never been anything but kind, but times change and so do people, and after dealing with Hastings, Richard was a little less trusting. "Even if they knew how weak we are, they would not have sent only three men if they intended to harm us. Come on, let's go." He started forward and Jordan stumbled beside him. He reached over and put Jordan's arm across his shoulder.

Whatever it is, friend or foe, the Ojibwa always let it expend its own energy first. The three men only moved forward when they saw that Jordan was about to collapse about a hundred yards from shore.

The eldest Ojibwa spoke first. "You are Holmwood. You are Captain, and you do not look well."

Richard smiled weakly. "We are indeed unwell, but I am looking for my wife and family, and we have walked a very long way. They were on the island," he said, gesturing back toward the island and calling it by its native name.

The elder Ojibwa smiled and said, "Little Dark Eyes. Yes, she came to us from the ice in a canoe."

"She is with you now?" Richard gasped.

"She is, yes, and she is well," he said.

Richard sobbed once, then asked, not daring to hope, "And my children?"

"They are all well," the old Ojibwa smiled, and then added, "You will walk into the camp now?"

"Yes, yes! Just take us there," Richard cinched Jordan higher across his shoulder and started forward. The Ojibwa men would not touch Jordan, though they were sympathetic to his illness. If he had been Ojibwa they would have helped him, or if he was alone, but they would not humiliate him in front of his own.

Richard and Jordan made quite a bit of noise getting over the top of the ice mounds and sliding down the jumbled blocks on the other side. First the dogs came charging and then people were coming out of their lodges to investigate the barking. Old Zagaswe, whose eyes were still sharp as a falcon's, recognized Richard as he came into the edge of the camp.

Mary was almost finished nursing Rose in her lodge while baby Lucy slept in a fur-lined basket next to the fire pit. Zagaswe entered and smiled her toothless grin, motioning for Mary to come to her. "Why are all the dogs barking?" Mary asked, frightened.

"This is good barking. You come, come with me. It is something wonderful," Zagaswe said and poked at Mary to make her move faster.

"Did they get meat, large meat?" Mary asked, thinking that would be wonderful as they had eaten the carcasses of the small animals the men trapped. She would love to have some venison. Zagaswe took Rose from her arms and motioned for her to button herself up, and then she shoved her out into the late afternoon sunlight. Two Ojibwa women had now taken hold of Jordan who had slowly followed Richard into camp. Richard was close by when Mary burst out of her lodge, shielding her eyes from the glare. She looked around and then stopped in her tracks and stared. For a moment she didn't recognize Richard, but when she did, she ran the short distance to him and threw herself into his arms. She pulled back sobbing and looked at him again to make sure he was there, "Oh, I thought I would never see you again."

Richard buried his face down into where Mary was wrapped in his arms and said, "Mary! Oh, Mary." He could say no more for nearly a minute, and then he pulled back and took her face in his hands and said, "My God, are you all right?" She nodded, and he said gasping for breath,

"The boys, are they both all right?" Mary nodded yes, and he crushed her to him again.

The women helping Jordan had now caught up to them, and Old Zagaswe came out of Mary's lodge, handed Rose to another woman, and then walked to Richard and Jordan. She looked at their sunken eyes and pushed their lips back to examine their teeth like they were horses. Zagaswe called to three women standing about twenty yards away, and they approached and listened to her and then scurried away to follow her instructions. She motioned for the men to follow her and then said to Mary, "These men need berry water and rest. I will bring your man back, and you may keep him in your lodge to sleep, but the other stays with me. Hurry, they will not walk much further."

Zagaswe led them to a small lodge, and Mary walked along holding Richard's hand, which he squeezed every so often smiling weakly at her to make sure she was still there. Zagaswe lifted the door flap and entered a low, dark room with a fire pit and a few piles of fur on a raised table almost like a dais. "There," she motioned to the furs and Jordan climbed onto the table and collapsed into them. He stayed there on his back with his eyes closed. Richard eased himself onto the table in a sitting position and when Zagaswe pushed him by the forehead he leaned back but was still rigid and tense. Mary whispered for him to relax. Zagaswe looked up as the three women returned, and she spoke to them in Ojibwa. They hesitated for a moment and then set about stripping the clothing off the two men on the table. Richard struggled and Mary took over telling him it was for the best. Once both men were naked, they were rubbed with snow and then roughly dried off. Richard struggled again, but once they dried him and tucked him into soft furs, he settled down.

One woman approached Richard with a bowl and motioned for him to drink. The other two women got behind his shoulders and propped him up. He bent to drink from the bowl, but turned his head away at the smell. Mary snapped at him gently, "Drink it Richard, it will help you. I had to drink it too when I got here." He gagged fiercely but kept it down. Mary wiped the liquid off his beard where it had spilled and then kissed his cheek.

"What was that?" he whispered.

"It's liquid pemmican," Mary whispered back, referring to the staple of the Ojibwa survival diet: pulverized dried venison, cranberries, and blueberries pounded to a powder, and then heavily laced with fat. In liquid form it never really dissolves but sits on top of the water like cocoa when it is first mixed. The liquid underneath simply helps wash down the powder. Richard nodded, understanding and closed his eyes. Mary looked over to where the three women were trying to get Jordan to drink his dose of pemmican, but they were having no luck. Mary went to them, took the bowl, and held it to his lips, saying softly, "Jordan, it's Mary

Holmwood. Drink this please. It will help you. It is just meat and berries. Please drink it down." Jordan's eyes snapped open and locked on Mary. He reached and put his hands on each side of her face and she urged him again. He nodded this time and gagged the liquid down, holding her wrists as he did so.

The three women built up the fire and put small birch branches on top, and the lodge began to fill with a fine, silky smoke. The two women were again scrubbing Richard and Jordan with handfuls of snow, and Mary shuddered thinking how it must feel. Zagaswe spoke to her now. "You go," Zagaswe tugged at Mary's arm, "and when we have sweated them, and they have slept, I will send your man to you." Mary nodded, looking over her shoulder at Richard, who craned his neck to see her as she was pushed firmly from the lodge.

The rest of the day when Mary wasn't taking care of the children she was pacing in front of the lodge where Zagaswe had Richard and Jordan under her care. The sky had that odd, gray-pink of winter along the western horizon that proclaims dusk, prompting Mary to return to her lodge to settle the children for the night.

At first Mary had been overly protective of them, but when she learned she was insulting the others in the camp by not trusting them with her children, she let them go to be raised by the entire camp as is the Ojibwa way. She now fed them a sort of a stew that had been simmering on the edge of the fire all day, and the boys squatted by the fire and ate quickly, wiping their mouths on their sleeves. Mary had given up trying to maintain any sort of table manners. She figured there was no sense when there wasn't even a table. Cassie ate quickly and then returned to the lodge where she had been sleeping for the last week or so with some girls her age. Cassie and the girls worked and conspired happily together, but Cassie returned several times a day to check on Mary. After she fed both infants, Mary quickly downed her stew while it was still practically scalding. She looked across at Jack who was fighting to stay awake as he leaned against Edward. They played so hard all day that they usually passed out after dinner. Mary tucked them in and almost had them both asleep when the door flap moved aside and two men helped Richard to a pile of furs near the fire. They mumbled something to Richard that Mary couldn't catch and then nodded to her and left. Richard sat on the furs and looked at them, smiling weakly. His hair was matted where he had sweated so heavily, and his color looked better, but the dark rings under his sunken eyes were still heavy. "Papa!" Edward jumped up from his pallet and ran to Richard, trying to climb in his lap. Mary stopped him and told him to sit right next to him, but not to climb on him. Richard hugged him tight, and then with a wink at Mary, pulled Edward onto his lap and held him close. He then looked over at Jack, who sat staring back at him.

"Hello, Jack," Richard said softly, but Jack leaped up and ran to Mary, hiding in her skirts. She picked him up and then sat next to Richard, so Jack could see him from a safe distance. "He doesn't even know me, does he?" Richard said.

"He will soon enough," Mary said, patting his arm. Jack stared with his huge, green eyes, trying to figure out who he was and why Edward wasn't afraid of him. Richard reached out gingerly and touched his cheek. Jack smiled. Edward told him it was all right, and Jack took the plump finger he had been furiously sucking out of his mouth and touched his father's face with it.

Mary let them sit for a few more minutes and then she got the boys back into their furs. Edward protested he would never sleep, but was soon snoring next to Jack.

Mary turned back to Richard to speak to him, but he was asleep as well, and she tucked him into the furs. She was rising to add more wood to the fire when Zagaswe appeared in the door. She had not made a sound as she entered and startled Mary. The old woman motioned, and when Mary came nearer, she said, "You must feed him as you would an infant. He will not want to, men are proud, but he must if he is to get strong. You will do this in the night when you wake to feed the babies." Mary nodded solemnly, and Zagaswe turned to leave, then added, "You must do the same for the other man too." Mary stared after her and then wrapped herself in her coat and sat next to Richard where she could see him in the weak light thrown from the fire.

She had still not slept when Rose woke crying to be fed. Richard jolted at the sound and opened his eyes. He was confused and dizzy. Mary whispered to him, and he relaxed again, but did not take his eyes off her as she moved around taking care of the baby he had not even noticed earlier. "Sleep, Richard. You are safe, and I'm not going anywhere."

"Baby," he gasped, and then closed his eyes and was asleep again in minutes.

Forty minutes later he stirred but did not waken when Lucy started to fuss. Mary fed her and then tucked Lucy back into her basket. She sat next to Richard and leaned close, whispering to wake him. He stirred and opened his eyes. "Richard, you must drink this." He started to shake his head no, dreading another dose of the pemmican, but Mary patted his face and opened her blouse. "Richard, drink this milk to get strong," Mary said, settling close to him and cradling his head.

He shook his head and struggled and then as he realized what she meant he turned his head away and whispered, "That's for the baby."

"You will be my baby tonight. Just drink it, so you can get strong," Mary whispered, kissing his cheek as she pushed her breast toward his face. "Drink it, please." Richard looked at her a long time and then opened his mouth and accepted the nourishment she offered. It hurt his teeth and gums to extract the milk, but more painful was the humiliation of being reduced to such a state. A silent tear of shame rolled across his cheek and disappeared into his beard as he continued to draw her strength into his throat.

Richard was able to nurse only about five minutes before he fell asleep again, and this time Mary didn't try to wake him. Instead she covered him well and went to find Zagaswe so she could provide the same sustenance for Jordan.

When Mary arrived at the medicine lodge, Zagaswe was sitting on the low dais next to Jordan. He had not responded as well to the pemmican, and he did not even open his eyes though he did drink the breast milk Mary offered him, simply drawing on the childhood instinct for nourishment and succor. In a way, Mary was glad he had not known she was there; it was awful enough that she knew it herself.

The next morning the dark circles under Richard's eyes were lighter. He drank some liquid made from steeped cranberry bark which Zagaswe said he must have. Richard claimed it tasted somewhat like limes, so it must be good for him. He immediately fell back to sleep, but was able a few hours later to drink some broth with tiny bits of muskrat meat and wild garlic. The broth brought a smile to his face, but it sapped his strength to sit up and drink it, and he fell back to sleep right after eating it. Mary checked with Zagaswe, and she assured her sleep was the best thing for him. Richard must have understood that as well because he slept most of the next two days.

When he finally awakened the morning of the third day, the first thing he noticed was that his gums and teeth no longer hurt. The human body responds amazingly quickly to proper nourishment. Richard had seen scurvy before and had even had mild cases of it, but to see it at such an advanced stage horrified him. As they walked day after day, he had constantly pushed at his teeth with his tongue, absolutely certain they would soon be falling out. He had heard that wounds which had healed years before, especially blade wounds, sometimes opened fully in the last stages of scurvy. With this in mind, he had noted an old sword wound on his side which had reddened again though it was years old. Zagaswe had noticed it as well when she stripped him in the medicine lodge, and she had applied a poultice of willow bark and sphagnum moss which had stung like the devil when she first pressed it to his side.

Richard sat up now and looked around the tiny lodge. Slowly he got to his feet, which still ached, and though his head felt swimmy, he was able to walk the few steps to the door flap. He stepped out into the sunshine reflected off the snow, and it nearly blinded him. He stood clinging to the door flap of the lodge, shielding his eyes, and when he could see again, Mary was standing in front of him, grinning. He smiled and touched her face and then noticed the child in her arms. "I didn't know."

Mary smiled back and said, "I didn't know when you left either."

"You had the child in the sloop, didn't you?" he asked, already knowing the answer. Mary nodded, led him back into the lodge, and sat down on the furs with the child in her arms. Richard sat next to her and gently took the baby and uncovered the face. He looked at the wide mouth and the blond fuzz on her head and smiled weakly. "I guess sometimes they don't look like either parent," he said, moving the child up and down, and then he added, "but what a hefty one."

Mary looked at him and then understood and said, chuckling, "No. This is not our baby. This is Stella's baby, Rose."

Richard mumbled, "Oh, thank God," but then he added, confused, "but I don't understand, didn't you have a . . . on the sloop we found." Mary took Rose from him and put her down in her fur-lined basket. She then picked up Lucy and placed her in Richard's arms saying, "This is our baby."

Richard gingerly pulled down the blanket to expose Lucy's face and peeked at her, "Much better," he said softly. He sat and shifted Lucy in his lap so she was propped against his knees and then smiled, "Born right on the gun deck! A true son of a gun. He nudged Mary with his arm and then turned back to the child and said, "You, my little man, are going to be a great sailor. It's in your blood, and no matter what your worrying mama says, you will love the sea and be a master of it." He turned and grinned at Mary, "Does he have a name?"

Mary smiled wickedly and said, "Lucy."

Richard looked at her and snorted, "Lucy?"

Mary smiled and said, "Richard, the baby is a girl."

"A girl?"

"Is that bad?" Mary asked, almost worried.

"No! Oh, heavens no! I just always threw boys and never even thought of a girl," he leaned down and grinned at the tiny infant, "but what a beauty you are. You look just like your mother, and you will break a dozen hearts." Lucy captured him as she had already captured her brothers, and he grinned at her transfixed. After a few moments Mary took Lucy from him and tucked her back into the basket and placed Rose next to her. Richard watched her and then asked, "Is Lucy a common name in your family?" Mary smiled softly and recited the tale of their crossing on the ice, and how Jack had reassured her he was going to hold "loosely" which became hold "Lucy."

"Those boys were so good on the trip," Mary shook her head remembering. "You would have been proud of them, Richard. They helped me so much, and I feel bad they had to go through it not understanding what was happening." Richard stroked her cheek, and she continued, "I can still see those three children wrapped in one of your greatcoats, sitting on furs, wrapped in more furs with Cassie and me pulling that canoe over the ice. It was horrible, and several times I didn't think we would make it." Mary recited her tale and then added, "Cassie was so much help to me that I had to take back anything unkind that I ever said or thought about her. I truly would not have made it without her help. She even helped deliver Lucy." Mary looked at Richard seriously and said, "She's not a bad person, Richard. It was Dorcas that made her seem that way."

Richard nodded, "She is welcome to stay with us as long as she likes." He touched her face and then said aloud, "Mary, you are amazing. How can such a tiny person be so strong?" Richard smiled, but Mary was looking away, and he asked quietly, "What is it?"

"Tell me what you found when you got to the island," Mary said, touching his face. "You have been saying horrible things in your sleep."

Richard nodded and recounted what he had discovered next door. He clenched his jaw, "Reggie had been partially cooked and eaten."

Mary's face contorted in disgust and she said, "Oh God, what about Dorcas?"

Richard looked at the floor as he said, "It appears she choked to death."

"She choked on her own son?" Mary said horrified, but then she looked up and said seriously, "She threatened to eat Jack or the baby, and she would have tried, wouldn't she?"

Richard nodded. "I think she would have tried. I don't know whether she shot Reginald on purpose or by accident or even if he did it himself, but I think that whatever way he died, she couldn't let him go to waste, so she started in on him. You were smart to leave when you did."

"You know Cassie hasn't even asked me if I know what happened to them. Does she have to know all this?" Mary asked, concerned.

"She needs to know they are both dead, and she can know Reggie died from being shot, but I for one don't think she needs to know more than that." Mary nodded, rubbing his arm. Richard looked into the fire for several minutes and then asked, very softly, "What happened to Wrennet?" Mary explained how she had died, and how they had covered her with snow. She also told him how Wrennet had nursed him as an infant and how he had taken the place of the child she had lost. After she finished, Richard smiled fondly and said, "That explains a lot. I never told her how much I loved her, but I think she knew just the same."

"I know she did," Mary said as she put her head against his arm.

Richard gained strength daily, and when he had been in camp a week, he determined it was time to bathe. Mary told him she had been washing herself and the children from a small wooden bowl, and Richard did the same. As he was finishing, Mary handed him a shirt. "Here, put this on. I brought it thinking I would need it to make clothes for the baby, but I have enough already." Richard slipped the shirt over his head, thinking clean fabric had never felt so good. His hair was long enough that Mary tied it at the back of his head with a strip of cloth. He then touched his beard and shrugged; it would just have to wait.

While Richard was getting stronger every day, Jordan lingered in a fevered state. Zagaswe had dosed him with everything she knew. He tossed and turned, drenched in sweat, only sleeping a few hours at a time. He had struggled this way for nearly a week, and then his fever raged even higher. Zagaswe told the woman helping her care for Jordan, "His mind is troubled, and it eats at his body. His mind may win if he has no reason to live. We must find out what troubles him."

Jordan opened his eyes and slowly became aware of his surroundings. His first image was a hazy ceiling and a fire. For a moment he thought the ship was on fire, and he struggled to get up, but a great weight held him down. He was too weak to move his head, but he swiveled his eyes until he could see a shaggy, gray-haired creature bending over him and pinning him down with strong hands. The creature bent closer, and Jordan could see it was an old woman. She touched his face with a hand that felt deliciously cool and murmured soothing words that he could not understand but that made him stop struggling. There was a roaring fire and the smoke swirled before it vented out a hole in the roof. He watched and the old woman tossed some water on the stones around the fire, causing a hiss that filled the lodge with steam. Jordan slept again, still shaking with fever.

Jordan dreamed that he rose from the dais and walked through the side of the lodge. As it is with dreams, he thought nothing of being able to walk through a wall, but simply took a few steps more and began to smile. He walked past other lodges and through another wall where he saw Mary sleeping on a pile of furs, flanked by sleeping infants. Richard was a few feet away on another pile of furs, curled up with Edward and Jack. The fire in the lodge had burned down to little more than embers, but the light reflected on Mary's face, and she looked beautiful.

Jordan bent closer until he was only inches away. Unlike the other dreams of her where he simply watched, he had free will in this dream, and he nudged the fur cover. He knew he was dreaming, but at the same time knew he was the author of what he dreamt tonight, so he knelt closer to her and pulled the fur blanket off her shoulder. He ran his hand over the creamy skin of her neck and touched her cheek. Mary stirred and brushed her face like she was shooing away a fly. Jordan smiled and carefully picked up Rose, who squeaked but then settled again. He carefully placed her next to Richard, and then did the same with Lucy, who startled and then fell back to sleep. Jordan noted what a beautiful child she was and then placed her next to her father. He returned to Mary and stretched out next to her. He hated himself for what he was doing, but he refused to stop. He leaned close, feeling the heat from her body, then held her face in his hands, willing her to wake. Mary's eyes fluttered and she looked at him. Rather than startle or jump, she simply mouthed his name, looking concerned. She reached up and held his face in her hands, asking what he needed. He closed his eyes to kiss her and he felt her hands on his head, but rather than welcoming him they became forceful as they pushed him away. Her fingers dug into his skull until he thought they would scoop out his brain, and he pulled away from her and closed his eyes against the pain.

He opened his eyes and found he was still in the sweat lodge with old Zagaswe leaning over him, holding his head tightly. She hissed at him in English, "No you don't. I saw where you went, and you won't travel in this fever to betray a man who has been like your brother."

Jordan closed his eyes and whispered, "I have known her since before I was a man. She came to me for years before he ever knew her. She belongs to me."

Zagaswe held his face and stroked it, saying softly, "She does not belong to you." She patted his face and hummed soothingly. Jordan looked at her, and despite the wild hair, wrinkles, and chin hair, there was a power and dignity to her that could not be denied. She reminded him a bit of his grandmother who had died when he was very young.

Zagaswe leaned close and said, "I see many things, some good, some bad, and some far in the future, and I'll tell you now what I see." She looked hard at him and said, "The day the woman in your dreams will belong to you will be the day stones can shed tears." Jordan groaned and closed his eyes.

Mary woke just at dawn and sat up alarmed. "Richard! The babies!" Richard sat up quickly and startled Rose, who began to wail. Mary looked over at him and asked, "When did you move the babies?"

Richard shook his head, looking around. "I don't remember moving them at all." They looked at each other and then at the infants who were now both howling. Old Zagaswe was passing outside their lodge just then and heard the commotion. The power of dreams should not be underestimated, she thought with a smile.

RICHARD MET with the Ojibwa leaders to get some information about the garrison and the others on the island. The men did not want to go to the island but agreed to so long as they did not stay more than three nights and waited until the moon was new. Richard now came back to tell Mary, who agreed that no matter what had happened she wanted to go back to their house on the island.

Richard left a few days later with three of the Ojibwa men, taking only the barest necessities. They completed the four miles in just a few hours.

When they arrived the Ojibwa men held back. Richard was able to get them moving again only after they had made a small offering and a birch bark packet of grass and mud and stones was placed on the shoreline.

They tackled the obvious problem first of burying the bodies of Reggie and Dorcas. There was no way they could get them in the ground, so they dug a snow pit and packed it tight. Richard covered the bodies with planks so they could find and move them in the spring. They then moved Wrennet's body from next to the doorstep to another pit and covered her again with snow. Richard ached with grief for the woman who had been like a mother to him.

Richard and the men then set about getting the Holmwood house in order. They built a fire again and swept up the evidence of Mary's hasty departure. They then moved down to the ship to find supplies. Mary had told him she gave everything to the other two ships when they came to her in the summer, but he hoped there would be at least something tucked away.

They climbed into the main hold which Richard thought was empty. To his delight, he saw half a dozen intact barrels. Upon inspection, he found they were filled with salt pork, oatmeal, and pickled cabbage. The four men lugged the barrels out of the ship and then rigged ropes around them one at a time and parbuckled them up the steep slope with ropes the same way they would up the side of a ship. When they were finished, they were exhausted. Richard tapped the barrel with the oatmeal, and they scooped out a panful. They boiled it up with pemmican they had with them and smoky-dried muskrat into a pottage stew. They then curled up in their blankets by the fire and slept like logs. Richard had offered them beds, but the three men declined. They didn't want to be on the island at all, but staying close together by the fire made it somehow more bearable, and even then they would take turns sleeping. They feared what might come upon them if they all let down their guard. Richard slept there with them, though he would dearly have loved sleeping in his own bed.

The next day Richard opened the barrel of salt pork, and the men cheered. Salt was a rare commodity in the Northern Territory and they had eagerly devoured the pork Mary brought with her like it was caviar. When he opened a barrel of the pickled cabbage the men had backed away shaking their heads. They wanted none of it, but they would certainly welcome the pork and oatmeal.

They fashioned some skids and lashed a barrel of pork and a barrel of oatmeal to it and prepared to head back across the ice. Richard stoked the fire as full as he dared, and then they returned to the encampment that afternoon. Smoke coming from the stove made the island look a little less lonely. He would bring Mary and the others, including Cassie and Rose, back tomorrow. They had talked it over, and though it would be lonely, they both wanted to be back with walls and a roof around them and a floor underneath. Mary dreamed of a real bath.

By the time Richard returned from the island, Jordan was well enough to sit up. Both Mary and Richard urged him to return with them to Mackinac. "Please, for your own good," Mary pleaded. But Jordan just looked sadly away and shook his head no. He said he would winter with the Ojibwa. Several of the girls a bit older than Cassie giggled at this and smiled.

They lashed the canoe onto the skids used to carry barrels. After making a fur nest for Jack, Lucy, and Rose, they left dragging it behind them as they slowly made their way home. Edward had begged to walk, and Richard let him, figuring he would be back in the canoe before they were a few miles out. Grub loped back and forth in front of them, occasionally dipping his open lower jaw in the snow which he would then hack back out, sniffing and snorting as he ran. He had not had so much as a wipe down from Mary in months, and the encampment had been a glorious place to find things to roll in. Grub seemed uncanny in his ability to stay upwind of them to give them the full effect of his stench.

They set the house to rights and divided up sleeping quarters. Cassie slept in Wrennet's bed with Edward in his own bed and Jack in his crib. In the other bedroom were Mary and Richard and the two babies. Perhaps it was good Jordan had turned them down. They had no idea where he would have slept.

There were nice things to be had at the Deems's, some of which would have made them more comfortable, but when Richard asked Cassie if she wanted him to go with her to get them, she adamantly shook her head no. There wasn't a thing in the house she wanted, and, in truth, would have felt better if it burned to the ground. She said quietly, "If you don't mind, I would like for the Ojibwa to take all of it." Then she added slowly, "If they even will."

They had plenty of food, but what they lacked was variety. For the next eight weeks they lived on salt pork, oatmeal, and pickled cabbage. Sometimes Mary would roll the salt pork inside a paste of oat flour laced with the slushy fat collected from the top of the boiling salt port and bake them like little rolls. Sometimes she fried the boiled pork with the rinsed cabbage or tried to make a soup of the three. Toward the end of the two months Mary would set the table and call people to dinner. What had earlier been a scramble for position and a rush through grace was now a sigh. Mary insisted they still say grace, but it was nearly sarcastic in its tone as they thanked the Lord for the food they were about to receive. Only Richard and Jack didn't seem to mind. Richard had lived on such fare for long stretches in his life at sea and little Jack didn't know any differently. What he did find different though was the enforcement of table manners.

When the relief ship finally arrived in April with its load of sugar, ham, olives, and the like, the Holmwood clan felt like heaven had been delivered to them. Robert Stuart stepped onto the island and looked them over carefully. They looked colorless and somewhat spongy from all the salt they had eaten, but nonetheless healthy. After a week of dining on supplies from the ship, their luster and spirits were restored. Jordan Ladysmith left with the ship as it returned to Welland, and from there he sailed on the *Draco Mare* which had brought more supplies and waited to take him back to the Atlantic. He had not seen Mary since the night of his fever, and he was quite certain he would never see her again in his dreams.

CHAPTER 20

WINTERS PASSED and each spring the sun found the Holmwoods blinking and pale but all alive and in good health. Spring turned to summer and Richard was home between charting voyages, sitting at the long kitchen table, when Mary came into the cottage in a flurry. "There is a man in St. Ignace that is going to be hanged in a few days," she said. "They say he was convicted of killing a man in Detroit, and then he escaped, but that he is suspected of killing and robbing dozens of others." Richard nodded, only half-listening, as he looked at a section of a chart that was still sketchy with detail.

"How do you know this?" he asked absently.

Mary explained what she had heard from some of the Ojibwa women and Richard nodded his head every so often, partially listening as she continued with her tale until she said, "They also said he has hair red like the sunset."

Richard's head snapped up at this and his heart began to pound. He looked up at her wondering if it was possible, but he asked casually, "Did you get a name?"

"They told me his name is Hastings, um, Reuben Hastings. Do you know him?" Mary said as she put down her basket and unloaded and sorted the vegetables she had picked. She turned to get Richard's answer, but he was already gone with the door left wide open behind him. She went to the door, but he was already striding down the path to the pier. "I guess you do," Mary said, looking anxiously after him as she shut the door to keep Lucy from walking right out of it.

Richard didn't even wait for the cutter to be tied up before he leaped off it and strode into the territory office in St. Ignace. Three men looked up at him as he closed the door. The territory agent knew Richard, but he was taken aback when Richard said, without any form of greeting, "Do you have a Reuben Hastings here?"

The tallest of the three men stood and said to the others, "This is Captain Richard Holmwood, and gentlemen, I believe he has had a run-in with our Mr. Hastings as well." Richard didn't answer, but nodded, trying his best to keep his anger in check. The agent then said, "Yes, Captain, we do. May I ask your business with him?"

Richard stated flatly, "I want to make sure you hang the right bastard."

The three men looked at each other and then the one who spoke earlier said, "Come with me, please." He led Richard to a storeroom on the back of the office and unlocked the door. Chained to a ring in the wall was Reuben, who looked like a schoolboy raising his arm to answer a question. His face lit up when he saw Richard.

"Captain! I am so pleased to see you alive! Tell me your young officer made it too," Hastings said with true concern.

Richard took a lunge at him, but the territory officer grabbed his arm. "None of that, Captain. Whatever issue you or any other man has with Mr. Hastings will end at dawn in two days. Those two men out there have come all the way from Detroit to see to it."

Richard shook his head, though his fists were still clenched, and Hastings said in his lazy way to the territory officer, "You will let a dying man speak to an old friend won't you?"

The officer looked from Richard to Hastings and then said as he closed the door, "If this is the way your friends feel about you, no wonder you are going to hang."

"Get on your feet," Richard said, low and menacing.

"Only for you, Captain," Hastings said, slowly rising and stretching until he was standing. Before Richard could say anything, Hastings said with a smile, "You want to ask me why. You want to know why I left you, right?"

"Damn right I do," Richard snapped, the green of his eyes hiding the tranquil blue with their rage.

"I can't tell you why I did it, any more than I can tell you why I have cheated and stolen from a hundred men," Reuben said, "but if it makes you feel any better, I will say, I thought about it for several days before I actually left you. Usually, it just comes over me and I act on impulse, but with you two, I really had to justify it to myself." He looked at Richard and nodded slowly, "If you hadn't had so much gold on you, I maybe could have resisted, but it was so much gold." Hastings said this as though it explained everything.

"I had already given you two hundred dollars in gold to take us back to Mackinac," Richard snapped.

"Yes, you did, and I thank you for it. I would have taken one hundred, but you offered two, and I have never been one to turn down gold," Hastings said, "but you see, you had more, and it was just there in the snow where you left it a few days back, and I wanted that too. I couldn't help myself." Hastings said this like a kid explaining why he stole a piece of hard candy.

"Why couldn't you have just slipped back and taken it? Why did you have to leave us stranded without even any snowshoes?"

Reuben couldn't answer. He just smiled and continued, "I hope it helps to know that it did bother me. Usually it doesn't, but this time it did. I almost turned around to find you again, but couldn't figure a reason to explain why I had left in the first place, so I kept going." Richard just stared at him in silence. Hastings continued, "Tell me Captain, did you find your wife and boys when you got there?"

"What?" Richard asked, stunned at his concern.

"I was hoping you would tell me that you found them all well," Hastings said. When Richard didn't answer, Hastings said, "I'll be gone in two days, just tell me you found them well, and it will relieve what little conscience I have. I really did like you." Hastings shifted his feet and leaned against the wall. "It has always been a wonder to me what a man will do for the woman he loves, and for her sake at least, it's good I never found a woman to love me."

"Why didn't you just shoot us when you left in the night?" Richard asked.

"You know that same thought has come over me a dozen times. Usually that is what I would do, but with you two, I just didn't have the stomach for it. As I said, I really liked both of you," Hasting said, smiling. Then he added, "And you know something? I still do."

Richard shook his head and started to leave. Whatever he had planned to do to Hastings when he found him was moot compared to what would be done to him in two days' time. It was over, and he put his hand on the latch to leave. Behind him, Hastings shuffled his feet and said, "Captain, one more thing." Richard turned and looked at him, and Hastings continued, "You know I went back and took all the gold and equipment we left behind, don't you?" Richard nodded, suspecting as much, and Hastings added, "The gold is long since spent, but if you will look in my pack there, inside the wide belt is a little flap, and there you will find the necklace and earbobs you got for your wife. I held onto them hoping to somehow get them back to you. As a matter of fact, that's what brought me north again." He then added, grinning, "Well, that and the knowledge that they were looking for me south." Hastings smiled ironically. "Think about it, Captain. The one good thing I ever do in my life, and it gets me caught to pay for all the bad things I've ever done."

Richard took the jewelry from the belt and put it in his jacket pocket and then said quietly, "They say that no good deed goes unpunished." Richard turned and looked at the prisoner one more time, and said, "Goodbye Hastings. I can't really wish you good luck, but I do wish that it be quick." With that, he turned his back and walked out, shutting the door behind him. The three men looked up as he came out, and he noted they now all had muskets, perhaps on the notion Richard was there to free Hastings. Richard said, "No need for those. I left him as I found him, a sorry piece of a man."

The territory officer said softly, "Well, he won't be taking up space much longer, so don't give him another thought."

"I don't intend to. Good day, gentlemen." With that, he left, wiping any trace of Reuben Hastings from his memory.

CHAPTER 21

MARY WAS PREGNANT again. She had been given a respite from bearing children for the last several years, but passion and nature had again coupled to leave her swollen and ungainly. They were now raising five children including Cassie and Rose. Word had reached them in the spring the year before that both Stella and Roger had taken a fever and died over the winter at their outpost. It was unthinkable to do anything else but keep Rose with her only living blood relative, her Aunt Cassie. Richard secretly wondered how Mary would have fared parting with her anyway, since she had raised her from an infant, feeding her as if she were her own.

Richard watched Mary struggling to pick up Jack who was now almost five and large for his age. He had not taken after his small mother as Richard feared, but instead was a strapping youngster. Jack looked up at him and grinned. He had Mary's curly, dark hair, but Richard's blue-green eyes, and the combination was startling. Lucy too had Mary's hair, but her eyes were strictly her father's, the same striking aqua and thick, long lashes. They were a healthy, attractive family and even Cassie's features had softened since she had been removed from the influence of her mother. With a better diet and some exercise, she had become quite pretty. Rose was a plump, pliant, bald little creature who mercifully promised to look more like her father than her mother.

Richard's five-year duty was nearly up when he received official word from Washington that treaty discussions were ongoing to disarm the Great Lakes. For all he knew the decision could already be made. After all, Jackson had completed his historic battle at New Orleans two months after the peace treaty was signed, but no one knew it. He was told in the communication to await the order and then remove any ships of war as soon after as possible. The English would do the same if the treaty was ratified. It was believed by the leaders of both countries that this would increase trade, but Richard believed it more likely that the United States had conceded this disarmament to the British in exchange for something it wanted more. Nothing in politics was done without some quid pro quo.

He talked with Mary about leaving, and though she had made a cozy home for them on the island, she was more than willing to leave. "It's beautiful here, and two of our babies were raised here, but I am ready to go home."

It was early October when the word finally reached them that the treaty had been signed. They decided to winter over in Detroit where there was some semblance of civilization. Richard had teased Mary about delivering children in the oddest places, and she had quipped, "Richard, if I were to have a baby in a bed with women around to help me, I would most surely die."

Richard told Robert Stuart about his decision to leave the territory. Earlier that day, Edward Biddle had arrived on the island and he was setting up a trading post connected to the American Fur Company. Robert introduced them. Biddle was married to an Ojibwa woman named Agatha and this connection to the Ojibwa nation would be an enormous benefit to him in trading. He was looking to build a house, and Richard said, "We are leaving in the next few weeks, and you are welcome to our cottage if you would like it."

"You would be willing to sell it to me?" Biddle asked.

Richard smiled and said, "We never actually bought it, and no one really knows who built it. We were basically squatters, but you are welcome to take it if you want it."

"I'll come and take a look tomorrow if you don't mind. I don't want to bother you now. I saw you have little ones who are sleeping by now," Biddle said politely.

"Then we will look for you tomorrow," Richard said.

Biddle was delighted with the cottage and it was his intention to move in right after they left. This caused a flurry of cleaning by Mary. "I won't have him think we lived like animals here," Mary said as she scrubbed the wooden floor planks. Miki was helping her and both women were crying at the thought of parting with each other. It would be folly to believe they would keep in touch over such a long distance. The whole family walked around the island the night before they sailed, and they marveled one last time at its beauty.

They reached Detroit and got settled about three weeks before Mary went into labor. This time she was surrounded by women, some of whom actually knew what they were doing and for the first time Richard was nearby.

He was downstairs with about half a dozen men from the ship and another dozen from Detroit, and he paced and started at any sounds from the floor above. One old seadog finally said, "This your first one, Cap'n?"

"No," Richard informed him, "this is my fifth child."

"Well, I'd a hated to see how you were with the first one if you're pacing around like this," the old salt said, chewing on his pipe stem. Richard realized with a start he had never been present for the birth of any of his children, so, in essence, he was like a first-timer.

After what seemed an eternity, there was a shuffling and a small cry from upstairs. Richard bolted up the steps, taking them two at a time, and burst into the room. Inside the door he ran into a woman carrying a basket filled with blood-soaked sheets. They were so covered in blood, it appeared to Richard as though she had used them to wipe the decks after a boarding party. Richard stared at the sheets alarmed, and two women began to shove him from the room. "No, sir, she is not ready yet. You cannot see her the way she is," they said as they pushed at him. He stood still and finally they stopped.

"I have seen more wounds and blood than you can imagine. I am going to see my wife, so please move out of my way," Richard said, pushing gently at them.

One older woman stepped forward and said, "It isn't for your sake we keep you away. It's for her. No woman wants to be seen like this, so you just wait a few minutes and then you can see them both." She looked at Richard like she meant business and could in another life easily have been a successful jailor, so he nodded and stood down. She turned to walk away and then said over her shoulder, "The child is a boy, and a big one at that." With that, she shut the door in Richard's face.

A few moments later he saw Mary propped on pillows. The other two women in the room stayed and watched as if checking to see that Richard behaved himself. Mary smiled weakly and patted the bed next to her. Richard sat down gently. "Are you all right?" She nodded and handed the infant to him. He didn't look at it right away but instead touched her face with his free hand and asked again concerned, "Are you sure you are all right?" The two women in the room smiled and nodded to each other in approval. They had witnessed too many instances where the husband grabbed the infant to show it off without so much as a glance at the recovering mother. Only after Richard had assured himself Mary was fine did he pull the blanket down to see the child. He tried not to let it show, but he could not help but grimace.

Mary saw his reaction and said, concerned, "What is it?"

Richard looked at the child and then at Mary and said, "Is there something wrong with him that they didn't tell you about?"

Mary took the baby from Richard in alarm and whipped the blanket back. She looked him over from his dark head to his bent and bowed legs terminating in tiny feet, and then said puzzled, "He looks fine to me."

"Are you sure?" Richard put his back between himself and the two women who had refused to leave the room and whispered, "He looks like he isn't quite finished or something. Does he have rickets?" He held one of the baby's tiny, bowed legs.

The truth dawned on Mary and she asked, "You have never seen any baby this small, have you?" Richard shook his head. It was true, and Mary laughed softly and said, "Give him a month, and he will look just like Jack did when you first saw him. Just give him a day, and he will look much better than he does now. His legs are crooked from being so cramped inside me, and his face is swollen and bruised from the birth. They all start out rather ragged and bruised."

DETROIT IN THE winter offered more civilization than Mackinac Island, but not much more. There were women for Mary to talk with, children their age for the Holmwood brood to play with, and men from both sides of the recent war to argue seafaring and the like. Richard would often make his way down to the tavern to catch gossip and to see who was there, and one night a few weeks after the baby, Christian, had been born, Richard stepped through the door and was greeted by the smiling face of none other than Captain Leteauce. "Captain Holmwood, I am very glad to see you. Is your family well, and are they with you?" Richard smiled and explained that they were fine and all returning to the East Coast. Leteauce, after a long pull on his beer, said, "I am leaving as well. Part of me will miss these waters and the wild beauty, but another part of me will be glad to never see them again. I have negotiated fickle waters, but none so changeable and tricky as these in my life." He leaned closer as if to share a secret and said, "I have to admit, I hurled my lunch over the rail the first time I came here. Can you imagine the humiliation of it?" Richard nodded and relieved Leteauce's shame somewhat by admitting it had happened to him as well. Leteauce took a large swallow and said, "Your wife and boy, are they well?"

Richard smiled, "My family is fine. We just added another son to the lot a few weeks back."

"Well done! I am glad to hear it." Leteauce smiled, then added, "I never quite forgave myself about what happened to your wife, but it sounds like all is well."

"Very well," Richard said, draining his glass. Leteauce drained his as well and then leaned back and looked at Richard oddly before he said, "During the war, I twice was nearly taken in by a captain who pretended that his ship was disabled, and then as we drew near, he righted himself and started firing. I was the last in line of a small convoy of three ships the first time and managed to escape. The second time a storm came up, and we broke off the engagement, but it was the most incredible thing I ever saw." Leteauce looked hard at Richard and said, "They called this captain 'The Killdeer,' after the meadow bird who pretends to be wounded."

"I've heard of him," Richard said. "Why do you ask?"

"Because I would like to buy him a drink. That was the finest sailing I have ever seen in my life," Leteauce said. He leaned back in his chair and nodded his head toward some men sitting around a table in the corner and added, "Those men said that you are the man we called Killdeer, and from what I saw of you in the battle with the *Siren* and the *Chanticleer*, I would say I tend to believe them." He put his elbows on the table and asked, "Are you the Killdeer?"

Richard looked at him for a long, few seconds, and then said, "No. I don't think that man is around anymore."

Leteauce looked at him quizzically. "I'd like to buy you that drink all the same," he said with a slight nod and a smile, and then added with a grin, "just in case he comes back."

THEY ARRIVED in Washington after wintering in Detroit and Richard promptly went to report to the Navy Commission. He barely got through the door before he ran into Stephen Decatur, and they hugged like school chums. Decatur exclaimed, "Look at you! Richard, you look absolutely wonderful. Being married has been good for you! Come and see us and bring Mary and Edward, please!"

Richard grinned sheepishly, but said with pride, "You may want to think that over, Stephen. There are a few more of us than when we left here five years ago."

"I don't care if you had a dozen, bring them. Susan and I love children," Stephen said and added, "Come right now, and say hello to Susan, so she can convince you to bring your family. Plus, you can see the house. It wasn't finished when you were here before, but it certainly is now." Richard agreed and they walked the short distance to the Decatur house which sat on the very edge of Lafayette Square. It was beautiful and would serve Stephen well in what was becoming a very promising political career. In the short time he had been back in Washington, Richard had heard snippets of talk that linked Stephen to a possible run for the presidency. He had never been much for politics himself, but Stephen had always liked the game of it, and Richard wished him well. They didn't speak of the political scene as they drank tea with Susan, but rather of Richard and Mary's adventure. Then Richard mentioned the children, but Susan interrupted him.

"Don't tell me any details, not even how many, just bring them. I want to see each one like a little surprise." Richard tried to explain the expansion of his family, but she cut him off, giggling. "Tonight, bring them all tonight," she said, then added with a look of concern, "unless Mary doesn't feel up to it after the voyage."

Richard laughed. "Mary is the finest traveler I've met in my life. We stopped in Boston to take care of a few things and Mary did some shopping while we were there. She was catching up with a vengeance for being fashionably in arrears, so I am sure she will be hinting heavily for me to take her out to show off her new gowns. I'll answer for her. We would be delighted to come tonight!"

Richard left shortly afterwards and when he got to their hotel and told Mary, she jumped up and down like the same girl he had taken down the James River five years ago. She began rummaging through boxes of gowns and stockings and finally Richard asked her what she was doing. "I'm looking for a gown that will go well with the emerald necklace you gave me," she said, holding up one in cream with deep, green embroidery. "What about this?" she said, holding it up against her body. Richard nodded his approval, noting Mary really looked almost the same as when he married her. It was difficult to believe she had borne three children, and though she still had the face of a girl, she had the unmistakable curves of a woman.

The Holmwoods arrived in front of the Decatur house, packed into their carriage like salted fish in a barrel. Stephen and Susan came out onto the steps as they unloaded, and Stephen described it later as, "I saw nothing but windows full of little faces when you pulled up."

Stephen came to the curb and laughed as Richard started handing down children. Susan Decatur's two nieces were standing on the steps anxiously waiting. They had come to stay with their Aunt Susan, and this appeared to be yet another fascinating family to which they would be introduced.

Edward, who was now eleven, was very tall and even more beautiful than he had been. His eyes were stunning blue against his golden curls, and he reminded her so much of his mother that Susan gasped when she saw him. Edward had Jack by the hand, and Jack looked up at Susan and Stephen with a frank perusal and then broke into a grin. They couldn't help but grin back at him. Cassie stepped out and looked around shyly, not wanting to stare, but wanting to take in every inch of the elegant Susan Decatur.

Susan had now joined them at the carriage and smiled as Richard handed over to Stephen the most beautiful little girl either of them had ever seen. Lucy smiled with perfect little teeth and blinked at them with her stunning eyes. Her head was completely covered with dark ringlets and she shook them like a grown lady. Stephen laughed at her and said, "And what is your name little princess?"

"That's Lucy, and she's no princess," Jack piped.

Susan led them into the sitting room and pulled the blankets from the baby and sat with him in her lap. He was five months old, very alert, and like his brothers and sister had been easygoing. He sat up against Susan's arm and smiled at her with his long lashes fluttering.

Cassie stood next to Mary, unsure of herself. Mary put her arm around her and pulled her close, "Susan and Stephen, this is Cassie Deems. She is going to stay with us from now on. I always wanted a little sister, and now I have one." Mary squeezed Cassie's hand while Cassie smiled shyly at the Decaturs. She too had heard tales of the great naval hero and tried not to stare at Stephen.

Cassie looked so much better than she had before. There was nothing she could do about the wide mouth or the thin build, but her hair now had magnificent luster, and she was quite pretty. Mary had helped her find some lovely gowns and had even teased her, "Seventeen is old enough for the gentlemen to start looking you over. I got married when I was only a year older than you."

They ate dinner in relative peace, and then the ladies and children withdrew to let Richard and Stephen conspire alone. Stephen caught Richard up on Navy gossip, and the political scene in Washington, and then he talked of the ongoing problem and hostility between him and Commodore James Barron. Barron still held a grudge against Stephen for testifying honestly at his court-martial all those years ago, and most recently the grudge had turned to threatening letters. Stephen said, "This will end badly, Richard. He has been spreading lies and at this point he threatens my honor." They discussed the matter further, and it was later than usual when the men finally joined Mary and Susan in the sitting room.

Susan asked Mary a dozen questions about their trip, and Mary answered in her matter of fact way. When Stephen and Richard came into the room, Susan said, "Stephen, you wouldn't believe what they have been through!"

Stephen nodded and said, "Yes, I would. Richard told me about it too. You are all lucky to be here and well." He looked at Mary and said, "You are a wonder!" Mary smiled and then fussed with Lucy's ribbon, not wanting to be the center of so much attention. Stephen and Susan wanted them to stay and talk more, but it was getting very late. Edward was dozing against Cassie, Jack had found himself a nest in the window seat and was fast asleep, and it was about time to feed Christian, so they said their goodbyes and piled back into their carriage, waving as they pulled away.

Stephen put his arm around Susan's waist and held her tightly as they watched them leave. "I wonder if they know how blessed they have been?"

Susan put her head against his chest and said, "I have a good idea they do, love."

THE FOLLOWING MORNING Mary woke to find that Richard had just finishing dressing. It was still dark, and she mumbled, asking where he was going. He kissed her and tucked her back in, saying, "I promised Stephen I would meet him early this morning. He wants some help taking care of an old problem that has been festering. I'll be back later." Mary nodded, snuggling deeper into the featherbed as she slipped back to sleep. Had she been fully awake, she would have caught the look of concern on Richard's face.

Mary nor any of the children got up very early that morning, so they skipped breakfast and were seated at the table waiting for an early lunch to be served when the girl serving their soup said, "I just heard that Commodore Decatur was involved in a duel early this morning with a Commodore James Barron." She began to ladle the soup into their bowls and added, "They say a man was hurt real bad, but I only got that from the butcher's boy a few minutes ago." She placed the top back on the tureen and left. Mary stared at Cassie, horrified.

"Mary, what is it?" Cassie asked.

"Cassie, will you watch the children for me?" Mary was already rising from the table.

Cassie nodded, "But what's wrong?"

Mary's face was pale as she said, "Richard went with Stephen early this morning." Mary left the inn wearing nothing to keep her warm but her shawl.

It was only a short distance to the Decatur house, but she could see carriages and horses filling the street while she was still several blocks away. As she approached the house, she saw blood on the walkway in great blotches and a partial boot print reddened with blood. A man grabbed her as she walked up the steps and pulled her aside.

"No, ma'am. It is not a sight for a woman's eyes," the man said kindly but firmly.

Mary struggled, "Who is hurt? My husband was with Commodore Decatur. I need to know who is hurt."

"What is your name, ma'am?" The man asked softly. Mary told him and then waited while he disappeared into the house. A few moments later, Richard appeared, but Mary barely recognized him. He had removed his jacket and waistcoat, but the front of his shirt was soaked in dried blood, and there were streaks of it on his face. Mary ran to him, but he held her away from his bloody clothes.

"I heard someone with Stephen was hurt! Where are you hurt?" Mary cried, looking anxiously at Richard's shirt.

"I'm not hurt, Mary. It's Stephen. The bullet is lodged in his abdomen." He looked at Mary and added, "The injury is fatal. He's lost so much blood already and they can't remove the bullet to stop the bleeding." Then he said, just above a whisper, "It's just a matter of time."

Mary looked past him at the doorjamb streaked with blood where they had carried Stephen into the house. She looked back at Richard,

"Poor Susan, does she have anyone with her?" Richard nodded and said her nieces and her sister were with her upstairs.

"I am going to stay here until it is over, Mary. I should have done more to stop him, but he wouldn't hear of it," Richard said. Just then William Bainbridge burst out of the door and vomited into the flower bed. He steadied himself and then turned to Richard.

"My, God, what have we let him do, Richard?" Bainbridge was oblivious to Mary as he stood staring at Richard with a haunted look on his face. "What will they do to us when they learn we were with him?" Mary shrunk behind Richard, who just shook his head at Bainbridge. After a few moments, Bainbridge returned to the house, got his coat and hat, and left in the same carriage in which they had carried Stephen home.

"Is that true, Richard? Will you be arrested?" Mary asked.

Richard went to put his hand on her lips, but pulled it back as it was caked with dried blood. He leaned down and said, "Sweetheart, you need to go back and stay with the children. Nothing will happen to me, but I cannot leave Stephen now. I must stay." He bent his head down to her ear and whispered, "I'll come back when it's over." He kissed her forehead and then watched as she walked back up the street toward the inn. When she had disappeared out of sight, he went back into the glorious house on Lafayette Street and gently shut the door.

THE FUNERAL for Stephen Decatur was the biggest thing ever to occur in Washington. Many people travelled day and night to attend. Word spread fast, and soon the mourners swelled to nearly eleven thousand people, larger than the inhabitants of Washington proper. The carriage with Stephen's body left St. John's Episcopal Church in his beloved Lafayette Square, and following in a carriage was Susan and her family. Behind her walked the officers who had served closest to Stephen. They lined up like a deep-blue wall and solemnly walked along, each remembering how Stephen had touched his life, and still trying to wrap their brains around the fact that this shining light of a man was gone, snuffed out by hubris and a lead ball. They had only walked about fifty yards when the horse pulling the carriage began to limp, and then it quickly became completely lame. Richard and five other officers, including David Porter and William Bainbridge, halted the horse. They took Stephen's casket and hoisted it until it was cradled on their shoulders and they walked with their arms stretched under the casket, resting their hands on the opposite man's shoulder. In this way, they carried the great naval hero's body to his gravesite, a much more fitting journey than moving him cold and alone on a carriage.

After the graveside service there was a wake at the Decatur house.

Mary did not attend the funeral or the wake, and Richard was glad she did not. She didn't really know either of the Decaturs that well and would have felt awkward there among those who really knew them. Richard stood off to one side with Jordan Ladysmith, and they looked over the crowd. "A beacon has gone out, Jordan," Richard said, and then added, "No one burned brighter than Stephen, and he loved every minute of it." He clinked his glass to Jordan's and tipped back his drink.

A man approached him and Richard was surprised to see it was President Monroe. The President smiled softly at Richard and Jordan and then said, "Stephen Decatur was the most vibrant man I have ever known. He loved the Navy, and he loved his life here in Washington too. His was a star that extinguished as it was rising. He spoke often of you, Captain Holmwood, and he said you were the finest seaman he had ever known."

Richard smiled sadly and said, "I take that as the greatest compliment."

Monroe said, "I never had the privilege of serving at sea, but in listening to Stephen tell of it, I was able to capture a grain of its glory and majesty." He then smiled solemnly, "Washington will be a much dimmer place missing the light that seemed to shine from him and from his wonderful wit. To Stephen Decatur," he said, as he raised his glass and both Richard and Jordan did the same.

The crowd mingled about, trying to comfort poor Susan Decatur. She had yet to really absorb that Stephen was gone. This seemed just like another ball or dinner to get through, but unlike the others, when she went to bed exhausted tonight, she would wake up alone tomorrow morning and for all the mornings to come.

Richard returned to the inn in the late afternoon and Mary greeted him cautiously. He took off his jacket and then stood looking at her for a moment. He wrapped her in his arms and said, "God, let me hold you." Mary stood holding him as he crushed her in his arms. Suddenly, Rose and Lucy burst into the room and wrapped their arms around his legs. He smiled down and then scooped them up. It was good to see someone not touched by this tragedy. The family had been cooped up in the inn for days due to the funeral, and though the children had been good as gold, they were restless. He smiled at Mary and said, "Let's get out of here and go home."

They were packed and ready to leave two days later, but before they went, Richard left to give his regards to Susan Decatur. She sat holding his hand, but said very little. Richard looked at her and said, "I have learned something about loss, and one thing you must do is keep Stephen alive in conversation. From the day she died, I never said Lorraine's name until a few months ago. I refused to talk about her, and in doing so, I acted like she never existed. Poor Edward doesn't even know the first thing about his own mother, and it is my fault. In refusing to speak of her, I dishonored her memory. Talk about Stephen and tell what he would have done, what he would have found funny, and what would have made him angry. Keep him alive in your heart, even when your heart is breaking."

Susan smiled and said with tears in her eyes, "I could do no less than talk of him. He was my life, and I will keep him alive in my memory." She looked at Richard and smiled sadly and then said, "I will never really live again, but you, though, need to live. Take that lovely little Mary and all of your beautiful babies and go and be happy."

Richard kissed Susan's hand and said, smiling gently, "I intend to." He looked down at her in her grief and offered, "If there is ever anything I can do to help you, I am a letter away."

Susan laughed softly and said, "Though it may take a year to catch up with you." Richard smiled at her and then left. He walked to the inn, mentally closing doors on rooms of memory that were too painful to visit just now, but later, in a few weeks perhaps, he would open them again, and rejoice in having known Stephen Decatur as a friend.

MARY STOOD holding the railing looking out over the water. They had just cleared the Potomac Shoals and were edging into the Chesapeake Bay when Richard asked, "Are you anxious to see your family again?" Mary nodded but said nothing. Richard stood now with his back to the rail facing her and said, "I suppose that once you get back to Scotland Neck and show off all your babies, you will never want to leave again? I don't suppose you will ever want to be away from your mother again?"

Mary caught the odd question and looked up at him, "I have been a thousand miles from my mother, and I would leave again to be with you. Why do you ask?"

"I am tired of living like a peasant, and now that I have resigned my commission, I want a change," Richard said and immediately noticed the hurt look on Mary's face. He touched her lips before she could say anything and added, "Don't you dare be hurt. You have me wrong. You made that little cottage a wonderful cozy place, but we deserve more." He waited to see her reaction and then said, "I don't want to go back to Scotland Neck to live." He took her hands in his and said, "Mary, I had another life before I moved there, and I would sort of like to revisit it, only this time with you." Richard was testing the waters.

"You've changed since Stephen died," Mary said with concern.

"Yes, I have. I ran away to Scotland Neck after Lorraine died. I ran there to heal, but I never did. I didn't heal until I was with you."

"Then what do you want?" Mary asked, confused.

"I still have a house in Hampton. It has been shut up for years, but it is, or at least it was, a beautiful place, and I think we could be happy there," Richard explained. He turned and leaned down to Mary's level. "Would you at least take a look and think about it?" Mary nodded silently. She knew that whatever decision she made, Richard had already decided. After being in the Northern Territory she could live anywhere.

They wouldn't have to make any decisions for a while because they were stopping to see Gabriel and the Holmwoods in Hampton before they went on to Scotland Neck to see the Spencers. They found Gabriel had aged rather well, and by evening the entire blond Holmwood tribe had descended on the house, clamoring and exclaiming over the new arrivals. The babies were passed around and poked and squeezed while the adults begged to hear of life in the Northern Territory. Both Mary and Richard retold their adventures, and it was rather late when they finally got back to their hotel. They had already been summoned for an encore the following evening, but during the day Cassie kept the children while Mary and Richard escaped to look at the house he had bought from Commodore Preble's estate so many years ago.

As they drove down the street, the houses progressively became larger and statelier. The Spencers had been the gentry of Scotland Neck, but their house paled in comparison to those lining the street they were on now. They finally stopped in front of a large, brick house set well back from the street. It had the silent, waiting feel of an empty house, but even with its untended beds and shuttered windows, it was beautiful. Mary stared at it, and for a second had doubts of whether she could pull off living in such grandeur. The house was almost as large as the Decatur's.

They got out and walked to the door. The carriage driver accompanied them carrying a large, wooden toolbox. "We will have to cut the lock," Richard said, nodding to the driver who rummaged around and found some large snips. He lopped off the arm of the huge padlock chaining the door shut, and it fell with a clang to the granite-topped porch. He handed it to Richard and then looked at them both, shaking his head. He drove off in the carriage promising to pick them up in three-quarters of an hour.

Richard tried to move the latch, but it was stuck fast. He picked up the lock and banged on the latch with the butt end of it, and it gave way. He pushed the door open and the hinges, which had not shifted or been oiled in over a decade, howled as they moved. The interior looked black like a cave, and the only light came from the open door and the dirt encrusted transom. "Stay here, Mary. Let me open a few of the shutters," Richard said and absently handed her the huge lock as he walked through the door. Mary stood in the doorway holding the lock, and she could see the deep tracks Richard's boots made through the dust of a decade. Where his boots removed the layer of dust, Mary could see beautiful, cream-colored marble, heavily veined with green and rust.

Richard banged around and opened a sash so he could reach through to unlatch the pin on the huge iron bar that ran through the shutters on the outside. He then walked back around to the porch and pulled the bar free. As he folded the shutters back on themselves and secured them with the ornate hooks in the wall, they also shrieked in protest. Sunlight filtered through the dirty windows and Mary could see elaborate molding and a sweeping staircase in the distance. She walked through the doorway trying to stay in Richard's tracks in the dust so she wouldn't ruin her new cream boots.

They located a lamp and a flintset and lit the lamp. Mary wiped the lamp chimney with her handkerchief and put it in place. Richard held the lamp up high, and Mary looked around as far as the light would penetrate the gloom. They walked from the foyer into the dining room where the long, mahogany table slumbered while its straight-backed sentinels stood guard all around. Not even the layers of dust could completely hide the gleaming wood. On the table was a dish that had contained fruit when the house was closed, but all that remained now were a few pits gnawed by long-dead vermin. There was evidence everywhere that mice had run rampant for a time after the house was closed, but the spoor was now old.

They moved into a sitting room which was decidedly feminine. The furniture was lighter and of a dainty build, and there were floral paintings on the wall. Mary slipped into the room and smiled, "This is a lovely room. I could see myself in here after breakfast."

Richard nodded. "That's what it was built for, and right on the plans it said 'lady's morning room.' In winter the sun comes right in those windows," he pointed to the shuttered twin windows, "and you can write or read in bright, warm light." Mary walked further down the hall and entered another room. This was definitely a man's room. It had the same feel as her papa's study, only the fireplace in her father's study was well-smudged while this one had barely any evidence of a fire. Richard, she supposed, wasn't at home enough to really smudge the fireplace, but the walls were covered with books, and there were piles of them on the tables and the floor. Mary noted two loggerhead fire pokers hanging next to the fireplace and remembered with delight her father heating a loggerhead poker in the fire until it was red hot and then thrusting it into a tankard of cider laden with sugar, cinnamon, and cloves. The hot poker would make the cider hiss and roil, and when it was removed what was left in the tankard was a sweet, spicy brew with a wonderful hint of bitterness like tea or coffee. "Do you like mulled cider?" she asked, touching one of the pokers. They had not had the luxury of cider while in Mackinac, and Mary now craved it.

Richard looked over at the loggerhead and said, smiling, "I prefer mulled wine, but cider will certainly do for me." Mary smiled back at him and then looked over his shoulder. Her smile evaporated, and Richard knew without turning what she had seen. Lorraine's portrait stared down from the wall above the fireplace, and ten years of dust couldn't dull her beauty. Mary looked at Richard with an expression nearing panic, and she started to back away. "Mary, stop," Richard said softly. He pulled her close and then turned to look at the painting too. Lorraine was beautiful, there was no denying it, but to Richard it was like he was looking at someone else's wife. He had been with Mary so long, and they had been through so much, it was difficult to remember ever having been with another woman. He realized too that he had spent more time in Mary's company than he had in Lorraine's even though they had been married longer. He had never spent more than three months with Lorraine at any one time; whereas, he had spent many long winters with Mary from November to April where they were never apart for a single night. He looked at her now and said, "That painting was made before I even knew Lorraine. I would think she was about your age when she sat for it."

Mary looked at the portrait and said, "Edward looks just like her."

"He always did, right from the start, but you are his mother, and he knows no other. If Lorraine were here now, she would be a stranger to him."

"She was beautiful," Mary said quietly. Richard put his arm across her shoulder and said, "Yes, she was, but not any more beautiful than you are right here, right now." He pulled her close and then guided her out of the room. Mary looked back as they walked, and she watched Lorraine's gaze fall back into the shadows as the lamp moved away down the hall.

They stepped into the kitchen and both of them gasped at the same time. It was here that the rodents had wreaked the most havoc. There were droppings and skeletons of mice and squirrels and even a rat or two. The pantry had been stripped bare. Anything that had touched food was also chewed. Wooden bowls and butcher blocks were gnawed deeply. Even the big pine preparation table that dominated the space was chewed until the edges appeared scalloped. There was also evidence that as the food ran out, some of the stronger vermin turned to cannibalism and the remains of a few chewed and scattered skeletons bore mute evidence of the victim's last stand. "They must have had a time of it for a while here," Richard said, shaking his head. "Let's look upstairs," he said, placing his hand in the small of Mary's back, guiding her to the stairs. They crunched through some skeletons hidden in the dust and climbed the curving stairway. They stood on the landing, and Mary looked left and right down the hallway that stretched the full length of the house. There were doors that opened on either side.

"How many bed chambers are there up here?" Mary asked, and found she was whispering in the stale closeness.

"Six, but one is very small," Richard said, opening the first door he came to. It was Owen's room and still full of what had been left behind when they fled to Scotland Neck. A look of pain washed across Richard's face, and then he closed the door and moved on. Some of the rooms looked like they had been used for guests only, but others like Wrennet's and the nursery bore evidence of personal items. Looming at the end of the hall were double doors. Mary glanced toward them, but Richard held back, and said, "Mary, there is no need to go there. I am certain the sheets on which Lorraine died are still right there on the bed. I think we can leave it alone." Richard took Mary's hand and led her back down the stairs to the foyer where the air was sweeter. "What do you say? Do you want to move here from Scotland Neck?" Mary glanced at the large foyer, and she could see beyond the dust and debris to a beautiful, glowing room and a home where there was plenty of space for everyone. Mary nodded her head and ran her finger along the doorjamb. Richard hugged her and laughed. "Your fingers are just itching to get at this place with a broom and a bucket, aren't they?" Mary nodded and held him close.

They stayed in Hampton with Gabriel until the cleaners got started, and then they travelled up the James River to see Mary's family. She insisted they send no word ahead, but that they just arrive at mealtime. It was about noon when all eight of them lined up at the door and Mary knocked softly. Arla answered and couldn't believe her eyes, but then she let out a whoop that brought the whole house running. There was a general mob of hugs and kisses. Richard grinned as Mary proudly introduced their tribe.

There was some swift bustling and banging, and the dining table was reset with places for everyone. Mary was disappointed that Adrian was at sea, and even more so that William was out, but Arla assured her he was expected back at any time. Emma and Diana stared dumbfounded at Mary, who was dressed in magnificent silk, and they were stung deeply at the change in her. She was no longer the naïve princess, but had instead turned into a beautiful and gracious little queen, and they both felt rather tarnished next to her.

Dinner was the loud process Richard remembered from years ago, and there was, as always, enough food to choke a horse, but they finally got through it. The ladies vacated the dining room after dinner, taking the children with them and leaving the men behind. They were burning to really grill Richard for information about the journey and the lakes, but had had to hold off until now.

In the drawing room, Cassie sat next to Mary, feeling overwhelmed. Mary patted her arm, and said, "You told me you wanted to be part of a large family."

"I didn't know it was so loud, though," Cassie said, laughing.

Just then a man poked his head in the door, and Mary recognized her brother William. He ran to her and lifted her off the ground, spinning her in the air. "Princess! When did you get back?"

"Just a little while ago," Mary said, all smiles, and led William into the room where the children were playing on the rug. "Look at all my babies, Will. Aren't they beautiful?" Mary said, beaming.

"Yours? All of them?" Will said as he pulled Edward into a squeeze and then squatted down on the floor next to the children. They didn't know who he was, but he looked so much like their mama they smiled back at him anyway, and Lucy even came forward and touched his face with a plump finger. He looked back at Mary and grinned, "Good job, Princess!" He then caught sight of Cassie sitting on the arm of the chair behind Mary and the smile vanished from his face. He stared at Cassie in wonder. Mary didn't see his distraction and continued to rattle off the names of the children for him, but when he didn't say anything, she looked up. She followed his gaze and saw him staring at Cassie.

Mary looked at Cassie and saw her blush under William's gaze, and she quickly responded, "Will, may I introduce Cassie Deems? She has been like a sister to me while I have been away."

Will bowed deeply and said, smiling, "Then I am sure we will see a great deal of you, Miss Deems." He sat back down to play with his new nephews and nieces, but kept stealing glances at Cassie, who was snatching them right back. Mary smiled at the two of them knowing Will would pull her aside as soon as he could and pump her for information about Cassie, and she was sure Cassie would do the same about Will.

They ended up staying at the Scotland Neck house for six weeks while the house in Hampton was put to rights by a renovation crew. Richard instructed them to remove the furniture from the master bedroom and from Owen's room and to donate it to an old sailors' home being built in Norfolk. They quickly assembled the things from the house in Scotland Neck that they were taking with them. Richard and Joshua Spencer had been spending a great deal of time talking in those weeks and the outcome was that Joshua wanted to throw in with him and make it one shipping company. Joshua had said in the latest of these meetings, "Of course, you have the larger fleet, and I always stay close to home, so you will be in charge. I don't have the head for business that you have, and frankly neither do my boys, but they are good sailors nevertheless."

It was finalized and the two ships that Joshua Spencer owned were purchased at an excellent price by Richard. He would insure them and arrange for their voyages. Gabriel had been dropping hints he would also like to be swallowed by Richard's company, and it was made final the week following Joshua's arrangement.

The Holmwoods moved into their refurbished home in Hampton and spread to the ends of the house, reveling in the space and privacy it provided. Mary had to admit it was a lovely house, and for all its size and grandeur, it felt like home.

Richard was preparing to go on his first voyage since they had moved back, and Mary was a bit anxious for him to leave. "I know you have to go, not just because it makes money but because you need to go for yourself. You need to be at sea, Richard, I know that. I just wish I knew when you would be back. I remember you told me two months, and it was three months when you went to Jamaica. It's even harder to explain to the children that I don't know when you are coming back, but I do understand that you need to go." Richard touched her face and pulled her close as they lay curled in their huge bed, shut away from the world for a few precious hours.

The house was very quiet, and Richard and Mary checked on the children to make sure they were settled. Only Cassie was awake, sitting up in her room reading the latest letter she had received from William Spencer, who had been diligent in his correspondence since he successfully sought out Richard's permission to write to her.

"Cassie must have that letter almost memorized by now," Richard said.

"It must be nice to get a letter from a man who loves you," she said, hinting heavily. It dawned on Richard that except for the note telling her she was eleven miles from home, he had never written a letter to Mary though they had been married for five years.

"Well, expect some letters from me then," Richard said, smiling. He pulled her close and turned the lamp as low as it would go. The room was dimly lit, and Mary's creamy skin glowed in the soft darkness. "I'll write you some you can share with the kids, but others you'd better read on your own," Richard said, chuckling deep in his throat.

RICHARD DIDN'T REALIZE how much he missed being at sea. Coming back down from Halifax had been nice, but he had to worry over Mary and the children. Now it was just him, the sea, and the men in the crew, and it was heaven. By the second day Mary and the children entered his thoughts a bit, and by the end of the first week he missed them terribly. He too wished there was some way to know exactly when he would be back. He swung in his bunk that night thinking how it could be possible to have the sea and a schedule that allowed him to see his family on a regular basis. As it was now, he had to wait until the ship was loaded with cargo to make the trip back profitable, and that could be weeks or months.

Richard awoke as the watch was changing, and he realized he had been dreaming. The nemesis of his teenage years, Theodore Yancy, was in the dream, and there he continued to say over and over, "Always on schedule, you son of a thief." In the dream Yancy would open his waistcoat and take out a huge crate that could not possibly have fit, but was possible through the elastic reality of dreams. He then ordered Richard to place the crate in the hold where he found his father, Gabriel, who admonished him not to let good tobacco sit on a wharf in the hot sun. As they were talking, a Spanish diplomat they had transported on the *Draco Mare* came down the steps of the companionway and took off his waterlogged shoes. It was here that Richard awakened and looked around him in surprise, realizing the answer had come to him in his sleep.

He had eight ships under his control. If he set up a schedule for them, and if they left exactly on that schedule, he could charge because he could assure his passengers and those for whom he was delivering freight that he was leaving and arriving on time. With eight ships, he could have one leaving every two weeks, and if they travelled to selected ports on a schedule, people would come to depend on that schedule. In the last few years, even he had heard about the vast numbers of people coming to America from Europe. American goods were in demand all over the world, and he could provide those goods and on a schedule to boot. He was so excited he fumbled getting out paper to write all this down. If his plan worked, it meant he could tell Mary exactly when he was coming and going to Hampton.

When he returned to Hampton, he discussed the idea with his father, Shaw, and Jordan. They all gave an enthusiastic endorsement. Richard put it into action six months later with his first advertisements for the circuit from Hampton Roads to Boston to London, and back to Hampton Roads again. When he was in London, he set up an agent there to schedule passengers and freight. The *Lorraine*, the *Fiona*, and the *Vindicta* would sail this circuit. The *Draco Mare* was set for a direct voyage from Boston to London every six weeks. If it was successful, he would expand the number of ships making the transatlantic trip, but for now the ships he received from his father and Joshua Spencer would provide a similar transit within the Chesapeake Bay.

As he was speaking with Jordan about the first of the trips to London, they spotted a small steam engine making its way across the Bay from Hampton to Norfolk, belching smoke and roaring but barely moving along. Richard shook his head at the stench and sluggish nature of the vessel, but when he turned to look at Jordan, he saw that Jordan did not feel the same. "I know they are noisy and not very good yet, but you wait, their time is coming and they will take over from sailing vessels. Think how handy one of them would have been in the Great Lakes where the wind was never coming from the direction we needed and the current was sometimes stronger than the wind," Jordan said with conviction. Richard snorted his disbelief, but Jordan just watched in rapture as the little steam engine huffed its way across the Bay.

CHAPTER 22

RICHARD'S REALIZATION of the sailing circuit was more profitable than he had envisioned. He now had twelve ships maintaining the various circuits and the family was gathered to see two new ones that had recently been built, bringing the total number of ships bearing the white-on-black "H" of the Holmwood line, embroidered on their mainsail, up to fourteen.

Jordan Ladysmith had taken a circuit to China that involved nearly three years of sailing. He had run the circuit three times and had not been back in Hampton at the same time as Richard for over twelve years, though they corresponded a great deal. Jordan was there now with the entire Holmwood family, gathered to see the new, sleek ships roll down the ways into the water. They had been built in Portsmouth, and Mary stood with the children waiting anxiously. All of her children were taller than her by at least a head. Even Lucy, now eighteen, was six inches taller than her mother. Jordan approached a little awkwardly and greeted the children. Edward was the only one who recognized him, and he wrapped Jordan in a hug, smiling and laughing. Edward turned to his brothers and sister and said, "I'll bet you don't remember Jordan, do you?" Mary stepped forward and kissed him on the cheek, and Jack and Christian shook his hand. Rose held back and just waved, shy as usual. Edward then said, "And this, believe it or not, is Lucy." Lucy turned slowly as she heard her name. She looked at Jordan. He tried not to stare, but he couldn't help it. Staring back at him was the true vision of the woman in his dreams, right down to the dark hair, the dimples, and the green eyes. Her face was not as round as Mary's and it appeared exactly like it had been in his dreams, with the exception of the small, red scar under her chin. He realized with a start that the woman who visited him in his dreams had never been Mary. It was Lucy. With that, his heart sank. Here was another Holmwood woman to torment him, for how could Lucy, at eighteen and as fresh as a flower, have anything to do with him, a man now in his thirties.

"I know you," Lucy said almost more to convince herself than him as she offered him her hand, "but I don't know how I could." She held it out, palm down, expecting him to kiss it rather than to shake it, and Jordan obliged. Lucy recovered and said, "I mean I don't remember you, but I know you from somewhere, almost like from a painting or a drawing." Lucy turned to her mother and asked, "Do we have a painting or a drawing of Mr. Ladysmith at the house?"

"Not that I know of dear. Why do you ask?" Mary said absently, watching the shipyard men taking turns pounding on the way supports with huge hammers, trying to get the ship to begin to move down toward the water.

"I doubt, Miss Holmwood, that there is a picture of me anywhere in the world," Jordan said quietly.

"What a shame," Lucy said, and just then the wedges gave and the first ship slipped down the ways, the heat of its movement creating smoke as it rolled toward the water. Everyone cheered, and it was quickly moved aside to make room for the second ship, which plunged into the water a few minutes later. It was rather anticlimactic because the ships would now be towed to shore and rolled over to have their masts and rigging installed and it would be months before they were actually ready to sail. Lucy had stared at Jordan, unable to look away.

Richard arrived and clapped him on the back. "Jory, I am so glad you could make it! What has it been, five or six years since I've seen you?"

"No, it has been at least double that," Jordan said as they all moved in the direction of a coffeehouse where they could eat and catch up. The whole family crowded around two tables and Lucy found herself directly across from Jordan. She stared at him openly and only looked away when Richard spoke to her the second time, asking what she wanted to drink. She mumbled something and then looked back at Jordan.

Throughout the afternoon, while Richard and Jordan caught up, Lucy listened, fascinated about the places Jordan had been and the things he had seen. She finally asked, "Papa, have you ever been to China?"

"No love, I have never been much beyond the Cape of Good Hope, so Captain Ladysmith here has me," Richard said, smiling at Jordan.

When they left the coffeehouse, they moved down the walk in a lazy, meandering manner and Lucy found a way to fall behind the rest of them and walk just ahead of Jordan. Richard noticed her and watched, but didn't say anything. Finally, Mary noticed Lucy had slipped behind and called, "Lucy, come up here and walk with Rose and me. It's getting dark, and I don't want you lagging behind." Lucy glanced over her shoulder at Jordan and then walked forward to obey her mother.

After she had taken her place well forward, Richard said to Jordan, "I bet you barely recognized Jack and Christian?"

"They have all grown up so much, I don't think I would have recognized any of them on the street other than the fact that the boys, even with their dark hair, look just like you," Jordan said, trying to keep Lucy in view.

"Lucy too, I mean it's remarkable how much she looks like Mary," Richard said, turning to Jordan who tore his eyes away and shook his head in agreement.

"They were all little children the last time I saw them, but they certainly aren't little anymore," Jordan said and looked at Richard.

Richard smiled at him and said, "Especially Lucy?"

Jordan didn't dare speak for fear he would give away just how much this young lady had affected him. He only nodded, and after carefully measuring his words, said, "She's very beautiful."

Jordan spent nearly every evening with the Holmwoods in Hampton and wonderful stories were told, and everyone laughed and teased him good-naturedly as Richard recited them. He was able to tell a few on Richard that even Mary hadn't heard.

Jack, now twenty, sailed with Richard, and Christian, who had just turned sixteen, had been reluctantly released by his mother to accompany his father at sea. While Jack and Christian loved the sea, to Edward it was only a means to get somewhere. He could not understand their love of sail plans and rigging and their delight in a stiff breeze. A breeze cooled him off or dried his paintings. Edward's true love was botany, and he had already published a manual on the wetland plants of the Hampton Roads region.

Edward's drawings were exacting, and his ability to sit and stare at a plant endlessly while capturing its features was the butt of many jokes by his brothers. "No wonder you don't have a wife yet. You'd never even look at a woman unless she had leaves growing from her head," Jack kidded. He told of a recent time when two young ladies had obviously been interested in Edward, who sat sipping a drink and studying fern sketches while at a coffeehouse in Norfolk. Jack added, "There they were, absolutely beautiful women, and what did you do, Edward? You asked the one closest to you if she could move to the right as she was blocking your light!"

It was true, the ladies found Edward absolutely entrancing. He was lovely to look at, not just handsome, but actually beautiful with his golden curls and his eyes like lapis, but he wasn't interested in them at all. It wasn't that he preferred men or anything of that sort, he liked the company of women and had spent more than a few of his hard-earned dollars on them, but he liked them on his terms, and he wasn't ready to settle down.

While they had been on Mackinac Island, Edward had travelled with Richard whenever Mary would let him go. He was very artistic and had helped the cartographers a great deal. It was something practically foreign to his father, but he encouraged Edward nonetheless. Edward at first tried to draw living creatures like bugs and frogs, but they moved, and he could never complete his drawing, so he began to draw plant life. His artwork and attention to detail improved and he amassed a large collection of excellent botanical drawings, detailing where they were found and the conditions in which they grew. He had been especially interested in some orchid-like flowers on Beaver Island. He found them nowhere else and returned to draw them whenever he could. Later, as an adult, he was unable to find them even mentioned in any plant journal and decided on returning to Beaver Island someday to see if he could find the orchids again. He put the drawings from the Territory away years ago, but Mary had unearthed them in the attic in Hampton and gave them back to him during the winter when he was home on holiday. He mentioned to Richard his desire to return to the Northern Territory. Richard said, "What a coincidence, because I was just talking with your mother about the opportunities for trade we are missing up there. If we could set up a scheduled circuit, it would be very profitable. People are pouring into the Territory, and they will need transport for themselves and supplies. I was actually thinking of going this spring. Would you be able to go?" Richard asked the question, knowing Edward was firmly held to his teaching schedule at the College of William and Mary in Williamsburg.

"I will find a way, especially if I can come back with new material. My term is up in May, but could you wait that long to go?"

Richard accepted when Edward was still quite small that he would never be a sailor. Edward did not love the sea. Perhaps it was wrong to admit it, but he had two more sons coming along who appeared to love it, so Richard had never pushed him.

Jack, on the other hand, was born to it. From the time he could talk he was asking to be taken on the ship with his father. Mary resisted at first, but in the end realized she was fighting a losing battle. Jack was as stubborn and strong-willed as his Ojibwa nickname suggested, and either she would let him go or he would run away to the sea as Richard had. He could learn more from his father about sailing than any other man, so she relented.

Her only stipulation was that Richard maintain his education while Jack was on board. Richard had hired a schoolmaster much to Jack's chagrin.

Christian was held firmly at home by Mary. One son lost to the glory of the sea was enough for her. He would stay at home and get his education there. Christian rebelled and balked and spent every spare moment he had sailing around Hampton Roads in a small sloop Richard gave him. By the time Christian turned sixteen, Mary had no choice but to let him go. She knew if she kept him after that, he would end up hating her.

Jordan Ladysmith had had enough of being on the other side of the world. He asked Richard if he could take up one of the shorter circuits for a while and let Shaw or someone else take the one to China. Shaw was more than happy to trade his Hampton Roads-Boston-to-London schedule for the one to China, so Jordan would now be in Hampton every three months or so.

Lucy connived many ways to be around Jordan in the next few months, and she saw another chance when she learned the *Draco Mare* was being refitted in Portsmouth. Christian often sailed his sloop over to see the progress, so when Lucy asked to go along it caught him off guard. He couldn't think of a good excuse to tell her no.

Christian and Lucy moored alongside the pier nearest the *Draco Mare* and saw Jordan standing near the shipyard office talking with several other men. As they got closer they heard him say, "I could stop over and see about it later tomorrow. I am going to be at St. John's attending the wedding of one of my crew in the morning." Jordan caught sight of them then and grinned as he introduced them to the shipyard manager. After the introductions, Jordan led them over to where they could see the latest repairs to the *Draco*'s hull. She sat looking terribly uncomfortable in her dry dock. Lucy pointed out that her draft was so deep it looked almost misshapen. Jordan turned to her and said, "That's what makes her so fast and stiff in the water, Miss Holmwood."

"Stiff is good?" Lucy asked, having no more feel for a ship than Edward.

"Very good," Jordan smiled. He looked at Lucy. She was absolutely beautiful, and she looked him in the eyes so frank and bold, unlike many women her age.

Lucy was very outspoken, and it caused no end of worry for Mary. Richard took it in stride, reminding Mary that Lucy was a good girl, and she probably couldn't help being spirited. "She was, after all, born right on the gun deck."

After looking at the repairs to the *Draco*, Jordan took them to get something to eat. The only place close to the shipyard that was at least somewhat reputable was a tavern. It was just after noon, so the drunks from last night were sleeping it off. The three settled at a table and ordered bread and cheese and some cold-roasted beef. There was no tea or coffee in the place, but there was cider, and though it was rather hard, they ordered it to go with their meal.

They ate and talked and Jordan was struck by Lucy's acumen. She asked him a dozen questions about places he had been. She fired her questions so fast, he was barely able to answer them. The cider was a bit stronger than any of them anticipated, and when they rose to leave, they were all a bit wobbly. Lucy exclaimed as she started to walk, "I think my bones have become invisible!" She latched onto Christian's arm for support and took hold of Jordan's as well. He could feel her touch through his coat like it was hot metal, and he realized he was barely breathing. Jordan suggested they walk a bit to sober up before Christian attempted to sail back home, so they walked the length of the shipyard looking at the various types of vessels in all stages of repair. When they returned to the sloop, the fresh air and exercise had done its work though Lucy, still held firmly to Jordan's arm. She had long ago abandoned Christian's and only took it now so he could help her into the sloop. They smiled and cast off and when they were at least fifty yards away, Lucy turned to see if she could get one last look at Jordan's ship, but she was more surprised to see he had not moved from the pier and was watching intently after them.

The following morning, Lucy got dressed early and fidgeted through breakfast, frequently getting up to look at the clock on the mantle. Mary asked, "What are you up to?" Lucy arched her eyebrows innocently, and Mary said suspiciously, "Lucy Catherine, whatever it is you are planning, you better give up on it. If it is causing you to be this nervous, it can't be anything good."

The clock chimed softly nine o'clock and Lucy leaped off her chair and grabbed her shawl. "You're right Mama, I better go to church instead," and with that, she blasted out the door like a ball out of the barrel of a musket hurtling toward St. John's Episcopal.

Lucy knew Episcopal weddings always took place in the morning, but she wasn't sure how early, so she walked to the church and waited. Seeing no one there, she walked back toward the churchyard and wandered there looking at the headstone inscriptions. She even pulled a few weeds and tried to look busy, though she doubted anyone would toss her out of the cemetery if they saw her. After about forty-five minutes, Lucy noticed people arriving. She checked her hair and then found a place near a large yew tree that gave her a good view of the church entrance but shielded her as well. Clouds had been building since dawn, and she hoped her plan would work before the rain set in. She wouldn't make much of an impression looking like a drowned rat.

The church continued to fill with people, and Mary saw the exceedingly plump bride and her family slip inside. She heard the bride's mother say, "Well, you'll just have to get through it as best you can. You are running out of time." The groom and his best man took up residence near the outer wall of the bell tower, and it looked to Lucy for all the world like they were passing a bottle, but she asked herself who would do that right before a wedding? The church was nearly full and the arriving attendees were down to a trickle. She began to worry that Jordan had somehow gotten into the church without her seeing him or had decided not to attend. Just as she was about to give up, she saw him walking briskly down the path. She summoned her courage and left her hiding spot, walking with her head down at a diagonal. She ran headlong into

Jordan on the path, and he grabbed her to steady her. "Miss, I didn't see you. Are you..." he stared, then said, "Miss Holmwood?" He let go of her arms. "Are you attending this wedding? Where is your family?"

Lucy looked around, trapped. She hadn't thought this far ahead. Her plan had only extended to meeting up with Jordan, and she now blurted, "I was just caring for some of the graves in the churchyard. I do that sometimes."

Just then a fat raindrop splashed on her arm and it hit with such force that Jordan looked at it as well. It was followed by several more drops and a cold breeze. "Come into the church with me. You will never make it back home before you are soaked. You can come as my guest," Jordan said, escorting Lucy into the church. The congregation was shuffling and shifting in the drafty and ancient church, waiting impatiently for the ceremony to begin. Jordan led her to a pew near the back, but they had barely sat down when the groom's younger brother came and escorted them to the pew right behind the family. It had been saved especially for Jordan, as almost the guest of honor.

Jordan quickly settled Lucy and then sat down beside her. She linked her arm through his in a most proprietary way and Jordan let her do so. The ceremony began with the bride being escorted to the altar by her father. What Lucy had interpreted as plumpness, she realized now, was in fact the very last stages of pregnancy. Lucy must have come to this realization at the same time as Jordan. They exchanged quick glances and then looked away, fearing they might giggle. The ceremony in basic Episcopalian terms was brief, but even then there were a few pauses between readings and prayers and in those lapses Lucy could distinctly hear the bride breathing heavily. She sounded almost like a horse after it reaches the top of a hill when pulling a heavy load. Just before the "love, honor, and obey" portion, Lucy noticed something glint on the stone flags of the church floor and realized it was liquid reflecting the light from the stained glass windows. She understood then the bride had urinated on the floor, and it was forming a puddle near her feet. The groom noticed it as well and then so did the priest, who spurred himself through the remainder of the ceremony in record time. Just after they were introduced to the congregation for the first time as man and wife, the groom quickly led her down the aisle and out of the church. Jordan leaned down to Lucy and said, "I hope they make it before the baby comes." Lucy realized with a start that the bride had not wet herself but that she was in labor, and her water had broken right in the church.

The groom popped his head back into the church and said, nearly in a panic, "All of you please go have some ham biscuits and cider and cake. I'll be right back to join you after I pick up the midwife!"

Jordan couldn't hold it any longer and he burst out laughing. Lucy looked at him and then looked away embarrassed. He rose and led Lucy out of the church and across to the vestry where the congregation was gathering to eat. It was terribly crowded as the little tables set out on the lawn were useless in the pouring rain. "Do you want to stay to eat, or would you like me to take you home. Are you hungry?"

Lucy said, "I'm hungry, but it is so crowded here. I don't think we will be able to eat."

Jordan asked, "Would you let me take you to the inn then?" Mary nodded and they dashed diagonally across the street and around the corner to the inn.

They stomped inside, shaking their clothes to shed some of the rain. Lucy's hair was sprinkled with raindrops and they looked like diamonds stuck to her dark tresses. They found a table near the fire, which was well-banked, and sat and ate their soup. They talked and laughed and the time slipped away as the rain let up outside. Jordan looked at Lucy with the firelight shining on the side of her face, and he wondered what she really thought of him. Did she think he was another father to take care of her, or did she see him as an older brother or what? Whatever her thoughts might be, Jordan's were not so tame. He was ashamed to say he could not help but see her rolling over in bed to greet him in the morning while she wore nothing but a smile.

In his travels to the Orient, Jordan had sampled many women. Some of them had been lovely Asian ladies, and others had been European, and one was even the wife of a British diplomat. He never thought much about them once he was out of their bed, and he never returned to any of them twice. Lucy entranced him though, and he wanted to see her as much as he could. It was more than lust, because for the first time in his life he had found a woman he wanted to be with always, to wake up with, and to long for while he was at sea.

When they were close to the Holmwood house, Lucy stopped Jordan and said, "I need to tell you something." He turned and looked at her, and she said, "I wasn't in the churchyard caring for graves." She swallowed hard and added, "I was waiting for you. I overheard you yesterday, so I knew you would be there. Was it bad of me to have done this?"

Jordan smiled softly, and said, "That depends on why you wanted to see me."

Lucy looked at him and then at the ground. "I wanted to see you, because, well, I wanted to see you. I like being with you."

"You like being with me as a friend of the family, or as an older brother, or what?" Jordan said, forcing Lucy to speak her mind.

"I don't know, but not like a brother," Lucy said, looking back up at Jordan, "definitely not like one of my brothers. Sometimes I can't stand to be around them, but I want to be with you all the time."

Jordan pulled her chin up, forcing her to look at him. He said softly, "Lucy, I am too old for you. You think you want to be with me because I am different, and I have been all over the world. To you that is exotic and exciting, but once the tales wear off and I become an everyday feature around here, you will feel differently, I'm sure."

"Don't tell me what I feel, Captain," Lucy said sternly. Jordan saw the strong will take over, and she actually stomped her foot as she said, "I am the only judge of that." With that, she whirled to leave and took about six steps and then came back with tears in her eyes. "I'm sorry. I'm just confused and say things I don't mean."

Jordan smiled sadly and said, "Lucy, I am nearly twenty years older than you, and I don't think it would work. I know lots of couples have this age gap, but you are not the kind of a woman who will slow down with age, or if you are I am sadly mistaken. You deserve someone who will not grow old on you too fast."

Lucy's green eyes snapped, "So what this comes down to is you are afraid I will not be happy with you later on? Is that it?" Jordan nodded, and Lucy continued, "Think of my parents. When they really look at each other, even now, it's like anyone else in the room vanishes. I want that. I want a man to look at me like that when I am my mother's age."

"This will not work." Jordan wanted to explain how it involved betraying Richard, for he had no doubts Richard had larger plans for his daughter than to marry a merchant sailor. He never got to finish because Lucy stood up on her toes and kissed him on the mouth. It was not the kiss a sister gives to a brother. After his initial shock, Jordan kissed her back, in broad daylight, within sight of her house. It was the most satisfying kiss he could recall.

Lucy pulled back from him and said, "Tell me that was terrible, and I will make sure I never bother you again."

Jordan touched her face and said, half-smiling, "You certainly do bother me, Miss Holmwood."

Richard was in his study when he saw Jordan and Lucy approach the house. He didn't think much of it because he had seen the way they looked at each other, but he found it odd that Mary had allowed Lucy to be out on her own. Lucy was known for her wild spirit, so Richard was not shocked when he saw her lean up and kiss Jordan. He thought it best for everyone's sake that Lucy tame herself with a husband, preferably one with some experience in life, for he was certain Lucy would run roughshod over a man her own age. What had surprised him was that Jordan had not come to him to talk about courting Lucy.

Jordan left for Boston when the repairs to the *Draco Mare* were completed the following day. Lucy wanted to see him off, but she acted so nervous that Mary kept her in the house. Lucy waited every day for a letter from Jordan, but none came. When he arrived back three months later, Lucy barely looked at him, she was so hurt and confused.

Jordan tried to get Lucy alone to speak with her, but she wouldn't have anything to do with him. Nearly a month later, Lucy still had not spoken to Jordan, and he tried once again to speak to her after dinner. He was frantic to get her to understand that he had not written because he felt he needed to speak to Richard first before he started corresponding with her. He had planned to do so as soon as he returned to Hampton, but after the way she acted, Jordan held off and didn't say anything to Richard.

Shortly before Jordan was to leave again on his circuit, and against all his good sense, he left a note with the Holmwood's maid asking her to give it to Lucy. In the note he explained how he really felt and asked if she would allow him to write to her. If so, he would speak with Richard about it.

Nearly a week passed, and when there was no response from Lucy, Jordan left for Boston. It would be three months at the very soonest before he returned to Hampton.

The entire Holmwood family, with the exception of Cassie, who had just delivered her fifth child with William Spencer, and Rose, who stayed to help her, were preparing to leave for the Great Lakes. Grub would not accompany them this time. He had lived with the Holmwoods, odiferous and beloved, for thirteen years, until he succumbed to having eaten most of a ham he stole and devoured down behind the privy. His old guts couldn't take such fare, and he died belching softly in his sleep by the very hearth where he had committed the crime.

The family was now packed and they boarded the *Vindicta* for their trip back to Mackinac Island. There had been such a commotion in getting everyone packed on time that Jordan's note to Lucy was misplaced, and she didn't get it until the day they were to leave. She hastily wrote back, then asked that it be delivered to the warehouse. Lucy spent the rest of the day trying to make up some excuse of staying behind in Hampton. The trip by this time had become a Holmwood odyssey of sorts, and there was no way she was going to be allowed to stay back. She reluctantly sailed with the family, and they entered the St. Lawrence River six weeks later.

Jordan returned from England and held his breath as he went through the correspondence waiting for him at the warehouse. Finally, he reached the bottom and there was no word from her. Months later the staff at the Holmwood house in Hampton were clearing up after a celebration they had thoroughly enjoyed. They dipped into the food stores a bit more than usual, and as there was no one to see, they made more than a few trips to fetch wine Richard had stocked earlier in the year. The evening turned out to be rather a wild time, and as they were cleaning up, they were moving a cabinet near the front door to dust behind it when they discovered a letter to Captain Jordan Ladysmith. "It looks like Miss Lucy's hand, but how long has it been there?" the cook said, taking the letter from the maid and wiping the dust off it to read the address better. The maid went pale realizing the letter had lain there for months. She quickly forwarded it to the warehouse the following day where it just missed Jordan as he sailed again for Boston and London. Three months would be gone before he returned.

THE HOLMWOODS planned to stay in the Northern Territory just over a year. In that time Edward could search for his orchids, and Richard could strike up some trade business. The Territory was growing like a rampant weed, and Richard and Mary were amazed at the change fifteen years had made in the area. There were a dozen new houses on Mackinac Island, but their little cottage was still there and still happily owned by the Biddle family. They paid their respects to the graves of Douglas and Dorcas on behalf of Cassie and Rose, and they planted a Lily of the Valley flower on Wrennet's grave. The flower had always been her favorite, and Mary had brought the pips to plant all the way from Boston where they stopped to pick up supplies.

They set up their camp on Beaver Island and Edward disappeared the following morning looking for his orchids. Richard said as he watched the foliage swallow Edward, "At least he will get some sun out there looking for his flowers."

Ram's Head Orchids with their almost checkered pattern are very rare, but unlike what Edward believed, they can be found in other places in the area. He set up his easel and began to sketch, and before he knew it, evening closed in on him. He was forced to nearly run back to the camp, swatting mosquitoes and clouds of biting black flies that crawled into his ears and nose. Mary heard him coming, and they all waited for him as they stood on the edges of the campfire where the smoke repelled the insects. They had all forgotten how thick and thirsty the flying insects were in the Territory. They spent three weeks on the island and then moved over to the northern shore of Lake Michigan and set up another camp.

Jack and Christian had been entranced by tales of silver mines being founded on the Great Lakes, and they searched the rocky shore for any sign of the precious metal. They found loads of iron pyrite, the glimmering fool's gold that had broken so many hearts and hopes over the years, and they tried unsuccessfully to smelt it in a huge open-pit fire nearly six feet across.

Mary shook her head at them, but the fire provided loads of smoke to drive the insects away, especially if some green branches or live grass were tossed onto it, so she kept quiet. Christian and Jack kept the fire raging all day, and it only stopped flaming at night when there was no one to feed it. By morning it would be a bed of ashes two feet deep. Every morning, Jack or Christian would rake the ashes to see if any silver had pooled in smelted nuggets at the bottom. They found some ore containing copper and melted it into a flat glob about the size of a man's palm, and they were exceedingly proud of their work, showing it around the camp. Mary shook her head at them. Jack, freed of his duties as ship's commander for a time, reverted to a kid and thoroughly enjoyed himself. He and Christian kept their fire pit roaring for weeks on end.

One day Richard was gone in the cutter, Edward was away sketching fireweed seed pods while Lucy had gone with Jack and Christian gathering ore from a promising site about a half-mile away. Mary was left alone in the camp, and she was knitting by the fire when she got an uneasy feeling. It was not the feeling that her children or Richard were in danger but more that the camp was not safe or that she was being watched. She caught herself several times scrunching her neck down toward her shoulders as if to protect it, and finally she went and stood by the shore waiting for some of the family to return. She was relieved when she heard Edward coming back to camp. He saw her standing by the lake and asked if she was all right. She nodded her head that she was, but he was still concerned. Just as she was about to ask him if he wanted tea, her peripheral vision caught sight of movement in the brush as if someone had passed through it. Edward hadn't noticed it, and Mary just passed it off to having lived in the city for too long.

They moved their camp about fifteen miles west and immediately Jack and Christian dug another pit and began gathering ore. Richard looked at them and said, "There is no greater fool for gold and silver than a sailor who wouldn't know what it looked like in the raw if it fell on his head." But even Richard helped them gather great buckets of the stuff. If it sparkled, then it went into the pit.

A man hiding in the brush had been watching them intently. The family never seemed to be in camp at one time except when they slept and when they ate the evening meal. He was a man bent on vengeance, and he had had decades to let it ferment and fester in his heart like a fungus. The time had now come to release the pent-up spores of hate. It was the girl he was most interested in because she reminded him of someone who had angered him long ago. She would be the first one to suffer, or maybe he would keep her until last, but in any event he would take his time and enjoy her.

The man had hidden his boat in a small cove about half a mile away, and he watched now as Edward returned to camp. Edward seemed excited as he told the others about a wonderful place he found about three miles inland. He described a waterfall in such magnificent detail that they all determined to go see it the next day.

Another fire pit had been scratched out, and after days of burning the seafaring miners were rewarded with a glob of something that looked like copper but not as shiny. Christian claimed this one as they set about to stoke their fire and toss in more chunks of ore. They piled on at least three feet of wood, most of which was pine, and the fire roared into the evening sky. They all had to move back at least ten feet to keep from having their faces scorched and their hair singed. "Can't the two of you just build a fire? Does it have to be this inferno every single night?" Mary asked, backing away from the heat, but grateful for the smoke which drove away the bugs.

The man didn't notice the bugs. He was used to pain. It had been several years since he had the first sore in his groin that signaled he was infected with syphilis, but the symptoms had gone away, and he thought he had beaten it. Several years later, when he had such terrible headaches he could barely see, he sought out a doctor in France. The doctor patiently told him the only cure was mercury injected into his penis with a syringe and that even after the painful procedure, it was probably too late. The man listened carefully to what he was told and then knocked the doctor over the head with a metal bar used to prop open the door, leaving the doctor's wife screaming after him. The doctor, before his talking was stopped, had warned the man not to have any relations with women, as it was possible to spread the disease. In response the mad man doubled his efforts to copulate with every woman he could find.

He stared now from his hiding place at the family getting ready for bed. They sometimes stayed on the ship and sometimes in their camp tents. When the mosquitoes were exceptionally bad, they slept on the ship, further out from shore. Tonight was one of those nights, and as the fire began to burn down, they took to the boat and rowed to the ship. He could see them moving about the ship settling down for the night, and when it was quiet, he crept out from his hiding place. He first went to the tent shared by Richard and Mary and after pulling back the covers on the neatly made bed, he urinated all over the sheets. He stole some food and a jacket and then ducked back into the brush to wait.

The following morning after breakfast the whole family, except Lucy, went up to see the waterfall Edward had found. Lucy was not feeling very well and decided to stay behind. Lucy found a spot in the shade to rest and slept for several hours. When she awoke, she realized her shade had moved with the sun and left her hot and thirsty. She noticed that Jack and Christian had really loaded their fire this morning because it was now like a hell pit with blazing red coals that must have been at least two feet deep below the flaming wood. As she backed away from the fire, a hand slipped over her mouth and pulled her to the ground. She tried to struggle and turn her head to see but was overpowered. She reached up and dug at his hands with her nails, and he released her long enough to punch her in the jaw. She tried to scream in pain, but he clamped his hand tighter over her mouth. She craned her neck and wrenched her jaw to bite his hand, but he saw what she was trying to do, and he punched her again. The pain shot through her head like she had been hit with a hammer, and she started to cry as she felt something sharp under her chin. The voice behind her said, "Don't you move, bitch, or I'll cut your lovely throat." He dragged her toward the tent, and she struggled despite his warning. She felt the point of the knife open a cut under her chin, and she was certain he had slit her throat. She stopped squirming immediately when she felt the blood flow down over her neck. The cut was not deep, but it terrified her just the same. The man removed his hand from her mouth and showed her the knife. "Now that you know I will do it, don't give me a reason." Lucy nodded her head quickly, but she was so frightened she was whimpering, and he screamed at her, "Stop that noise!" He shoved her into the tent, and she fell onto her knees, but jumped up and looked around for a weapon. She was in her own tent, and there was nothing there but clothes and a washstand. Without really looking, she flung the washstand at him, and it caught him on the shoulder. He glared at her in the gloom, and she gasped as she caught sight of her attacker. He looked just like her father, only cruel and unkempt.

"Owen!" she stammered. She had never met him, but had heard from Edward and others about him. He was, as they said, the image of his father. "Owen Holmwood is dead, and I took his place. Now, I'll let you guess what I'm going to take from you," he said, enjoying her shock and horror.

Owen had not been back in the United States even once until nearly a year ago. He had lived under several names and fathered numerous bastards all over the world, but they held no more interest for him than the women who bore them. He had convinced himself that there was only one woman he had ever really loved, and his father had stolen her. This girl standing before him looked so much like her, he couldn't believe how satisfying it would all be.

Owen returned to Scotland Neck to seek revenge only to find the family had moved to Hampton, and by the time he got there, they had left for the Northern Territory. He was in such a rage, he got into a fight outside a tavern and killed a man. He fled from Hampton Roads and hid for a while and then travelled north taking work as he could. He finally located a ship in Boston that was sailing to the Territory, and he signed on to the crew. When he got near Mackinac, his quarry was relocating from Beaver Island to the shoreline. Owen jumped ship then and watched the family for weeks, stealing from them when he could, grateful they didn't have a dog guarding the camp.

Owen had stolen a ship's boat, and though it was not much bigger than a jolly boat, he used it to follow the Holmwoods around Lake Michigan.

As Lucy now backed away from Owen in the gloom of the tent, he chuckled deep in his throat, and it sounded just like her father. Richard was the kindest man she knew, and it was horrible to see such a satanic image of him. She was nauseous with the fear of being raped by her half-brother. Her panic made Owen want her even more. He leered at her and said, "I came back for your mother to claim what should have been mine, but in taking you, I will in essence fuck my father. This is too good to be true." Lucy backed away until her hands touched the sailcloth from which the tent was made. She was trapped, and she looked around frantically for something, anything, to throw at him. She squatted down, keeping her eyes locked on Owen, and felt around with her hands on the ground. Her hands found shoes and a brush and she threw them at him as hard as she could. Owen just laughed and deflected her futile tosses. He started forward and said flatly, "You know, I'm sick, and I shouldn't be with women, but we'll be good citizens and keep it in the family." He lunged at her in a feint and enjoyed how she gasped. Owen said, without really expecting an answer, "Do you know what I mean, little one, about being sick, or have you been so sheltered that you don't even know what I am talking about." Lucy stared at him, and he said, "You look so much like your mother. I used to have a mother, and she was beautiful, but my father killed her. I'll bet you didn't know that, did you?"

Lucy lunged at Owen, pushing hard against his chest as she screamed, "Liar!" Owen was so shocked at her outburst, he lost his footing and tumbled backward, pulling Lucy down with him. He lost his grip on the knife. Her screams reached the crew on the ship. Owen could hear the whistles and other sounds indicating that a boat was being lowered. He grabbed Lucy and pulled her over into the brush near the camp and threw her on her back. She fought to get away, and he slapped her hard with the back of his hand, splitting her lip against her teeth. She steadied herself against the ground with one hand while she held her lip with the other. She could already feel it starting to swell. Owen picked up a stone about twice the size of an apple and threatened her with it. "If you fight me again, I swear I will crack your head open with this." He brought it down hard on the hand Lucy was using to steady herself and she screamed. Owen grabbed her and tore her blouse down the back so it hung from her arms. He then grabbed the thin fabric of the chemise front and ripped it down to her waist. She tried to cover herself, but he pinned her to the ground.

MARY AND RICHARD and the others were still at the falls. It was such a beautiful place, they decided to eat their noon meal there, and Jack and Christian offered to go and get some food from the camp, but Mary spoke up, "Let Edward go. He has better sense when it comes to food." She added, "Perhaps he can talk Lucy into joining us."

Edward was fairly close to camp when he heard a whistle on the ship and banging of the block and tackle. It sounded like they were lowering a boat, so he picked up his pace. He called to Lucy and found some scuff marks in the dirt and several items from Lucy's tent on the ground outside. The boat being rowed in toward shore was nearly a half-mile out. Edward, alarmed, searched the camp, and he thought he heard a whimper. He listened again, but could not place the sound exactly. He started for the brush at the side of the camp, and suddenly heard Lucy scream, "Edward, watch out!" He turned and saw a blur behind him, and then everything went black. When he came to, he could hear Lucy struggling, and he tried to move, but his legs would not obey. His head was throbbing from where the stone had hit him, and he realized then he was tied securely and could only move his neck. Standing before him was the brother who tormented him so many years ago. "Owen?"

"Ah, it speaks," Owen said mockingly.

Edward cleared his throat, "Lucy, are you all right?" Lucy was now gagged, but she shook her head yes. Owen came over then and cupped one of Lucy's breasts in his hand, grinning wickedly. Edward yelled, "For God's sake, Owen, she is your sister. Leave her alone!"

"Sister?" Owen sneered. "I don't have a sister. As a matter of fact, I was an only child. You don't count even as dung on my boot." Owen smiled horribly and leaned close to run his tongue down Lucy's shoulder. She curled her head away and shut her eyes. Just then, Jack and Christian came into camp having been sent by Mary to help Edward carry the food. They were stunned by the bizarre scene and stopped abruptly. Owen looked up, recognizing his father's features in their faces and swore out loud, "Christ, what do you people do other than breed like rats? How many more are there of you?" Christian and Jack charged him, but he told them to stop as he held his knife to Lucy's throat and hissed, "Since I won't be able to do what I wanted, I have very little use for her now. You come one step closer to me and I will slit her throat. She won't be the first woman I have disposed of this way." The brothers stopped and stared at Lucy. She was naked from the waist up, crying in fear and humiliation; but emboldened by the arrival of two more, she swung her legs at Owen, who was crouched next to her, and he tipped on his side and the knife skidded away. As Owen fell, Christian jumped on him, but Owen swiveled around and hit him with the rock he had grabbed. Christian's body shuddered as if he had been shaken, and he fell limp to the ground. Jack grabbed the knife and cut Edward's hands loose, then handed him the knife to slice through the cords around his ankles. Jack turned to attack, but Owen had moved toward the tent Mary and Richard shared. A musket lay on a little table outside the tent. Owen swiftly picked it up and found it was loaded. He now leveled it at Jack and cocked the hammer. Jack froze, but from the expression on Owen's face, he knew he was going to shoot, and he dove sideways. The musket ball slammed through the thick muscle just below his collarbone, miraculously missing his lungs and heart. The impact knocked Jack to the ground, and in that instant Edward came in low, catching Owen just above his waist. Owen dropped the musket and Edward picked it up by the barrel and swung it in an upper cut that caught Owen under the chin and propelled him backwards several feet to the very lip of the fire. He teetered for a moment, then his boots slipped, and he tumbled into the huge fire pit landing on his back. Owen jumped up, but the blazing embers were halfway up his thighs, and his back burned furiously. He tried to step from the blaze, but fell face down. He reared up once more, but this time Edward heard the steam escaping from Owen's ears as his brain vaporized. With one final scream, he flipped onto his back in the ashes and the flames covered him. Edward stared in horror as Owen's limbs twitched and flailed. Edward whispered, horrified, "I figured you would end up in hell, Owen, but I never thought I would have to witness it."

Edward turned to Lucy and wrapped his jacket around her. Christian was moaning as he held his head, and Jack was on his feet, but bleeding heavily. Edward walked quickly to him and turned him around to look at his back. The musket ball had passed right through Jack, and from what limited experience Edward had with gunshots, he understood that this was a good thing. Jack would heal if they could staunch the blood.

Mary and Richard arrived hurriedly, alerted by the musket shot, and stared at their wounded family. Mary didn't know which one to mother first, but Lucy and Edward directed her to Jack. The ship's doctor had arrived then, and between them, they patched Jack up nicely. Christian was talking now and making good sense, so his injuries didn't seem permanent. Lucy held a cold cloth to her lip and Mary wrapped her hand in soft bandages. She didn't think there were any broken bones in Lucy's hand, but it was difficult to tell with all the swelling. Now that everyone was mended, Richard asked Lucy and Edward what happened. Edward led him to the fire pit.

"It was Owen. He came all the way up here to get back at you and Mary. When he saw Lucy, he decided to vent his rage on her instead." Edward told them what Owen had planned to do and how he had fired at Jack. When he finished the tale, Edward asked, "How does a person become so evil?"

Richard didn't answer for a long time, and then he said softly, "I don't think they become evil, Edward. I think they are just born that way."

Richard, Edward, and several of the crew shoveled sand and rocks over the fire pit until it formed a mound. They poured barrels of water over it to put out the fire. They left a simple headstone made of a rounded lake stone on which the ship's carpenter chiseled Owen's name and the date of his death. Richard added the same date next to Owen's name in the family Bible and then closed it softly and walked away. Lucy followed him. Richard looked out over the water and when Lucy saw that he was crying, it terrified her, but she stepped forward and held his arm. "Papa, I'm sorry Owen died. I know you loved him."

Richard put his arm around her shoulders, and said softly, "Owen died several times before today, but today I accepted it at last. I hope he is at peace. You know I never understood him, not once, but I loved him. God I loved him."

"Papa, he was sick. He had syphilis. Doesn't it make you do crazy things?" Lucy asked, trying to find a way to justify what Owen did.

Richard turned to her and said, "Yes it does, and for all our sakes, let's believe that is what happened."

They relocated about two miles down the shore which was actually closer to the beautiful, lacy waterfall Lucy had not had a chance to see, and they all spent a great deal of time there. Six weeks passed and everything for the most part had returned to normal. Lucy had been quiet and almost depressed since the incident, but then again she had been quiet and depressed since they left Hampton, over a year and a half before.

Mary and Richard went for a walk along the shoreline, and they had gone about a mile west of the camp while Jack and Christian were fishing from a small boat about a half-mile away in a cove. The only ones left in the camp were Lucy and Edward, and Lucy had already gone back to the waterfall to collect plants for Edward. Some very unique ferns and some lady slipper orchids in both yellow and white grew there, and Lucy had a knack for collecting them without damaging the plants. She had gone ahead, and Edward was supposed to follow in about half an hour.

Edward heard a strange throbbing sound and looked up, startled to see a small steam launch approaching around the headland of the beach where they were camped. There appeared to be only three people aboard, and when it got closer a man jumped overboard and swam to shore. The swimmer came up dripping and smiling from the water, and Edward was stunned to see Jordan Ladysmith. The little launch came about and anchored offshore and released some of its steam in a great hissing cloud as Jordan clapped Edward on the back and shook his hand. Edward said, "Good God, Jordan, what in the world are you doing here?"

"I'm looking for your sister, Lucy. Please tell me she's here with you," Jordan said wearily.

Edward eyed him and then said, "We're all here, the whole family, but I am the only one in camp. Lucy is gathering plants for me to catalogue." Edward fingered the yellow lady slipper orchid he was holding. It had already bloomed and now, flowerless and leafless, it was a bland little knot like a ginger root that would not show its glory until next spring. He pointed with the plant still in his hand, "Lucy went up that way, collecting at the falls. If you wait a minute, I'll show you." Jordan shook his head, smiling, and had already started in the direction Edward had pointed. Edward called to Jordan's back, "Follow the stream, and you can't miss her." Then as an afterthought, he said, "You are staying with us for a while, aren't you?"

"I hope for quite a while," Jordan said as he walked. He followed the stream until he found a small, marshy area below a veil-like waterfall. He skirted the little marsh, which was simply a shallow bowl in the gray limestone that retained water, giving life to delicate moisture-loving plants, and edged around to the front of the falls looking for Lucy.

The waterfall was about twenty feet wide, but the water spread out so evenly across its lip that it appeared to be a fountain constantly dripping. Behind it was a deep hollow, almost like a cave, and just inside it he saw Lucy digging around the edges of a delicate fern. She put the plant in a small, canvas box and draped more canvas over the top to protect it from the bright sunlight. Lucy walked forward to the fall and rinsed her hands. She cupped the water and let it run over her face. She closed her eyes, enjoying the feeling.

Jordan sprinted across and stood on the outside of the falls while Lucy was still on the inside. He waited for her to open her eyes, and when she did she yelped and jumped back into the cave. Jordan walked through the veil of water and smiled at her.

She stood back up from where she was crouched and stuck out her chin. Her hands were clenched as she snapped, "How dare you come here and just smile at me!"

Jordan looked confused. "Lucy, I got your letter, and I came right away."

"Right away! I wrote that letter," she looked exasperated, "years ago!" She hissed, "You're late."

"I never got your letter until six months ago. It travelled all the way across the Atlantic and back trying to catch up with me before I finally got it. I turned over heaven and earth to get back to Hampton, but when I got there, I found your whole family had come up here." He looked at her and said solemnly, coming closer, "Lucy, I have done nothing but try to find you since I read your letter."

Lucy started to cry and Jordan reached for her, but she backed away. "It's too late," Lucy sobbed.

"What do you mean 'too late?' Have you found someone else? My God, are you married?" Jordan, alarmed, fired his questions one after the other.

"No!" Lucy wailed. "But I gave up on you. At first I cried, and then I called you the most horrible things, and I could never take them all back now!"

Jordan laughed. "I'll never know what you said, and you'll never understand what I went through to get here, so, I think we're even." Jordan touched her cheek and leaned closer, "Lucy, I am so sorry if I hurt you." He backed up a bit and looked at her, "Did you mean what you said in your letter, that you wanted to be with me?"

"Yes, God help me, I did," Lucy whispered. Jordan grabbed her face in his hands and kissed her, almost crushing her mouth. Lucy wrapped her arms around his back, holding him tight. Her heart was pounding so fast, she could hardly breathe, and when Jordan pulled back from her face to speak, Lucy began fumbling with the buttons on his shirt.

He looked at her startled and put his hands over hers to stop her. "Lucy, don't do that. I won't be able to stay away from you if you do," Jordan gasped.

Lucy shook his hands loose and returned to his buttons. "You have been away from me long enough, haven't you?" Jordan looked at her and then held her wrists firmly and said, "I want you more than you could possibly know, but we are going to do this right. I'm not going to sneak around. We are going to tell your family, and then we'll be together, I promise you." Lucy tried to go for his buttons again, and Jordan pulled her hands away from his shirt and kissed them, teasing her, "You certainly have your father's blood. No one enjoyed boarding the enemy more than he did!" Lucy smiled back and finally relaxed her hands.

They gathered Lucy's plants and tools and stepped through the veil of water. The sun came out from behind a fluffy cloud and lit up the little falls. Lucy shielded her eyes and looked at Jordan. After all the years of waiting, it was the exact vision from his dream, right down to the little, red scar under her chin. He smiled at her, and then looked around at the falls. "Does this place have a name?"

Lucy said, "The Ojibwa call it Weeping Rocks. Why do you ask?" Jordan just smiled, remembering old Zagaswe's words, *The day the woman in your dreams will belong to you, will be the day stones can shed tears.*

Jordan said as they started to leave, "You do intend to marry me, don't you?"

Lucy said with fake archness, "Mr. Ladysmith, the sooner the better for both our honors."

Richard had heard the steam launch and had returned like the others to see who it was. Edward came running to meet them, "You won't believe who's here!" he shouted while they were still yards away and added, "Jordan Ladysmith is here, and he wants to see Lucy!"

Christian jumped out of the canoe and shouted, "I'd better go and see if he found her."

"No! You stay put," Richard said with a sly smile. "I don't think he will have any trouble tracking her down. He came all this way. Let him win his prize on his own."

"Prize? You mean he wants Lucy?" Christian said with assurance, "She won't have him."

"I have a feeling she will," Richard said under his breath.

About an hour later, Lucy and Jordan walked into the camp and Richard rose to greet them. He said to Jordan, "I should beat the tar out of you for breaking Lucy's heart, but I was never sure what happened back in Hampton." Jordan looked worried for a moment and then caught Richard's smile. They hugged each other warmly and Richard said, "You look like you've had a rough trip, and you also look like you have something to ask me." Richard grinned wickedly and then said, "I'll make this easy for you. Jordan, are you here for my Lucy at last?"

Jordan smiled, and said, "I think it would be for the best." He smiled at her, and Lucy moved next to him and held his hand.

"Lucy, this is what you want. I can see it on your face," Richard said, smiling at her lovingly.

Lucy moved closer to Jordan. "Yes, Papa, it's what I want more than anything."

Jordan spoke up now, "I love her, Richard, and I promise I'll take care of her.

Mary stepped up, looking from Jordan to Lucy, and then she turned on Richard. "You knew about this, and you didn't tell me?"

Richard pulled her close and spoke for both of them. "You have our blessing."

Mary nodded and hugged them, then trained her sights back on Richard, "Why didn't you tell me?"

"I just did," Richard said, grinning with his arm around her.

"Papa, I want you to marry us now, right here," Lucy said, and Richard looked at her startled, but not as startled as Jordan.

"Lucy!" Mary said shocked. "That wouldn't be proper."

Lucy turned to Jordan and said, "You told me we would tell my family and then we would be together. I thought you meant what you said."

"Lucy, I do mean it," Jordan said and started to add, "but don't you need a dress and cakes and all that stuff?"

"Jordan, you better take her now. She has a fearful temper, and she may say no by tomorrow morning just to spite you," Richard chuckled.

"Richard!" Mary said even more shocked.

Jordan said seriously, "I will marry her this instant if you will do the service."

Richard looked from Lucy to Jordan and said, "I will do it on one condition. You will go to Sault Ste. Marie in the next few weeks and make sure you are legally married. I have never been sure if this really sticks."

The service was brief and straight from the "Book of Common Prayer." Richard had them sign the ship's log and then he and Mary signed as witnesses. They entered the same information in the family Bible and that was it. There was no ring, but Jack had snipped off a small rod of whatever it was he smelted in his pit and formed it into a ring that would fit Lucy's finger.

Jordan transferred Lucy's things to his steam launch and they spent their nights there. A week later the entire family travelled as a tiny convoy to Sault Ste. Marie where a priest married Lucy and Jordan. They then travelled to Mackinac Island and docked at the pier which had been greatly enlarged since the first time they saw it. That night they discussed the future. "I see you haven't lost your love of steam," Richard said, eyeing the launch as it idled, belching tiny puffs of coal smoke.

Jordan nodded, "I said before that this is the place for steam. The wind is never right here, and you spend all your time tacking, but the shoreline is pocked with miners, all anxious to transport their ore and bring in men and supplies. You could do a smashing business here with a small fleet of steam launches."

Richard leaned back in his wooden chair, sipping his wine, and Jordan said, encouraged, "I was so determined to find Lucy, I didn't even think what I would do when I finally found her. Other than buying this boat, I have most of the money I have ever made, and I actually thought about starting up a small steam line somewhere."

Richard looked at him, "Do you need to start your own line, or could you join up with me? It would be a simple matter of extending our services here, and I have to tell you, I was already determined to get in on the crest of the shipping wave that is bound to come out of the Lakes. Hell, coming up the St. Lawrence this time was like coming into Philadelphia Harbor, there were so many ships. The shipping traffic is only going to grow, so we might as well get in on it, and this is the perfect place for your damned steamboats. I think that if you talk with Christian, he might stay here. He has become a slave of the steam engine as well." Richard looked at Jordan and said, "So what do you say? You can have complete control of what you do up here. I will be a silent partner."

Jordan smiled, "I can't think of a better plan, but I doubt very much you will be silent." Richard smiled and then, raising his glass, tipped back the last of his wine. It was now completely dark. Jordan walked with his lantern to the steam launch where Lucy was already in bed waiting for him. Richard looked over toward the ship and saw the light from his cabin where Mary was waiting. He tossed a few sticks on the fire to leave it as a beacon on the shore and went to join her.

AUTHOR'S NOTE

MUCH OF THIS STORY is based on fact and the lives of real people embellished with fiction. Richard Holmwood did not exist, but he could have. There are certainly hundreds of fine men from the War of 1812 whose names have slipped through the sieve of time, and they have disappeared from our history. They are gone, but you can capture a sense of them and their time by visiting the two ships from that era that remain with us today. The *Constitution* lies in Boston Harbor, and the *Niagara* has been raised, restored, and is berthed in Erie, Pennsylvania. Go and touch them and I swear they will touch back. They are a living link to the past and are teeming with stories if you will listen.

Scotland Neck and all the other places in Virginia are real, as is Mackinac Island in Michigan. The island clings stubbornly to its history, and if you go there you will step back in time for there are no automobiles allowed even for full-time residents. You must ride a horse, bicycle, or walk if you want to visit the magical limestone arch, the Devil's Kitchen, or the Crack in the Island, and even the Biddle House. The garrison at the fort is still on active duty, and you can find them all there on that fabulous rock which straddles two of the largest fresh water lakes in the world. If you are truly daring, choose the largest of them all and venture into Superior to see the magnificent caves, dunes, and the painted rocks. If you are brave enough, go out in Superior beyond where you can see land in any direction, and then tell yourself it's just a lake.

CPSIA information can be obtained at www.ICGtesting.com
Printed in the USA
BVOW032307071212

307629BV00001B/7/P